THE FIRES OF THE GODS

THE FIRES OF THE GODS

A Sugawara Akitada Mystery

I.J. Parker

This first world edition published 2010
in Great Britain and in 2011 in the USA by
SEVERN HOUSE PUBLISHERS LTD of
9–15 High Street, Sutton, Surrey, England, SM1 1DF.
Trade paperback edition first published
in Great Britain and the USA 2011 by
SEVERN HOUSE PUBLISHERS LTD.

British Library Cataloguing in Publication Data

Parker, I.J. (Ingrid J.)
  The fires of the gods.
  1. Sugawara Akitada (Fictitious character)–Fiction.
  2. Public officers–Japan–Fiction. 3. Japan–History–
  Heian period, 794-1185–Fiction. 4. Arson investigation–
  Japan–Fiction. 5. Murder–Investigation–Japan–
  Fiction. 6. Detective and mystery stories.
  I. Title
  813.6-dc22

ISBN-13: 978-0-7278-6989-0 (cased)
ISBN-13: 978-1-84751-321-2 (trade paper)

Severn House Publishers support The Forest Stewardship Council [FSC],
the leading international forest certification organisation. All our titles that
are printed on Greenpeace-approved FSC-certified paper carry the FSC logo.

MIX
Paper from
responsible sources
FSC
www.fsc.org   FSC® C018575

Typeset by Palimpsest Book Production Ltd.,
Falkirk, Stirlingshire, Scotland.
Printed and bound in Great Britain by
MPG Books Ltd., Bodmin, Cornwall.

ACKNOWLEDGMENTS

First, I owe thanks to my friends Jacqueline Falkenhan and John Rosenman for their generous comments and suggestions on the early version of this novel. Their steadfast support and encouragement keep me going. Next, the editorial assistance at Severn House is superb, and special appreciation goes to Rachel Simpson Hutchens for her excellent insights and for catching my errors in detail and style. And finally, as always, I am indebted to my agents, Jean Naggar and Jennifer Welsh, for their continuing efforts on my behalf.

CHARACTERS

(Japanese family names precede first names)

MAIN CHARACTERS:

Sugawara Akitada	nobleman, senior secretary in the Ministry of Justice
Tamako	his wife
Tora	his retainer and sidekick
Genba	another retainer
Seimei	his secretary; a faithful family servant
Hanae & Yuki	Tora's wife and baby son
Kobe	superintendent of the Capital Police

CHARACTERS INVOLVED IN THE ARSON CASE:

Tojiro & Takeo	homeless boys
Koichi, Shinichi & Seiji	three deaf mutes; 'collectors' for a protection gang
Haruko	Koichi's daughter
Jirokichi	burglar, aka 'the Rat'
Hoshina	his girlfriend; owner of a wine shop
Kaneharu	a small merchant
Watanabe	a rich merchant
Abbot Shokan	abbot of the Seikan-ji temple

CHARACTERS INVOLVED IN THE MURDER OF A SENIOR OFFICIAL:

Kiyowara Kane	the Junior Controller of the Right
Lady Kiyowara	his wife
Katsumi	his son and heir
Lady Aoi	Lady Kiyowara's cousin; a shrine virgin
Ono Takamura	a court poet
Prince Atsunori	the Minister of Central Affairs

Fuhito   Lord Kiyowara's major-domo

OTHERS:
Munefusa   Akitada's subordinate in the
                               Ministry of Justice
Nakatoshi   a former subordinate
Fujiwara Kaneie   the Minister of Justice

THE DANCING DEMON

Tora stepped into the dense summer night and looked up at the roiling black sky above the jagged lines of roofs. Trees tossed their branches in the hot wind, and the dust swirled under his feet. Then thunder crackled and a flash of lightning momentarily lit up the empty street. Ducking his head, Tora clutched the batch of loose gold and silver coins inside his jacket and hurried towards home.

The streets were dimly lit here and there by garish paper lanterns marking wine shops or houses of assignation. They swung and danced in gusts of wind, throwing weird shadows across the street and on the walls of houses. A nasty night!

Tora did not care. He had been lucky. Playing at dice most of the night and buying a lot of wine, he had won magnificently. It meant that he could make the final payment on the small farm outside the capital. Sucking in a breath of warm air, he flexed his muscles, and felt blessed. Being a son of farmers, he had longed for many years to own his own bit of land.

His glee faded a little at the thought of telling his wife the good news – he was bound to get another lecture. Hanae disapproved of gambling.

He was preoccupied with this problem when, somewhere in the Sixth Ward, someone rushed from an alley and collided with him. They both went sprawling in the dirt, scattering Tora's dubious fortune across the rutted street.

Tora scrambled to his feet and saw in a flash of lightning that the stranger was scooping up his coins with amazing speed and dexterity. 'Hey!' Tora shouted and lunged for the thief. They fell together, rolling around in the dirt, punching and kicking. The thief was slight and wore silk. A woman? Tora relaxed his grip. The next moment, his attacker had slipped out of his grasp.

'Drop my money, you little tart!' Tora lunged for her wrist. She sank her teeth into Tora's hand and put a fist in his eye. He howled and let go.

The eye hurt badly, and Tora felt it to make sure it was still there, then he groped around for the thieving little whore.

She was gone. He got to his feet. Lightning lit up the street again and he saw her blue and white robe disappear around the far corner. Some of his gold pieces lay scattered a few steps away. He went to pick them up, but more people had erupted from the dark mouth of the alley. He was dimly aware of young faces and hissing breaths. Something struck his head, and he fell to his knees, retching. They laughed, then a clap of thunder drowned out all sounds. The darkness was filled with swirling, multicolored stars, and Tora stayed down until the stars dimmed and he was sure that the sour taste in his mouth was not followed by the wine in his stomach.

By then, his attackers were gone. People came from a wine shop to help him to his feet. They commiserated, but one of them bent and palmed a coin before they left. He stayed, cursing and unsteady on his feet. His small fortune was gone, and with it any hope of convincing Hanae that he had gambled for their welfare. Glumly, he brushed himself off and looked around for coins the thieves might have missed. There was nothing but a small blue silk bag with a broken string, the kind people used for an amulet. He picked it up and was about to leave when his nose caught a hint of smoke.

There is smoke, and then there is smoke. The nights in the capital were redolent with the scent of burning pitch pine from the torches used to light the streets and gates. This smelled serious. He turned his head to sniff the air, then hurried into the dark mouth of the alley.

It was short and led to another street of shops. There, in the distance, Tora saw a reddish light flickering. People shouted. A thin, high wail rose above the noise.

It was another fire.

This street passed between rows of adjoining small shops with homes attached in the back. In such streets a fire could jump from roof to roof and race across the quarter in an incredibly short time. Already the front of one of the shops was filled with flames, and thick smoke spread over the area. As he ran towards it, Tora saw a small figure that seemed to be dancing about in front of the conflagration. The creature was shouting and waving its arms as if it were cheering the fire on. To Tora's horror, its body was covered with small flames. It looked like a demon had come straight from hell. Tora slid to a halt, his hair bristling.

They were calling them the fires of the gods, and the capital had been plagued by them for weeks now.

In another flash of lightning, he saw shadows creeping from the darkness to watch. The dancing demon seemed to make several attempts to jump into the fire, and someone was praying to Amida.

Tora shuddered. He joined the watchers and, with a nod to the fire demon, asked, 'What is that thing?'

An elderly woman, her eyes wide with horror, said, 'It's Young Kaneharu.'

'Young Kaneharu?' Tora looked more closely and saw now that the demon could well be a human on fire.

He rushed forward and grabbed the man. He looked scarcely human, his nightclothes aflame, his face blackened, the whites of the eyes and the open red hole of his mouth the only features. A clap of thunder drowned out his words. Tora threw him on the ground and rolled him in the dirt. The burning clothes seared his hands, but he did not stop until the last flame was extinguished. Young Kaneharu moaned and babbled.

Chaos broke out in the street; people shouted and rushed about in a panic. A few came to look at the burned man, who finally became quiet.

Young Kaneharu twitched and opened his eyes. He said in a clear voice, 'My father's in there,' and struggled to get up.

Someone explained that the man was the owner of the shop and had been trying to get his aged father out.

Tora looked at the fire, which by now filled the entire front section of the house and was coming through the roof. He asked the injured man, 'Where's your father? Where in the house?'

The old woman said, 'He's all the way in the back.'

Young Kaneharu nodded. His hands looked charred. Tora was afraid to look at his own. They hurt viciously, but the man was in worse shape with burns all over his body. The skin that showed through the holes of his clothes looked blistered. He must be in dreadful pain. Even so, he reached for Tora with his charred hands. 'Please save my father.'

It seemed hopeless. These houses were built of wood, bamboo, and grass matting. The fire had gained the upper hand, and Tora could see past the shop to the back where the flames were leaping up to the neighbor's roof. There was no way to get through those flames.

Tora got up and shouted at the gaping crowd, 'Don't stand around. Get sand and use buckets to bring water from the nearest canal. Make a chain and pass the water along. Throw it on the fire and pass the buckets and pails back.'

They knew the routine, kept a bucket of sand in every house in case of accidental fire, but this fire was already much larger than what a single bucket of sand could extinguish. They started running, though, and perhaps it would rain in a moment. Tora turned back to the moaning man on the ground.

'Is it possible to get in from the back? From an alley?' he asked.

The man looked dazed with pain. Tora had to repeat the question before he nodded. 'An alley, yes. An alley. Save him.'

'I will. Rest now.'

Tora left the fire to the weather and the neighbors. They had the most to lose if the flames spread and so would do their best to put them out. He ran down the street, the first raindrops cooling his face, looking for an opening between buildings that would lead to the backs of the houses. He found it five houses down and, guided by fitful lightning, scrambled over rain barrels, bamboo staves, empty chicken crates and other objects to reach the narrow alley.

As he doubled back towards the fire, he ran into the thick, acrid smoke produced by wet wood. The wind had shifted, and it choked him, making him cough and his eyes water so that he could barely see. Through the murk appeared the orange light of flames. To his relief, the fire had not yet reached the back of the house. Covering his mouth and nose with a sleeve, he vaulted a low fence into the yard of the burning house. The yard, too, was choked with odd objects, hazy shapes that got in Tora's way. The hot air carried burning bits that started small flames among the debris.

Tora's lungs labored for every breath and burned as painfully as his hands. He knew he had very little time to find the old man. Half-blinded, he found a shuttered door and pulled with hands that felt raw. A thick cloud of hot, suffocating smoke came out and drove him back. He coughed and gasped, then plunged into the dark room, holding his breath and feeling his way. His foot touched a body, and he bent to feel for the old man. There was no movement or response, and Tora needed air. Staggering back outside, he drew in a lungful of smoky air and choked.

Suppressing the coughing bout, he dived back in, found the old man's ankles and pulled him outside. There his strength gave out and he fell across the old man, his last conscious thought of Hanae and his little son.

OBLIGATIONS

After the night's brief rain, it should have been another fine summer day in the capital, but Akitada woke to the acrid smell of smoke. The Sugawara house was built of wood and cedar shingles.

He got up quickly and stepped on the veranda, looking anxiously about and sniffing the air. The smoke hung like a thin dark fog above the cedar-bark roof of his house and the tree-tops of the garden, but the fire had been elsewhere. The reassurance was brief.

There had been too many fires in the capital lately. Homes and businesses had been destroyed and some people had lost everything. Of course, the danger of fire was always present, what with candles, oil lamps, open braziers, and torches. It was particularly bad in the inner city, where people lived in flimsy houses built close together. Not infrequently a whole quarter went up in flames, and if the wind was high and blew north-ward, the fires could reach even the imperial palace, though this year there had been fires started in the palace grounds.

Frowning, Akitada went back inside to put on his clothes and prepare to go to work at the ministry. He already had a bad feeling about the day.

When Seimei crept in, balancing his master's gruel and a pot of tea on the household account ledger, Akitada shifted his worries to more personal matters. Seimei was well past seventy and plagued by aches and pains that were always much worse in the morning, yet he insisted on serving his master as he had done all his life.

Because he felt guilty, Akitada said a little peevishly, 'Thank you, but I wish you'd let me fend for myself. I'm perfectly capable of going to the kitchen to get my breakfast. Where is the fire, do you know?'

Seimei placed the dishes carefully before answering. 'It was in the merchant quarter again, sir. The rain put it out, but the wind still carries the smoke our way. People are talking of divine retribution.'

Akitada paused with his cup halfway to his lips. 'Why?'

'They demand reinstatement of Prince Atsuyasu as crown prince. He was passed over in the succession.'

'Nonsense.' Akitada took little interest in court politics and did not believe that the gods started fires because they disapproved of political shenanigans. Whenever such notions took hold of the simple-minded populace, great mischief ensued. Seeing Seimei still hovering with the account book, he said, 'Sit down and have a cup of tea. What's this all about?'

Seimei accepted the invitation. 'There have been so many fires lately. People say it isn't natural. They also say there have been omens and portents that a great disaster will befall the capital.'

'Unsubstantiated rumors.' Akitada did not know the prince. He was a mere secretary in one of the ministries, and lower-ranking officials did not come into contact with those who lived 'above the clouds'.

But Seimei was not so easily deterred. 'His Majesty has ordered the reading of sutras by eight priests and the reciting of prayers and making of offerings in all the Amida halls of the temples.'

Akitada frowned. 'Hmm. They do that sort of thing frequently anyway.' Putting the matter from his mind, he changed the subject. 'How is my wife this morning?'

Tamako, who was due to give birth, slept very poorly these days, and he had not wanted to disturb her during the night. The fear of losing her and his unborn child was with him all the time.

Seimei smiled. 'Her Ladyship was in good spirits yesterday. She walked a little in the garden with Oyuki. I believe she is still asleep.'

Oyuki, Tamako's maid, had returned to her service after the death of her husband. Akitada had reason to be grateful to Oyuki these days, and to Tora's wife Hanae. He was useless in matters of pregnancy and childbirth, and seeing his wife in her present shape terrified him. He said, 'I'm glad. In that case, I won't trouble her, but tell her I'll see her tonight.'

Seimei nodded. He watched his master finish the bowl of gruel, then said, 'Tora just came home.'

'What? At this hour? Is he visiting the wine shops and gambling houses again?'

Seimei pursed his lips. 'I cannot say, sir, but he looks terrible.'

'The rascal is probably drunk.' Akitada suspected he had slept in some harlot's bed and felt angry on Hanae's account. He had come to like Tora's pretty wife, who filled the house with her singing and had given Tora a bouncing baby son. Tora did not know how lucky he was in having her and that fine little boy.

The door opened, and Tora walked in. His clothes were in tatters and his face and hands were an angry, sooty red. Gray ashes covered his hair, making him look prematurely old.

'What happened to you?' Akitada demanded. 'Where've you been all night?'

Tora's eyes were red-rimmed. He made a choking sound and swallowed. 'There was a fire,' he rasped.

Akitada looked him over. He did not like the labored breathing or the dazed look in Tora's eyes. 'Are you hurt?'

Tora shook his head and winced. 'Don't think so. Passed out and got singed a little. A constable pulled me out.' He cleared his throat and coughed. 'I don't seem to be able to catch my breath.'

Akitada glanced at Seimei. The old man was frowning. 'But how did you come to be at a fire?' he asked.

Tora hung his head. 'Went out for a cup of wine. Was going home when I smelled smoke. Went to see if I could help.' He paused to cough again.

'Don't talk any more,' Akitada said, regretting his earlier suspicions.

'The old guy was dead when I got to him,' Tora said. 'I know it was stupid.'

Akitada did not like the way Tora looked and sounded. He seemed dazed and sick. 'Well, go now and get cleaned up,' he said. 'Seimei and Hanae can tend to your injuries. If you feel well enough afterwards, you can tell me all about it.'

Tora struggled to his feet and walked out slowly.

Seimei cleared his throat. 'He must have breathed in too much hot smoke,' he said, shaking his head. 'And there is some blood in his hair. I wonder if the house fell on him. I'll go and prepare an ointment for the burns and perhaps a special tea for his throat. Purslane and honey, I think.'

Akitada poured another cup of tea and looked at Seimei's

household accounts. Though meticulously accurate, they were unsatisfactory, as expected. The income from his farms had disappeared after the smallpox epidemic. The harvest had been lost because some of the peasants had died or fled the land. Meanwhile, there were more mouths to feed here on the modest salary of a senior secretary in the Ministry of Justice. He wondered again if he could afford to continue keeping two horses in the city.

Tora returned quickly. He had washed and changed his clothing and looked much better, his eyes steady, and his color back to normal.

Akitada gestured to a cushion. 'Sit down. Are you sure you feel well enough?'

'Yes.' Tora touched his head gingerly. 'A few blisters don't matter, but I got hit on the head pretty hard. And then later the smoke got to me.' He swallowed. 'Seimei made me drink something.' He grinned. 'It tasted pretty good for once.'

'You got hit? By accident?'

Tora grimaced. 'No. The bastards meant it.'

Akitada wondered how badly Tora had been injured. 'What bastards? I thought constables pulled you from a burning house?'

'Yes, later. I was attacked on my way home. Some female jumped from an alley and knocked me down. The thieving bitch was scooping up my money when a bunch of street kids came, and one of them hit me on the head with a piece of wood.' He rubbed his head. 'Come to think of it, maybe *she* was really a *he*. What I had a hold of didn't much feel like a woman. Didn't fight like a woman either.'

Akitada stared at Tora. 'What money?'

Tora blushed. 'I won it at dice. Silver and a few pieces of gold. Enough to pay off my little farm. I hope the bastards roast in hell where they belong.'

'You've been gambling?'

'Don't tell Hanae, sir. She wouldn't understand.'

Akitada was about to snap that he did not understand either – or rather, that he understood only too well that Tora had returned to his old ways. He swallowed his words and asked, 'What of the fire?'

'When I got up, I smelled the smoke. The fire was one street over. A shopfront was blazing when I got there, and the owner was jumping around looking like some demon. His clothes were on fire – that's how my hands got burned. He asked me to get his father out. I tried, but as I said, the old man was gone. Smoke, I think, because the fire hadn't reached the back of the house yet.'

Akitada said, 'I see. Well, I'm very glad you're alive. We'll forget about the gambling in view of the good deed you tried to do. I'm sorry that you lost the money, but if you waste your time in low pursuits, you attract the notice of criminals. No doubt they worked together, your attacker and his or her companions.'

Tora pulled something from his shirt and laid it on Akitada's desk. It was an amulet bag with a broken string. 'One of them dropped this,' he said. 'I was hoping you could tell who it belonged to and I could try to get my money back.'

Akitada reached for the small bag. The material was blue silk with a pattern of golden wheels. 'I doubt this will help. The wheels are symbols of Buddha's law. I expect they stole it also. Or if you tangled with a female, she may have dropped it. Prostitutes are superstitious and get such presents from wealthy clients.' He fingered the pouch. 'The silk is very good, and there's something inside.' He started to open it.

Tora said quickly, 'Don't! You'll break the spell.'

'What do you care? It's not your spell.'

'Oh.'

In the bag was a small but finely made ivory figurine of the Bodhisattva Fugen riding a crouching elephant. Akitada turned it this way and that. 'This carving is extraordinarily good. I doubt anyone would give it to a woman of the streets. More likely, it's stolen.' He put the figurine back, pulled the drawstring and returned the amulet to Tora. 'Sorry.'

Tora opened the pouch and peered in. 'Is it worth a lot of gold?'

'I don't know. You'd have to take it to a dealer in religious objects.'

Tora sighed. 'Will you keep it for me? I'd rather not explain it to Hanae.'

DISMISSED

Akitada's day did not improve at work. Munefusa, an unpleasant and ignorant junior secretary, had made several mistakes in a legal document. Akitada did not relish discussing the matter with him. He missed Nakatoshi, that bright and eager young man who had worked with him a year ago during that dreadful summer. But Nakatoshi had moved on and now served as junior secretary in the Ranks Office of the Ministry of Ceremonial.

He made the corrections and was debating how to present the matter most diplomatically when a clerk appeared with a summons from the minister.

Since the minister seldom appeared at work, Akitada decided to have a word with him about Munefusa. Fujiwara Kaneie was approachable and seemed to like Akitada. Today, however, he greeted Akitada stiffly and would not meet his eyes. After Akitada was seated, he said, 'You may be aware that His Excellency, the new chancellor, has been reviewing the positions in the various ministries?'

Akitada's first thought was that Kaneie, a pleasant and harmless young man, had lost his position to another stupid purge of anyone connected to the previous crown prince. A number of high-ranking noblemen had resigned lately or accepted reassignments. He said cautiously, 'I hope there is no bad news, sir.'

Fujiwara Kaneie was younger than Akitada by nearly ten years. He had the sort of smooth skin that flushes easily and he flushed now. His eyes briefly met Akitada's, then he looked down at the sheaf of papers studded with official seals on the desk before him. 'I am afraid you will think it so,' he said in a voice so low that Akitada leaned forward. 'You are to be demoted to the rank of junior secretary.' He heaved a sigh and raised his head. 'Believe me, Sugawara, this was none of my doing. I was told that one of the controllers, Kiyowara Kane, questioned your qualifications. Kiyowara has the chancellor's ear. I tried to tell them about the good work you have done for me, but you probably know that my voice has no weight these days.' He sighed again unhappily.

Akitada had difficulty digesting this news. 'Junior secretary? But we already have a junior secretary. Not that he is qualified. I had my hands full this very morning with the mistakes he's been making. Still, the position is filled.'

'Hmm, er, not exactly.' The minister shifted on his cushion and bit his lip. 'Er, Munefusa will trade places with you.'

'What?' Akitada was shocked. 'The man knows nothing of the law, let alone of the duties of a senior secretary. You know very well that you have always relied on me to see that things are done properly.'

The minister flushed more deeply. 'I wish you would not imply that I am also unqualified for my duties,' he said testily.

Akitada was only dimly aware that he had overstepped his bounds. He was still wrestling with the unfairness the decision. Of course, Fujiwara Kaneie *was* unqualified to run the Ministry of Justice. Most of the high-ranking nobles were merely figure-heads. Only a year ago Kaneie had taken the place of the villainous Soga, who had died in the epidemic. At the time, Kaneie had admitted to Akitada that the work was beyond him. Akitada had covered for him. What would happen now if the inexperienced minister had to depend on an incompetent secretary to carry out the duties normally assigned to this office? More to the point, what of all the hard work Akitada had done to make sure that no one realized the minister was unfamiliar with all but the social and ceremonial functions of the office? Meanwhile, Akitada's reward for his loyalty and effort would be a drastic loss of income just when they needed the money most. And to be replaced by the incompetent Munefusa was an insult.

Clenching his fists, Akitada snapped, 'Don't pretend you tried to defend me. I don't believe it. I think there's some political advantage to you. You know very well that you were unqualified for your duties the day you arrived. In my view you've made little effort since to grasp the basic aspects of our work here. I have covered for you, and the thanks I get is a demotion. No, worse than that. You're putting an idiot in my place.' Seeing the minister begin to bluster, Akitada raised his voice a little. 'Don't bother to deny it. You've buckled down to the new chancellor's demands. And that was not only ungrateful, but also cowardly, sir.'

He regretted his outburst the moment the words left his mouth, but it was too late. Kaneie shot to his feet, his face an alarming shade of scarlet. 'I believe,' he said in a shaking voice, 'it will be best if you take a leave of absence. Immediately. Clearly, the news has deranged your mind. You will be told when – or if – to report back.'

Akitada stood also, his face hot with anger and embarrassment. He considered resigning or apologizing, but in the end he just bowed and left.

Breathing hard, he stalked back to his office, thinking to sit down to gather his thoughts and calm the rage that had caused him to lash out at Kaneie. The minister was the last man he should have attacked, and he had acted with little foundation, too. He had no proof that Fujiwara had not made an attempt to defend him. In fact, the minister himself was on shaky ground with the present administration. Besides, Kaneie had always been fair with him, had even been a friend in the past.

He was considering the situation more rationally until he walked in on Munefusa rearranging the furnishings in his office.

'What are you doing?' Akitada snapped, seeing his desk pushed against the opposite wall.

'Oh,' said Munefusa with a silly grin, 'I got the news before you and thought I might have a look at my new office. You're to take mine, I believe.' He turned to eye the array of books and scrolls on the shelves and went to take down a large tome.

'Those are mine,' said Akitada quickly. 'Aren't you rushing things a bit?'

Munefusa put the book back and turned, smiling more widely. 'Not at all, Sugawara. You've always said yourself we shouldn't waste time. Do you want some help moving these things?'

Disarmed by the offer, Akitada nodded sourly. Munefusa was not to blame for the vagaries of fate.

Munefusa clapped his hands and told the man who appeared, 'You will assist the junior secretary by taking a few things to my old office.' Then he looked around one more time and said, 'I'll leave you to it, Sugawara. Make sure to take the inventories in the Tomonori case with you. I'd like to see them finished and on my desk by this afternoon.'

Akitada glared at him, then said coldly, 'I am to take a leave of absence. You'll have to find someone else to do your work.'

Munefusa raised his brows. 'Dear me, it's worse than I thought. What did you do?'

Akitada turned away. By now completely demoralized, he made no attempt to settle into Munefusa's small office, but took only a few of the most valuable books and his father's writing box before leaving the ministry. In better days, he could have summoned one of the ministry's servants to carry his things, but seeing the secret smirks and blank stares, he did not have the courage to ask. He had thought he was well liked, but in this world a man's value was judged by his influence.

The smoke had been dispersed by a hot wind. Walking from the ministry in his official robe, while carrying a heavy and awkward armful of objects, caused him to perspire. He thought of Tamako and the bad news he was bringing, thought of her condition and the discomfort she must feel in this heat. They could ill afford it, especially now, but he would go later and purchase some lengths of hemp. Oyuki and Hanae could soak the panels in water and hang them around Tamako's room. Then fanning the air might bring her some relief. He envied the wealthy, who were accustomed to large vessels of ice cooling their houses. The ice was brought into the capital in winter by their servants and slaves and stored in cellars or earthen pits until it was needed during the summer heat. But the Sugawaras could not afford such luxuries. And now, after the way he had insulted the minister, he would surely be dismissed, and times would get much harder.

He expected his early return with his books and writing box would cause instant consternation among his people, but only an astonished Seimei greeted him.

'Back already, sir?'

Akitada said, 'I shall want to speak to you about our expenses.'

Seimei stared at the box full of books. 'But we discussed the accounts only this morning, sir. Is anything wrong?'

'Later,' Akitada said brusquely and went to Tamako's pavilion, clearing his throat outside to give her warning and steeling himself for the sight of his grossly pregnant wife. It was strange that he had not felt either fear or this shameful reluctance to be near Tamako during her first pregnancy. But they had both been younger then and full of life and hope. Tamako had been rosy and healthy and happy. When they had lost that child, his beloved Yori, a few short years later, they had both changed.

Tamako called out, and he opened the door. The room was nearly dark with the shutters closed against the heat. Tamako sat alone, enveloped in a loose gown of stiff rose-colored silk, and moved her fan listlessly to stir the stagnant air.

'How are you?' Akitada asked, scanning her pale face and the dark-ringed eyes. As he came closer, he sniffed the air. It smelled vaguely still of smoke, but also of sweat and illness.

'Well. Thank you,' she said and looked away. 'I'm sorry this is taking so long. You must be tired of waiting.'

'No, not at all,' he said quickly, but he knew she was right. Instead of a wife and companion – a lover, even, in happier moments – she was an invalid and, frighteningly, a reminder of death waiting just beyond the closed shutters. Would he be trading her life for that of another son? Men everywhere faced that fear and bore the guilt of having caused their wives' deaths.

He sat down beside her, taking the hand that rested on the swollen belly. 'I'm afraid, Tamako,' he said more honestly, bowing his head. 'You're not as strong as last time. I blame myself.'

She squeezed his hand and, for a moment, her eyes twinkled. It occurred to him that he had not heard her laugh for weeks now.

'No, no,' she said. 'You mustn't worry. I wanted this child as much as you. Besides, I'm quite strong. I'm just tired, and it has been so hot. It won't be long now. I can feel it. Be just a little patient with me.'

That almost brought tears to his eyes. He said nothing and raised her hand to his cheek and lips.

'You're home early,' she said. 'Is it because of me or has the ministry run out of interesting cases?'

He lowered her hand, cradling it in both of his, and looked away. 'Neither,' he said bleakly. 'I've been given a leave of absence.'

'Oh, how nice!' she said brightly.

For a moment he considered hiding the truth from her, but he knew she would guess, perhaps had guessed already. Yes, she was searching his face. He heaved a sigh. 'It may well be a mistake, but someone close to the new chancellor decided that my promotion to senior secretary was premature.'

'What? How stupid! You're the best man they have.'

He liked the fierceness in her voice and squeezed her hand. 'Thank you, but I'm not as wise as you think. I lost my temper with the minister and that is why he told me to take a leave of absence. I expect it will be permanent unless I can convince them to reconsider.'

Tamako was silent. She just looked at him and curled her fingers around his. He had not really intended to beg for reinstatement, but seeing Tamako's eyes full of faith and loyalty, her free hand on the unborn child, he suddenly felt a powerful bond between the three of them. Yes, of course he would humble himself for Tamako and his unborn son.

He smiled at her. 'I still have friends and must see what can be done. Don't lose faith, my dear.'

'Never,' she said.

He returned to his study, pondering his options. His friend Kosehira, who had once briefly filled the post of minister of justice, had long since been dispatched to the desirable assignment of governor of Yamato province. It was not too far from the capital, but Akitada did not want to make the journey when Tamako was so close to her time. He must, of course, apologize to the current minister. That was only just, even if it would be shameful and likely be interpreted as an attempt to reverse the demotion. He imagined the detestable Munefusa's sneering comments. Then a dim memory surfaced. The minister had mentioned the name of the man who had spoken against him.

He cursed his inattention. The name had not registered because he had not recognized it, but it must be someone important to have the chancellor's ear. The family name escaped him, except that it was not Fujiwara.

Seimei waited, his face anxious.

Akitada sighed. 'I'm afraid there's bad news, old friend. I expect to be dismissed from the ministry.'

Seimei's eyes widened. 'What happened? You've been promoted, and you've always been hard-working. Whatever you are charged with, sir, it must be a mistake.'

Akitada winced. People would quite naturally assume that he must have committed a serious offense – or at least a stupidity – to be treated as he had been.

'I don't know what happened,' Akitada said, 'but I suppose I shall find out. Only, don't expect that the matter will be righted. In my experience, that never happens to men in my position.'

THE ANGRY GODS

When she saw Tora's face, Hanae stopped bouncing little Yuki on her knees and asked, 'Are you in pain again?'

Tora shook his head and winced. 'No, I'm fine,' he lied. 'I'm going out. Don't know when I'll be back.' He looked for his boots.

Putting the baby on the floor, Hanae jumped up. 'Don't go. You aren't well.' She shook his arm when he ignored her. 'Surely the master wouldn't make you run errands after what's happened to you.'

The abandoned baby started crying, and Tora went to scoop up his son, wincing again. 'Where are my boots? The master doesn't know. And don't tell him. This is my business.'

Hanae stood in front of the door, her arms folded. 'You're not leaving,' she said. 'It could be your death to walk around with that big swelling on your head. We need you alive.'

Tora's face softened. He kissed the baby and handed him to Hanae. Retrieving his boots, he sat to put them on. 'I just want to look in on the man whose father died last night.'

Hanae looked uncertain. 'Is that all you'll do? You'll come right back afterwards? You won't get into any more fights?'

He nodded, kissed her and, moving his wife and son out of his way, left the house.

The street that had seemed a living inferno the night before looked merely depressing by daylight. He recalled the urgency and excitement of the flames, sparks, moving shadows, and screams. Now there was only the wet, smoking pile of rubble. The houses on either side were scarred by the heat, and a few neighbors moved about, making repairs. No one bothered with the ruin.

The Kaneharus had made and sold *tatami* floor mats. The grass mats, of course, were a great fire hazard, and so the disaster might be blamed on carelessness with open flames and cooking fires, but Tora recalled the old woman's calling to the gods. He shuddered. That fire had seemed unnatural. Could the gods really be so angry that they would kill an old man?

He walked up to a man on a ladder who was ripping charred boards from the wall of his house and asked what had happened to his neighbor.

The man glanced down. 'He's dead,' he said and returned to his work.

The curt finality sickened Tora. It wasn't right that people cared so little about each other. Maybe life was just a matter of accepting tragedy and making repairs. 'What?' he persisted. 'Both the father and his son have crossed that bridge?'

The man now paused to look at Tora more closely. He took in his bruised face and the blistered hands. 'You were here last night, weren't you? You're the one that tried to get Old Kaneharu out.' When Tora nodded glumly, he climbed down and said, 'The old man walks that path alone, but Young Kaneharu's very bad. He's staying with a cousin.' He gave Tora directions, then added with a bow, 'We're grateful that you told us what to do to save ourselves and our houses. May the Buddha smile on you.'

Tora waved that away. 'Buddha sent the rain, and you did the rest yourselves.' He glanced once more at the steaming pile of blackened timbers that had been a shop and a house and was now unrecognizable. The smell was acrid, but he knew it would have been much worse if it had not rained. The whole street would have gone up in flames. Other people would have died in the fires. Perhaps the rain, too, had been the gods' doing.

The neighbor looked at his damaged wall. 'Old Kaneharu was cheap. A regular miser. Look at what his fire did to my place and the others.'

This astonished Tora. 'What do you mean?'

The neighbor shook his head and started back up the ladder. Tora looked after him and reflected that neighbors were like family. You had no choice in the matter. And this man was clearly unhappy about the damage to his house. Then he had a thought and shouted up, 'You have much trouble with thieving kids around here?'

The man looked down and shook his head. 'Not lately.'

The search for Kaneharu's cousin proved frustrating. After trying several streets in vain, Tora passed a large house of a rice dealer. A sign read 'Watanabe – Best Rice for Eating or Seeding'. Bales of new rice were stacked near the door, and from the back came the sound of pounding: someone was grinding rice into a fine meal. A fat man stood in the doorway, filling it with a broad belly covered in gray silk. He was counting the bales and shouting numbers to a clerk, who was making entries in an account ledger. The fat man's round, shiny face rested on several chins, and the bulging eyes and thick lips suggested that his body could barely contain so much good living.

When the merchant had finished counting, Tora greeted him and asked about the umbrella maker who was married to Kaneharu's cousin.

The merchant pursed his thick lips. His face reminded Tora of a large koi. The man compressed his lips and said, 'Two streets back. Number sixteen. Is it about the fire? The gods' anger is a terrible thing.' He shook his head. 'It's criminal to let this go on. Now a man has died, and they say the son's not going to make it.'

The umbrella maker's shop was one of the poorest in this quarter. He was not as well off as the Kaneharus. The owner sat cross-legged in his small shop, splicing bamboo. When Tora asked for Kaneharu, he made a face and shouted for his wife, then went on with his work of splicing and cutting umbrella ribs. His pale, thin wife took Tora to the back room, where her cousin lay on a pallet. He was shivering continuously and his teeth chattered. His chest, arms, and legs were covered with stained bandages, and his swollen, crimson face shone with oozing burns and the ointment the cousin had applied.

'He's bad,' the cousin whispered. 'The fire's eating him up from inside. He says he's got nothing to live for now. His business is gone, and so is Uncle.'

Tora nodded and squatted beside the injured man. 'Kaneharu,' he said, 'can you hear me?' The eyes flickered open, rested on Tora for a moment, then closed. Tora tried again. 'Do you remember me? I tried to get your father out last night. It grieves me that I failed.'

This time the eyes flickered and stayed open longer. The blistered lips moved and sounds emerged, but Tora could not make out what Kaneharu was saying and bent closer. 'What?'

His cousin offered a translation. 'There's no shame in that. You were very kind.'

Tora doubted that the shaking and shivering patient had said all of that, but he accepted it, asking, 'Did your cousin say what happened? How the fire started?'

Kaneharu moaned loudly and said something.

The cousin gave a little cry and put a hand over Kaneharu's lips.

'What? What did he say?' Tora asked.

The cousin shook her head. 'He blames the gods, but it was an accident.'

The dying man – Tora no longer doubted that Kaneharu was dying – rolled his head about from side to side and said quite clearly, 'Father paid the money. He *paid.*' Then the shaking got worse, and he started to wail.

His cousin reached into a basin for a moist cloth and laid it on his head, making soothing noises as if to a whimpering child. She gave Tora a pleading look. 'He's not in his right mind,' she muttered.

Tora nodded. He bent to Kaneharu. 'Please forgive me for troubling you. I'll pray for you.'

Kaneharu said nothing.

Tora let himself out. Perhaps the cousin was right and he was out of his mind with pain. Tora wondered if he should go back and talk to the neighbors again, but he did not feel up to it. His breathing was still shallow and painful and both his head and his hands hurt. It would have to wait.

More importantly, he had given his word to Hanae.

THE INAUSPICIOUS VISIT

A kitada hated pleading, but he stiffened his resolve with an icy determination. The image of Tamako's pale face was before his eyes, and the hardships they would all soon suffer were on his mind.

He had sent Genba with his horses and the dog Trouble to the farm to save on feed. The farm did not produce much in terms of saleable rice, but there was plenty of grazing. It had been hard, because he loved his own horse and enjoyed riding it. They would now be forced to rent horses. It meant they would not go anywhere they could not walk to, but it was more important to feed his family.

And he would miss the dog. In spite of the well-earned name, Trouble was a member of the family, and Akitada thought that the dog had shown particular affection to himself.

His best hope lay in avoiding dismissal. He must try, even if it involved groveling. The prospect sickened him so much that he had not been able to eat.

He decided to start with the minister. Here, at least, he had been in the wrong. To his dismay, however, Fujiwara Kaneie was not in – though on second thought it would have been more unusual if he had been.

Unfortunately, his request to speak with His Excellency was overheard by the detestable Munefusa, who came running, full of glee at Akitada's disappointment.

'Come to apologize, have you?' he asked, loud enough for everyone to hear. Heads popped out from doors as clerks and secretaries expected another confrontation. 'Won't do you much good, I'm afraid. The minister was very angry.'

Akitada bristled. 'You've got it wrong again, Munefusa. My purpose was to find out the origin of a certain false rumor about me. No, I don't suspect you. You haven't got the intelligence or the reputation to carry a convincing tale.'

Someone snickered, and Munefusa flushed. 'Whatever you may think of me, I know who's responsible, while you don't.'

Akitada was already sorry that he had let his temper get away from him. He said more calmly, 'Do you? Well, then I needn't trouble His Excellency. Out with it.'

Munefusa raised a brow. 'That wouldn't be very professional, would it?'

'Why not? It should be your first interest that those who are connected with the Ministry of Justice are above reproach. I'm merely clearing my good name.'

'There's a matter of confidentiality involved here.'

Akitada took a step towards Munefusa. 'So you've lied again. You know nothing. You just like to make people think you have the power to hurt them.'

The hallway had filled with clerks, scribes, and servants. Munefusa looked at them, then told Akitada, 'I happen to know because His Excellency told me. The person who complained about you to the chancellor is Junior Controller Kiyowara Kane. And I wouldn't recommend approaching him. You might find yourself thrown out of his house.' With that, Munefusa turned and ducked back into his office.

Akitada looked after him with a smile. 'Good!' he said and winked at the audience before walking away. He was nearly outside when quick footsteps sounded and an elderly clerk caught up with him.

'Sir,' he said, a little out of breath, 'we wanted you to know that we all think very highly of you and pray that justice will be done. Munefusa will be the death of us all. He doesn't know anything.'

Akitada was very touched, but he said only, 'Thank you, Shinkai, but you mustn't let me, or anyone else, hear you speak this way about a superior again.'

They bowed to each other and parted.

Who was Kiyowara Kane? The name seemed vaguely familiar: not because he had met the man, but rather because someone had mentioned him as being one of the new chancellor's supporters or friends. Akitada, who was excessively non-political for a civil servant, had paid little attention to the recent shifts of power in the administration. Now he stopped at the tax office, a place he visited occasionally when he needed to consult its archives for cases involving property disputes.

The archives were just as dim, dry, and dusty as he remembered. 'Kunyoshi?' he called. There was no answer. It was too silent. On the other hand, the head archivist was old and nearly deaf. Akitada had long since expected him to leave the service to become a monk. He went to look for him, making his way through a warren of rooms filled with shelving, down narrow halls lined with more shelving, into larger spaces divided by yet more tall stacks of shelving. The shelves were stacked high with dusty boxes and tagged with wooden markers.

He found Kunyoshi in the last room: a small cubbyhole with a desk. Kunyoshi was folded forward over the desk, his white head resting on a stack of papers. His brush had dropped from lifeless fingers to the floor.

Akitada felt the familiar tightness in his belly when in the presence of death and took a deep breath. Poor Kunyoshi – taken in the midst of a loyal service to the emperor that must have exceeded fifty years. It would have been what he wanted. Too many of the dead in Akitada's past had died prematurely, violently, because they stood in someone's way. This made him suspicious of all sudden deaths. So he peered more closely, then felt very foolish; Kunyoshi's breath caused one of the sheets of paper to flutter slightly. The old man was asleep, drooling a little on one of his documents.

Akitada touched his shoulder, and Kunyoshi came upright with a cry. Staring up at Akitada, he clutched his thin chest. 'Wha— what? Who . . . Is something the matter?'

'I beg your pardon, Kunyoshi.' Akitada felt guilty. 'I only wanted to ask a question, but you were so preoccupied that you did not hear me call out.'

'Ah. Ah so. Yes, quite,' mumbled Kunyoshi, glancing down at the half-finished document and brushing at the spittle with his sleeve. He looked around for his brush, then gave up. 'It's you, Lord Sugawara,' he said and made an attempt to struggle up, but Akitada gently pushed him back.

'Don't disturb yourself. It's a small thing and hardly worth interrupting your work. Still, I would be very grateful for the information. Do you happen to know anything about a Kiyowara Kane?'

Kunyoshi blinked. 'Certainly. He's a new man. His first lady is the chancellor's second lady's sister. You haven't met? He's very eager, they say.' Kunyoshi compressed his lips. 'Being a provincial no doubt has something to do with it.'

Some of this made sense to Akitada. Kiyowara had garnered an important position in the central government because of his connections to the new chancellor's wife. Since life in the provinces held little charm for the nobility, Kiyowara was now very eager to make a name for himself. The old guard, like Kunyoshi, despised such men. But why was this provincial gentleman bent on persecuting him? Unless it fell under the heading of busywork to impress his brother-in-law and others in power. Akitada thought his case might look a little more hopeful if Kiyowara simply labored under a misconception and could be made to see reason.

'What exactly is his position?' he asked.

The archivist made a face. 'Junior Controller of the Right.'

Impressive. That put him in the senior fifth rank, many steps above Akitada and several above Kaneie. More importantly, as a controller he had a significant voice in the administration of those ministries that formed the right arm of the government, and that included the Ministry of Justice.

'I see,' said Akitada. 'Do you happen to know where he lives?'

Kunyoshi cackled. 'You should know his house well. It used to belong to your former chief.'

Akitada was taken aback. The Soga villa had been the home

of his old nemesis, the late Minister of Justice, Soga. The know-ledge brought back memories of being ordered to report there to feel the lash of Soga's tongue and hear threats of immediate dismissal.

Under the circumstances, it was a very bad omen.

It suddenly struck Akitada that he was reliving the past. A little more than a year ago he had also faced dismissal. And though he had kept the position, while Soga had died, the same plague that took Soga had taken Akitada's son. He was not by nature a superstitious man, but fear seized him again: a year ago he had lost Yori. Would he lose Tamako and another child this time?

Akitada left Kunyoshi with muttered thanks.

His earlier determination now quite undermined, he set out to make the acquaintance of this official who had happily destroyed a stranger in order to make himself appear conscientious and hard-working.

The Soga house had always been far more luxurious than his own, which had fallen on hard times. The Sugawara family had suffered the disfavor and persecution of the Fujiwara rulers and had eventually sought refuge in the anonymity of poverty. Thus, the Soga villa occupied a much larger property, allowing for extensive gardens, many courtyards, and separate service build-ings. The new owner had found it necessary to embellish the property further. The thatched roofs of the main hall and front gate had been replaced with shiny new green tiles, and fresh white sand covered the entrance courtyard. Trim, railings, and banisters were newly lacquered in brilliant red.

Numerous servants in white uniforms with black sashes were busy placing tubs of ornamental trees about. An older man in a dark silk robe, who had a long, pale face, supervised them. When he saw Akitada, who wore his second-best silk robe and his court hat with the rank ribbons, he came to greet him.

'Sugawara Akitada,' said Akitada in the brusque manner likely to get service. 'From the Ministry of Justice. I'm here to see Lord Kiyowara.'

The man bowed deeply, identified himself as Major-domo Fuhito, and led him past the main hall, through an interior court-yard with artistically placed rocks and bamboos, down a hallway, and into a reception room, where he offered him a silk cushion and promised to announce him.

The room was elegant but sparsely furnished. Akitada looked around at a number of handsome paintings, one of which depicted a large manor house surrounded by rice fields cultivated by many peasants. No doubt this was Kiyowara's provincial home, here displayed to demonstrate a background of wealth and importance.

Open doors to a veranda overlooked a part of the private garden. There, too, improvements had been made. The shrubberies were neatly trimmed; an elegant pagoda-like roof with gilded bells rose above them – by its size and decoration it was probably a garden pavilion in the Chinese style – and water glistened between tree trunks where he could not remember seeing any before.

Akitada sat for a while, pondering this visible wealth and the power that went with it, and felt his anger fade to despair. Ostentation was meant to impress, but now he saw that it also intimidated. The best he could hope for in the coming encounter was that he might convince Kiyowara that it was better to sacrifice someone else to his ambition. There had probably been nothing personal in Kiyowara's actions. The irrational notion that somehow Soga's vengeful spirit had taken possession of Kiyowara's body in order to continue his persecution was ridiculous. He bent his thoughts to making a convincing argument for reinstatement.

The sudden appearance of another visitor interrupted this. He was an older man, as formally dressed as Akitada, but with rank ribbons that caused Akitada to kneel and bow deeply. The other man gave him only a casual glance, nodded, and sat down. After a moment, Akitada did the same. He knew Prince Atsunori, Minister of Central Affairs, from the official meetings he occasionally attended. A son of the late Emperor Reizei, the prince was said to be reserved, efficient, and trusted by the young emperor. He also appeared to be haughty, for he refused to speak or look at Akitada beyond the first glance.

How important was Kiyowara if he could make a man like the prince wait? It was not a long wait, however, for the door opened again and a harried-looking Fuhito dashed in, bowed very deeply, and muttered, 'Sincerest apologies, Your Highness. The stupid servant made a mistake. My master asks that you join him.'

The prince rose, lips compressed with irritation. Both left without speaking to Akitada.

Time began to hang heavy, especially when Akitada's thoughts
turned again to Tamako's condition and their precarious finances.
After a while, he rose and stepped out on to the veranda to
distract himself with a look at Kiyowara's grounds.

He saw now that the water was an artificial lake, fed by a
small stream that seemed to meander around the various buildings that made up Kiyowara's villa. It was the sort of stream
where nobles would gather during poetry month to compose
verses and drink cups of wine sent floating downstream by
servants.

The sound of a woman's laughter made him look towards the
pagoda. A moment later, the figure of a gentleman appeared on
the narrow path that skirted the stream. He was about Akitada's
age and handsome in the smooth-faced way that was much
admired at court. As he strolled closer, he glanced back over his
shoulder and smiled. He touched his narrow mustache, perhaps
to make sure that the encounter with the woman had not left
tell-tale traces.

Akitada turned away, embarrassed, but the gentleman suddenly
exclaimed, 'The crickets cry: I sense the coming cold.'

Akitada swung back, but the stranger was not looking at him
– was, in fact, unaware of him. He stood, his arms spread a little
and his head cocked as if he were listening. Then he nodded.
'Yes. Not bad.' He walked closer to the small stream and paused
to stare into the water. After a moment, he raised his hands once
more and declaimed, 'Everywhere the wind moves through dead
grasses, and I shiver in the darkening night.'

It seemed a madman's comment on this hot and humid summer's
day, and Akitada watched him nervously. Just then the man looked
up from the stream and saw him. Far from being embarrassed, he
called across, 'Hello, there. I'm Ono. Well, what do you think?
Will it do? What about "darkening night"? Is that too repetitious?
I was thinking of loneliness and thoughts of death.'

Not a madman then, but a poet. Perhaps there was little difference. Akitada suppressed a smile. He had never been consulted
about poems before, because his lack of talent and interest in
that direction was too well known among his friends. After a
moment's hesitation, he said, 'I like it, but how do you find the
inspiration in this weather?'

Ono looked astonished. 'What does the weather matter?' he
asked and walked away.

Akitada returned to his cushion. So this was Ono Takamura, the famous poet who was said to be working on a collection of poetry to be presented to the emperor this year. What had he been doing in Kiyowara's women's quarters? But it was none of his business.

Surely the prince's visit could not have lasted this long. The sun was already high in the sky, he was hungry and thirsty, and he had been kept waiting for almost two hours. That was insulting. Even high-ranking nobles could at least dispatch a servant to express their regrets at the delay. Clearly, Kiyowara had no intention of receiving Akitada and did not care how rude he was. Akitada was tempted to leave, but sneaking away like a beaten dog did not sit well with him. He jumped up again and stalked angrily to the door, flinging it open to call for a servant.

The gallery outside was empty. To his right lay the way to the entrance courtyard; to the left, a pair of elaborate doors must lead to Kiyowara's quarters. Akitada opened his mouth to shout for a servant, when he heard raised voices behind Kiyowara's door. At least one of the voices was male; the other, slightly higher, might belong to either a man or a woman. Both sounded very angry, but he could not make out words.

Akitada hated to be caught eavesdropping and ducked back into the reception room, closing his door softly. He considered that his errand had just become even less likely to be successful. Kiyowara would be in a bad mood.

A door slammed and steps rushed by outside. Then there was silence. He waited a few moments longer and peeked out again. The gallery was empty, the doors closed just as they had been before.

It would be best to leave and return at a more auspicious time. Akitada tiptoed away and quietly left the Kiyowara compound. Someone in the courtyard saw him pass and called after him, but Akitada simply walked faster until he regained the street outside. There was little point in telling a servant about his futile visit and why he had decided not to wait any longer.

UNDER SUSPICION

The rest of that day and the following one passed without bringing any hope of positive change. The heat continued, and there had been too little rain to assure a good harvest. Tamako was feeling feverish, and Akitada and Tora set about hanging wetted hemp panels over curtain stands in her pavilion, while the maid Oyuki plied a large fan to cool her mistress.

Akitada was increasingly anxious about Tamako, even though she kept assuring him that she felt quite well again now that the room was so much cooler. He placed his hand on her forehead and found it still very hot and dry. Jokingly, he said, 'Let's hope this heat doesn't mean our son will turn out to be a hothead.'

She did not smile. In fact, he thought she looked near tears. Perhaps his words had reminded her of Yori. Yori had not really been a hothead, just a very lively and clever child. He had been born in the bitter cold of northern Echigo, where the three of them had survived despite the extremes of climate and hardship. It was ironic that the comfortable life of the capital should have proved so much more dangerous.

Back in his study, Akitada was looking through old correspondence for the name of some past friend who might be willing to speak up for him when Seimei appeared with tea and news.

'There has been another fire,' he said as he poured. 'They say the people will petition His Majesty to appease the anger of the gods.'

Akitada was cynical about such superstitious delusions. 'Fires happen all the time, and the emperor is still very young and no doubt busy with his wives and concubines. His first duty is to give the nation an heir. And the chancellor supports him in this. His granddaughter has just joined the emperor's ladies.'

Seimei looked disapproving. 'The petition asks that the first prince be declared heir because the gods have turned against the second prince.'

'Not very likely to be successful,' muttered Akitada, sipping his tea.

Seimei switched to another topic. 'One of the new appointees died very suddenly yesterday.' He paused to see if his master was interested. 'It seems even the nightingale in the plum tree cannot escape misfortune,' he pointed out.

This was a mistake because it put Akitada in mind of his dead son and the possibility that this time he could lose both Tamako and his unborn child. He snapped, 'What are those people to us? Less than nothing. Rather tell me that an old friend has come to town, or that there's a promise of a good harvest.' Or, he thought, that my wife has given me another son.

Seimei said defensively, 'This Kiyowara Kane was the Junior Controller of the Right. He was one of your superiors. When he is replaced, it might mean some changes in the ministry.'

Akitada stared at him. 'Kiyowara Kane has died? You must have misheard. I was at his house yesterday. He was alive and well.'

'Nevertheless, he is dead today.' With a certain morbid satisfaction, Seimei went on: 'A man's karma is a turning wheel. You can no more stop it than flowing water. And he had just achieved high office, too. They say Heaven never bestows two gifts at the same time. He may have been given wealth and power, but what is that if he has not life?'

The subject had brought forth a spate of Seimei's sententious sayings, and Akitada interrupted quickly: 'When did he die?' And then, remembering the overheard quarrel: 'And how?'

'The servants found him yesterday in the afternoon. They say he fell and hurt his head, but people are already muttering that the gods struck him dead for having had a hand in passing over the first prince for the succession.'

Akitada did not believe that the gods had struck Kiyowara dead. Still, it had nothing to do with him, especially when he was on a leave of absence. His only regret was that he could not get Kiyowara to withdraw his censure.

Seimei sighed heavily. 'Fate is with Heaven.'

Akitada gave him a look. 'And man must adjust to the blows of misfortune. Let's discuss ways of raising funds for the Sugawara household or of reducing its expenses.'

The discussion proved unproductive, and the rest of the day passed uneventfully until sunset, when Seimei brought in Kobe. The superintendent of the capital police was Akitada's friend and sometimes rival. They had known each other for a long time and had frequently worked together on criminal cases. These days, Kobe was in the habit of dropping by from time to time for a cup of wine and a friendly chat.

Akitada greeted him with a smile, and Seimei busied himself with wine and cups as they exchanged greetings.

'How fares your lady?' asked Kobe.

Akitada sighed. 'She's very uncomfortable. I hope it won't be much longer. I suppose you know how it is.' Kobe had two wives and five children by now and would be familiar with the worries over childbirth.

'My best wishes to her and to you.' Kobe gave him an encouraging smile. 'Come, all will be well. Perhaps it will be another son. An heir to the Sugawara name.'

'We must hope, but life is uncertain.' Akitada thought he was beginning to sound like Seimei. 'How is your family?'

'Thank you, thriving. My oldest wants to be a soldier. It would be safer to attend the university and become an official like his father, but a part of me is proud of him.'

Akitada laughed. 'Only a part of you?'

'To sons!' Kobe raised his cup with a smile.

Seimei slipped out and closed the door. The two friends drank, and a brief silence fell. Akitada thought of his impending dismissal, but decided not to mention it. There was nothing Kobe could do.

Kobe watched him for a moment, then said, 'And how is the estimable Tora – and his family? And Genba?'

Akitada was grateful for the change of topic. 'Genba's gone into the country, but Tora is here, resting after an unpleasant encounter with hoodlums and a fire two nights ago. His wife and baby son are glad to have him home for a while.'

Kobe looked surprised. 'Hoodlums? Why, what happened?'

'He was attacked and knocked out by some youths in the street. When he came to, his money was gone. Then he smelled smoke. He went to investigate and found a business and home in flames on the next street. He tried to save an old man, but it was too late.'

'I heard about the fire. Probably carelessness – an old man falling asleep and knocking over his candle. We don't need any more unexplained fires.'

'True enough.'

Another silence fell. Akitada sensed that something was wrong. Perhaps Kobe had heard of his troubles and was too polite to ask, waiting for Akitada to tell him. He sighed.

Kobe leaned forward a little. 'Is something else on your mind?'

'Yes. I expect to be dismissed. I'm on a leave of absence because I told the minister a little too frankly what I thought of him.'

'Ah.'

The 'ah' disconcerted Akitada. It suggested that Kobe already knew, but surely a friend should say more than 'ah' to such news. He waited.

'Go on,' said Kobe.

'There is no more. Someone close to the chancellor and regent blackened my character, and in response the minister gave my position to an idiot. It reminded me of Soga and his persecution – the same story all over again – and so I lost my temper. Yes, I regret it now, but I'm afraid it's too late.'

'The someone close to the chancellor was Kiyowara Kane?'

Akitada raised his brows. 'Yes. How did you know?'

'According to his servants, you went to see him yesterday.'

Akitada still felt out of his depth. 'Yes, I waited quite a long time and finally left without speaking to him. Seimei says he died later the same day.'

'Can anyone prove that you did not speak to Kiyowara?'

'What do you mean? I was seen to arrive and to leave. By Kiyowara's servants. Prince Atsunori and Ono Takamura also saw me in the waiting room. I exchanged a few words with Ono, but frankly, he didn't strike me as the sort of person who'd pay much attention to anything but his poetry. And the prince did not deign to take notice of me. Why do you ask?'

'Kiyowara Kane was murdered.'

'Murdered? How?'

'Someone hit him on the head. It would help if someone knew you left without seeing him.'

'Look, Kobe, my visit was embarrassing enough. I certainly didn't want to draw special attention to myself. I left as soon as I realized that I'd come at a bad time.'

'A bad time? How so?'

'Kiyowara was quarreling with someone. They were shouting. I decided to speak to him another time.' Akitada stopped. The reason for this interrogation had finally hit him. 'Do you suspect *me* of murdering him?' he asked incredulously.

Kobe's lips twitched, but he did not smile. 'Someone certainly does,' he said dryly. 'I was told of several people in your ministry who are willing to testify that you were furious when you heard that Kiyowara was behind the loss of your position and that you took great pains to find out where he lived. Shortly afterwards, according to Kiyowara's servants, you arrived at his villa and demanded to speak to him. And when you left, much later, you rushed away in an almighty hurry.'

Akitada shook his head. 'But that's ridiculous. I don't know Kiyowara, and I never saw him yesterday.'

'Are these people lying?'

'No.' Akitada was becoming angry. 'You should know that all sorts of interpretations can be put on a man's actions. It is true that I went to see Kiyowara in hopes of clearing up a mistake, but I never got a chance to do so. Killing the man was surely the last thing I would have wanted to do. Now that false report will never be corrected. And apparently I have many enemies.' He took a deep breath, then said accusingly, 'I would not have expected *you* to doubt me, though.'

Kobe relaxed a little. 'I don't. Mind you, you do have a temper. In any case, it was my duty to come and ask you about this.' He lifted his cup, found it empty, and put it back down.

Akitada refilled it and his own. His hand shook a little. They drank. He was shocked at being suspected and wondered if he should mention that the poet had visited Kiyowara's women's quarters, but decided against it. His business there might have been as harmless as his own presence. Perhaps he had flirted with one of the maids. 'That quarrel I heard. It wasn't long after the hour for the midday rice. Did you find out who was arguing with Kiyowara?'

Kobe shook his head. 'Apparently, you're the only one who heard it.'

'I know that the prince went in to see Kiyowara.'

Kobe shook his head. 'A man like Prince Atsunori doesn't need to go to someone's house to kill him. He has the power to ruin men and send them to their deaths quite openly. And if he killed Kiyowara in a fit of anger, we could not prosecute anyway. Are you sure they quarreled? What did you hear?'

'I don't know if the quarrel was with the prince. And I only heard raised voices, not words. One voice was higher than the other. It could have been a woman's. I'd been there a very long time by then – perhaps as much as an hour after the prince went to see Kiyowara. It might have been someone else by then.'

'There you are then.' Kobe looked glum. 'I would ask you to look into the matter, but I'm afraid that might implicate you further. Someone doesn't like you. You are the suspect of choice.'

An uncomfortable silence fell as Akitada wondered what other disasters were awaiting him.

Kobe sighed and got to his feet. 'Well . . . I must be on my way. Best wishes on the impending birth.'

Akitada walked the superintendent to the steps into the courtyard, then returned to his study. People were in a great hurry to lay the blame for the murder on him. It proved how powerful and dangerous the resentment against him was. The progress from implicating him in the murder to his arrest, trial, and exile required only small steps for those in power. He had relaxed too soon, thinking that his former enemies had either died – like Soga – or lost interest in him. Apparently, recent shifts in the administration had once again created an atmosphere where he became a handy scapegoat for the offenses committed by others.

The worst of it was that this time he had no idea who was behind it.

JIROKICHI, THE THIEF

There were five of them. All were in their teens, but strong and fast. Five against one.

Despite his age, Jirokichi was agile, but they cornered him. Somehow, in his hurry to escape the first two, he took a wrong turn down an alley, which brought him to the abandoned temple, and then there were suddenly five, and he took another wrong turn into the temple grounds, hoping to double back towards a busier part of the city.

But they worked together and herded him into the farthest corner, where he ended up boxed in by walls too tall to scale – though he was agile enough – and now they were walking towards him, slowly, with grins on their faces.

Stray dogs closing in on a rat.

'Hey, Rat,' said the one in front, a stringy youth who was their leader, 'why so unfriendly? We just want to chat. We heard business was good lately.'

Business had been good. He had found gold and a finely carved and gilded Buddha figurine he hoped to sell at a great profit to an abbot of his acquaintance, but these five could not know about that. They were guessing.

They closed in around him, their eyes bright with excitement. 'What do you want?' he squeaked. He was small, deceptively frail looking, and when nervous, his voice rose to a piercing squeal.

'Whatever you got, Rat,' said the leader, still grinning. He was an ugly kid with a broken nose and a knife scar running from one ear to the corner of his mouth. His teeth were broken, too, and then Jirokichi saw that the fists he clenched had scarred knuckles – from beating up other victims.

Jirokichi shrunk away a little more until his back was against the wall. The boy next to the leader eyed him with a hungry look. 'Let's take his clothes off and see what he's got.' He fingered the knife in his belt. 'Maybe we'll cut off his jewels.' They laughed.

Jirokichi was close to wetting his pants. He stripped off his jacket and tossed it to them. 'I've got nothing. See for your-selves. You got the wrong fellow.' They searched the jacket and tossed it aside. He started to undo the rope that held up his pants, but the leader's arm shot out and grabbed Jirokichi's wrist. He jerked him forward, against himself, until they were nose to nose. Jirokichi was short, and the other had to lean down over him. Jirokichi felt hands on his body, checking to see if anything was hidden in his pants. One of them twisted his genitals so viciously that he screamed. The leader dropped him, and he fell sobbing and moaning into the dirt.

'Wasted our time,' said one of the youths and kicked Jirokichi in the kidneys.

'Maybe not,' said the leader. 'He left it at home. Up, you turd,' he told Jirokichi.

Jirokichi stayed on the ground, rolled up in a ball and trem-bling. One of the youths grabbed him by an arm and jerked him upright. Another slapped his face with both hands until tears, snot, and blood dribbled down on Jirokichi's bony chest.

'Where's your place?' demanded the leader.

'B–by the f–fox shrine.'

The leader slapped him only once this time. 'What fox shrine, turd?'

'Umajiro koji.'

'Well? Are you going to take us there or not?' the leader asked.

Jirokichi moaned and nodded. He tried to take a step, but crumpled.

'Wipe his face and put his jacket back on,' snapped the leader, 'Walk him between you. Arms around his shoulders. Like friends walking home a drunk.'

They did, and Jirokichi hung between two of them, legs bent and head drooping.

The leader seized Jirokichi's topknot and jerked his face upward to show him a knife. Jirokichi blinked. 'If you try to call for help, you're dead. Understand?'

Jirokichi drooled a little, but nodded again. He accepted that he would probably die anyway.

Tora wore old clothes that were slightly too small and ripped in places where his muscular arms and chest showed to best advantage. His loose hair was tied up in a twisted rag, and he strode through the city with the bearing of a man who could handle himself in any situation.

He felt almost well again. His breathing had returned to normal, and the blisters on his hands had scabbed over. He planned to find the gang of young thieves. The money the bastards had stolen from him had been a small fortune, and the fact that he had been attacked in such a brazen manner in a decent neighborhood rankled.

His destination was the warren of poor tenements that adjoined the Western Market and the deserted ruins and barren fields where the capital's criminals lived like animals in their burrows. Not even the armed constables of the city's police went there willingly. He did not really think he would find the culprit and get his winnings back, but at least he could get information about youth gangs for the police, and that might teach the young bastards a lesson.

When he reached the outskirts, where shacks and warehouses were interspersed with large open areas, he kept a sharp eye on the people he saw. They were poor laborers and their families and outcasts, scrabbling through the garbage of ordinary people to make a living. Not all were criminals, but frequently a father, brother, or son provided for the family with ill-gotten income and was caught, and so all of them hated the police and officials.

That was the main reason Tora was dressed in rags. He hoped to be taken for a tough, a street fighter they wouldn't dare jump in some dark alley.

Even so, he still met some hostile looks from the men. Outside one of the plank huts, a skinny girl with a small child tied to her back gave him a gap-toothed smile and sang out, 'What's your hurry, handsome? Why don't you stay awhile?' Tora quickly turned the corner and walked through a series of dingy alleys with ragged clothing drying on broken fences and hungry dogs barking at him. Where he emerged, a ruined temple, part of its roof collapsed, rose from a grove of trees. He turned that way and almost immediately encountered an oddly assorted group of people.

Five young men in flashy clothing accompanied an older man, who seemed to be having trouble walking. A drunk? Tora had little faith in the charitable nature of the young in this part of town. He had once been their age and poor and had had no regard for anyone else. The young are first of all survivors. Here, in the capital, they were frequently raptors. As he got closer, he saw that the man they supported had been beaten. There were bloodstains on his jacket, and his face was swollen. And they were not supporting him. They were forcibly taking him somewhere.

Their prey was middle-aged, short and frail, his clothes a grayish brown. He did not look strong enough to tackle even the smallest of the five louts.

Tora gauged their strength. Five of them, young and tough-looking. No doubt they carried knives. They were probably no better than the thieves that had taken his money.

He was unarmed. Bad odds, though he outweighed the biggest one and knew a good deal about fighting. Their victim would be no help. On a second glance, he looked like a crook himself. Perhaps the youths had merely repaid him for something he had done to them or their families.

But Tora did not like it when the young and strong abused the weak. He slowed and stepped in their path.

The tallest youth, walking behind, moved around the two who held the beaten man. 'Get out of the way,' he said in a threatening manner.

Tora grinned and raised both hands in a conciliatory gesture. 'Taking your old uncle home from the wine shop?' he asked. 'Got into a little trouble, did he?'

The tall one's eyes shifted to the group. He relaxed a little. 'That's right,' he said. 'My auntie sent us for him. Got there just in time.'

Tora shook his head sadly. 'Some people never learn. Can I give you a hand?'

'No, thanks. We're five of us.' He sounded as if he was making a point.

'Help me,' croaked their victim and cried out as one of the youths twisted his wrist.

'Hush, Uncle,' said the tall boy. 'We'll get you home to Auntie, don't you worry.' He took a step towards Tora. 'You'd better let us pass.'

Tora rocked back and forth on his feet, as if undecided, his eyes on the limp figure between the two young thugs. Then he studied his boots a moment before launching himself at the tall youth, swinging his right foot forward, aiming the heel at the youth's groin. The kick was powerful and unexpected. The youth left the ground and flew a few steps back, landing on his back with an almighty scream.

Tora had already pivoted towards his companions, the two whose hands were free. He used his fist to strike the first one on the temple and send him crashing into the dirt. 'You're next,' he growled to the other. But that one pulled his knife and rushed Tora.

Tora feinted, jumped back, caught the youth's knife arm at the wrist, and twisted it back until it snapped. The knife fell to the ground, and the youth shrieked, cradling his broken arm.

Tora scooped up the knife and turned to the two, who gaped, still holding the limp figure between them. They dropped their burden and ran.

Tora surveyed the wounded trio that was left. The one he had hit with his fist sat on the ground, looking groggy. The tall one lay curled in a ball. He was cursing steadily. 'What were you doing to the old guy?' Tora asked. 'And don't lie to me.'

The one with the broken arm blustered, 'He's a thief. We caught him. We were gonna turn him in.'

Tora fingered the knife. 'And I'm the Empress Jingo. Try again.'

The other backed away. 'He's got a lot of gold hidden.' He glanced at his companions and offered, 'We might share with you.'

Their victim raised his voice. 'They're lying.'

'Hmm.' Tora eyed the small man and decided that he did look like a thief, but a poor one. He turned back to the trio. 'Let's see. What should I do with you? I could call for the constables.'

They merely stared at that suggestion. For some reason, the victim was the one who cried, 'No.'

Tora glowered at the youths. 'Get out of here before I change my mind and cut you up a little.'

The one with the broken arm hesitated only a moment, then turned and ran. The tall one staggered to his feet, cursed Tora, and pulled his groggy friend up. They limped off, clutching each other for support.

After making sure they were gone, Tora checked the miserable heap still sitting on the ground. His shoulders were heaving, and he made a strange wheezing noise. Tora thought he was weeping, but when he bent down, he saw that the wheezing was laughter. The little fellow shook with it. A small claw-like hand shot out and pointed. Down the street, the tall youth Tora had kicked was bent over, vomiting.

'Hehehe!' wheezed the small fellow. 'Hehehehe. Son o' a bitch knows how it feels to get kicked inna balls! Tha'ss worth a piece o' gold, that.'

He had trouble speaking and stopped to feel his front teeth. One of them was loose and started bleeding again. 'Damn bassards beat me,' he said unnecessarily.

Tora reached out to help him to his feet. 'Who are you? Are you really a thief?'

The other stood gingerly and groaned a bit. Then he looked up at Tora. 'Yes,' he said simply. 'I'm Jirokichi. And you, my hero?'

Tora stared. '*You're* Jirokichi? Jirokichi, the thief?' he asked, dumbfounded.

The other nodded. The little fellow was anywhere between thirty and fifty, for all Tora could tell. With his buck teeth, sharp features, and close-set eyes, he resembled a rodent, but Jirokichi, also known as the Rat, was a legendary and magical person, and this creature looked altogether insignificant in his plain and dirty brown cotton clothes. And his manner was ingratiating.

'Well,' said Tora, 'whatever. I'm Tora, and you look like you could use a cup of wine. Come along. I'm buying.'

The little man gave a chuckle and followed obediently. Tora

headed back towards the market. After a while, Jirokichi mumbled, 'Don't believe me, do you?'

Tora looked back, hesitated. The real Jirokichi could make himself invisible. Because of this, he could enter wealthy people's homes while they slept to steal their gold. Among the poor, a kind of religion had developed that venerated the image of a rat, presenting gifts to it and praying that Jirokichi share his wealth with them. There were claims that such prayers had been heard, and that people had found gold in their empty rice bin or under a wooden bucket, or stuffed into their outdoor shoes.

'Maybe your name is Jirokichi, and maybe you're a thief,' Tora said cautiously. 'It doesn't matter. We both need a drink.'

But the fellow tugged at Tora's sleeve. 'It matters to me.' The broken tooth caused him to make whistling sounds when he talked.

'OK, I believe you,' said Tora, suppressing a grin.

At the market, Jirokichi pointed to a small wine shop with benches outside. This time of day it was nearly empty. Tora saw only a few other guests. Inside, a monk ate something from a bowl and two old men drank wine and played *go*. Outside, a shifty-eyed man sat and watched the crowd. He gave them a brief glance, then turned his attention back to the market.

Jirokichi lowered himself gingerly on to the bench and shouted, 'Hoshina! Wine.'

A large young woman appeared from the back of the shop, crying, 'Jiro, my little turtle, is that you?' She glanced at Tora and then at Jirokichi. 'Amida! What happened, lover?'

Jirokichi waved her away and looked at Tora with a blush. 'She's great in bed,' he muttered.

Hoshina reappeared with wine and two cups in a basket. Tora marveled at her size. She was one of the biggest women he had ever seen. Jirokichi's head would barely reach her ample bosom. She took a wet cloth from the bottom of the basket and knelt down beside the little man, touching his bruised face as lovingly as a mother. 'You look terrible. Who did that to you, my love?' She dabbed at the traces of blood.

Jirokichi winced, snatched the cloth away from her, and held it to his swollen lip. 'Don'ask.'

Tora reached into his jacket to pay for the wine, but Jirokichi pushed his hand away. 'On me,' he mumbled through the cloth.

'I thought those hoodlums picked you clean?'

'Hoodlums?' cried Hoshina.

Jirokichi took the cloth away to say, 'No, no. I had a fall. Now pour us some wine, precious.'

'Precious' leaned over him like a pine over a mushroom. 'My poor darling. Whatever you say,' she murmured. She poured. 'Will I see you tonight?'

'I'm not quite up to it.'

She pouted. 'Liar. You're always up to it.'

Jirokichi blushed again and shot Tora a glance.

She raised her chin. 'Maybe I'll ask your friend. He looks like he's up to it.'

Jirokichi gasped, then shot Tora an anxious glance.

Tora laughed. 'Thanks, but I'm a married man.'

'Pity.' She poured the wine, whispered something in Jirokichi's ear, and left.

They drank deeply and sighed in unison. Jirokichi – or whoever he was – certainly looked like a thief. Ask a thief if you want to catch a thief. His color was better, and Tora liked that the little man had not complained about the loose tooth or the pain in his jewels.

'About those louts that attacked you,' Tora said. 'You don't look like a wealthy man.'

Jirokichi gave him a quick glance, then looked down at himself and brushed some dirt from his pants and jacket. 'Whath wrong with my clothes? I'm a working man, and I was clean before those bastards got hold o' me. Leth forget about it.'

Tora's eyebrows rose in disbelief. 'After what they did to you?'

'No' so loud.' Jirokichi looked around, then leaned closer. 'See, where I come from, we don't make trouble for people like us. We help each other.'

Tora snorted. 'After what those cruel bastards did to you?'

Jirokichi frowned. 'They'll be taken care of.'

Tora changed the subject. 'I take it you only steal from the rich to give to the poor?'

Jirokichi ignored the sarcasm. He poured more wine, drank, and felt his tooth again. 'Rich people steal our rice and our labor. I'm taking back what belongs to us,' he explained.

He seemed serious, but Tora did not believe him. 'What if someone turns you in to the police?'

Jirokichi raised his shoulders. 'Life is full of surprises,' he said.

'Then you live dangerously. Is it worth it?'

'Yes. I'm a great man to my people. I'm an artist. I'm no different from a poet or a painter or an archer. I practice my art and polish my style. I watch and I listen. I pick my target. I plan my approach. I execute it perfectly. My body and my mind are trained like a master swordsman's.'

The little man was full of himself. The only thing he had practiced was telling tall tales. And he had not wanted to talk about the youths that attacked him. There was little point in it, but Tora asked anyway, 'Since you do all that watching and listening, do you know anything about that last fire in the Sixth Ward?'

Jirokichi stared at him. 'What?'

'Come on. You must know about the fires. I'm looking for some young hoodlums just like the ones that grabbed you today. They robbed me of a large amount of gold and silver not far from there. If you're such a famous thief, surely you know others like you.'

Jirokichi glanced over his shoulder towards the shifty-eyed guest, then leaned closer. 'I know nothing about any fires.' He glanced at passers-by. 'See that boy?' he said, pointing.

Tora looked. A youngster dressed in blue and white figured silk walked past with the grace of a dancer. 'He's nothing like that devil's spawn you were with or the gang that jumped me. He's some rich kid or an actor,' Tora said dismissively. 'Or someone's toy boy.'

Jirokichi shook his head. 'Wrong. He's also one of the lost boys. The city's full of them. They have to live.'

'You think he's a thief?' Tora narrowed his eyes as he looked after the youngster. 'I don't believe it. The guys I want were street fighters, not pampered boys.'

Jirokichi's eyes widened. 'You saw the boys near the fire?'

'Not well,' Tora admitted. 'But they were together, and they may have a female working with them. She knocked me down and got most of my money.'

Jirokichi raised his brows. 'A female knocked you down?'

Tora flushed. 'I thought it was a woman. I was drunk and didn't see her coming.'

'Ah.' Jirokichi grinned and nodded. 'Careless. How much did they get?'

Tora told him in an aggrieved tone. 'It was to pay off a little piece of land for my wife and son. I'll never have that sort of luck again.'

Inside the wine shop, the monk was gathering his staff and leaving. The old men clicked their *go* pieces as before. 'Plenty of gold around,' Jirokichi muttered, frowning.

Tora grasped the small man's wrist. 'Come on, Jirokichi, you owe me.'

Jirokichi jerked his arm away. He looked both frightened and angry. 'Leave it alone,' he snapped. 'You'll get your gold back.' He got up and hobbled away.

Tora left some coins on the bench and hurried after Jirokichi, but the little man had disappeared.

AKITADA PLAYS WITH FIRE

A kitada woke up to a furious anger.

For years he had struggled against hostilities from members in the administration. Though his family name linked him to the spectacular rise and unjust fall of his ancestor Michizane and he still bore the resentment and fear that that name aroused, he had never become disloyal to the emperor or to the ruling Fujiwara family. At no time had he refused to make sacrifices in his service – risking his life and limb and the lives of his family and people. And, invariably, his loyalty had been rewarded by new demands or punishments. And now someone was trying to pin a murder on him.

Enough was enough.

Notwithstanding Kobe's gentle hint to stay away from the Kiyowara case, he could not wait for others to clear his name.

What Kobe had implied – without saying it in so many words – was that any effort Akitada made to clear himself of the suspicion would make things worse. If the chancellor himself was behind the demotion, Akitada might clear his name, but he would lose everything by interfering.

Perhaps he would have to take his family and seek modest employment in a provincial administration. His friend Kosehira would surely let him serve as his secretary or as a district prefect in his province.

He knew that no official had ever managed to return from such disciplinary dismissal to a career in the capital. He was taking an enormous risk, but if he did nothing, he would also be lost. Kobe would try to help him, but Akitada did not think he would succeed.

He got up and dressed – soberly, to fit his mood. Then he went to tell Tamako of his decision and its likely outcome.

It was early, but he found her awake. She looked drawn and tired – and still much too flushed. He almost changed his mind, but she had as much to lose as he, and they were both concerned for the unborn child's future.

'Forgive me for troubling you,' he said humbly. 'I'm afraid I've made up my mind to take a step that may affect us all. As I seem to be under suspicion for Kiyowara's murder, I will try to clear my name, but this, as Kobe tells me, may cost me my position and rank. We would have to give up this house and move to one of the provinces.'

He saw her tense and fold her arms protectively around her belly. 'Forever?' she asked with a little gasp.

He regretted his abruptness, but it was too late now. 'It may not happen, but if it does . . . I can barely maintain this house at the best of times, and we shall need the funds I can raise on the sale to make a new life.'

'It is your ancestral home, Akitada,' she protested, her voice breaking. 'It has been in your family since Heian-kyo was founded. Oh, Akitada!'

He flushed with shame. 'I know you're disappointed in me – not perhaps on your account, but on behalf of our unborn son. I can only say how very sorry I am. I have tried, Tamako, but I cannot fight against the determination of those in power. The best I can do is to protect my family by removing them from danger and poverty.' He put his face in his hands. 'I've failed to protect you once before and lost my son. Even if I lose my position, I shall at least not fail to protect you again.'

She said nothing.

He lowered his hands. When their eyes met, he saw tears in hers.

'Thank you,' she said, 'but I wonder if you understood my concern. It isn't for myself or our unborn children that I protest, but for you. It isn't like you to give up so easily. This house is a symbol of Sugawara persistence. Don't sell it. We shall find a way to keep it, even if we must go wherever fate takes us. Only, can it wait until this child is born?'

'Of course. I never . . . You did not think we were to leave immediately?'

She chuckled weakly. 'You came with such a fierce look on your face that I thought you wanted me to start packing at once.'

Relief washed over him. 'But the rest . . . You would not mind my losing both position and rank? I doubt I shall ever be able to regain them after this.'

'I'm your wife,' she said firmly. 'Have I ever given you cause to doubt my loyalty?'

'No. Never.' He had doubted her in the past, but he had been wrong. It had been he who had been disloyal to her. Ashamed, he took her hand and held it to his heart. 'I shall try to be a better husband,' he said, then left quickly.

He went to see Nakatoshi first. Nakatoshi had been his clerk when he had run the Ministry of Justice for the absent Soga. Meanwhile, the able Nakatoshi had been promoted and transferred. He was the only man he knew who would help him in this undertaking and be discreet about it.

He found the young man in an office in the Ministry of Ceremonial. He sat behind a very neat desk, dictating a letter to a scribe. His fortunes had changed quickly: he was now a junior-grade secretary in the Bureau of Ranks.

Dismissing the scribe, Nakatoshi rose and greeted Akitada with effusive pleasure.

'I'm impressed,' said Akitada, when seated, looking around the fine room. 'You've done well for yourself. But no one deserves it more, and I expect you'll rise quickly now.'

Nakatoshi made a face. 'The fact is that I miss working in the Ministry of Justice. This is all pretty dull stuff. But one must consider the welfare of one's family. I'm married now, and we're looking forward to a child.' He blushed a little with pride. 'It's wonderful that you stopped by and I could share my news with you.'

Akitada felt guilty that he had not looked in on Nakatoshi before, all the more so because he now wanted a favor. He said, 'My heartiest congratulations. We also – my wife and I – are expecting. Any day, in fact.'

Nakatoshi's face broke into a huge smile. 'Oh, excellent news, sir. I'm so very glad. I'm sure you're particularly looking forward to this child. After the tragedy of last year, you'll finally enjoy the happiness of being a father again.'

Happiness? Akitada was acutely aware of not being happy.
The impending birth had raised all his fears of death again –
Tamako's and the child's this time. And if Tamako survived the
birth, children were so frail. Most did not grow to adulthood.
The joys of raising another small son like Yori were doubly cruel
if that son was also taken away.

'Is anything wrong, sir?' Nakatoshi asked, eyeing him nervously.

Akitada did not want to speak of his private terror and plunged
instead into the murder of Kiyowara Kane and of his having
become a suspect in the case.

Nakatoshi barely let him finish. 'But that's absurd,' he burst
out. 'Anyone who knows you, knows that. Besides, you had never
met the man, had you?'

'No, but I was very angry that he, a stranger, should speak
against me. I'm still angry, only now I can see that I must not
let my enemies use their tricks against me again. I've been warned
away from the case by Superintendent Kobe, but I think doing
nothing is worse. I've come to you for some information about
Kiyowara's family and his friends and associates. Someone must
have had a strong motive for the murder.'

Nakatoshi nodded eagerly. 'The accusation is ridiculous, but
you see, already my life becomes exciting again.' He had such
a look of fervor on his face that Akitada felt uncomfortable.
'Thank you for your trust, sir,' he said. 'I shall not disappoint
you. Allow me to take a part in the investigation – however
small.'

Akitada was dismayed. Any active participation was likely
to ruin Nakatoshi's promising career because he would be
working against a powerful Fujiwara faction. Akitada's enemies
– and Akitada now counted the chancellor among them – would
not think twice before destroying Nakatoshi, who, though
talented and hard-working, did not have the advantage of
Akitada's old and noble name and would be much easier to
remove.

'Thank you for your friendship,' Akitada said. 'I shall not
forget it, but at the moment all I need is some information. This
being the Bureau of Ranks, I thought you might know something about the man.'

Nakatoshi clapped his hands. When his scribe rushed in, he
requested the documents pertaining to Kiyowara Kane. The man
bowed and disappeared. Nakatoshi said, 'Kiyowara is – was –

provincial gentry. His family is said to be quite wealthy, with holdings in Bingo and Izumo provinces.'

'Yes. He bought Soga's villa and has spent a great deal of money on it,' said Akitada.

Nakatoshi smiled. 'I bet you hated going there.'

'I did.'

The scribe returned with a box and left again. Nakatoshi started sifting through the papers inside. 'His father served as governor of Izumo and made a number of very generous gifts to the emperors at the time. No doubt because of that, some of the women of the family were invited to serve at court.' He held up a document and looked at Akitada. 'That would explain Kiyowara's marriage to a daughter of the Minamoto chieftain. His mother was lady-in-waiting at the time and arranged the match. It turned out to be a brilliant move. The following year her sister married Fujiwara Yorimichi, our current chancellor.' He returned to the rest of the papers in the box. 'Kiyowara quickly received appointments. The latest one made him a junior controller.' Nakatoshi closed the box. 'That is all we have. I'm afraid I know nothing of any enemies, but a man who rises so quickly may count on opposition.'

Akitada nodded. 'True, but envy rarely leads to murder. I think there must have been greater provocation. What of his reputation?'

'People say that he was a hard worker. Mind you, since this is the Ranks Office, there was some gossip about what honors he might be striving for next, but it was just gossip. Still, he seems to have been an ambitious man.'

'Yes, I think we can take that for granted. What of his personal life?'

Nakatoshi frowned. 'I seem to recall someone mentioning that he was too fond of women.'

Akitada smiled. This sort of gossip attached itself to many men, and some positively cultivated such rumors. 'You think that perhaps his wife lost her temper?'

Nakatoshi looked doubtful. 'Why didn't she object earlier? I have a feeling that she enjoys being the wife of a man who is rising in the government. You know, of course, that Yorimichi will be making more appointments soon?'

'There have been rumors.'

'Yes. Since Michinaga finally retired to his new palace at Uji,

there have been many changes in the government. Now four of
his sons hold the highest offices, and Yorimichi, the eldest, is
regent and chancellor. Michinaga rules from retirement.'

Akitada remembered the rumors about the fires. 'The people
are still very unhappy about his choice of Crown Prince. Do you
think he will listen?'

Nakatoshi shook his head. 'He's never listened before. Last
year they blamed the smallpox epidemic on this, and now it's
the fires. Still, he must be worried. The court astrologer has done
a reading, and he says the gods are indeed angry.'

They were getting away from the murder case. 'What about
Kiyowara's children?'

'His son by his first lady is the heir, I believe. He's the only
one old enough.'

'If he was a womanizer, it could mean jealous husbands or
lovers.'

Nakatoshi spread his hands in a gesture of helplessness. 'I
can try to find out more.'

'No, better not stir up suspicions. At least, not yet. Besides,
there's another suspect. Prince Atsunori went in to speak to
Kiyowara before me. He may be the man who quarreled with him.'

Nakatoshi reacted much as Kobe had. 'Atsunori? He's an imperial and outranks Kiyowara. If they quarreled, Kiyowara would
be the loser.' He thought. 'Could it have been suicide?'

'No. Apparently Kiyowara's head was bashed in. I did wonder
what a man of Atsunori's rank was doing there.'

'Yes, it's strange.'

'I also saw another famous gentleman. Ono Takamura was
coming from the women's quarters.'

'The poet? He's a favorite of the court at the moment. They
say the collection he's working on will be brilliant. A lot of
people hope to be included.' Nakatoshi pondered a moment, then
said, 'I would have thought him harmless. All he cares about is
poetry and his comforts. He makes himself pleasant to people
in power because they supply him with praise and luxurious
surroundings. Did you know that he lives as a guest in the Crown
Prince's Palace?'

'Does he really? I had much the same impression of the man,
but I think I must try to talk to him. He may know something
about other visitors that day. How does he come to be acquainted
with Kiyowara's wives?'

'I don't know, sir. Perhaps I can find out.'

'Better not.' Akitada rose. 'Thank you, Nakatoshi. Please don't mention this to anyone – for your sake as well as mine.'

Nakatoshi stood also. 'Of course. But I wonder if it might not be better if I asked the questions. It's easier for me to get access to some of the people close to Kiyowara. Won't you let me help, sir?'

Akitada knew what he meant. Doors would be closed to him in too many quarters now. Nobody wanted to be seen to associate with those in disfavor. He smiled at Nakatoshi. 'Not quite yet,' he said. 'Perhaps later.' But he knew he would not involve this very nice young man in his troubles.

'Be careful, sir.'

'I'll try to be, Nakatoshi. My best wishes to your wife.'

Nakatoshi blushed and smiled. 'And mine to yours, sir.'

THE COURT POET

Ono's reputation might have entitled him to quarters in a palace, but his room lacked the luxuries Kiyowara had enjoyed.

When Akitada was shown in by a palace servant, he found a somewhat mean space dominated by a small, old desk and shelving overflowing with books, scrolls, and document boxes. But the writing set on the desk was new and very beautiful. Boxes, brush holders, water containers, seals, and even the brushes were lacquered the color of autumn maples and heavily decorated with golden leaves and mother-of-pearl flowers.

Ono himself wore a casual green silk robe open over a heavy white under-robe and brilliant red trousers. This effeminate attire suited him, as did the lassitude with which he gestured towards a cushion, saying, 'You find me hard at work, Sugawara. Please forgive the lack of amenities. When there are fires every day, one does not want to burden oneself with possessions. Alas, I cannot even offer you wine. I do not take my meals here, and my servant has gone out for ink.'

Akitada sat down. 'Don't concern yourself, sir. It's very good of you to see me.' On closer inspection, Ono was not only a handsome man, but also older than Akitada had thought. His hair, now that he was bare-headed, was turning quite gray, though the eyes were still large and bright and his face smooth. 'I wonder,' Akitada asked, 'if you recall our meeting at Kiyowara's house two days ago?'

Ono looked blank. Clearly, he had not recognized Akitada. But he smiled quickly and nodded. 'Ah, yes. Of course. Poor Kiyowara. He has died, you know.'

'Yes. The very day we met. I'm afraid he was too busy to see me.'

'Ah.' Ono nodded, but volunteered nothing else.

Akitada thought perhaps the poet was still confused and explained, 'You were walking in the garden, reciting poetry. I was on the veranda of the reception room. Do you remember?'

Ono's eyes lit up. 'Oh, *that* poem. I've rewritten it completely. Wait a moment. Now, where did I put it?' He stared at the shelves with their boxes and scrolls, shaking his head. 'It's a very great undertaking, putting together an anthology of the best poems of our time. There are so many submissions that my own work gets lost among them. Sometimes I despair.'

'Please do not trouble on my account,' Akitada said quickly. 'It's the murder of Kiyowara I came about. Being a close friend, you must have some thoughts on who could have killed him.'

'Oh, I'm not a friend. No, not at all. I didn't like the man. And I haven't really thought much about his death.'

That was an astonishing and – under the circumstances – fool-hardy admission. Akitada cheered up a little. The poet's lack of common sense could turn out to be very helpful. He said, 'Oh? I thought as a frequent visitor . . .' and let his voice trail off.

Ono glowered. 'Only of Hiroko and her children. I avoided Kiyowara. The man had neither taste nor talent. His was the soul of a bureaucrat.'

Being a bureaucrat himself, Akitada was not sure he liked this. 'But if you consider his murder now, do you have any suspicions?'

Ono looked up at the ceiling and frowned in concentration. 'I don't know . . . there was some rumor. Some official was dismissed because Kiyowara insisted on it.' He stared at his over-flowing shelves for a moment, then shook his head. 'No, I don't recall exactly. Why do you ask?'

With an inward sigh of relief, Akitada accepted that Ono was simply too self-absorbed to care about those around him. Getting information from him was hopeless. He said blandly, 'Just a matter of interest. With Kiyowara gone, there will be changes in appointments. Someone else will be put in his place. That can make for a powerful motive.'

'You think so? In my world, men feel most strongly about love and art.'

'In mine, ambition and greed are more common,' Akitada said dryly. 'I assume his son will succeed to the estates?'

This time, Ono got his drift and glared. 'Katsumi is a very fine young man. He is devoted to his mother, who is my friend. I've known her and her son since both were children. I will not have anyone spread slanderous lies about them.'

Akitada raised his hands. 'Forgive me. I put it badly. As I said, I know nothing of the family.' He wondered if Ono was truly naive or so full of his own importance that he saw no need to hide his own motive or his relationship with another man's wife. 'I take it that the lady has influence at court on her own account?'

Ono was still irritated. He snapped, 'Naturally. Kiyowara owed his position to her. The Minamoto daughters were raised to be great ladies, perhaps empresses. Their education and refinement are superb. Her sister is married to Yorimichi.'

Meddling in the affairs of the *kuge*, those of the highest rank in the nation, was like playing with fire, and Ono clearly considered his continued interest offensive. Akitada changed the subject. 'Speaking of Lord Yorimichi, is he aware of the rumors about the rash of fires in the city?'

The poet relaxed a little. 'Dear heavens, yes. They said the Biwa mansion would burn. Michinaga's daughter and grandson, the retired emperor, reside there. Both Michinaga and Yorimichi went to touch their heads to the ground before the Buddha and prayed for rain. Well, there was a big fire, and then there was rain. They saved most of the palace. It is clear that the gods inspired the rumors.' There was a pause, during which Ono stared at Akitada. 'Fire,' he said after a moment. 'Now that you mention it, fire has great poetic possibilities. My own ancestress, Komachi, wrote that she was consumed by the fire of her passion. So powerful.' His eyes grew distant. 'I must discuss fire with Hiroko's cousin Aoi. Yes, the sacred fire for purification – or destruction, leaving nothing but ashes – ashes to be blown away by the winds

– the winds of fate.' He swept out an arm to describe vast distances, then tapped his mouth with a forefinger and fell into an abstraction.

Akitada tried to find something to break the spell, but Ono blinked after a moment and focused on him again.

'Umm,' he said, 'a very pleasant chat, my dear fellow, and so kind of you to stop by, but you can see I'm dreadfully pressed for time. You must forgive me.'

Akitada went home, not much wiser about Kiyowara's murder and at a loss how to proceed. He changed into his old clothes and then looked in on Tamako. She was sleeping, her maid Oyuki sitting nearby sewing some tiny clothes. Seeing the small garments moved him deeply, but he was not sure if they made him happy or afraid.

He spent several hours sorting through his papers, separating ministry materials and boxing them, and looking for forgotten promises. He had never sought preferment as a reward for helping someone, but most officials relied on just that sort of thing to protect their positions or win better ones. From time to time men had thanked him, adding that he might call on them for future benefits. But he knew it was a hopeless task. He had ignored all such offers, even received some with stiff disapproval perhaps. Now that he needed help, they would claim ignorance.

Discouraged, Akitada fled outside to see if Tora was home. He found him on the small veranda behind his and Hanae's living quarters. He was playing with his son, swinging the baby up and down as the child gurgled with laughter. Akitada's spirits lifted.

'Careful,' he cried out, when the baby's head nearly hit the roof overhang.

Tora turned, laughing and cradling his son against his chest. 'Did you want me, sir? I just got home, and Hanae was needed in the kitchen.'

'No, no. I came for a chat.' Akitada sat down, dangling his feet over the edge of the veranda. 'How Yuki has grown! He'll surely be a big man like his father.'

Tora grinned. Holding the baby away, bare legs kicking, he looked him over proudly. 'Better than looking like his mama. Not that it's not very fetching in a female. Will you hold him, sir, while I get us some wine?'

The baby was bare-bottomed, but Akitada received him

gladly, almost reverently. Yuki was a fine boy and a happy child. His parents doted on him. He settled the baby, pleased that he did not cry in his arms, and fell, willy-nilly, to cooing and tickling, admiring the bright eyes, the tiny, perfectly formed fingers and toes, the smiling toothless little mouth. Soon, very soon, he would hold his own son and feel a father's pride again. There was deep joy in such brief moments – joy that would surely make up for the fears that also lurked in the corners of the mind.

Tora returned with the wine and said, 'Wait till you hear what happened to me.' He poured two cups, then took the baby back and set him down next to a wooden ball, a couple of smooth bamboo sticks, and a small carving of a dog.

Akitada watched the child rolling the ball back and forth and decided to buy him a toy in the market. 'So, what have you been up to?'

'I met Jirokichi, the Rat.'

'No! Did you?'

'Well, he claimed to be Jirokichi. Five young thugs were dragging him off after giving him a bad beating. I came along just in time. They thought he had gold hidden away someplace.'

'More mischief by young ruffians. It's becoming a city-wide problem.'

'My thought, too. I figured the little man would be grateful and help me find the bastards that got my gold, but when I started asking questions, he clammed up and ran.'

'Hmm. Probably afraid of retaliation.'

'Maybe, though he's a spunky little guy.'

'Did you check on the fire victims?'

Tora's face fell. 'Yeah. The son's not going to live either. He was delirious. About the only thing on his mind was if his father had paid some debt.' Tora related the dying shopkeeper's words: 'But Father paid the money,' and the neighbor's comment that the old man had been a miser. 'It's almost as if they thought the gods punished them in some special way.'

Akitada frowned. 'What did the cousin have to say about that?'

'Nothing. She said he was hallucinating, but maybe he wasn't.'

'No, I don't think he was. I think she's afraid to talk because there's a protection scheme going on. Some masterless warrior has sold his skill with the sword to tradesmen who want protection against thieves and robbers. She and the neighbor think the fire was set because they didn't pay.'

Tora gaped at him. 'You mean it wasn't the gods?'

'Of course not, though it could have been carelessness.'

Tora said eagerly, 'Let's go investigate it, sir, and turn the bastards in.'

'I have my hands full, trying to clear my name. You should report this to Superintendent Kobe.'

Tora's face fell, but it was not in his nature to be discouraged for long. 'You'll solve the Kiyowara murder in no time, sir. I'll help if you need me – only, I'm not much good at chatting up the important people. I think I'll look for Jirokichi. He's a thief, and he knows something he doesn't want to talk about. Maybe I can find out if there are fire setters. Then you can report it to Superintendent Kobe and the ministry, and they'll be so pleased that they'll beg you to come back.'

Akitada had no hope that things would work out so smoothly, but Tora's optimism always cheered him. His eye fell on the baby. Yuki was pursuing a shiny green beetle to the edge of the veranda and was about to tumble off into the weeds below. He lunged to snatch him back to safety. 'Let me hold him,' he said, bouncing the baby on his knee. 'You can't be trusted to look after him properly.'

At that moment, there was a loud knocking at the gate, and Tora ran off to see who it was. A moment later, Akitada heard him shouting, 'Sir? It's a messenger for you.'

Carrying the baby, Akitada walked back to the courtyard, where he found a member of the palace guard mounted on a splendid, red-tasseled horse. The officer stared at him. 'Are you Secretary Sugawara?'

'Yes.' Akitada became aware of warm moisture spreading between the baby and himself.

The guard pulled a thin rolled-up document from his tunic and handed it down. 'No answer is expected, sir,' he said with a sharp nod and turned his horse to trot back out into the street.

Tora closed the gate behind him and came to take his son. 'Sorry, sir,' he said when he saw Akitada's robe. 'He's not quite housebroken yet. What is it?'

Akitada had undone the silk ties and unrolled the letter. The thick inky brush strokes swam before his eyes after the first lines. He had to force himself to go back and read the whole document again. It spelled disaster. He rolled it up again and said, 'It's not good, I'm afraid. I've been dismissed and have to hold myself ready for an investigation by the censors.'

'The censors? I thought Kiyowara's murder was a police matter.'

'Officials in the imperial administration are also subject to review by the Censors' Bureau. It's a good rule. They make sure that officials who have committed crimes never serve in any responsible capacity in the government again.' He did not add that such investigations usually led to exile.

He had to bear the blame for this. When you touch fire, you get burned. Far from being an absent-minded poet, Ono must have gone to report his visit, and the chancellor had acted much more quickly than even Akitada could have expected.

RAT DROPPINGS

Tora woke to the chatter of his son Yuki. The baby normally slept between his parents, but last night Tora had wanted to make love to his wife, and on such occasions they took their son into the small kitchen area and made him a bed in a large basket.

Hanae, who had been busy in the main house for the past week, was still soundly asleep. Being a considerate husband, Tora got up to make some milk gruel for the baby.

The little kitchen was still dark. Tora struck a flint and lit an oil lamp. It was unusual for Yuki to wake up before daylight. When he raised the lamp to check on his son, he saw to his amazement that Yuki seemed to be sitting on a blanket of shining gold coins. The baby squinted against the light, then crowed with laughter at the sparkling new toys.

Tora's jaw dropped. What the devil was this? So much gold. Was it a miracle? Had the Buddha heard his bitter complaints when he had lost his winnings the other night? But there was much more here than he had lost. Tora picked up a coin and bit it. It was real. Setting down the lamp, he gathered the gold, ignoring Yuki's wails. He counted twenty pieces. Where had they come from?

He finally picked up the baby – who was making enough noise to wake Hanae – and set him on the floor with one of the coins. Then he started the kitchen fire under the pot of gruel Hanae had prepared the night before. It was only after these chores that he turned his attention to the wet bedding in the basket. A crumpled piece of paper fluttered to the floor.

Tora snatched it up before Yuki could grasp it and flattened it out. There was writing on it – thick, poorly shaped characters – but the message was short and simple. Tora had no trouble deciphering it.

Thank you for your help. Forget about the kids.

There was no signature; instead Jirokichi had drawn a small rat.

Tora was profoundly shocked. It was not only the very large amount of gold that upset him, but also the way it had been left in his house. How had the bastard got in? And when? Had he been spying on them while they were making love? A man was not very observant at such a time. In fact, someone probably could have ripped the roof off the place, and he would not have noticed.

So, instead of gratitude, he felt a hot fury when he looked at the gold. He wanted to shove it down the little bastard's throat.

Yuki reminded him of the gruel by whimpering. Tora hid the gold in an empty jar on the high shelf, then mixed a small amount of gruel with some cow's milk and, taking his son on his lap, fed him his morning meal.

He decided not to tell Hanae about their night-time visitor, because it would frighten her. His master, on the other hand, must know about it right away.

As soon as Hanae joined them, yawning widely, then smiling at husband and son, he went to wash at the well, combed his hair and tied it, and put on a clean robe.

'You look very handsome, husband,' Hanae crooned when he came back. She came to stand on tiptoe and kiss him.

Tora briefly considered postponing his errand, but better sense won. He released Hanae regretfully and watched her take Yuki for his bath, then he scooped the gold out of the jar and hurried to the main house.

Akitada was in his study, bent over the account ledger, his face looking drawn, as if he had not slept.

'Here,' said Tora and deposited the two handfuls of gold coins on Akitada's desk. 'I found them this morning. They're yours.'

His master regarded first the gold, then Tora. 'Found them? Is this the gold you were robbed of?'

'No. I suppose I earned it. It's from Jirokichi.' He laid the slip of paper next to the gold.

His master read the note and shook his head. 'I can't take this. It's yours,' he said, pushing the gold towards Tora. 'Why are you so angry?'

Tora explained about the shocking intrusion into his home. 'I was going to ram the gold down his throat, sir, but I figured you might have a need of it. For that matter, if the bastard got into our place, he may have done a bit of thieving in your house. Maybe you'd better check.'

Akitada called Seimei, and together they made a brief search of the valuables. The money box was untouched, and everything else was as it should be.

'A clever burglar,' said his master. 'You may do with the gold as you see fit, but find him and see if he can help us with the fires.'

'I thought you didn't want to become involved in that.'

'I have reconsidered. I may as well try to earn a living by investigating crimes.'

Tora left the gold in his master's strongbox and went to look for Jirokichi. He started with the thief's girlfriend.

Hoshina's eyes narrowed when she saw him come into her wine shop. 'Tora,' she cried brightly. 'You haven't forgotten me.' Every man in the wine shop turned to look at him.

Tora was embarrassed. The woman was almost as tall as he and nearly twice as wide. Her arms and shoulders would have done credit to any man. Besides, the hungry way she looked at him made him uncomfortable. He liked women to be dainty and a little shy.

'Why, you're even more handsome today,' she trilled and sidled up close enough to stroke his chest through his blue robe.

One of the men shouted, 'Hey, Hoshina. I want some more wine before you drag him off to have your way with him.' The others laughed.

Tora glared around and stepped away from Hoshina. 'I need to talk to Jirokichi,' he told her in a low voice. 'Where can I find him?'

She stroked his cheek. 'Why bother with him?' she cooed and pressed her body against his. This brought more shouts of obscenities and laughter from the audience. 'Sit down,' she said, pushing him. Tora sat. She blew him a kiss. 'We'll talk about it over a cup of wine.' She walked away slowly, moving her hips to the hoots and whistles of the men.

So much for Jirokichi's romance. Tora almost felt sorry for the little rat – almost, but not quite, seeing that the encounter was proving more embarrassing by the moment. Hoshina returned to more applause, with wine and freshly painted lips. She bowed to her audience, then sat down so close to Tora that their thighs touched. The other customers watched avidly.

Tora moved away a little, but she wiggled closer and whispered in his ear, 'Bet I can make you much happier than that wife of yours.'

'Then Jirokichi must be a lucky man,' Tora said hoarsely and gulped some wine.

She put a hand on his thigh and let it wander higher to whistles and a bawdy request that she offer such service to all the guests. Tora had had enough. He removed her hand from his thigh, put some coppers down, and left, his face flaming. More shouts and laughter followed him out.

His failure grated. He had got nothing from the disgusting woman, and that was not like him. Perhaps marriage had ruined his style. In the old days, he would have made up to her and taken her to bed. She was crude, but that large body was voluptuous and promised a good lay, and she would have ended up telling him whatever he wanted to know.

A sudden suspicion gave him pause. Had she performed that flagrant and very public bit of seduction to drive him away because she did not want to answer questions about Jirokichi?

Tora glowered and clenched his fists. He had expected to find Jirokichi quite easily and was wearing his ordinary clothes. The trouble was that they marked him as a retainer belonging to the household of an official. And that meant he would get no information on the whereabouts of a thief.

He wandered aimlessly around the Western Market in hopes of seeing Jirokichi on his way to Hoshina. It was a waste of time, but when he passed the vegetable sellers, he encountered the handsome youth he had seen outside Hoshina's wine shop the day before. The boy was haggling over a daikon radish and a small cabbage.

Tora gave him a nod and a grin. Being caught by another male at such an embarrassingly feminine activity made the boy flush and turn his head away.

THE DUMPLING MAN

A little cheered by the fact that others had their troubles, too, Tora decided to have a look at the Kiyowara residence before going home. He would not be admitted, but outside the houses of great nobles there were always people who knew all about the inhabitants. Street vendors and beggars quickly assembled where the wealthy lived. The common people, largely invisible to the powerful nobles, kept themselves extremely well informed about their betters. When you are poor, you spend a good part of your life watching the wealthy.

As he had expected, there was a dumpling seller at one corner of the property, and a woman selling fans at the other. Some ragged children hung about in hopes of holding horses, running errands, or begging for a copper coin.

For a house in mourning that had all the attendant taboo signs posted to warn visitors of contamination in case they intended to worship at a shrine or make a pilgrimage, the Kiyowara mansion's gates not only stood invitingly open, but people were also going in and out.

Two of those leaving were police officers; the others looked like merchants making deliveries or looking for business. Tora gauged his chances between the dumpling seller, a thin man of middle age with a hungry look about him, and the fan woman, who looked senile, and approached the dumpling man.

He spent a copper on a stuffed dumpling and remained to chat while he was eating. The dumpling man was not busy and welcomed the company.

'Good dumpling,' Tora commented. 'You'll be busy when it's time for the midday rice.'

The man looked depressed. 'Thanks, but it's been slow since the murder.'

Tora pretended surprise. 'Murder? Here in the street?'

'No. Inside. Lord Kiyowara.'

Tora gaped at the open gate and the rooflines beyond the tall wall. 'A great lord! Karma is in the turning of a wheel,' he said piously.

'Makes you think,' said the dumpling seller, waving away a wasp attracted by his sweet bean paste. 'They say it's all decided when you're born. So does that mean the murder's also planned before the killer's even suckled at his mother's breast? If that's so, then he can't help himself when the time comes. He has to kill the man he's ordained to kill.'

Tora stared at him. Dumpling sellers were not, as a rule, philosophical. 'My master doesn't believe that,' he said after a moment. 'Murderers are selfish bastards who please no one but themselves. That's what we have the devils in hell for. To punish them for taking another person's life.'

The dumpling seller smirked. 'Lord Kiyowara needed killing. He was an evil man. What about that? Does the murderer still deserve to go to hell?'

Tora frowned. He did not want to engage in a pointless argument about karma, but it was an opening. 'How was he evil?' he asked.

The dumpling man barked a nasty laugh. 'Stupid question. All the great lords do evil things. They wouldn't be great otherwise. This one took what he wanted and never cared what happened to others.'

'What did he take?'

'Anything he wanted. Land, money, women.'

'Women? He chased women?'

The man rolled his eyes.

Tora finished his dumpling and wiped his hands on his trousers. 'All real men chase women. What did he do? Rape a nun?'

But the dumpling man shook his head. Perhaps he thought he had said too much already. 'There's talk,' he said vaguely. 'Don't quote me.'

Tora changed the subject. 'Were you here the day he was killed?'

The man looked at him a moment. 'You want another dumpling while you're wasting my time?'

Tora laughed at this – the dumpling man had not had any other customer and nobody had stopped at his stand – but he shelled out another copper. 'Well?' he asked, biting into the dumpling.

'I was here.'

'So maybe you saw the fellow that did everyone such a big favor. Anybody in particular?'

The man gestured at the street. 'People come and go here all the time. How should I know what their business is?'

That might be true, but having been conned out of another copper, Tora was not giving up so easily. 'Come, you're a man of experience, a man who thinks. I bet you noticed something out of the ordinary.'

'Nothing to do with the murder.'

'Ah! Something did happen. Let's hear it.' Tora swallowed the last of the dumpling and adjusted his sash, causing his string of coppers to clink.

'Well,' the dumpling man said, eyeing the sash, 'not that it means anything, I'm sure, but the young lord rode down the fan seller.'

'Rode down the fan seller?' Tora glanced at the old woman in the distance. 'Why?'

The vendor shook his head. 'He's a good rider as a rule and well-behaved for one of them. He even threw me a piece of silver once. But that day, the kid came galloping out of the gate as if demons were after him. He whipped his horse mercilessly and had a face as black as the thunder god. The old woman was standing down there, at the street corner, selling her fans – it was hot as blazes and business was good. He took the corner too fast and the horse knocked her down. You could hear the crack it made up and down the street. Her stuff went flying everywhere. She screamed and fell into a fit. One of the boys ran to get the constables and they carried her away like a dead woman. It's a miracle she didn't die from it.'

'His face was black? You mean he painted his face black?' Tora asked, astonished.

The man gave him a look. 'No. Of course not. Black with anger. He looked like the god of thunder or . . . well, like Fudo. You do know who Fudo is?'

Tora nodded. Fudo was one of the heavenly generals. He was always depicted as snarling ferociously. 'So what do you think made him so angry?'

But the man did not know.

Down the street, Tora saw a tall female who looked like a fortune-teller. She was coming slowly in their direction. He nodded towards her and asked, 'Is she a regular?'

The dumpling man looked. 'She comes and goes. I don't know what she's up to. She walks right in and out through the gate.' He shuddered. 'With that look on her face, she must frighten customers away.'

Tora watched her with interest. She was tall, and both her expression and appearance were off-putting. Her clothes were made of rough white hemp, and her shawl was a deep red. Thick strands of beads and amulets hung about her neck and decorated her arms and the ankles above her bare feet. And her hair was a wild and tangled mane. But Tora looked beyond the scowl and saw that she was young and beautiful.

He grinned. 'Why would a man be scared by a beauty like that?'

The dumpling man eyed him slyly. 'Why don't you go talk to her?'

Tora went to meet the fortune-teller at the open gates. She was going to enter, but Tora stepped in her path, flashing his wide smile. Few women could resist him when he smiled, but this one stopped and stared back with a face like stone.

What a beauty, he thought, even with that wild hair and those angry eyes. A man could lose himself in both. She was like some wild thing, and he itched to tame her. Not that he was being disloyal to his Hanae, but no real man could resist dreaming a little with such a challenge.

'Greetings, my pretty little sister,' he said, making her a bow. 'I could use a good fortune told by a beautiful woman. How much will you charge me?'

She gave a shudder. 'I'm not your sister. Go away.'

She had a striking voice, deep, almost masculine, but this was not the way to do business. Tora's eyes narrowed, searching her face and body. Could it be a man in woman's garb and a wig? He was not easily fooled in sexual matters, but her robe was full and he could not make out the shape of breasts under those thick strands of beads. Her hands were somewhat large but slender enough for a woman. And the face was smooth, but some men had little or no beard.

'Are you deaf?' the fortune-teller asked, raising her voice. 'Scram! I have no time for lazy louts.'

Tora had no time for males in women's clothing, but the

problem was an interesting one. If this was a man, what was he doing here, dressed as a woman, and going to the Kiyowara mansion? And if a woman, why did she turn custom away?

He was about to follow up on the mystery when voices and hoof beats sounded inside the compound. Then a young rider on a very fine dapple-gray horse rode out of the gate. They both stepped out of the way.

Tora sucked in a breath. The horse was magnificent, tail flicking, ears perked, and red tassels swinging at every step. He loved fine horses, and this one was superb. Its rider was also easy on the eye: a slender youth dressed in a fine dark-green silk robe over full white trousers tucked into embroidered black boots. He sat the animal well and had a very handsome face.

He stopped before the fortune-teller, who bowed. 'Mother asked for you,' he said, then he spurred his fine horse and rode away. The fortune-teller watched his receding back for a moment, then walked through the gate.

Tora decided she was a female. She was tall for a woman and moved with great economy, walking erect and with a firm step, but her gait was a woman's. What a creature! His face grew hot at the thought of bedding her.

Mildly ashamed, he rejoined the dumpling man, who said, 'That was the young lord I told you about. Did he tell her to go in? I wonder what they want with her.'

Tora decided to share the information. You never knew when the dumpling man, so conveniently positioned, would become useful again. 'Her Ladyship sent for her, it seems.'

The dumpling man shook his head in wonder. 'Who needs a medium after a death?'

'You got me there,' Tora said. 'The world's full of strange things.'

He bought another dumpling – for Hanae because he felt guilty – and they parted on friendly terms.

As he was walking homeward, he pondered something even stranger than the beautiful fortune-teller. The young Lord Kiyowara had looked a lot like the boy in the market.

FOREBODINGS

As if things were not bad enough for the Sugawara household, Tamako's condition suddenly took a dramatic turn the next day. She had spent a restless night and refused food in the morning. She complained of feeling feverish again. Akitada went out early to buy some things in the market, hoping to tempt her with oranges, sweet plums, mushrooms, chestnuts, a fresh bream from nearby Lake Biwa. He paid a boy to carry his purchases home and called on Kobe to find out how the investigation was going.

Since Kobe was out, Akitada returned home – to hear a monk chanting. Monks were generally called only if someone was seriously ill or near death. Akitada rushed into the house and burst into his study, where Seimei was bent over paperwork.

'What's wrong?' he gasped.

Seimei looked up. 'Nothing. When the pains started, Her Ladyship thought it was time. She sent for the doctor, but the pains subsided again. The doctor left a draught for her fever.' Seimei shook his head. 'Some unusual concoction. I could not find anything about it in my herbals. I hope the man knows what he is doing.'

Fear had drenched Akitada in cold perspiration. He loosened his collar. 'But how is she now? Never mind. I'll go see for myself.' He turned on his heel and dashed off, bursting into Tamako's room without announcing himself. His wife was resting on her bedding with a picture scroll open beside her. The monk's chanting was so loud that he must be sitting outside her lowered shades. 'I heard you were unwell,' Akitada shouted. He was relieved that all seemed normal, but was becoming angry with himself for his unwarranted panic.

Tamako rolled up the picture scroll. 'It was nothing. I was a little feverish, and there were some pains, but they stopped. I'm very sorry to disappoint you.'

Weak with relief, Akitada sat down abruptly and brushed the film of moisture from his face. 'I was afraid,' he said. 'The chanting and the doctor . . . I suppose I . . . I keep remembering last year.' He heaved a deep breath to steady himself. 'Never mind. All is well? The pains are gone? You're feeling quite . . . all right?'

She smiled a little and nodded. 'Poor Akitada. This is harder for you than for me. Be patient. The child will be born, and the gods will protect it.'

They had to raise their voices.

'Yes . . . but must we have the monk? It's impossible to talk with that howling going on.' He glared at the shades.

She hesitated. 'They won't like it if we send him back so quickly.'

He recalled that it was customary to have the sutras chanted to protect mother and child during birth, but they had not done so in Echigo when Yori was born because the heavy snows had prevented it. Akitada had experienced chanting only for the deaths that had occurred in his family. He shuddered. 'If it makes you feel better, let him stay,' he decided.

She reached for his hand. 'No,' she said. 'Let him go. He makes me nervous, too.'

Back in his study, Seimei waited with his house robe.

'How much is in the money box?' Akitada asked, taking off his robe and untying his full silk trousers.

'Apart from Tora's gold, fifteen pieces of gold, about thirty of silver, and twenty strings of copper cash.'

So little.

'Tell the monk he's not needed quite yet and give him what you think is adequate for his work.'

'Very well. But perhaps we should speak to a yin-yang master, sir. To cast the child's fortune and to perform proper purification rites.'

Akitada stared at the old man, appalled. 'Another expense? Purification rites? Next you'll suggest we build a birthing hut out in the garden so the house won't become polluted.'

Seimei did not look at him. 'Such things are customary, sir. The empresses leave the palace when their time comes. The gods are offended by pollution.'

'I'm not the emperor,' thundered Akitada. 'I simply cannot afford all that expense. Besides, I can't imagine that Tamako would be more comfortable in a hut.'

Seimei folded his hands in his sleeves and raised his chin. 'It is meant to protect your lady's life and that of the child, sir. We should also have someone twanging a bowstring to drive the evil spirits away.' He paused a moment. 'And a medium to pray to the gods.'

'Are you mad?' Seimei knew very well his master's aversion to anything that smacked of superstition.

Seimei fidgeted a moment, then said softly, 'Better to lean on a stick than to fall down.'

That took Akitada's breath away.

Theirs was a family where death had struck not long ago when his son Yori had died. Perhaps Seimei believed that had happened because they had not taken such precautions at his birth. In spite of the warmth in the room, Akitada shivered. He had no choice in this matter. Not if he did not want to be blamed again if anything went wrong.

'You may speak to the yin-yang master,' he said after a moment. 'And the monk can come back at the time of the birth. Tora can twang his bow. But I will not have a half-crazed witch casting spells in my courtyard.'

Seimei smiled. 'Very good, sir.'

There was a brief silence while Akitada mentally totted up expenses for the monk and the yin-yang master.

Seimei cleared his throat.

'Anything else you'd like me to spend our dwindling funds on?' Akitada snapped.

Seimei flushed a little. 'No, sir. Tora went to the Kiyowara mansion to talk to a street vendor. He stopped by to talk to you, waited a while, but then said he'd be back later. I was to tell you that the young Lord Kiyowara was in a very bad temper the day of the murder. He rode down an old woman in the street.'

Akitada exploded. 'What was Tora doing there? Any meddling in the Kiyowara case will make my situation worse. How will I explain to the Board of Censors why I sent my retainer to cause more trouble after they notified me of their displeasure?'

'I am sorry, sir.' Seimei shrank into himself. 'I believe he was trying to help.'

Akitada grasped his head in frustration. 'I wish everybody would stop helping me. If that is all your bad news, I think I'd like to be alone now.'

Seimei bowed and departed on silent feet, but Akitada heard the soft shuffle of dejection and felt guilty. His people suffered his misfortunes along with him and did not deserve his ill-tempered tongue-lashings. Especially not Seimei, that faithful man who had devoted himself to him, never asking for a life of his own or protesting against his master's ill humor.

As a penance, he spent the day composing his defense against the accusations the censors were likely to bring against him. He had no doubt that they would build a monstrous case, a case that would use the murder of Kiyowara as only the latest in a long string of treasonable and rebellious acts.

The task was painful because he disliked bragging about achievements that seemed to him frequently flawed by misjudgements along the way or successful only by some lucky chance. But he weighed against this the injustices done to him over the years.

He began with his family background, reminding them of his illustrious ancestor, Sugawara Michizane, that brilliant, good, and loyal servant to the empire who had suffered exile and death at the hands of his political enemies. The Fujiwaras had believed for two centuries that Michizane's ghost had visited misfortune upon them. Perhaps they might believe that he would also protect his descendant against unjust charges.

He mentioned his distinguished university career and the fact that he had placed first in the examination. Then he moved on to the special assignments he had accepted and brought to successful conclusions against everyone's expectations. The case of the lost tax convoys from Kazusa, where he had foiled the plot of a treasonous abbot, was one of these. The removal of Uesugi, the warlord in Echigo who had attempted to seize control of a province, was another. He reminded them of the island province of Sado, where he had almost died and had suffered wounds that still caused him pain. In Sado, the emperor's exiled brother had attempted to join with the hostile forces in the North to seize the throne. Oh, yes, they owed him better treatment than this.

At this point, Akitada interrupted his work to look in on Tamako. The women – she was with Hanae and Oyuki – were busy sewing, while Yuki crawled about between them and played with bits of colored cloth. It was a cheerful scene, and the slight fever made Tamako's face rosy so that she looked deceptively healthy. They were cutting and sewing small garments from old robes. He thought he recognized a lovely rose-colored silk that he had particularly liked on Tamako. But for a boy? He said nothing about this, however, and instead chatted about the absent Genba and the dog Trouble, and how he missed them – yes, even that shaggy dog. For their part, they also kept their comments to happier times.

When Yuki began to whimper and pull on his mother's sleeve, Hanae said, 'He's hungry,' and put him to her breast. Akitada thought that soon he would see his own child at its mother's breast. That made him smile, and he reached for Tamako's hand.

Tamako looked first at him and then at Hanae with the baby, understood, and said, 'What a very fortunate thing, Hanae, that you're still nursing.'

What did she mean by that? Did she expect Hanae to nurse their child also? She had nursed Yori. Would she not do the same for this child? True, women of his class rarely nursed their own children, but Tamako had never behaved like them.

Hanae shot him a glance and said, 'Don't fret, My Lady. I won't be needed,' and Akitada understood that Tamako had made preparations for her death. Deeply shocked, he jumped up and left without another word.

The fears were back, and they were more real than ever.

In his study, he paced without finding any consolation or hope. In the end, he did what he had not done for a long time now. He retrieved his flute and walked outside with it. Playing his flute reminded him of Yori's death. He would always associate it with death now. It was a great pity because before that dreadful time, the flute had given him many hours of pleasure and brought him peace when he had been troubled.

He was still playing, fumblingly because he had forgotten the tunes, when Seimei joined him on the veranda. His mind on death and dying, Akitada lowered the flute and asked anxiously, 'Is anything wrong?'

'No, sir. A messenger has arrived with a letter for you.' Seimei held it out with both hands. 'From Lady Kiyowara.'

Akitada was so astonished that he gaped at the prettily folded square for a moment before opening it. He caught a whiff of expensive incense, and the paper was thick and beautiful. The handwriting also was quite exquisite. The message was short: 'Lady Kiyowara begs Lord Sugawara to call on her.'

'She wants to see me,' he said blankly.

'Shall I get out your good robe and trousers, sir?'

Akitada looked up at the sun. Ladies of her rank expected promptness. 'Yes,' he said. He heard Seimei's footsteps receding and called after him, 'Thank you, Seimei. For everything.'

The steps paused. 'It is a pleasure, sir. Always.'

THE WIDOW

In his second-best robe, the same one he had worn on his previous visit, Akitada presented himself to heavily armed retainers at the Kiyowara gate.

They had not been here before, and their martial demeanor struck an unpleasant note in this normally peaceful quarter of the city. Kiyowara's rank and position permitted them, and they might have been brought from his provincial seat to attend his funeral and to protect the widow and her young son against unwelcome attentions, but Akitada felt as though he were walking unarmed into an enemy camp.

Still, they admitted him readily when he identified himself. A house servant, dressed in white hemp because of his master's death, took him to the main reception hall and indicated a single silk cushion placed before an empty dais at the end of the large, dim room.

The dais was new since Soga's days and suggested aspirations beyond Kiyowara's recent rank – that or the expectation of an imperial visit. The coffered ceiling was lacquered dark brown, the heavy beams had gilded mounts, and the squares between were painted in a red and white design – probably the Kiyowara crest. The dais was covered with thick *tatami* mats edged in red brocade, and on the wall behind it was a large painting of flowering branches and birds. Someone had set up a lacquered curtain stand with costly brocade hangings and had placed three silk pillows, one in front of the others, on the *tatami* mats before it.

It was to be an official reception, something resembling an audience. In a way it was reassuring – the Kiyowaras did not intend to have him cut down by their soldiers. But Akitada's placement below the splendor of the dais was also insulting. He considered his own descent far more ancient and noble than that of a Kiyowara.

At least they did not make him wait. A door slid open in the painted panel, and three people slipped in. Lady Kiyowara and her companion were gorgeously robed in scented silk, but wore short hemp jackets over their many-hued gowns. They were followed by a young male. Akitada guessed that this was the son and heir. He also wore expensive silks under his hemp jacket and looked pale and nervous.

Lady Kiyowara seated herself in the center of the dais, while her son and companion took their places behind. The arrangement meant that Lady Kiyowara intended to conduct the interview. It also implied that she would speak for the heir because of his youth.

Akitada was curious about the son, but could not get a good look at him, except to note a high forehead over slanted brows that met above his nose. He seemed to be fifteen or sixteen and was subdued for a young male who had just succeeded to his father's title.

He had a slightly better view of the elderly companion, who held a small box. Neither woman had applied the thick white paste and heavy black and red paint common among upper-class women. Though this, too, was meant to signify mourning, Akitada preferred it. He disliked the custom, and Tamako rarely painted her face.

Both women held up fans, but these did not always hide the face and never the eyes. Lady Kiyowara appeared to be a few years older than Tamako, perhaps by five or ten, but she had fine features. Her elderly attendant was extremely plain. Neither looked particularly distraught.

Akitada hoped the son, at least, grieved for his father.

They exchanged bows. Lady Kiyowara studied him carefully over her fan. The fan was plain paper with a faint dusting of gold – very proper. Her eyes were thinly outlined in black, so subtly that they looked natural. It was very attractive. He must tell Tamako about this, he thought, then became impatient with the formalities.

'You asked to see me, madam?' he asked without preamble.

She blinked at his abruptness and shot a glance at her companion before saying softly, 'Thank you for coming so promptly, sir, and at such an inauspicious time. Allow me to introduce my son and my lady-in-waiting. I sent for you because I have need of your advice. You are said to have a certain expertise in matters of this sort.'

Akitada made her another slight bow. 'If Your Ladyship refers to Lord Kiyowara's murder, I must tell you that I have been warned away from the case. It seems people have seen fit to suggest I might have had a hand in it myself.' There, that was blunt speaking and should cut through other circumlocutions.

She raised her fan a fraction higher, but he could see her eyes flashing. She was surely an intelligent woman. He must be on his guard.

After a moment, she said, 'Yes, it is best to speak plainly. The police have assured me that you are not considered a suspect. Perhaps you would explain your previous visit more fully yourself?'

He had been right about her intelligence. And Kobe had protected him. He kept the explanation short. 'I was recently passed over for a position I held for more than a year. An incompetent man was put in my place. When I discovered that this was done on your husband's order, and since Lord Kiyowara and I were strangers, I came here to see if some mistake had been made. Now I am thought to have come for revenge. I did not, of course, though I would have been angry to find out that Lord Kiyowara had ruined me simply because it suited him to do so.'

She looked at him silently, as if weighing his words. Then she said, 'I am sorry. My husband's affairs were not mine.'

That was surely a bald-faced lie. Her brother-in-law was Chancellor and Regent Yorimichi. Akitada said coldly, 'Many would say that your husband owed his career to you.'

She stiffened. 'He owed his career to his ability and his past service to the emperor.'

'My case exactly, but that did not prevent Lord Kiyowara from replacing me with an inferior.' Akitada bit his lip. He would gain nothing by further antagonizing the lady. 'Perhaps you had better tell me why you called on me under these circumstances.'

Her eyes narrowed, and he realized that she was smiling. 'You are still angry, and yet you are here,' she said.

He said nothing.

'I asked you to come because the policeman speaks highly of you, and because I want a separate investigation into my husband's murder.' She gestured to her companion, who got to her knees and shuffled over, setting the small box down in front of her. Lady Kiyowara flipped open the lid and turned the box towards Akitada. It was filled to the brim with gold. 'This should replace your lost income for the year. Allow me to offer this gold for your services. When you have completed the investigation, you will receive another box just like this. Together, I believe, they equal two years of your salary as senior secretary in your ministry.'

Akitada's face burned with shame. It was one thing to be paid a salary for his service to the emperor, and quite another to be bribed by this woman to protect her family. Worse, most likely he was here because he was Kobe's friend. He wanted to reject the offer disdainfully, but his circumstances did not permit empty gestures. Still, he was very angry.

'I am flattered, but Superintendent Kobe is well able to handle this.'

She frowned. 'Nevertheless, I would like you to act for me.'

'It is impossible to say where a murder investigation leads. If you think I can avert an arrest of yourself or a member of your family, you give me too much credit.' He saw that she was offended and pressed on. 'Besides, it is too early to say what I may find, or if what I find out is going to please you. For example, it may be that your son quarreled with his father –' that had been Tora's opinion, but one that had surely been correct – 'or that you yourself preferred another man to your husband.'

The elderly lady gasped, and Lady Kiyowara dropped her fan and stared at him in shock. 'W–what?'

'Your son's anger was observed by others. He rode down an old woman in the street outside. And as I waited in the anteroom on the day of the murder, I overheard shouting in your husband's room. As for Your Ladyship: Lord Ono and I met the afternoon of your husband's murder. Ono was coming from your quarters. I assume he has informed you of my visit. He did not hide his close relationship with you.'

'Then he lied about me,' she snapped. 'And so did the people who accused my son. He was not here at the time of his father's death. Who told you those things? If they are servants of mine, they will be dismissed.'

He liked her less for that outburst and said, 'That will hardly stop the rumors. I expect Superintendent Kobe is already aware of them.'

Her shoulders sagged abruptly, and she bowed her head. 'What shall I do?' she said softly. 'Oh, what can I do? I hoped you would help me, but what good are you if you believe those tales?'

That disconcerted him. 'Neither your relationship with Ono nor your son's anger necessarily prove guilt,' he said, 'but I will not be bought.'

She looked up, startled. 'Bought? Oh . . . Oh, I did not . . . That was not . . . I beg your pardon.' She quickly closed the lid on the box as if to remove the offensive sight from his eyes. That almost made him smile. 'But if you thought that,' she said more calmly, taking up her fan again, 'then you must think us guilty, my son and me. Individually or together.'

'Again, no. But if I am to undertake the work you propose, then it must be on the condition that I shall find out the truth no matter who is hurt by it.'

She quickly pushed the box towards him. 'Of course. It shall be as you wish. I must trust that you are infallible, sir,' she said. 'Now, what do you wish to know?'

He did not touch the box and glanced at her companion. The woman looked frightened.

Lady Kiyowara said quickly, 'My lady-in-waiting is in my confidence. She knows we have nothing to fear. Ask whatever you wish.'

He wondered if that also meant that the attendant approved of Lady Kiyowara's relationship with Lord Ono and asked, 'Lord Ono has expressed his complete devotion to you. Do you know of anything that might have caused him to kill your husband?'

'As you have spoken to Ono Takamura, you must know that nothing would cause him to commit an act of violence. He is a poet.'

'Poets express powerful emotions quite frequently,' Akitada pointed out.

'In poems, yes. But poetry is an exercise of the mind, not of passion. Do you write poetry?'

'No, My Lady.'

'Ah.'

Akitada blushed at that and asked quickly, 'Did you know that your son quarreled with his father?'

'No, but it is likely. Katsumi wished to join the guards. His father forbade it because he is only fifteen and our only son. He did not kill his father. You must believe that. I know my son.'

The young lord said nothing and remained hidden behind his mother. Perhaps, thought Akitada, but mother love could be as blind as romantic love. That thought caused him to ask, 'Were you and your husband happy together?'

She did not blink, but the hand holding the fan tightened. She said tonelessly, 'Of course.'

That was her second lie, but it was too soon to press her. Akitada asked, 'Do you know of anyone who might have wished your husband dead?'

She frowned. 'My husband rose quickly in the government and was a rich man. Surely that makes enemies.'

'Anyone in particular?'

This time she hesitated. 'Wives are rarely in a position to know their husbands' associates.'

In general, this was very true, but perhaps her answer had hinted at something she did not want to mention. He let it go. Earning his fee would not be easy. He suppressed a sigh. 'Very well, My Lady. I accept your offer with the conditions I made. Can I be given ready access to everyone in this house?'

'Certainly.' Nodding to her companion, she made him a slight bow, rose, and left by the door she had entered. The companion hurried after her. They left behind the memory of a swishing of silks and the scent of orange blossoms and sandalwood. The young lord, caught unawares, stared at Akitada with frightened eyes. Then he seemed to remember himself and got to his feet and out of the room quickly.

Akitada took up the heavy little box and tucked it under his arm, where the fullness of his sleeve hid it. He walked homeward, filled with new hope and a pleasant interest in solving the mystery of Kiyowara's murder.

THE FRAGRANT PEACH

Tora looked forward to reporting the young lord's furious departure on the afternoon of the murder. It surely meant that the quarrel his master had overheard had been between Lord Kiyowara and his son. In that case, most likely young Kiyowara could have been the killer. A rash-tempered youth was prone to knocking people out, and this one's temper was proved when he had ridden down the old woman.

And if this information did not solve the case, then at least another suspect could be offered to the police.

All in all, a good day's work, though it would have to wait. The next morning, the master was busy. Tora changed back into his rags.

Hanae's face fell. 'Are you going out again?'

'The master thinks someone's setting those fires. You know he needs all the help he can get.'

Her eyes widened. 'Amida! Someone setting fires?' She bit her lip and nodded. 'Go then, but be careful and don't stay out too late.'

'Never fear.' He ogled her. 'Just be ready for me when I slip into bed.'

That made her giggle.

This time Tora passed through the Western Market, skirting Hoshina's wine shop, and wandered through the dingy streets beyond. From time to time, he stopped a man or woman to ask for Jirokichi. People either denied knowing of him, their faces closing like slammed doors, or they smiled and nodded but had no idea where Tora might find him. It was frustrating.

Near midday he was in an especially depressing part of the city. Hunger gnawed and his legs were growing tired. He decided to look for a place where he might eat and drink and rest for a while. He found a low dive in the very next street.

The curtain hanging across the doorway bore the name of the establishment: Fragrant Peach. It was so old and tattered that the painted blossoms looked like dirty snow falling from a cloudy sky, and its smell resembled that of dung. Still, from the sounds within, there would at least be wine, and after a drink the place would look much better.

Tora pushed aside the curtain and stepped down into a dirt-floored room with a low, dark ceiling. It was a hot, airless hole. Fumes of smoke, burning oil, sour wine, and sweat hit him like a fist. A few oil lamps, fixed to the walls, accounted for the stink of oil. The smoke came from a central fire pit. At first glance, the place contained several customers, both men and women, all of them poorly dressed and dirty.

A few faces turned his way but showed no interest. In a dark and lonely alley, these men, and a few of the tattered females, would probably just as soon shove a knife in a man's back to rob him of a few coins.

Tora gritted his teeth and looked for a place away from the fire. He would have his cup of wine, try for some information and, if things turned ugly, he would get out. Then he saw a familiar figure on a sort of dais in the far corner.

The fat rice merchant from Kaneharu's cousin's ward was standing there, talking to a couple of juveniles. Tora wondered what would bring him to a place like the Fragrant Peach. The merchant was waving his chubby hands, and the youngsters, who had their backs to Tora, nodded and laughed. Tora searched his mind for a name, found it, and started forward.

'Hey, Watanabe!' he shouted.

The fat man's head jerked around. For a moment, there was puzzlement on the broad face, then he said something to the youths, who slipped away, and raised a hand in greeting.

Tora put a hand on his shoulder. 'Well met, my friend. I'm parched and hate drinking alone. Join me in a cup.' The merchant hesitated, but Tora called for wine and made him sit down. 'You look surprised,' he told Watanabe. 'The name's Tora. We talked outside your house about that fire the other day. Any news of Young Kaneharu?'

Watanabe's double chin creased. 'Ah, yes. He died yesterday. A release. He was in terrible pain – terrible! Ah, the anger of the gods!' Jowls quivering, he shook his head.

Tora's heart sank. So he had not been able to save the son either. 'That's a pity,' he said heavily. 'You don't think it could have been an accident?'

Watanabe pursed his lips and suddenly resembled a frog. 'I see what you mean. A senile father and a house full of dry grass and bamboo. Perhaps. But even then it might have been a sign. Did you notice the altar at the end of their street? I paid for that, and for the priest to perform rites.'

Tora had not, but he nodded. 'Very pious,' he said. 'You're probably right about the gods being angry. So many fires, that's just not normal.'

A very young waitress in a stained pink robe slouched up and plunked down two cups. Her robe gaped open as she bent, revealing firm young breasts. She filled the cups from a flask, set down the flask, and held out a dirty palm.

Tora eyed her. She looked not much more than fourteen or fifteen and was surprisingly pretty. He felt pity for her. Already, she had lost her childhood. Her smooth face was painted like a trollop's, and she looked sullen. Children grew up fast in this part of the city. Tora fished out three coppers and placed them in her palm.

'Hey,' she said with a pout. 'That pays for the wine. What about the service?'

Tora flashed her a smile and let his eyes sweep over her again. 'I don't know. What do you offer?'

Watanabe shook with silent laughter. She glared at both of them and flounced off.

Tora looked after her. 'Not bad looking, but she needs a bath.'

With another rumbling belly laugh, Watanabe said, 'Around here, men don't care. She's both young and willing.' He winked.

So the girl was a whore already, and Watanabe had probably slept with her. Tora was disgusted and said nastily, 'I thought your interest was young boys. Or isn't that why I saw you talking to them?'

The rice merchant reached for his cup. 'I take a charitable interest in poor youths,' he said coldly.

Right!

Tora smirked. 'Well, to each his own. I prefer females myself.'

Watanabe choked. 'You misunderstood. I'm a married man,' he squawked, coughing.

'So am I, but that doesn't keep me from ogling a beauty.' The girl was at the open back door now, talking to someone outside. A moment later, she slipped out.

Watanabe was still protesting his innocence. 'I'm just helping poor boys find work. Working keeps them out of trouble.'

'That's very public-spirited of you.'

Watanabe eyed Tora resentfully. 'If you don't mind my asking, what are *you* doing here?' he asked. 'And why are you dressed like that?'

'I'm looking for a thief. It seemed like a good idea to blend in.'

Watanabe's bulging eyes widened. 'Why are you looking for a thief? Are you a constable?'

'No. This one paid a visit at my house.'

'Ah. Did he get away with much?'

'Not really. I have nothing to steal. Have you heard of a Jirokichi? The one that steals from the rich to give to the poor?'

Watanabe's belly quivered with mirth again. It reminded Tora of boiling bean paste. 'Sure, I've heard of him,' he said. 'It's a great story. Fools will believe anything. Some even pray to him for gold – just like some god.'

Tora flushed. He did not like being called a fool, and while he knew Jirokichi was human, he had great respect for miraculous events. 'You can believe what you want,' he said ungraciously.

Watanabe became apologetic. 'No offense. I knew you were joking.' He thought a moment. 'You know, speaking from a business standpoint, a man could make a lot of money out of a thing like that. Being thought a god, I mean.' He started to laugh again.

Tora watched him with barely hidden disgust. The man was made of whale blubber. 'How so?'

'Think about it. All sorts of things can be done if people think they are done by the gods. The police don't trouble themselves with arresting the *kami*.' He leaned forward to refill their cups. 'Oh, no! The *kami* are quite safe.' He fell into another bout of laughter.

'Pretending to be a god would be a sacrilege,' Tora pointed out, but he wondered if Jirokichi was the sort of man who would dishonor the gods. And that brought up another thought. 'Is that what's going on with all those fires, do you think?' he asked Watanabe. 'You know, someone's setting them and blaming it on the gods?'

Watanabe was shocked by the notion. He stopped laughing. 'Of course not. Much too dangerous. And what's in it for him?'

The wine had warmed Tora's belly. He was wasting time with Watanabe. Emptying his cup, he got up. 'Well, I'm glad I bumped into you, but it's time I was off. My wife's not as understanding as yours.'

Watanabe's grin was strained. 'Thanks for the wine, Tora. And good luck finding your thief.'

As Tora walked away from the Fragrant Peach, he passed the alley next to the building. A closely entwined couple leaned against the wall. The young waitress had her pink robe pulled up to her waist and a pale thigh clasped around a young male in a blue and white robe. His hips moved energetically against her.

Tora was amused. When he was young, he had known such uncomfortable but exhilarating moments himself, but these days he had something better waiting for him at home.

THE DEAF MUTES

There was another fire overnight. The home of a minor official burned down.

The news was a painful reminder of Tora's lack of progress. His mood was not improved when he learned that his master had been angry with him for going to the Kiyowara house. He postponed the tongue-lashing as long as possible.

When he finally reported at the main house, Seimei greeted him with a smile. 'Good news, Tora,' he said. 'The master has a new assignment and has been paid. With such an auspicious turn of events, we sent for the yin-yang master right away to cast the child's fortune. And what do you think he said?'

Tora waited expectantly. Maybe things would be all right after all.

Seimei rubbed his gnarled hands. 'He declared the child would be blessed with health, wealth, and happiness. And when the master presented him with an additional gift, he said that fate would elevate the unborn even past the father's rank and position. Past his father's rank! What do you say to that?'

Tora blinked. 'He'll be greater than his father?'

'Yes. Such excellent news!' Seimei chuckled. 'Well, the master said this would not be hard to achieve since he was without rank and position at the moment, and that he trusted his son would fare better. But I could tell that he was very happy.'

Tora's spirits lifted. He found his master bent over his accounts and looking very pleased. 'I hear there's good news, sir,' Tora offered, intent on keeping things cheerful.

His master looked up and smiled. 'Ah, Tora. I'd hoped to see you sooner, but you must've been busy with that fine son of yours.'

Tora let him think so. 'Seimei says you've had a great fortune cast for yours.'

His master looked a little embarrassed. 'Well, it's customary – not that I put much faith in it. It seemed a good idea now that we have a little money. Did Seimei tell you? I've been employed by Lady Kiyowara to find her husband's murderer.' He put on a stern expression. 'As it turned out, your information about the son was useful, but don't take matters in your own hands again. It may cause me a great deal of trouble with the censors.'

Tora made a show of hanging his head. 'Sorry, sir. I wasn't thinking.'

'Well, don't do it again. Now please report.'

A chastened Tora told everything he had observed and been told outside the Kiyowara gate. When he was done, he asked, 'So, do you think the son killed the father?'

'Too soon to know. It may be more complicated than a quarrel between father and son. The son cannot have been very surprised by his father's decision. I suspect the young man was merely frustrated and expressed himself by shouting. The young frequently lose their temper. I did myself once.'

'He could have done it.' Tora felt cheated of his contribution. 'Maybe there was more to it than the military service. Maybe that was just the last straw.'

'Perhaps. We'll see. What about your own case?'

Tora reported what had happened in the western city.

When he finished, his master frowned. 'You'll have to be careful in those low dives. There has been gang activity in the city, and those hoodlums that robbed you may work for one. Remember, that peculiar thief knows where you live. That means that he also knows what you do and who I am.'

'Amida!' Tora slapped his forehead. 'What a fool I am! I should've thought of that. I bet the nasty little bastard is in it up to his skinny neck and has warned his gang by now. Sorry, sir. What do you want me to do?'

'Well, leaving you the gold suggests that he's not without honor. He may or may not belong to a gang, but it seems more important than ever to find him. A clever thief like that may well overhear secrets as he creeps into people's houses. I don't like this business with the fires. Just be careful in the future.'

Tora left, thinking about the situation. He would go back to the Fragrant Peach when he was done with his chores. After a light snack, he put on clean but nondescript cotton clothing of the sort worn by coach drivers, stable hands, or mounted messengers. Next he sought out Seimei for help with a note for the elusive Jirokichi. Since he could not run the thief to ground, he hoped the note would make him come to him.

Seimei balked a little when he saw the threat. He said, 'You may be Tora the Tiger, but remember that a cornered rat attacks the cat.'

That made Tora smile. 'You still have a way with words, old man,' he said. 'I'll remember it. The master's already told me to be careful. I'm carrying a knife. I have a family to consider.'

Seimei shook his head, but he wrote out the message for Tora.

When Tora stopped to leave the note at Hoshina's wine shop in the Western Market, Jirokichi was not there, but Hoshina came from the back with a tray. She saw Tora and glared briefly before she went to serve her customers. When she came to greet him, she was all smiles and seductive wiggles again.

Tora growled, 'Forget it, girl. I'm wise to your tricks. Here, give this to your boyfriend.'

She took the note, unfolded it, and stared at it blankly. Tora saw she could not read and snapped, 'It says I have to speak to him. It's a matter of life or death.' He let that sink in, then added, 'His!' and walked out.

The sun was low, and the fading golden light turned the market buildings and flimsy stands into an unearthly scene – like one he had once seen in his lady's picture book. Towards the north, dark clouds were gathering. Perhaps another thunderstorm would clear the mugginess from the air. A stray dog wagged its tail at him and went to investigate the refuse beside the fish stall. He gobbled something, then lifted his leg on the rest. Somewhere, temple bells called to evening prayers.

It turned dark quickly, and Tora lost his way. The streets were deserted at this hour. He'd meant to return to the Fragrant Peach to learn something about the activities of local gangs, but after wandering aimlessly through unfamiliar sections of run-down homes and empty fields for what seemed like hours, he found himself among warehouses and storage yards. There were no lights, and the new moon was no help. He turned down a long passage between tall fences and the backs of blind buildings because of a glimmer of light in the distance. The darkness was dense. He stumbled into holes and over discarded debris, cursing and rubbing a bruised knee, but kept moving forward towards the small gleam up ahead.

Somewhere midway between the light and the point where he had entered this dark hole, he became aware that the darkness was no longer empty of life. The warm air seemed to breathe and pulsate with danger. He swung around.

Nothing. Just the impenetrable darkness.

The only sounds of the summer night were the chirping insects in some weeds, a dog barking in the distance, and the flapping wings of a night bird. It should have been reassuring, but there was still a powerful sense of something lying in wait. Tora shuddered at the thought of fox spirits or other demonic presences.

Above him stretched a starry sky. Taking courage, Tora walked on. But within a few paces, he was certain that he was not alone and moved quickly aside against the blind wall of a warehouse. There, he crouched and waited, watching a space between two buildings on the other side where his pursuer's head and shoulders would become visible against the stars.

No one appeared.

He counted to twenty and decided that he had imagined the whole thing.

As he rose and took a step, something whirred and struck the wooden wall where he had been a moment before. Tora burst into a wild dash towards the light up ahead. He reached a cross street out of breath and saw the lantern of a wine shop gleaming ahead. Gulping air, he slowed and looked back. Whoever had been back there – and already the incident seemed unreal – did not come after him. Tora's heart still hammered in his chest as he walked to the wine shop. He badly needed a drink.

Near the wine shop, a gray shape separated from a wall. Tora jumped back with a curse.

'Spare a copper, brother?' quavered a voice.

Tora saw a bent old man with a dirty white beard and put a few coins into the outstretched hand.

'May you live a thousand years,' said the creature to his back.

To Tora's surprise, the wine shop turned out to be the Fragrant Peach, proving how much the appearance of things changes after dark. Feeling a little foolish, he walked in.

In the daytime, the place had merely looked depressing. Now, in flickering firelight, it seemed to pulsate with danger. Several men were drinking and gambling with dice. They were poorly dressed and looked hungry. Tora had no doubt that most carried knives.

The crippled beggar had limped in behind him. 'Koichi's doing a good business tonight,' he said. 'You one of the sergeant's men?' He peered up at Tora with bleary eyes.

When Tora did not answer, the beggar moved off towards the gamblers to try his luck there.

Near the fire pit sat three tall and burly males. The young waitress stirred something in the large iron pot suspended over it. She almost dropped the ladle when she saw Tora. This pleased him, because it meant that his good looks had impressed her even in the ragged clothes he had worn. The burly man in the middle turned to stare at him.

The fellow was gray-haired and gray-bearded and very ugly.

Tora ignored him. 'Hello, beautiful,' he called out to the girl. He went to sit on the other side of the pit, giving the three men a friendly nod. They stared back. Tora sniffed the air. 'Something smells good. What's in the pot?'

She gazed at him, frowning a little. 'Cabbage and rice.'

'I'm hungry. Let's have some of that.' He let his eyes travel over her body. 'How's the boyfriend?'

She flushed and shook her head while ladling out a serving of the food.

The three burly men watched. They were muscular and had the brutish faces of men used to carrying out dire threats against ordinary citizens. One was bald and had the broken nose of an ex-wrestler. The other's face bore knife scars. Tora decided that they were almost certainly criminals. They would not spill any secrets and might spell trouble. The girl was another matter.

'I'm a plain fellow,' he told her as she handed him the steaming bowl. 'Plain fare's good enough for me. And better when it's been cooked by a beautiful woman.'

She did not respond to his flirtation, but glanced towards the three silent men.

The baldpate made some sort of gesture to the other two. The gray-beard, who had a face as ugly as Shoki's and wore a dull red jacket, scowled at Tora. Then he, too, gestured to his neighbor, who gestured back. The third man laughed, then got in on the act by moving his fingers around and waving his arms.

Tora watched the flapping and waving of hands in amazement.

When they kept glancing his way, he decided that they were making fun of him.

'What's with you guys?' he shouted across. 'Lost your voice?'

The girl snapped, 'They can't talk. Or hear you.'

'What?'

'They're deaf mutes.'

Tora gaped at her. 'All three?'

'Yes.'

That seemed strange. Tora looked at them, and they looked back. There was nothing friendly about their faces. They were dangerous thugs daring him to make some comment. He looked around the room and decided to let it go. If they were deaf and dumb, they were no use to him anyway.

The girl was waiting. He took up his bowl and tasted. 'Not bad,' he said. 'You do all the cooking yourself?'

'Yes.'

Being hungry, Tora made short work of the soup and was considering another bowl when he realized that she was still standing there. He put down the empty bowl. She snatched it up and held out her hand. Apparently, she wanted him to pay and leave. Tora dug out a couple of coppers and put them in her dirty palm, then snatched her wrist. 'Since the deaf mutes can't talk to me, how about you keeping me company?'

'I'm busy.' She tugged back.

Tora held on, grinning. 'Come on,' he wheedled. 'I'll show you a very good time if you'll let me. Better than the young fellow in the blue and white robe.'

She gasped, 'Shut up!'

'What do you care? They're deaf.'

'They can read lips.'

'Really? Never mind. Come, give me a kiss and I'll buy you a cup of wine.' Tora jerked her arm suddenly and she fell into his lap.

That was when he heard a growl. The gray-beard was up and coming for him. He had a heavy tread, his fists were clenched, and his face was red with anger.

Tora pushed the girl off and jumped up. The thug was older than he, but he was large and looked strong. And he was not alone, for his companions joined him. Tora considered pulling the knife in his boot.

At this point, the beggar intervened. He approached the

gray-beard with a bow and said, 'How're you feeling tonight, Koichi? Lively and strong as ever, I hope? Greetings, Seiji and Shinichi. Has the sergeant been good to you? And Lady Haru grows more beautiful every day.' He performed more bows, the last to the girl, then cast a longing glance towards the kettle.

The girl smiled at the beggar and told the one called Koichi, 'Leave it be, Pa. He's a stranger. We don't want trouble.'

Koichi looked over the beggar's head at Tora and glowered. Then he gestured towards the beggar, and Haru filled a bowl for the old man. Koichi and his companions lumbered back to their seats, and Tora sat back down.

The beggar received his bowl of food, bowed his gratitude to Koichi and the girl, and sat down beside Tora to eat.

The girl Haru said, 'Koichi's my father. He gets protective.'

'It does him honor,' Tora said. He was not sure what he regretted more: her father's affliction or her relationship to him.

She looked a little wistful. 'He doesn't like me seeing men.'

Tora nodded, grinned. 'That does make it hard, but maybe we can talk outside?'

She smiled a little. The beggar belched and returned his bowl for a refill.

Tora fished out another three coppers and gave them to her with a polite bow. 'The soup was delicious, miss,' he said aloud. 'Please forgive my bad manners.' He raised a hand to the three deaf mutes, nodded to the beggar, and left.

Outside, Tora stepped around the corner into the alley and waited. The stars had disappeared and he heard distant thunder. The girl did not come out. Maybe she was busy. Or maybe she had never intended to. A gust of hot wind stirred the dust of the street. Tora sighed and decided to go home.

But first he went back to check the road between the warehouses. Lightning flickered and he saw that the stretch lay empty. It was really a mere lane that passed between two rows of warehouses and storage yards. He walked down quickly, checking the walls. When he found the place where he had cowered, he waited for more lightning. Then he saw it, a deep slash in the weathered wood exposing pale splinters. It was the sort of gash the knife in his boot would have left, had he thrown it hard from a short distance.

So! Some bastard had tried to kill him.

He was not a likely object for robbery. Whoever had followed him had had another reason.

Shaking his head, Tora hurried homeward.

The storm moved in very quickly. Thunder rumbled, and flashes of lightning threw the streets into an eerie light. When Tora reached Suzako Avenue the first large drops splattered into the hot dust at his feet, and the trees tossed and turned in the wind. The darkness and the storm reminded him of the night of the fire. He looked around and sniffed the air. There had been too many fires and not nearly enough rain. Then he saw it: a thin line of red above the roofs of the merchants' quarter to his right. It was unreal and hellish in this darkness and with the thunder and lightning of the storm. He shuddered. Perhaps the gods were angry after all.

Suzako Avenue had been empty of people, but now Tora heard a shout and saw four our five dark figures running. They were coming towards him, laughing as they came. Lightning flashed and lit up the excited faces of boys. They passed him and disappeared.

Tora turned down a side street. The rain was coming down more heavily. As he ran, Tora thought one of the boys had looked vaguely familiar. He could smell the smoke now and saw the red glow flickering and fading. Near the gateway to the quarter, he collided with another youngster. Like the others, he had been running.

He was strong and agile, but this time Tora was not drunk. He clasped the struggling figure against him, had a weird feeling of going back in time, but held on. He managed to twist the youngster's arm, bringing him to his knees. No point in being gentle. The boy cried out.

'Why are you running from that fire?'

'I'm not,' moaned the other and made a valiant effort to buck upward and throw Tora off. Tora twisted the arm a little harder, and the boy went limp and sobbed.

'Be still,' Tora snapped, 'or I'll break your arm. I think it was you who stole my gold the other night. And you were running from that fire, too.'

'It wasn't me. Let me go or I'll shout for help.'

'Go ahead.' Tora put a little more pressure on the arm and got another groan and more sobs, but the boy did not cry for help.

'Well?'

'W–what do you want?'

'My gold. Think. Near Nijo? That's where you picked up my gold, didn't you?'

A pause and then, 'Maybe. But I didn't mean to take it.'

Tora gave a snort, twisted again, and got another wail. 'You didn't mean to pick up my gold?' he sneered.

The boy ground his teeth. 'I was going to give it to you. You can have it back, if you let go.'

Tora laughed. 'I think I'll let you explain to the constables.' He shouted, 'Hey, police! Over here!'

The boy jerked and wailed, 'Don't! Please.'

A flash of lightning lit up the boy's face. Tora had caught the handsome boy from the Western Market.

The one that looked like the Kiyowara heir.

'Who are you?'

The boy groaned. 'Tojiro.'

Tojiro's blue and white robe also looked familiar. Tora had last seen it in an alley, in the passionate embrace of Haru. Tojiro certainly got around.

In his astonishment, Tora relaxed his hold. The boy twisted free, and a moment later he was running down the street.

A NOBLE HOUSEHOLD

The late Lord Kiyowara's major-domo was called Fuhito. Akitada had not paid much attention to him on his last visit and made up for it now. He was a slender, reserved man in his early sixties and exhibited a sense of extreme propriety. As was appropriate in a house of mourning, he wore a pale hemp robe over the dark-brown silk that was probably his usual attire. In a great noble house, even the major-domo could be a gentleman, perhaps a member of a junior branch of his master's family.

True to custom, Fuhito was stiffly formal. He spoke in a refined voice, and his speech was that of an educated man. His bow and his welcome to Akitada were precisely gauged to the occasion and to the visitor's rank. He led Akitada to his own office, which resembled a gentleman's study, and had him served with refreshments before their conversation began.

Akitada was impatient with such punctiliousness. Violent death seemed to him to call for a relaxation of customs. 'I expect Lady Kiyowara has informed you of the purpose of my visit?'

Fuhito bowed. 'She has. We are to answer all your questions truthfully. I have so instructed the other servants. You are to be given access to everyone and shown around the property.' He seemed to want to say something else, but decided against it.

'Do you know who came to see Lord Kiyowara the afternoon of his death?'

'I do. I keep myself informed of such things—'

Akitada interrupted, 'I mean, do you know from your own observation?'

Fuhito looked taken aback. 'Not personally, sir, but the servants keep me informed. I assure you, they are very well trained.'

'Servants may lie for their own reasons or they may come to mistaken conclusions.' Akitada thought of his own aborted visit.

Fuhito shifted a little. 'I assure you, sir, our people are very honest. I know them all.'

It was all very proper, but Akitada sensed that the man was holding himself in an iron control. He cast about for some way to penetrate the shell of loyalty and found none. Eventually, he said, 'I am sure you wish to see your master's killer found.' Fuhito bowed his assent. 'Being a trusted member of the household surely means that you were in your master's confidence?' A slight hesitation, then another bow of agreement. Akitada wondered why Fuhito never changed the fixed expression on his face. The man had superb control – or else he had something to hide.

'Since life is never without its disagreements, you might inform me of anyone who has quarreled with Lord Kiyowara, or who had a reason to wish him dead.'

If such a thing were possible, Fuhito stiffened even more. He compressed his lips tightly. Akitada knew from experience that this meant the major-domo refused to reveal some important and relevant piece of information. Most likely it was something that implicated him or reflected badly on a family member. To Akitada's surprise, however, the major-domo spoke.

'You will have heard that Lord Kiyowara's son was upset with his father,' he said. 'Lord Kiyowara refused to let the young master become a soldier. You must not read too much into that. Those of us who have watched the young lord grow up, know that there is no viciousness in him. That particular disagreement you may therefore ignore. It happens – happened regularly; at least once a month.'

Akitada acknowledged this with a slight smile. 'You are right that I have been told about the quarrel, but Lady Kiyowara seems to take it more seriously than you. In fact, I believe she expects me to find a more likely candidate quickly, before her son is arrested.'

Fuhito's eyes moved around the room. 'Quite so, My Lord. I'm sure you know that a man of His late Lordship's temperament and position in the government may make many enemies that his household knows nothing about. Did not Her Ladyship tell you this?'

'But the murder happened here, in Lord Kiyowara's house. If the murderer came from the outside, either someone admitted him or he came by stealth. Since it happened in the daytime, the former is more likely. That is why I hope one of the servants will know who the killer is.'

Fuhito blinked. 'I must warn you that there are nearly thirty house servants here. And another eighty-five have various duties at the gate, in the stables, the kitchens, the bath house, and the gardens.'

It was an impossible proposition, and the major-domo knew it. Akitada said coldly, 'I expect a man in your position has questioned them already. Perhaps you would share what you have learned?'

Fuhito looked at his clenched hands. 'Not everyone, sir. But I did speak with those on duty in the house, at the gate, and in the gardens. I made a list of all the visitors who entered the compound that day. Neither the servants in the house nor in the gardens observed anyone who was not supposed to be there. The list is in the hands of the police.'

'Did you make a copy?'

Fuhito flushed. 'No, sir. I did not know it would be needed. I have some rough notes, which I used to compile the final list.'

That was better. Akitada asked to see the notes, and Fuhito went to a bamboo stand with shelves, where he took several sheets of paper from a writing box. These he passed to Akitada with a bow.

Akitada studied them closely. Fuhito wrote in an excellent hand. In fact, his brush strokes marked him as university-educated, though sometimes graduates of the Imperial University were forced to teach in the provinces, and Fuhito might have benefited from one such instructor.

He saw his own name, and that of the poet Ono. In each case, the purpose of the visit was noted. He himself was identified by his former rank and position and his intention 'to speak to His Lordship on a matter connected with the Ministry of Justice'. Ono was unidentified, perhaps because he was a familiar and regular visitor. He had paid a call on Her Ladyship. The others were tradesmen, messengers from various offices of the Greater Palace, and people from the Kiyowara estate. They had been seen by Fuhito or the head cook, because they had brought supplies or received orders.

When Akitada had read the notes carefully, he looked up. Fuhito met his gaze. 'I see the name of His Highness, Prince Atsunori. He and I met briefly in the waiting room. Why is the purpose of his visit missing?'

The major-domo seemed astonished by the question. 'His Highness was shown into the waiting room by mistake. I was horrified when I discovered what an ignorant servant had done and rushed to remedy the situation. His Highness should not have been asked to wait. He was angry.'

Akitada recalled the air of outraged importance that had enveloped the Minister of Central Affairs. 'But why not list the reason for his call? Did you also leave that off the list you gave the police?'

'I saw no need to demand a reason from someone of such exalted rank. He probably stopped on his way to the emperor to remind Lord Kiyowara of some small matter. I took him in myself and waited outside the door. He left after only a moment. His lordship was alive then.'

Ah, that helped narrow things, though Akitada, in a perverse humor, was a little disappointed that the prince was cleared of suspicion. He said, 'Thank you. May I ask you to make a list for me also? And then perhaps you might show me the house and the room where your master died. As you know, I never got farther than the waiting room the day I came here.'

Fuhito accepted his notes back. 'As you wish, sir.'

'Did you by chance attend the university here in the capital? Your calligraphy is excellent.'

This time, the major-domo blushed with pleasure. The man's

eyes became moist. 'Thank you, sir,' he stammered. 'Yes, I was so fortunate. Those were happy days. Long gone, I'm afraid.'

Seeing so much nostalgic emotion, Akitada felt like apologizing, but he desisted. Fuhito jumped up, tucked the notes away, and rushed to open the door for him.

The tour of the house was enlightening about the dead man's wealth and his hopes for the future. Clearly, he had aimed for palatial appointments, rejecting true elegance like the austere simplicity of the emperor's own residence. Costly fabrics, objects, and paintings abounded. The room where he had died was no exception.

More to the point, Akitada suspected that it had been cleaned after the police left and the body was removed.

In addition to Kiyowara's own desk, there was a smaller second desk meant for a secretary rather than a scribe. Akitada asked about this and was told that the secretary had not been employed yet, but that Lord Kiyowara had been casting about for a suitable man.

'Why was the job not offered to you?' Akitada asked. 'Surely your background would have made you an excellent choice.'

Fuhito bit his lip. 'Not at all, sir. I am too old. His Lordship hoped for someone younger and with connections among the court nobility.'

Was he bitter that he had been passed over? Or relieved? The position would surely have meant constant exposure to Lord Kiyowara's whims. Akitada found Fuhito increasingly interesting. What were his true feelings about his late master? So far, he had not seen signs of grief.

Since the room had been cleaned and rearranged, he could learn nothing from it. No doubt the police had noted whatever clues there might have been. Akitada went to look at the scrolls and books on Kiyowara's shelves. Much of it was what you would expect to find: the great poetry collections, the law books, the *Records of Ancient Matters* and some other chronicles, translations of the Chinese masters, and the court calendars.

Akitada turned away from the books. The desk was handsome, but bare of anything but the writing set. 'Where are Lord Kiyowara's papers kept?' he asked.

'His official documents are not in this house, and the estate documents are kept at the provincial mansion. I myself keep those documents that pertain to household expenses.'

'Then Lord Kiyowara did not work here?'

'His Lordship used the room for meetings.'

'Who served as his secretary on those occasions?'

'It was rarely necessary to keep notes. His Lordship's son occasionally sat in on a meeting. His Lordship wrote his own letters.'

That was very curious. A man as wealthy as Kiyowara should have had both secretaries and scribes at his disposal. It sounded very much as if Kiyowara had not trusted anyone with the transactions taking place here. Akitada eyed the desk thoughtfully. 'Who found your master's body?'

'I did.'

'Ah. Could you describe the scene?'

Fuhito thought a moment. 'He was on his side near the desk. His face was in a puddle of blood. And his head – his head had wounds, one dreadful wound just there.' Fuhito gestured to his right temple. 'His arms were by his sides, and one leg was straight, the other bent at the knee.'

'And where was he?'

Fuhito indicated a place halfway between the desk and the doors to the garden. 'His feet were towards the doors.'

Akitada frowned, then went to the closed doors that must lead to a veranda. Opening these, he stepped out. The garden stretched before him. He saw that this spot was around a corner from the place where he had first seen Ono step from the shrubbery. The sound of women's voices came from the other side of a bank of shrubs.

'Were these doors open when you found your master? I recall it was a sunny day, and the doors of the waiting room were open to the garden.'

'I believe one of the doors was slightly open. His Lordship usually kept them closed when he expected visitors, but it was a warm day.'

Akitada nodded and turned back to scan the room one more time. 'Did you see anything that could have been used as weapon?'

Fuhito shook his head. 'The police captain asked that. I was very shocked at the time and tried to bring him back to life, so I did not pay attention. Alas, I was too late. The police said he died from the wounds to his head.'

'That means he must have been struck with something. Do you know if the police found the weapon that had been used?'

'No, but I don't think so.'

The wounds and their location suggested someone lashing out in a sudden fit of fury while facing Kiyowara. An unplanned act? Akitada thought of the son again. But what had he used? There was nothing that was both heavy enough and easily grasped and swung. But perhaps the murderer had come with a blunt tool, say a heavy cane, and taken it away after the murder. In that case he would have had murder on his mind. Alternatively, the weapon had been something he'd found here, used, and then carried away.

Fuhito had withdrawn into silent propriety again. All along, he had seemed too detached. Perhaps he was simply being careful not to give something away that might involve him or another.

Akitada asked, 'Is anything missing from the room?'

Fuhito glanced around, frowned. 'I don't know, sir. It looks as it should. But I don't always come here, and on the day of the murder I did not look at everything. I think I would have noticed something large, though.'

Akitada gestured to the outside. 'A stranger could have entered Lord Kiyowara's room from the garden and left that way.'

The major-domo said quickly, 'No. The garden is walled. Strangers – and most of the servants – would have had to come through the house.'

'Walls can be climbed.' Akitada had once climbed such a wall in pursuit of a criminal.

Fuhito shook his head stubbornly. 'Surely not in the daytime. Someone would have noticed from the outside. Allow me to show you.'

They made a thorough inspection of the walls that separated the garden from the entrance courtyard and the stable area on one side and the streets on the others. They were high and in excellent repair. A gate to the stable enclosure was barred from the inside.

'I admit the gardeners myself and close it again after they have finished,' Fuhito explained. 'They had finished that day.'

'What about gates to the street in the back of the compound?'

'Also locked and rarely opened. I have the keys.'

So much security seemed too good to be true. Akitada regarded the major-domo with a frown. 'And there has never been a single instance of someone getting in without your knowledge?'

Fuhito paled slightly. 'Never. The rules in this household are quite strict. None of the servants would disobey them. And they are therefore very watchful of anyone who does.'

Akitada was not sure of this, but changed to another subject. 'Which family members are currently in residence?'

'Her Ladyship and the young lord. Her Ladyship's cousin. No one else.'

'What about the other wives? I take it that Lord Kiyowara had secondary wives and also other children.'

'Two other ladies. And five smaller children: two boys and three girls. All of them remain in the country.'

'Isn't that unusual?'

'Not at all, sir. The children are small, and neither of the ladies have family in the capital.'

Unlike the first lady. Yes, it made sense. Still, it limited the options. A jealous wife might well have attacked her husband. Women could be quite vicious when they felt themselves slighted. But Lady Kiyowara was small. Could she have delivered such blows? It was barely possible, given the right sort of weapon. Akitada sighed and started off towards the building beyond the shrubbery.

Fuhito hurried after him. 'That path leads to the women's quarters, sir,' he cried.

Akitada stopped. 'I thought Her Ladyship had instructed you to give me access to all parts of the property?'

Fuhito glanced towards the roof of the distant pavilion and bit his lip. 'Perhaps I had better go ahead and announce you.'

'Very well.' The ladies might be in a state of undress on a hot day like this and have their doors open to the garden. Akitada twitched his shoulders where his own robe was sticking to his skin and thought of Tamako, doubly miserable at this time of year.

Fuhito disappeared into the shrubbery just about where Ono had emerged the other day. The poet's relationship with Kiyowara's wife was surely dubious. Had Kiyowara really been so tolerant of another man's comings and goings?

Akitada wandered along the small stream where Ono had paused to recite his verses. The water was very clear and flowed over smooth river stones that must have been gathered in the mountains, because none so large and smooth were available in the capital. It seemed to him, as he looked around him, that access to Kiyowara's room had been easy and would have been unobserved. No one would be in the gardens around the main house unless the gardeners were at their supervised chores. The verandas would have been empty in the midday heat.

The waiting room was around a corner from Kiyowara's room. Each shared a view of part of the winding stream and of the more distant roofs of the women's pavilions, but from the waiting room it was impossible to see Kiyowara's room or his veranda or that part of the garden.

The sun blazed down out of the cloudless sky, and Akitada moved into the shade of a catalpa tree. There he stood, raising his eyes to the far blue mountains in the north. They looked hazy through the shimmering heat that covered the capital on this scorching summer day. Far above him in the sky, a hawk circled slowly. He smiled at the notion that it, too, was searching for prey.

Gravel crunched, and Fuhito reappeared.

'Her Ladyship wishes to speak with you, sir,' he announced.

He sounded and looked disapproving. It was understandable. This was a house where mourning had been disrupted by police searching for a murderer, and now strange men were being admitted to the women's quarters. All he had expected was a glimpse of the layout of the grounds.

Akitada followed him through a small thicket of shrubs, trees, and tall grasses, along an overgrown path that might well give a husband romantic notions of seeking out a new beauty in her hidden and derelict house. He was shortly disabused of such thoughts. Lady Kiyowara's pavilion was large and ornate with red-lacquered railings and banisters. Several maids, their many-layered silk dresses now covered with hempen jackets, had stepped on the veranda to watch their approach. They seemed astonishingly unattractive or elderly. Perhaps this suited their mistress's vanity.

When Fuhito clapped his hands, they scattered.

Lady Kiyowara's room was most luxurious. She was seated, surrounded by several folding screens painted with flowers nodding against a background of gold. As before, she wore little paint on her face – just a dusting of white, a thin outline of her eyes in kohl, the high eyebrows barely brushed on, and the merest touch of red on her lips. She seemed younger for that and was still a desirable woman. Raising her fan, she smiled at Akitada.

'Please be seated, Lord Sugawara.' Her voice was pleasant but cool. 'You, too, Fuhito, for propriety's sake.'

They bowed and sat.

Akitada took in the presence of two other women, sitting together at a distance. One was the same woman who had been with Lady Kiyowara on his last visit. The other was a handsome young female in a very odd-looking costume of white hemp covered with a red stole, and thick ropes of beads and shells hung about her neck. Her hair was thick but disheveled, and she stared at him boldly, almost hungrily. He looked away, wondering why the major-domo was required when there were other women present.

An odd thought seized him. If Ono was not the lady's lover – he had only claimed brotherly affection – then a middle-aged woman like Lady Kiyowara might well have chosen a man like Fuhito to be her lover and confidant. True, the man was in his sixties and his hair was sprinkled with white, but he was, for all that, tall and handsome enough. Besides, he was well-educated and conveniently available.

Lady Kiyowara gestured with her free hand. 'You have met my companion,' she said. 'The other lady is Aoi, a spiritualist and *miko*. She is consulting the gods to find out the truth about my husband's murder.' She paused to let Akitada absorb this, then said, 'And you, sir? Have you made any progress with your methods?'

It was a humbling moment. Akitada was clearly valued no higher than the local witch. He decided to ignore it. 'I assume from your major-domo's explanations and an inspection of the grounds that the attacker must have come from the inside,' he said.

Lady Kiyowara frowned. Her eyes moved to Fuhito, who shifted uncomfortably on his cushion. 'From the inside?' she said sharply. 'Can you be certain? My husband received visitors from the outside that day, yourself included.'

Akitada understood the implied hint that he had better come up with a stranger or he would become a suspect again. He said stiffly, 'My assumption is based on the information I was given.'

She turned on Fuhito. 'You know as well as I that no one in this household would lay a hand on my husband. Why then do you suggest this to Lord Sugawara?'

Fuhito paled. 'I know it, My Lady, but I also know how

careful all of us have been to protect our lord from unwelcome visitors.'

This surprised Akitada. It seemed to make a point of ready access for welcome visitors. Could the major-domo mean Ono? But he focused on something else. 'What unwelcome visitors?' he asked. 'If Lord Kiyowara feared anyone, surely this is the time to mention names.'

Fuhito compressed his lips and looked down at his clenched hands. Lady Kiyowara fidgeted with her fan.

'Well?' Akitada urged.

Lady Kiyowara shot Fuhito a furious look and said sharply, 'My husband was an outsider at court and widely resented by his colleagues. I assumed that you would answer this question yourself. I turned to you for help because you have access to government circles that are closed to the Kiyowara family.'

A very neat turning aside of his request. While she was far off about his real position in the government, Akitada had to accept her point. He was to find the murderer among her husband's enemies. Still, he was not at all sure that the solution did not lie within the Kiyowara household. For that matter, what better place to hide a murder weapon than in the women's quarters? The police would hardly dare search them. He said stubbornly, 'It does not answer the question how an outsider could have entered the compound unseen, My Lady.'

She snapped her fan angrily. 'Then you must look harder. You and Fuhito. I wish you luck.' She did not look at him this time, but sketched a slight bow.

Thus dismissed, Akitada and Fuhito withdrew.

As they walked back to the main house, Akitada asked, 'How secure is the compound at night?'

Fuhito seemed dejected. His shoulders slumped and his head was bowed. 'The gates are closed, and there are watchmen,' he said listlessly.

'I take it, if a thief were caught trying to enter, you would be called. Has there ever been a disturbance at night in your memory?'

'There have been some minor alarms. Once a group of drunken officers of the guard drove a carriage up to the outer wall and tried to climb in. They were noisy, and the servants stopped them quite easily. Another time, the guard in the front courtyard heard noises and rustling in the garden. They investigated, but found only some wild cats fighting. I was not called on either occasion. I am not here at night.'

Akitada stopped. 'You don't live here?'

'No, I have my own house in the western quarter. I go home at sunset and return at sunrise.'

Akitada left after this exchange, wondering more than ever about Fuhito. It was very unusual for a house servant, even a major-domo, to reside anywhere other than with the family. The fact that Fuhito owned property and preferred living there suggested again that he did not belong to the servant class. Surely some tragic circumstance had forced him to accept his present humble position. Akitada decided to check into the major-domo's background first thing the next morning.

Unfortunately, several events were about to intervene and drive all thought of Fuhito from his mind.

ANOTHER SUMMONS

Akitada was tired when he got home. To his relief, he found Tamako looking better. Hanae was with her, fussing to make her comfortable as Yuki whimpered in a nest of bedding. Nodding to the women, Akitada went to pick him up. Yuki fell silent for a moment and looked at him with large, sorrowful eyes. Akitada smiled and clicked his tongue. The baby scrunched up his face and wailed.

Putting the child over his shoulder, Akitada patted his back and asked, 'Isn't Tora back yet?'

Hanae shook her head. 'The rascal's out late again. He says he's working for you, but every night I can smell and taste the liquor on his lips.' She sounded irritated.

Taste?

Akitada glanced at Tamako. Their eyes met, and a smile tugged at the corners of her mouth. They knew that Tora was deeply in love with his dainty wife and that she returned his affection ardently. Akitada often felt envious to see them so passionate about each other. In the early months of his own marriage, he, too, could not get enough of making love to Tamako. They had gloried in their physical closeness. But he was older now, more settled. They both were.

Still, it was a pity.

He said to Hanae, 'Tora is looking into those fires that keep starting up all over the capital. You know how he felt about not being able to save the two men. I think someone may be responsible for them, and I've encouraged him to keep his eyes and ears open. Now he believes that it will help me if he can prove arson. This gossip about the gods punishing the capital is ridiculous; still, it must be unpleasant for Lord Michinaga and the chancellor. I hope you'll be patient. You know how Tora is when he becomes an investigator.'

'I know.' Hanae chuckled. 'I'm really very proud of him.' Seeing how Akitada struggled to calm the fussy child, she said, 'He's hungry, sir. If you'll stay here a while, I'll go nurse him and start our supper.'

He had not planned on staying, but now he handed over the baby quickly. 'Of course. By all means feed this fine boy.' Yuki stopped crying the moment his mother took him.

When they were alone, Akitada sat down and looked at Tamako worriedly. Was she so fragile that Hanae was afraid to leave her alone for even a short time?

Tamako smiled at him. 'Soon I'll have our own child to nurse,' she said happily. 'I hope I remember how.'

They both chuckled at that. Outside, the sun was setting and the sounds of the city faded. Akitada began to relax a little. He told Tamako about Lady Kiyowara and the men who might be her lovers. She was interested, and time passed agreeably as they explored motives and personalities. Hanae did not return, but Akitada did not mind. This was like old times. When dusk fell and a warm wind started up, tossing the branches in the garden, Akitada got up to close the shutters.

'Another storm is coming,' he said, looking out at the angry black clouds.

Tamako struck a flint and lit an oil lamp. 'Good. It will cool the air and refresh the plants. I have not been able to look after my two gardens.'

He turned and watched her. In the pool of golden light, she seemed to him more beautiful than ever.

His wife – the mother of his children. He felt a surge of gratitude and affection.

Going to her quickly, he knelt and took her into his arms. They clung to each other and kissed. Her lips were soft, responsive. Desire stirred. He kissed her more deeply, tasting her sweetness and thinking: Tora is not the only one.

But Tamako returned his passion only briefly – if deliciously – before drawing away. 'Akitada,' she murmured, 'it may not be good for the child.'

He released her with a sigh. 'Of course. Please forgive me.'

'Not at all,' she said. 'I am highly gratified.' She looked at him quizzically and murmured, 'Will you return after your supper? There are surely other ways that I may please you.'

He jumped up. 'We'll have supper together. I'll tell Hanae we've retired early and bring the food back myself. Then we can have the whole night together without being bothered.'

He left, humming to himself. No doubt, Hanae would inform Tora of his master's ardent attentions to his pregnant wife.

They dined on small delicacies he had coaxed out of the cook, and then they lay close together, while the storm passed over the city. He put his hand inside her gown on her swollen belly and felt the child moving against his palm. The touch of another life filled him with joy and wonder. 'Tamako,' he murmured into her ear, 'I have been so afraid to lose you.'

She looked at him and traced his lips with her finger. 'I know. My heart is full.' Then she raised herself on an elbow to kiss him while she undid his sash and then the bands of his trousers.

The wind buffeted the sturdy roof, and the rain fell in torrents outside. Inside, they explored a hundred ways of giving and receiving pleasure. Akitada discovered a boundless gentleness in himself and profound gratitude to Tamako. When the noise outside abated, they fell asleep contentedly in each other's arms.

When he left Tamako the next morning and returned to his study, Tora was waiting for him. Seeing Tora's broad grin, Akitada flushed and snapped, 'What are *you* so happy about?'

Tora's grin faded. 'Is anything wrong? Your lady . . . is she . . .?' He trailed off.

Akitada straightened his collar and tied his sash. He had hoped for an early bath and time to change his clothes. With a sigh, he sat down behind his desk.

'Nothing is wrong. My wife is very well.'

'The gods be thanked,' said Tora with feeling. The grin returned. 'I caught the little bastard.'

Akitada had no idea what Tora was talking about and found it hard to think before he had had his customary tea. 'Hem,' he said, searching his mind. 'You did?'

Tora looked smug. 'Yes.'

From the hallway came the sound of Seimei's shuffling steps. Akitada brightened. 'Here comes Seimei with tea. Save the story so he can hear it, too.'

Seimei came in and nodded to Tora. 'I looked for you earlier, sir,' he said to Akitada. 'No one told me that you spent the night with your lady.'

Tora chortled. 'Caught me unawares, too.'

'I'm parched,' Akitada said, 'and Tora is anxious to tell us his adventure.'

Seimei took his time pouring and stirring, and Tora fidgeted. It looked as if he wanted to comment on the sleeping arrangements again, but fortunately he thought better of it. He refused tea and, as soon as Seimei was seated with his own cup, he told the story of catching the boy Tojiro running away from the latest fire.

'He admitted stealing my gold.'

'What did you do?' Seimei asked.

Tora's face fell a little. 'He got away before I could find a constable, but I reported it to the police.'

'This is the young man who looks like the Kiyowara heir?' Akitada asked. 'I don't know, Tora. There's something very odd about your bumping into him all the time. Are you quite sure he set last night's fire?'

'Absolutely. This is the second time he was at a fire. He's the one all right. I told the superintendent that it was all your doing that the arson problem is getting solved.'

With a sinking feeling, Akitada set down his cup. 'I wish you hadn't done that.'

Tora's jaw dropped. 'What? You've changed your mind? I thought you wanted me to find out about those fires. I wish you'd told me. I wasted a whole night on this. And the police weren't exactly eager to arrest the little bastard. I did it because I thought it would help you get your job back.' He clamped his mouth shut in disgust and folded his arms across his chest.

Akitada felt guilty – as he was meant to feel. 'You didn't let me finish, Tora,' he said.

Tora said nothing and looked sullen.

'You know I'm investigating the Kiyowara murder. That means we have enough money to see us through the rest of the year. And besides, I never wanted you to risk your life in this matter.' He paused, then added in a softer tone, 'But I'm very grateful that you should have cared so much.' When Tora looked slightly mollified, he went on: 'I've been trying to keep Superintendent Kobe out of our activities because he ordered me away from the Kiyowara case. He may see a conflict of interest because of our past friendship.'

'But the fires have nothing to do with the Kiyowara murder.'

'Well, perhaps no harm is done.' Akitada paused. 'Unless, of course, you happened to mention this Tojiro's resemblance to young Lord Kiyowara?'

Tora mumbled, 'I might have said something about it in passing. Not to make a point of it, you know.'

'Not to Kobe, I hope. He would wonder why you should be familiar with Kiyowara's son.'

'I may have—' Tora broke off and cocked an ear towards the courtyard. 'Someone's calling.' He jumped up and left.

Akitada had not heard anything. He thought Tora had fled because he did not want to face his anger, but then there were voices.

A visitor? This early in the morning?

Seimei hurriedly put away the tea things. The door opened, and a strange monk stepped over the threshold, followed by a puzzled-looking Tora, who announced, 'This is Saishin, sir. He comes with a message from Abbot Shokan of the Seikan-ji Temple.'

The monk, middle-aged and slender, approached silently on bare feet. He bowed and presented a letter.

Akitada returned the greeting and unfolded the heavy paper. It was the expensive kind with leaves of dried grass embedded in it and not what he would have expected from a cleric. Furthermore, it was written in an elegant courtier's style. The letter was brief: 'Abbot Shokan begs Lord Sugawara's help in a matter very close to his heart.'

Astonished, Akitada asked the monk, 'Do you know what this is about?'

Saishin compressed his lips. 'I know only that it concerns one of the acolytes running away.'

It sounded as if the monk disapproved either of the acolyte or of his flight. Akitada speculated that the combination of 'acolyte' and 'close to my heart' suggested a male love affair, not unheard of in monasteries. He was mildly curious, but he hated to leave the house when Tamako was so close to her time. So he told the monk, 'I'm very busy at the moment. Perhaps the abbot could come to see me?'

Saishin raised shocked brows. 'The abbot never goes out unless the emperor, his nephew, requests it.'

Damnation! Akitada should have recognized the name and the temple, but there were so many male relations of emperors who served as abbots and bishops that he had never made the attempt to memorize them all. In any case, he could not refuse the summons now.

'When may I call on the Reverend Shokan?'

'The abbot is very anxious to have your advice as soon as possible.'

'Today?'

'I think that is what His Reverence had in mind.'

'Very well.' Akitada thought quickly. Tora had already rented a horse for the trip to the farm. They could postpone that journey for another day. He said, 'It will save time if I ride.'

Saishin nodded. 'Good. I have other errands. May the Buddha smile on you and your house.' He bowed, turned on his heel, and left.

Seikan-ji temple and monastery were to the north-east of the capital and on the other side of the Kamo River.

Akitada checked on Tamako before leaving. She looked better than she had for weeks and greeted him with a smile. Hanae was with her, making a list of supplies they wanted brought from the farm. Hanae asked, 'Should they bring Trouble back, sir?'

Tamako giggled. It was a familiar joke. The dog's name fit its disposition well enough and frequently caused merriment. A good omen, Akitada thought, and joined in the laughter. 'By all means. I'm fond of the beast. But we'll have to confine him when it's time for the child to be born. Seimei and Tora have invited monks and a yin-yang master for the occasion. I'm afraid to think what Trouble would make of that.'

'What about a medium?' Hanae asked and started laughing again. 'Can you imagine him chasing after that paper wand while she dances? Perhaps she could cast a spell on him.'

'No medium,' Akitada said firmly. He thought of the strange Lady Aoi in the Kiyowara house. She had even upset Tora. It occurred to him belatedly that she might have information about the family. Perhaps she would be willing to provide it, if he asked her to perform an exorcism for him.

THE ABBOT

On horseback, the journey to the Seikan-ji Temple took less than two hours. It gave Akitada a chance to pass through the center of the capital before turning towards the river. He had not been in the city for weeks. Earlier, his work at the ministry had kept him busy in the *Daidairi*, the greater palace enclosure in the northern part, and now he spent his time near Tamako as much as possible.

He observed for the first time the uneasiness the fires had brought to the city: piles of sandbags and stacks of buckets gathered at street corners, makeshift altars with gifts of flowers, rice, and fruit stood near shrines and entrances to city quarters, carts of charred rubble lumbered towards trash piles, and Shinto priests and their attendants performed ceremonies to appease the angry gods.

After he crossed the broad Kamo River, he entered the wooded mountains to the east of the capital. The heat and noise of the city faded, and a fragrant green world embraced him with peace and silence. Akitada had accepted the summons in a very ill spirit, but now he found pleasure in his journey. Part of it lay in being on horseback again, even if the rented horse was far from perfect and tried to bite the rider at odd moments.

Seikan-ji was a small temple and monastery, but like many imperial retreats, it was situated in a beautiful setting. The halls were rustic and of the same simple elegance as the emperor's palace. Since it housed a member of the imperial family, the wooded grounds and buildings were beautifully kept and resembled more a series of villas in gardens than a religious retreat.

The monks wore simple but very clean brown hemp robes, but Akitada also saw groups of young boys, acolytes or students, at play. Most were probably scions of noble families and wore the colorful and expensive silks of cherished children.

He had given his name and purpose to a young monk at the gate. Another monk had taken his horse, and a third showed him to the abbot's quarters.

In theory, an imperial prince who took the tonsure lost all claim to special honors and privileges enjoyed in his past life. His family and friends would grieve as he passed into another physical realm: that of a poor monk. In reality, that step was very carefully planned. He would choose his monastic abode from the most pleasant spots near the capital and take with him certain comforts of life, such as fine clothes, books, musical instruments, as well as favorite servants. And he stayed in contact with family and friends. In exchange, he would give up women, public life, wine, and his hair. Since, by middle age, those things had frequently lost their appeal, and official duties had become burdensome, many emperors and imperial princes took up a religious life because it allowed them to enjoy a life of leisure.

His Reverence Shokan was no exception. He resided in a small, but elegantly appointed hall among fine objects and paintings. Monks and acolytes competed for a chance to be of service, and the monastery kitchens served excellent meals, even if they tended towards the vegetarian.

Akitada had little respect for those who shirked their duties to the nation in order to indulge in a contemplative life, but even he felt an ingrained respect towards men of imperial blood. He prostrated himself before His Reverence.

Shokan received Akitada with a strange mixture of reserve and eagerness.

Like many Fujiwara relatives, he was prone to pudginess and jowls in middle age. Waving a white and dimpled hand, he said, 'Please. I am a simple monk. Be seated, Sugawara.'

He had a high voice and lisped a little. Akitada wondered if he had been born with a speech defect or if he cultivated the childish manner. His Reverence wore black silk of such volume and stiffness that it was hard to make out his figure underneath. A finely patterned purple brocade surplice, glistening with gold threads, was draped over one shoulder.

Akitada waited politely to be told why he had been summoned and hoped His Reverence would not waste time with idle chit-chat. Some of the abbots he had met tended to make up for their absence from public affairs by getting news, gossip, and information from their visitors.

But the twitching hands and the searching eyes meant the abbot was anxious. Shokan waited only until Akitada had been served fruit juice and a bowl of pickled nuts before saying, 'I am told that you are good at solving mysterious events.'

Akitada said cautiously, 'Until recently it has been my honor to serve His Majesty as senior clerk in the Ministry of Justice. In that capacity, I have from time to time come in contact with puzzling criminal matters and may have offered suggestions to the police. I cannot be said to be working with the police, or as part of my official duties, or indeed regularly.'

Shokan waved that aside. 'But you have solved difficult cases, and it is your intelligence that is needed, and perhaps your knowledge of the law.'

'You are too generous, Reverence. My modest skills are at your service.'

'Thank you.' Shokan gave him a tremulous smile and dabbed a sleeve to his eyes. 'My apologies. I am very emotional. This is the only thing that still matters to me in this life.' He caught a breath, then burst out, 'Oh, what does it matter? You see before you a grieving father, Sugawara. It is as if I had lost my only son.'

Akitada was mystified. He was uninformed about Shokan's family – many noblemen did not take the tonsure until late in life – but then the abbot had said it was 'as if' he had lost a son. So not a son. 'May I ask if this young man has died?'

'Oh, no, I hope not.' Shokan shuddered. 'I could not bear that. A monk strives to give up the things of this world, but for me the struggle has been hard. How do you turn your back on someone you love?'

'Perhaps Your Reverence had better tell me more. Your messenger said it concerns an acolyte?'

'Yes. He is a youth now, but he came to us more than ten years ago. Right away, he was seen to be special – beautiful, gifted, and eager to learn. I saw him grow into a youth on the threshold of manhood.' Shokan flushed a little and gave Akitada a beseeching glance. 'You know, that delicious age when a boy is almost a man, ardent and full of heroics, yet still capable of childlike grace. Kansei looks exactly like one of those depictions of the young Prince Siddhartha before he attained Buddhahood. Oh, I hope you will find him before he is lost.'

Akitada had formed a shrewd guess of just what the relationship between Shokan and the boy had been – certainly not that of a father and son. He was irritated. As a rule, he did not judge men for engaging in sexual relationships with other men, but that Shokan should compare such bonds to those between a father and his son sickened him. What could this man know of a father's love – or his grief when his son died? How dared he snivel over the loss of a lover who had probably simply run away from a cloying relationship with an older man. Akitada still wept for his son a year after smallpox had taken him. He still felt as if part of his flesh had been ripped away and he was no longer whole.

His silence had grown too long.

'Well, what will you do?' demanded His Reverence. He was staring at Akitada.

'I beg your pardon, Reverence. I lost my only son a year ago and was remembering how that felt. Er, what was the young man's name again?'

Instantly, Shokan's face softened. 'Oh, you know my pain,' he said, nodding. 'That is good. I gave the boy the religious name Kansei. The syllables are those of our temple, Seikan-ji.'

Apparently, Shokan considered the youth his own creation. How the youngster must have resented that. Akitada thought that any effort of returning Kansei to the abbot would prove futile. Kansei would not want to come back, and if forced to do so, would run away again. Akitada approved of that, but he could hardly say so. He asked, 'When did Kansei leave?'

'On the twenty-sixth day of the last month.' A shuddering sigh implied the extent of suffering Shokan had endured since.

Akitada raised his brows. 'He has been gone for nearly three weeks? Have you tried to find him?'

'Not right away. Kansei is young and impatient. We thought he missed his mother or his former friends and had gone to see them. But if he went to his mother, she would have brought him back.' Shokan fidgeted unhappily.

'Did you speak to her?'

'No. I sent for her, but she was gone also. The neighbors said she moved soon after Kansei came to us. No one seems to know what has become of her. That was when I became really worried. I am afraid that something very bad has happened to my boy.'

Akitada fished for an excuse to extricate himself. 'Surely that isn't likely. It seems more a matter of the youngster having taken a vacation from his religious duties.' At that age, the acolyte might have wondered about forbidden fruit and sought out the prostitutes of the capital. 'Did you consult the police about his disappearance?'

'Oh, no!' Shokan looked horrified. 'We cannot go to the police. They are much too heavy-handed. No, no. This situation requires discretion. And loyalty. That is why I sent for you. One of my cousins, Bishop Sesshin, spoke very highly of your discretion.'

Sometimes obligations have a long reach. Sesshin had been another princely monk, one who had proved both kind and generous. A debt was being called in. Akitada sighed inwardly and reconsidered. It was possible that he had jumped to conclusions about Shokan. Perhaps the abbot had only taken a needy youngster under his wing and become fond of him. The young needed protection.

And Akitada must keep an open mind.

He said, 'Bishop Sesshin has done me too much honor. He was a truly saintly man. I shall try my best to help you find Kansei. What does he look like and what sort of background does he come from?'

Smiling with relief, Shokan gave a glowing description of Kansei's appearance, adding, 'He has the most noble bearing. His mother came to me when he was small and asked me to take him because she was unable to raise him properly.'

'What about his parentage?'

'I assume she was a poor woman who found herself without a husband. What can it matter? The boy is exquisite. He deserves better than to live and die in the filth of the gutter.'

Akitada said nothing.

'She claimed to have served in a noble house. I did not question this, but it may not have been true. She implied the child was the master's son. Sometimes an official wife is jealous and dismisses a maid in such cases. It is easy to believe the boy has noble blood.'

Akitada doubted the tale; still, such things did happen and caused much unhappiness. 'Thank you, but that isn't much to go on. Why are you opposed to the police being involved?'

Shokan bit his lip, then reached for a small package beside him. It was tied up in a piece of blue silk. He unwrapped it, revealing five gold bars. 'I will pay you whatever you ask,' he said. 'If this is not enough, there is more.'

Akitada swallowed. Between Lady Kiyowara and Abbot Shokan he had been offered payment that far exceeded his modest annual salary as senior clerk in the ministry. But such generosity sounded like a bribe and shamed him. He said stiffly, 'You have not told me why you should wish to keep the police from knowing about the boy. Has he committed a crime? I will not protect a guilty person or cover up his offense.'

'Of course he has not committed a crime,' Shokan cried. 'How can you accuse me of such a thing?' He snatched back the gold and shoved it out of sight. 'It seems I have made a mistake,' he said and assumed a stiff and remote demeanor.

Akitada was sorry that he had not handled this better. He had no business making an enemy, and perhaps he had wronged the man. Probably, his years of poverty made more of five bars of gold than they were in Shokan's estimation. He bowed and apologized.

Shokan was quickly – perhaps too quickly – appeased. 'I can see you have your reputation to protect, Sugawara. I do not expect you to do anything improper. It is just that Kansei, being young and a little foolish, may not have gone to his mother, but become involved with dubious company. The young are easily tempted. I should like him found before he is corrupted.'

Akitada wondered what Shokan was afraid of. Most likely the novice monk was hanging around the brothels. A handsome boy could earn good money selling his body to older men. 'Do you have any proof that he has taken up bad company?'

The abbot shifted uncomfortably. 'He was seen by one of the monks. In a bad part of the capital, near the Western Market. With hoodlums.' Shokan shuddered. 'You see why I am desperate to find him before he is arrested?'

Akitada sighed. 'Very well, I shall do my best, Reverence. You need not give me more than one gold bar until I have results. But if the youngster should have become guilty of some crime, I shall have to turn him over to the police.'

'Agreed.' Shokan nodded. 'But please hurry!'

RAT BAIT

Jirokichi was in a quandary. He had thought a gift of twenty pieces of gold would satisfy anyone, let alone a young man with a family who depended on this lord who had neither wealth nor position. Yet the man who had saved him from the damned louts had returned to Hoshina to threaten Jirokichi's life.

What was he to make of that?

It was crass ingratitude, of course. And maybe this Tora wanted to extort more money. Why else would he demand to speak to Jirokichi in person?

Hoshina was afraid and wanted Jirokichi to stay in hiding. 'That one's a sly one,' she said. 'Mark my words, he's big trouble. And he works for an official. You shouldn't go out at all for a while.'

Jirokichi shook his head. 'I don't know. Why did he help me in the first place? There was nothing in it for him. He couldn't know I'd pay him. Something else is going on. I think it's got something to do with the fires. He wanted to know about those.'

Hoshina's eyes grew big. 'You aren't going to meddle in that, Jirokichi? That's very bad trouble. That'll kill you. And me, too.'

Jirokichi sighed and nodded. 'You're right. We'd better stay as far away from that as we can. But I still feel bad. It's that fellow Tora that'll get killed if he keeps poking his nose into this.'

'Serves him right then.'

Jirokichi did not know what to say. Hoshina sometimes surprised him. He had not thought that she could be so cold about another human life. Perhaps he should be flattered that she loved him as much as all that, but in reality she frightened him.

'All right, love,' he said, 'I'll stay away from the fire business, and I'll be careful when I go out. But there's a job to do tonight.'

Jirokichi set out right after the hour of the rat had been called by the night watch. The time had always seemed to him preordained. It was the hour for thieves, his own time, decreed by the gods since the very beginning of the world. And the gods had blessed his work.

But his funds were running low after he had left the twenty gold pieces for Tora. There were several families in need. One of them had just lost their small tailor shop when it had burned down along with all their clients' orders. The tailor had gone into a deep depression over what he owed to those who had trusted him with their property, and his wife had left a plea for help at one of the small altars set up to Jirokichi.

Jirokichi was embarrassed by the little altars, but they were really very useful places for people in need to leave their requests. He visited them on his nightly rambles and read the notes people had left. If he found one worthy, he paid the petitioner a surreptitious visit to make sure he or she was telling the truth.

Since the fires had started, he had found several good families in tragic need. Tonight he would steal something for the tailor.

The night was nearly perfect for his work: warm, but no longer as hot and oppressive as in the daytime. Instead the dark had a velvety smoothness that was almost a caress. A new moon hung in the sky, and stars sparked brightly, but Jirokichi was dressed in black and had blackened his face, hands, and bare feet. His shirt and pants were molded closely to his body so they would not snag when he wriggled through small windows or openings. He stayed on the shadowed sides of houses and chose alleys and narrow streets whenever he could. Moving quickly and silently, he reached the back of the large dwelling in good time.

The house was one of those ample and steeply roofed buildings like large farms in the country. Jirokichi had been here several times already to note the layout and construction of the house and outbuildings. The shop was in front and the merchant's office right behind it. House and outbuildings were surrounded by a wall that gave access to an alley in the rear. Jirokichi had talked to neighbors about how many people lived there and had been very pleased to hear that the servants slept elsewhere. Only the merchant and his new wife remained in the living quarters at night.

The previous night he had returned to climb the roof of the main house and peer in through the hole that let the smoke escape. Below him lay the family's large common room with its open hearth. To his surprise, there had still been a light in the office in spite of the late hour, and he had heard the murmur of male voices.

Jirokichi had contented himself with a good look around to remember the layout of the cross-beams, and then he had left quickly. It was disappointing, but when he had heard the rumble of thunder, he had been relieved. Navigating a steep thatched roof when it was wet with rain was very dangerous. The thatch turned as slick as ice.

Tonight there was no danger of rain. He climbed the rear wall and peered in. Yard and house lay silent and dark. Flinging a leg over the top of the wall, he turned on his stomach with both legs dangling inside, then lowered himself by his arms. His profession had not only made him quick and silent in his movements, but it had also given him very strong arms and legs.

He landed with a faint thud and immediately slipped behind a pile of boxes and large containers.

All remained still.

Jirokichi had not been making empty boasts when he had told Tora that he was successful only because he prepared carefully. Not all of his attempts turned up good targets. Some wealthy men's houses were inaccessible because of night-time guards, or a noisy dog or mewling cats. The latter problem he had once thought to solve by returning with several live rats in a cloth bag. These he had let loose to distract the cat, but the ensuing clatter as the cat scampered after the rats while the panicked rats looked for escape in unfamiliar surroundings had woken the owner more surely than if Jirokichi had simply strangled the cat. He had almost been caught – with the owner's full money purse on his person. Only the fact that the merchant had blamed the racket on the rats had saved him. It was this incident that had later given Jirokichi the nickname the Rat.

He climbed to the top of a small shed that gave access to the roof of the main house, then made his way up it, walking softly on the thick thatch until he reached the small opening near the top that let the smoke from cooking fires escape. Here he stopped and peered down. The fire in the hearth was out, and the place lay in darkness and silence, except for faint sounds of snoring. He made his move.

At this point, things got tricky. Because of the darkness, he now had to work by touch and memory. He pictured the wide cross-beams in his mind and squeezed through the opening, letting his bare feet dangle down until they found the beam. He felt around with his toes and stood up.

Only the fact that Jirokichi was as small and slight as a child of ten permitted such work. A larger man would not have been able to fit through the roof opening and would have been too heavy to traverse the tops of flimsy interior walls.

By now his eyes could make out a few things, and he walked along the wide beam to the opposite side of the house. Jirokichi never suffered from vertigo. He had apprenticed with one of the rope walkers in the market when he was a boy, but given up the profession as too uncertain a year later.

The lower part of the house was open to the roof, and only the eave chambers were enclosed by walls. The center of the house was the common room. Jirokichi reached a place above the merchant's office via one of the cross-beams. There he sat down and fished a key from the secret pocket Hoshina had sewn into his pant leg.

This was one of several thin gadgets fashioned of hard steel by a clever smith who believed that Jirokichi traded in used furniture and needed to open chests where the owner had lost the key. This particular 'key' fit locks like the ones on merchants' money chests.

He prepared to drop down to the floor when a loud pounding made him freeze in place. He listened.

The sound was too muffled to have come from the front of the house, but it was certainly loud enough to wake the owner.

There it was again. And now he heard other sounds, and a light sprang up in one of the eave rooms. The merchant had woken and was muttering angrily.

Jirokichi briefly considered making his way back to the roof opening, but the light would catch his moving figure, and the merchant might look up and see him. The main support beams were visible from most of the rooms below. Instead of risking capture, he scooted as far as possible into the dark corner where the roof descended and two beams crossed. There he cowered and waited.

The merchant's heavy steps receded. Somewhere in the back of the house, a wooden bar slid back and a door opened. Jirokichi heard excited male voices and the merchant's angry growl. Then the door slammed, the bar fell into place, and more steps returned. The merchant was bringing visitors into the common room.

When they appeared, lit eerily by the flickering light of the merchant's oil lamp, Jirokichi's heart skipped a beat. He recognized the two scruffy young louts instantly. They were the ones that had maltreated him so brutally. One of them was the ugly bastard with the knife scar on his cheek. The other was the thin one with the hungry look. He had a black eye.

They looked around curiously, but seemed polite and deferential. Their presence here surprised Jirokichi. Wealthy merchants like the one below did not associate with such scum. Besides, he would have expected them to use their knives to rob the older man.

Instead of being suspicious, the merchant merely looked angry. He snapped, 'Wait here,' then turned his back on them and padded off towards his office. Jirokichi wondered at that, and he wondered even more that they obeyed meekly.

The merchant now stood directly below him. Jirokichi drew in his arms and legs as the light crept towards his crossed beams. Oblivious of the thief cowering above him, the man pulled out a bunch of keys on a string he wore around his neck and unlocked the money chest.

When he lifted the lid, Jirokichi clamped a hand over his mouth to keep from gasping at the size of the treasure. Gold and silver in loose coins rose in piles, and bundles of bulging bags were stacked beside the piles. Golden ingots filled the sides, and more lay underneath the coins and bags. Jirokichi had never seen so much gold in one place.

He knew from the neighbors that the merchant was lending money at high interest, but even that did not explain such wealth. Even as his mouth watered at the sight, he knew that there was far too much for a small man like himself to carry away.

He considered various desperate methods of raising heavy weights up to the roof and lowering them outside. All proved impracticable. He watched in misery as the merchant counted out some gold coins, then closed and locked the chest.

Jirokichi tried to console himself with the thought that even the amount of gold he could comfortably carry offered a rich reward for his trouble. Soon the merchant would get rid of the youths and go back to bed, leaving Jirokichi to reap the fruits of his labors.

The merchant handed the gold to the scar-faced youth. 'Here,' he said, 'that should take care of the next one. It's more than you deserve. You've been getting careless. Two people dead already. Stay away from mat makers and paper merchants.'

The youth took the gold, but he blustered a little. 'It wasn't our fault. We made sure to wake up the guy. Who knew about the old one in the back?'

'You should've known better. And if you're seen again, you'll be useless. That's when you'll disappear permanently.'

The rat saw the fear in their faces as they slunk off without another word. The merchant followed them out, then closed and barred his back door and returned to his sleeping quarters. The light went out.

Jirokichi stayed in his cramped position for a long time, even after he could hear the merchant snoring again. He thought about what he had heard. The young punks weren't the only ones who were scared. He eyed the money chest longingly and clutched the key in his sweaty hand. After a while, he started shivering. Not even the immense treasure below could tempt him to steal from this man. If he were caught here tonight, he would be a dead man, and if he were merely suspected of having been here, he would be hunted down. When he finally got up to leave, he still trembled so much that he almost slipped off the beam on his way back to the exit hole.

Outside, on his way down the steep roof, he had to force himself to move carefully, but when he gained solid ground, he sped away as if all the devils of hell were after him.

THE WITCH

The new closeness Akitada had found in Tamako's arms was both deeply moving and upsetting to him. She was clearly feeling better but, far from being reassured, he now realized how profoundly her loss would affect him. And that thought kept him in an almost continuous panic – a panic that was always worst in the mornings when he left her bed.

The morning after Akitada's meeting with Abbot Shokan, Akitada was once again pondering the thin line between happiness and despair, when an unsmiling Superintendent Kobe arrived. He was shown into Akitada's study by Tora, who withdrew again quickly.

In spite of a sinking feeling that he would not like what Kobe had to say, Akitada offered a jovial greeting: 'Good morning, my friend. You're out and about early, but it's always a pleasure to see you.' When Kobe did not respond to this and continued to glower, he asked, 'Is something amiss?'

'You might say so.' Kobe sat down and glanced around the

room, then seemed to remember his manners. 'I hope all is well with your lady?'

When he had left her, Tamako had been curled up under the quilt and smiling sleepily up at him. Akitada, putting aside his perverse fears, said, 'Thank you. She is feeling much better.'

'I'm very glad to hear it,' Kobe said stiffly and fell silent.

'Will you take a cup of wine?'

'No.'

This blunt refusal was an unpleasant surprise. Akitada tried to ignore it. 'How may I be of assistance, then? Have there been more disturbances in the city?'

'Another fire night before last, but I expect Tora told you about it. I'm here on the other matter.'

The other matter could only be the Kiyowara case. Hoping to distract Kobe, Akitada said, 'Tora reported his suspicions of some young hoodlums, but I'm afraid he was too generous in giving me credit. I had nothing to do with it.'

Kobe fidgeted impatiently. 'It has come to nothing. There's no proof. The fact that they were near two fires was probably due to curiosity. The young don't have enough to do and roam the city at night.'

Raising his brows, Akitada said, 'Tora caught them twice running from a fire. Surely that's a little too much coincidence, don't you think?'

Kobe scowled. 'Don't waste my time with the fires,' he snapped. 'I'm here because you're in the pay of the Kiyowaras. In spite of my warning! I won't speak of the effect your involvement in the murder is bound to have on the Bureau of Censors or of the repercussions for your career. If you wish to ruin yourself and your good name, that's your business. But I will not tolerate your ruining mine.'

Akitada gasped, then sputtered, 'I'm not in the pay of the Kiyowaras, as you call it. And in what way am I ruining your career?'

Kobe seemed to swell with anger. 'When you use our relationship to interfere in a murder investigation and to protect the guilty, you call my honesty and my loyalty to my emperor into question. I came to warn you that you may not count on the police to help you, and I have already informed Lady Kiyowara of this. Naturally, she was unhappy that you won't be able to protect them from us.'

The room had become chill. Akitada felt as if all his blood had drained from his upper body and was forming a painful knot in his belly. Kobe's figure swam before his eyes. What had he done to deserve this from a man he had counted his friend for years? They had fallen out before, but Kobe had never insulted him like this, not even when Akitada had worked on a memorial to the emperor that criticized the police. He sat frozen, searching for an explanation, and finally hit on his dismissal from the ministry.

'I see,' he said bitterly. 'This is a mere pretext. Now that I have lost my position in the government, you're using this to cut the bonds of friendship. I had no idea you felt that way.'

Kobe's face flushed. 'That's a damned lie. How dare you accuse me of such cowardly behavior?'

The knot in Akitada's belly dissolved into red-hot fury. He shot to his feet and shouted, 'Because it *is* cowardly. And I shall *not* stop working for Lady Kiyowara to please you.'

Kobe was on his feet also. He had turned nearly white. 'Then I must warn you that you're cutting your own throat and ruining your family. Given your refusal to stay out of this case, I shall have to assure the chancellor that I cannot be responsible for your actions now or in the future.'

Akitada snapped, 'So you also plan to ruin my chances of getting another appointment. When have you ever been responsible for my actions? Not once. But you liked it very well when you benefited from them because you were inadequate to the job. No, I had it right in the first place: now that my enemies have the upper hand, you consider me a heavy stone that threatens to drag you down. You're nothing but an opportunist, Kobe.' Akitada clenched his fists to control the tremor in his voice. 'The fact that I have to earn a living outside the civil service is lost on someone who is in the pay of corrupt officials. No wonder you think me so dishonest that I would use your name to subvert the truth and protect a murderer.'

They stood glowering at each other for a moment. Suddenly, Akitada felt drained. 'You'd better leave,' he said and turned his back on Kobe.

He heard receding steps, and then the door slammed.

The sound echoed in Akitada's head as he walked unsteadily towards the veranda and looked out at the garden without seeing it.

Eventually, he realized that Seimei and Tora had come into
the room. Seimei cleared his throat, but Akitada did not turn
until Tora plucked at his sleeve.

'What was that all about, sir?'

'Superintendent Kobe has accused me of . . . dishonorable
behavior.'

Tora sucked in a breath, then muttered a curse.

Seimei came up. 'It is said that we must inquire seven times
before we doubt a friend. Surely there was a misunderstanding.'

'No misunderstanding.' Akitada turned and looked at them
bleakly. 'Tora, your report has come to nothing. Kobe says the
boys were not involved in the fire.'

'What about the one that stole my gold?' Tora clenched his
fists. 'Did he think I lied?'

'Forget it, Tora. Take the horse and ride to the farm to get
Genba and the dog. I'll give you money for old Matsue so he
can pay the workers and buy more seed rice.'

Tora and Seimei looked at each other, then Tora left while
Seimei remained to help count out coins and enter the new
expenses in the account book. Neither Akitada nor Seimei referred
to the quarrel again, but Akitada's hands shook as he handled
the silver and gold.

When he was alone again, Akitada took out his flute and
returned to the garden. The sun was already high, and the leaves
of trees and shrubs drooped in the heat. Even a bird flying from
branch to branch seemed listless. The hot wind hissed in the
miscanthus and moved a tendril of the wisteria vine across an
open shutter with a dry, scraping sound. Akitada tried a complex
melody to distract his mind, but the music jarred, splintered, and
broke into dissonance. Silence fell. The city beyond the trees
seemed to be waiting fearfully, and Akitada searched his heart.

What had he done that his old friend should reject him so
harshly? Surely Kobe could not believe that he would protect
either Lady Kiyowara or her son if either should prove guilty.
Perhaps Lady Kiyowara had believed it, but that did not make
it true. And Abbot Shokan – had he also called on him because
he thought the payment of gold bars would keep his protégé
from being arrested? Did they all see him as a corrupt or corrupt-
ible official?

He knew he was innocent, but he had taken their gold. They
would consider that a tacit acceptance of a bribe. He laughed

bitterly. Maybe he should have asked for more since he was selling his honor.

It did not matter. They needed the money. He would earn his pay quickly and honestly and prove them all wrong.

But that was easier thought than done. He had no idea where to start on either case.

In his misery, he sought out Tamako to share his troubles.

'How odd,' she said when he had explained. 'I wonder what happened.'

'Happened? Nothing happened, except that Tora mentioned the Kiyowara son, and Kobe became suspicious.'

'Oh, I don't think so. I expect he knew already. Your visit there would not be a secret when the police were in and out of the house.'

Akitada considered that. 'But then I don't understand why Kobe was so very furious all of a sudden.'

'Yes, it's very strange. Perhaps you had better wait a while before judging your friend.'

Akitada made a face. 'Much too late for that. He said some things . . . and I'm afraid I said some things . . . Well, I was naturally very angry.'

'Naturally.' She hesitated, then laid her hand on his. 'I'm sorry. You have much to plague you just now.'

He felt a little better for having talked with Tamako and returned to his study. It was time to see Tora off on his trip. He had missed Genba – and Trouble. The dog was something of a clown who performed foolish tricks and made them all laugh. And Genba would bring his horse so he could ride into the countryside again. He had almost forgotten how beautiful the mountains were until his visit to Abbot Shokan. He would manage quite well without Kobe.

At this point, the witch walked into his study.

Customarily, women did not pay visits to strange men unless they were nuns or courtesans and entertainers belonging to the outcast class. The only other exceptions were *miko*, who were nominally shrine maidens, but more usually promiscuous females versed in exorcisms and fortune-telling. He assumed his visitor belonged to this group. Tora, who had let her in, gaped at her with an awed expression.

Akitada had last seen her at Lady Kiyowara's, and then she had been sitting in a dim corner. Standing, she was astonishingly tall

for a woman. The chains of beads and shells around her neck
clicked softly as she lowered the red shawl from her head and
draped it around her shoulders. Her hair was as wild and tangled
as before, and the large brooding eyes in her handsome face fixed
him as boldly. She neither knelt nor bowed, but stood before him
as if she expected him to bow to her.

'Umm,' said Tora a little shakily. 'This is the Lady Aoi, sir.
She has something to ask you.'

'Thank you, Tora. You may leave.'

The strange female looked after Tora with a slight frown and
shook her head.

Lady Aoi? It was probably a professional name. Many courtesans chose fanciful names for themselves, and Lady Aoi was
a famous character in Lady Murasaki's novel *Genji*.

As the door closed behind Tora, she turned her eyes back to
him and measured him coolly. Akitada said, 'Please be seated –
er, Lady Aoi. Did Lady Kiyowara send you?'

She knelt gracefully, then sat back on her heels. With a nod
towards the door, she said in a rather deep but pleasant voice,
'Your servant is as ignorant as you are.'

While he would admit to his own ignorance in the Kiyowara
case, the criticism of Tora irritated Akitada. He said curtly, 'I'm
very busy. Could you get to the point?'

She eyed him for a moment. 'Have you made arrangements
for a *miko*?'

Somehow she must have discovered that Tamako was about
to give birth. His irritation grew. 'I don't believe in fortune-
tellers.'

She responded with a mocking smile. 'You see? That is why
I am here. You don't believe in anything. How can you find the
truth when you don't believe?'

Akitada snapped, 'Do you have a message for me or not? Is
this visit in any way related to Lord Kiyowara's murder?'

The mocking smile was back. 'Of course. You know nothing,
and you suspect the innocent. I told Hiroko as much, but she is
another unbeliever.'

The familiar use of Lady Kiyowara's personal name made
Akitada cautious. 'Perhaps you should explain your relationship
first. Who are you?'

'Oh, I am a cousin. She has many. I help her look into the
future.' She fixed him with those extraordinary eyes and said

with great seriousness, 'There is only the future, and it is already ordained.'

'If that were true, it would be pointless to try to change it. Why are you here?'

She frowned, then returned to the former subject. 'Your wife suffers from a fever. Most likely she is possessed and will need an exorcism.'

Akitada compressed his lips. The fact that she also knew about Tamako's fever did not surprise him. It was easy enough to get gossip from neighbors. 'Thank you. No exorcism is required. She is quite well again,' he said flatly. 'Why do you say I suspect the innocent? Do you know who killed Kiyowara?'

She shook her head impatiently. The beads around her neck clinked softly. 'Your house is filled with angry ghosts. They intend harm to mother and child.' She paused to listen and shuddered. 'The atmosphere here is almost more violent than at my cousin's.'

Akitada suppressed his rage. If she was indeed Lady Kiyowara's cousin, he could hardly throw her out. There had been some disturbing tales of high-born ladies who had gone mad and imagined they were shape-shifting foxes or hungry ghosts. Such sick fancies were part and parcel of the worst superstitions, and females were prone to them. One could understand the common people believing in such things, but he was not about to encourage them. If she was indeed mad, he must meet her crazed comments with calm.

'My wife is a sensible woman,' he explained, speaking slowly, as if to a child. 'She has never offended anyone. She will be quite safe from ghosts.'

Lady Aoi nodded. 'That may be so, but the same is not true of you, I think. You have offended many. There is a female spirit in this house who hates you with special venom. Hers is the most powerful presence here, but there are also many others, both male and female, whom you have harmed.'

He was taken aback. His stepmother had hated him. She had died in this very house, cursing him. It was also true that he had caused many evil men and women to be judged and condemned. But Lady Aoi's words were vague enough to fit anyone's situation. For that matter, the difficulties he had had with his stepmother might be known to her. He said firmly, 'Unless you have information about the Kiyowara murder, I regret that we have nothing to discuss.'

Lady Aoi looked at Akitada with her large, glittering eyes. Then she pulled her shawl back over her hair and got to her feet. Akitada noticed that she had come barefoot, and that ropes of beads also decorated her ankles.

'Foolish man,' she murmured.

Akitada clapped his hands. Tora appeared so quickly that he had probably been listening at the door. 'Sir?'

'Lady Aoi is ready to leave. Please see her to the gate.'

Lady Aoi walked out, beads clicking and robes rustling, without a bow.

Tora gave Akitada a look and shuddered, then followed her, leaving his master to wonder when Tora would finally lose his fear of magic.

When Tora returned, he looked pale. 'Sir, she speaks to the gods and knows what will happen. She told me to be prepared, that there is very great danger. And then she said it was probably too late already. Let's call her back and ask her to perform a service.'

Akitada was irritated. 'Nonsense, people cannot see the future. She is either mad or hopes to fool us into paying her in golden coin for her tricks of the trade. More likely she's merely mad. I'm sorry she frightened you.'

Tora looked stubborn. 'I just thought . . . if she's a proper *miko*, she could do an exorcism for when your lady gives birth.'

'Did you tell her that my wife is about to give birth?'

'She asked.'

'If she can see the future, she should have known,' Akitada pointed out.

Tora held his ground. 'It's hard to know everything. I know nothing. You know a lot more. Isn't it possible that some people know things you and I don't?'

'Certainly. In her case, I was hoping that she could tell me about the Kiyowara murder. She's the wife's cousin. But she had absolutely no idea.' He saw that Tora wanted to argue the point and said, 'Never mind. I've decided to postpone your trip into the country. I have a job for you.'

'A job? What about getting Genba and Trouble?'

'That can wait. I want you to find a young monk who's gone missing. His name is Kansei. The abbot says he was seen with some hoodlums in the western quarter. Frankly, it seems far-fetched for an acolyte. I would have thought he'd spend his time in the brothel quarter.' He mentioned Abbot Shokan's worries that his protégé was getting in trouble with the law.

Tora smirked. 'Lost his pretty boy, has he?'

'Perhaps, and perhaps not. The abbot is an imperial prince. He may simply have taken a fatherly interest.'

Tora guffawed.

'Look, it won't be helpful if you approach this task with preconceived ideas. Boys get into trouble all the time. Whatever the situation, we need to find him.'

'It won't be easy. Those hooligans are everywhere. No more begging or sweeping the street for a bite of food. As for mischief, we know some of them are setting fires, even if the police don't believe it.' He thought a moment. 'I wish I'd known sooner. That fellow Tojiro might know him.'

'Perhaps, but even if you find him, what makes you think he'll talk to you after you tried to have him arrested?'

Tora grinned. 'I know where his girlfriend works.'

Akitada decided to leave matters to him. 'Very well, but no violence and be careful. If you're right about the fires, you could find yourself in some real trouble.'

Tora thought of the knife attack in the dark alley. 'I'll watch myself.'

RAT TRAP

His heart beating madly, Jirokichi practically vaulted over the outside wall of the merchant's property and came down on the other side so carelessly that he twisted his ankle on the uneven ground. Muttering a curse, he hobbled away, down the alley between property walls and out into the side street. His mind on his painful leg and on getting as far away from the house as he could, he did not notice his danger until it was too late.

No more than fifty feet away from the mouth of the alley stood the two louts, engaged in an altercation. They saw Jirokichi the moment he saw them.

'Hey! What's he been doing back there?'

Jirokichi gasped, turned, and started running.

Almost immediately a sharp pain shot up his leg and he stumbled. He heard their steps behind him. One of them shouted, 'Grab him!'

They dragged him up by the collar and saw who he was.

'It's the Rat,' cried the leader, astonished and pleased. 'This time, shitface,' he told Jirokichi, shaking him like rag, 'you're not getting away.'

Jirokichi believed him.

'Been spying on us?'

Jirokichi shook his head.

'Let me search him,' said the other lout. 'I bet he's just robbed some rich bastard.' He started feeling Jirokichi's body.

'Wait. Not here,' said the tall one. 'Someone may come. We can have some fun with him at our place.'

Jirokichi risked a loud yell for help. He got a fist in his mouth and nose and spit out a tooth in a gush of blood. The pain and the blood shut him up, but his tormentors were not satisfied. While the big lout held the limp Jirokichi, his companion tore strips off Jirokichi's shirt and gagged him. Then they set off, dragging him between them like a bag of garbage.

They went quite a long way. Jirokichi choked on blood and convulsed a couple of times, but was shaken into proper compliance. It was late, and they kept to side streets until they reached the poorer part of the city and entered an abandoned warehouse. There they dropped Jirokichi while one of them struck a flint and lit an oil lantern. Jirokichi was again choking badly. The blood had closed his nose and the gag allowed very little air into his lungs. He twisted his head, trying to loosen the gag a little. They kicked him, then dragged him upright and ripped off the gag.

'Go ahead and cry your head off, turd,' said the leader, grinning. 'Nobody'll hear you.'

They searched him more carefully, but found no gold on him. Disappointed, they took turns pummeling him and laughing. Jirokichi accepted that he was about to die and passed out.

He woke to even greater misery, thereby proving that life was worthless, as the monks had taught him in his youth.

He was hanging from his arms. His feet barely touched the ground, and the pain in his arms and shoulders was so agonizing that he did not feel his other wounds. He had no idea how long he had been hanging like this, but his nose and mouth had bled freely down the front of his torn shirt and made a puddle on the floor that had mixed with piss when he had lost control of his bladder.

In a corner nearby, his two tormentors sat together with some other louts. They perched on sake barrels, discussing the events of the night.

'So,' the leader's skinny companion was asking, 'do we kill the Rat and tell the fat slug that he's been spying on him? Or will the slug get mad that we touched the saintly little bastard?'

'Kill him,' cried two of the newcomers. The third turned to look where Jirokichi was swaying in the semi-darkness.

'Hey,' he said, 'His eyes are open. He's been listening.'

Instantly, they were on their feet and around him. Jirokichi cursed himself. He closed his eyes and pretended to be unconscious, but they weren't fooled. A hard slap across the face made Jirokichi's eyes pop open again. Their eyes gleamed with anticipation.

One of them gave Jirokichi a push in the chest that sent him swinging and twisting like a pendulum. They laughed and spent some time pushing him back and forth on his rope, harder and harder. Jirokichi shrieked when his shoulder separated.

'Stop that noise,' snapped the leader, halting the human pendulum, 'or I'll do it again. Now talk. You were coming from that alley. What were you doing back there?'

Jirokichi blubbered, 'N–nothing.'

Instantly, he got another push and shrieked again. This amused the others, who hopped around, laughing.

Their leader steadied Jirokichi's body and brought his face closer. He was not laughing. 'You were down that alley spying on us, right? I want to know what you saw and heard.'

But Jirokichi knew that the truth would mean certain death. A lie had to be good, and even then they would probably kill him eventually – after lots of torment. He pretended to faint again.

Immediately, blows rained down on him, into his belly, face, groin, and back. He shrieked again and again. Hot pain exploded everywhere in his body, and he passed out for good.

THE BLIND BEGGAR

Before Tora left on his new assignment, he lectured Hanae about watching the baby and not wandering about town alone. He was so firm about this that Hanae got frightened.

'What have you done now?' she demanded, her eyes flashing. 'You and your master are getting to be more and more alike. You care for nothing but your work. I cannot imagine what makes foolish women agree to marry men like you.'

This caused a delay, as Tora had to reassure his wife he had done nothing and that she and Yuki were the treasures of his life. He was afraid to tell her what Lady Aoi had said. Hanae forgave him eventually, sealing his pardon with a kiss that he took such pleasure in returning that one thing led to another.

When Tora finally set out, it was nearly the hour of the midday rice. He walked quickly to the Western Market. He meant to visit the Fragrant Peach again. With luck, he would find Tojiro with his girlfriend; if not, the young waitress could be made to talk.

He skirted Hoshina's place at the market corner and was about to pass through the market gate into Nishi-Horikawa Avenue when he heard a female voice shouting his name. He turned his head, and there was Hoshina herself, galloping after him. She cried, 'Wait, Tora. Please!'

Please? Her eagerness astonished him. He waited. She came to a halt before him and caught her breath.

'It's Jirokichi,' she gasped. 'He didn't come home last night.'

Tora raised his brows. 'So?' He was still resentful about the tricks she had played on him. 'Is he your husband, then? And has he run off with another woman?'

She flushed. 'Shut up. It's serious.' She glanced around, but they were alone for the moment. 'He went out on a job last night,' she said in a low voice, 'and didn't come back.'

Tora snorted. 'In his business, that probably means he got caught. Check the jails.'

Hoshina burst into tears. 'I did, and he isn't there. I think those bastards got hold of him again. I think he's lying some-where, bleeding to death. Oh please, Tora, help us. Find him. I'll do anything. I can pay you.'

Tora's eyes narrowed. She wasn't trying to seduce him this time. She looked really desperate. But the old anger at Jirokichi welled up again. 'I don't want your money,' he said coldly and shook off her hand.

She grasped him again, this time with both hands. 'What do you want?'

'Information. And I bet he's just late getting home. Maybe he's been celebrating with whatever he stole.'

'No, he always comes home directly. Always. He knows I wait up.' Her voice got shrill, and a couple of women, passing with their shopping baskets, gave them sharp looks. Hoshina pulled Tora back towards her place. 'We can't talk here. If you'll come with me, I'll tell you about the fires.'

Tora stopped resisting. He did not trust her, but could not pass up this chance. It would be a fine thing, if Superintendent Kobe could be made to eat his words.

In Hoshina's wine shop, a couple of men were waiting to be served, but Hoshina snapped, 'Go away! I'm closed,' and pushed them out the door, locking up behind them.

'What about your business?' Tora asked, astonished.

'Never mind the business. This is more important. Are you going to find Jirokichi?'

Tora shook his head. 'If I recall, I asked you where he was hiding last time we talked, and you wouldn't tell me. If you don't know where he is, how am I going to look for him?'

She ignored that. 'You want to know about the fires. He didn't want to tell you about that because he liked you.' She snorted. 'He's a fool, but I want him back.'

Tora tried to puzzle that out and failed. 'What about the fires?'

'Someone's been setting them.'

'I know that already.' Tora made for the door.

'Wait. Jirokichi's really frightened about those fires. I think he may have found out something and . . .' She wailed, 'Maybe they killed him because he knows who's behind it.'

'Oh, stop crying,' Tora said. 'You don't know that. It could be something else altogether. Where did he go last night?'

She sniffled and wiped her nose with the back of her hand. 'He never says exactly, but he thought there'd be a lot of gold at this place. He needed the gold because of what he gave you.' She shot him an accusing look. 'And he got no thanks for it.'

'I don't want his damned gold. He'll get it back. I got angry because he snuck into my house at night and . . .' Tora tried to explain and failed. 'Well . . . it's the way he did it. Besides, I can't take gold for helping some poor bastard who's getting beaten up by hoodlums. It wouldn't be right.'

She was astonished. 'What do you mean, "It's the way he did it"?'

Tora blushed. 'He was in my place at night while me and my wife . . . I mean, anyone would be furious if strangers wandered around their house at any hour of the night.'

She stared at him, then burst into hysterical laughter. 'You thought he was spying on you and your wife making love?' she gasped. 'Wait till he hears! Oh.' She stopped laughing and put her hand over her mouth. Her face crumpled again.

Tora said, 'Maybe he got caught and someone decided to teach him a lesson for snooping.'

She wailed, 'That's what I'm afraid of. Only, it must've been about the fires.'

'Oh, I didn't mean anything serious. He could be dragging home with a black eye any moment. Aw, for the gods' sake, Hoshina. Tell me where he went, and I'll go take a look.'

She stopped wailing. 'Some rich man's house in the Fifth Ward. I don't know his name.'

'A merchant? What sort of business?'

'I don't know.'

'He must've said something. What about the house? Did he describe it?'

'No. But he was afraid of rain because steep roofs get slippery then. It didn't rain last night. Do you think he's gone and broken his neck?'

'My guess would be that he's good at his job, so don't worry. I'll see if I can find him. Now, maybe you can tell me something else. I'm looking for a young monk. His name's Kansei. He may be with the same crowd that got hold of Jirokichi the first time. Did Jirokichi mention a monk?'

She shook her head. 'What would a monk be doing with those bastards?'

Tora sighed. Maybe Tojiro's girlfriend would know something.

'You ever hear of three deaf mutes? Middle-aged and mean-looking?'

She nodded. 'They're collectors.'

Tora was pleased. Collectors worked for armed men who sold protection against thieves and robbers to merchants, but such a business was often run by the criminals themselves. The dying Kaneharu had talked of his father paying, but his neighbor had blamed the fire on the old man being a miser.

'You mean someone's running a protection racket?'

'They collect anything owed: rent, loans, and service. It's a way to make a living.'

'But they also collect for protection? Who's behind that?'

'An ex-soldier and his men. They keep watch over the market and some businesses that had trouble with vandals and thieves.'

'Would they be setting the fires?'

She shook her head. 'No. Jirokichi isn't afraid of them. He's afraid of someone else. Now please go. Maybe Jirokichi can tell you more when you find him.'

What Tora had learned was interesting, if not very helpful, but he retraced his steps, returning to the eastern city and the Fifth Ward.

Each ward in the more densely populated areas consisted of sixteen blocks arranged in a square and had a gateway on its southern periphery. The Fifth Ward contained mostly the homes of lower-ranking government officials and a few wealthy merchants. The first fire Tora had encountered had been in the adjoining Sixth Ward, a commercial area, but even here, there was fear. He saw a small altar erected and fresh flowers and fruit before it, and a holy man with bells around his neck danced around it, singing songs as people watched.

Stopping at the warden's office, Tora asked if any trouble had been reported the night before.

The warden was eating his midday rice and was not inclined to be interrupted by someone wearing threadbare clothing. He shook his head and continued chewing.

'Did you see or hear of any gangs of rowdy boys hanging about?'

Another shake of the head.

'I know they were busy in the Sixth the other night. They knocked me down as they ran from the fire there.'

The warden frowned, swallowed, and said, 'You the one tried to save the Kaneharus?'

News clearly traveled between wardens. Tora said, 'That would be me. My name's Tora. You keep yourself well informed.'

'My business,' said the warden, taking another bite and chewing thoughtfully as he studied Tora.

'So? About those gangs?'

'No gangs in *my* ward.'

'How can you be so sure?'

'I'm sure. No gangs here. No trouble.' The warden was becoming angry at the imputation that he did not keep good order.

Tora sighed. 'Thanks. Enjoy your meal.'

He wandered about for a while. Most of the houses were substantial, and quite a few had steep roofs. He asked people on the streets if they had heard any fighting or strange noises during the night. Mostly, the answer was no. People slept at night, and their sleeping quarters were in the backs of houses. One maid, who was airing out the family quilts, claimed she had heard screams, but her mistress shouted from the door that the girl was given to nightmares.

Tora left after that, feeling that he had done more than enough for Jirokichi and his troublesome girlfriend. What was he doing anyway, helping a common burglar? Jirokichi would turn up safe and sound, and Tora would give him back his gold.

End of story.

He left by the covered gateway that led out on to Rokujo Avenue, a broad street that passed between the Fifth and Sixth Wards. On the steps of the gateway sat an old beggar on a pile of rags. He held out an empty wooden bowl to Tora. The man was blind, his eyeballs bluish white below thin lids. Tora dropped a couple of coppers in the bowl.

'Thank you, thank you,' muttered the beggar, bowing from the waist in the general direction of the passer-by. 'May the Buddha bless you, sir.'

'You're welcome, uncle.' Looking at the beggar's emaciated figure, Tora asked, 'Have you eaten today?'

The old man thought this over, pushing his lips in and out in concentration. 'Not today,' he finally decided. 'But I'll eat now.' He grinned, revealing a few yellowed teeth, and shook the bowl, making the coins rattle around inside.

Tora felt a little ashamed of his small gift. 'Do you live nearby?'

The beggar nodded and pointed over his shoulder.

'You live in the Fifth Ward?' Tora thought that extremely unlikely. Wealthy people tended to keep beggars out of their neighborhoods.

'There's a hole in the wall of the gate. I sleep in there. Not bad in the summer, but I near froze to death last winter.'

Tora walked back under the roofed gateway and looked. Sure enough: there were a few loose boards in the wooden wall on one side. Perhaps a cart had backed into it and loosened them, and the beggar had helped matters along. Inside, he glimpsed more rags and an earthenware water pitcher. A thought occurred to him, and he returned to the beggar.

'By any chance, did you see . . . I mean, did you hear anyone passing last night? Anyone who might have been in trouble? Or some young hoodlums?'

To his surprise, the beggar nodded. 'Right. On both counts. Two boys going in. Recognized their voices from my hole. Talking about the Rat.'

'The Rat? You mean an animal, or someone called the Rat?'

'The Rat's no animal. He's a saint. He left me something when he passed by.'

Tora crouched beside the beggar, holding his breath against the stench that met his nose. 'That was last night? The Rat passed you last night, and then the boys came?'

The beggar nodded.

'Those boys, they're the ones I mean,' Tora said. 'Did they come back out? Were they alone?'

'Came back dragging someone. He was moaning. Don't think they caught the Rat, though. He can make himself invisible.'

Tora's heart beat faster. 'Thanks, old man,' he said, jumping up. 'I'll be back.'

He loped off looking for a food vendor. Near a bridge, he found a couple selling hot fish wrapped in cabbage leaves and rice cakes filled with vegetables. Spending nearly all his money, he bought one of each and ran back to the beggar.

'Here,' he said, placing the food in the beggar's hands. 'Eat. And then, if you can tell me where I can find those two boys, I'll come back tomorrow with a gold coin.'

The blind man took the food with trembling fingers. For a moment he just sat there, then he muttered a choked, 'May you live in paradise in the next life, young man. I don't know where they came from. They just came. I could smell them, and then I heard them talking.' He extended the food. 'Do you want it back?'

'No, of course not. Eat.' Tora crouched beside the beggar and watched him eat fish and cabbage leaf in large gulps, then take huge bites from the rice cake. 'Slow down,' he said, 'or you'll choke.'

The beggar promptly choked and turned nearly blue coughing. He gestured frantically behind him. Tora slapped his bony back, then recalled the pitcher and dashed to get it. It was half full of water. The beggar drank, caught a deep breath and wiped the tears from his face.

'I'm blessed,' he said. 'If you'd left me, I'd be dead now.'

Tora saw nothing blessed about the beggar's life, but did not say so. Instead he pursued the question of the hoodlums. 'You said they just came. Have they ever come before?'

'Maybe. I seem to remember the smell.'

Tora sighed. Putting his hand on the old man's shoulder, he said, 'Thanks, old man. Keep out of their way. They'd just as soon kill a man than walk around him.'

'You're right about that.'

Tora got up to walk away, then stopped and turned. 'You recognized them by their smell, you said?'

'Yes. People smell. You smell of baby spit. They smelled of malt.'

Tora grinned. The old man had a very good nose. Yuki had, in fact, spit up on his shoulder that morning. Malt, he thought. Malt is used by sake brewers. It was something. He thanked the old beggar again and went off whistling.

His good humor did not last. If the same hoodlums had Jirokichi, the poor Rat was most likely already dead. Still, he suddenly felt a great urgency and walked more quickly.

At the Western Market, he pounded on the door of Hoshina's wine shop. She opened it a crack, saw him, and threw the door wide.

'What is it? Have you found him?' she asked, the words spilling out in mingled hope and fear.

Tora stepped in and closed the door again. 'No. But I picked up something. A blind man in the Fifth Ward heard some young louts talking about Jirokichi. He says they smelled of malt. I wondered if you might know where I could look for them.'

'Oh, I hope those evil bastards haven't got him again. They nearly killed him last time.'

'Malt,' Tora reminded her.

She looked confused. 'You mean a place that sells malt? Or a brewery?'

'I don't know. It's got to be someplace where they either work or live.'

'Them, work?' She snorted. 'Never. They're thieves and robbers.' Seeing Tora's impatient face, she thought. 'About six blocks west of here are warehouses. Some belong to breweries. They're supposed to be watched, but a lot of scum hang out around there. Some of the warehouses are empty.

'Where?' Tora had his hand on the door.

She described the place where he had almost got a knife in his back.

He nodded. 'Wish me luck.'

He covered the distance at a steady trot, fearing already that he would find the bloodied corpse of Jirokichi in some corner among garbage and at the mercy of wild dogs. Then he would have to go back and tell Hoshina. He had not been very good at saving lives lately.

When he reached the alley – for the third time – he sniffed the air. Yes, there was the unmistakable, if faint, smell of malt. Glancing first one way, then the other, he decided that the most likely warehouse was near the middle of the block and on the right side. The Fragrant Peach was just down the road and around the corner. Tora decided to have a look at the warehouse first.

He walked down the deserted lane, which was little more than two weedy ruts where an occasional cart had passed.

The warehouses were long, low buildings, their flat roofs made of boards weighted down by large stones. The fourth building was the one with the malt smell. It looked abandoned, its chained gate leaning drunkenly, the access unmarked by wheels. The fence was unbroken, but the gate gave enough to allow a man to slip in and out.

Tora pushed it cautiously and peered inside. The warehouse lay still in the afternoon sun, its doors closed. It was hot in the barren yard, and flies buzzed nearby. Tora did not like the idea of flies. He shuddered and withdrew his head. The dust around his feet showed the footprints of people going in and out, some in shoes and some barefoot. Then he saw something else: a small

brown spot in the pale dirt. And there was another a few feet
away. He bent down, licked a finger and touched the spot. A
sniff verified his suspicion: someone had dripped blood here.

He studied the tracks more closely. Among the footprints he
found some straight lines – double lines, as if from someone's
feet being dragged through the dust. The lines came from the
street and passed into the warehouse yard. He had found the
place. Jirokichi had been brought here, probably alive but
bleeding.

Tora considered the situation. He was alone and did not know
how many of the bastards he would have to deal with. It was
unlikely that there would be only two of them; the place looked
like a hang-out for the whole gang. He did not dare check more
closely, because they might have put out a guard. And he could
not hang about outside on this deserted road either, in case one
or the other decided to leave or come back.

Torn between the urgency of saving Jirokichi and his promise
to Hanae to be careful, he chose duty to his family. He walked
quickly to the Fragrant Peach.

By now the hour for the midday rice was past, and the place
was dimly lit and empty of customers. The fire in the hearth had
been banked, and the heavy cauldron was gone. Only the girl
was there, sweeping the dirt floor.

'Well met, pretty flower,' Tora called out, hoping to overcome
her hostility with charm. 'Where do I find the local warden?'

She glowered at him. 'We're not open.'

'Oh, come, you can answer a simple question.'

'No time. Go away.'

Tora stood his ground. 'How about your boyfriend, then?'

She flushed and cast a glance towards the back door. 'I have
no boyfriend,' she snapped.

Tora grinned. So, the young scamp was hiding out back there,
probably just biding his time before jumping her again. Boys
his age never thought of anything but sex. 'I saw you two together.
You were very friendly to him in the alley outside.'

She stopped working and stared at him.

'Maybe this is something you do on the side for money and
to keep customers happy.'

With a shriek of fury, she raised the broom and rushed him.
Tora jumped up easily, sidestepped her with a laugh, and caught
her round the middle with one arm, while he twisted the broom

from her fingers with the other. She struggled and spat in his face. Tora dropped the broom and gave her a good shake. 'All right, my girl,' he said. 'Enough of this nonsense. Someone's in bad trouble and I need help. It's either the warden or Tojiro.'

She stopped fighting him. Holding on to her, Tora swung about and found himself face to face with the gray-haired deaf mute.

Her daddy.

Carrying the cauldron.

Tora saw the coiled-up violence in the man's eyes and knew it was about to explode like a volcano. The brute's right hand started swinging the cauldron.

Tora released the girl so suddenly that she almost fell. She staggered away from him, leaving nothing but air between Tora and the volcano. The man's right arm moved back. Tora scooted away a couple of steps. 'No,' he shouted at the top of his voice. 'Don't. I came for help.'

No use shouting at a deaf mute.

Daddy measured the distance and adjusted his aim. Tora took another step back and was up against a wall. Seeing the black cauldron coming at him, he pleaded with the girl, 'Tell him Jirokichi's in trouble.'

To his surprise – he had not expected it to work – her father stopped the swing of the ugly weapon and turned to his daughter. She gestured while he looked from her to Tora and frowned. Then he set the cauldron down to respond.

Tora took a shuddering breath.

She said, 'He wants to know what this is about.'

Tora explained, still doubtful that it would make a difference. She translated, and her father's face grew longer and he clenched his fists. Tora became nervous again, but the big man only gave him a sharp look, then nodded, and ran out the back door with surprising speed.

The daughter eyed Tora without much favor. 'How come you know Jirokichi?'

Tora explained about how they had met, then asked, 'Where did your father go?'

'To get his friends. Come on,' she said. 'They'll meet us there.' She started for the door.

He caught her arm. 'No, you'd better stay here. There'll be a nasty fight. It's not safe for a girl.'

She shook his hand off, glaring. 'Shut up.'

With a sigh, he tagged along behind her. It would make things more difficult, having to look out for a slip of a girl. Still, he liked her spirit. But when he saw that she knew the way to the warehouse, he became uneasy again. He was confused by the strange relationships between Jirokichi, the girl, her deaf mute father, Tojiro, and the arson gang.

When they reached the leaning gate, there was no sign of reinforcements. She turned to him. 'We wait,' she said.

Tora eyed her suspiciously. It was beginning to feel like a trap. 'Why is your dad willing to help Jirokichi?' he asked.

'Jirokichi's our friend.' After a short pause, she asked, 'Why do you keep coming and making trouble for me?'

'Kids have been setting fires. I think those young bastards that have Jirokichi are the ones. And your boyfriend's one of them.'

Her eyes had widened with surprise, but now she flared up. 'That's a fucking lie!'

'Nice language for a young lady.'

She raised her chin. 'You sound just like Tojiro. So what? I'm no lady, and Tojiro loves me anyway. But he'd never hang out with them.'

'Then why do I keep finding him with them every time there's a fire?'

'I don't believe you. And what makes you think they're the ones setting the fires?'

'I've seen them.'

It was not entirely true. It had been too dark to recognize anyone both times they had run past him. The only faces he had seen belonged to the five that had manhandled Jirokichi. That reminded him of the poor Rat. He peered through the gate. Nothing had changed. Fear seized him again that they were too late, that the pitiful corpse of Jirokichi would greet them inside the warehouse. 'We can't stand around chatting,' he snapped. 'Where's your father with the others?'

'He's bringing Shinichi and Seiji.'

'The two old guys I saw with him last time? There could be ten or more young men in that warehouse.'

'Don't you worry about my dad and Shinichi and Seiji,' she said. A moment later, she glanced down the lane. 'Here they come.'

The three deaf mutes came loping towards them, armed with

cudgels and lengths of bamboo. They offered spares to Tora and the girl. Tora accepted a bamboo pole, weighed it in his hand, and executed a few stick-fighting swipes. They watched, impressed. Then Daddy kicked open the gate, and they stormed in.

THE MAJOR-DOMO

As soon as Tora left his study, Akitada got up to pace. A new energy had seized him. He wanted to run off and do any number of things immediately. Foremost in his mind was Kobe's visit. Tamako's suggestion that Kobe's behavior could only be explained by some event Akitada knew nothing about made him want an instant explanation, but he could not confront Kobe, not after what had passed between them. He wasted time wondering who might know, and eventually accepted that he must wait for the answer.

Well, he still had two cases to solve. Tora was making a start on Abbot Shokan's lost acolyte, though perhaps that would not bring any results. What then? He would have to return to Seikan-ji and talk to the other acolytes and the monks who knew him. It struck him that he had neglected to probe for details about the mother's background – an embarrassing oversight, even if it was likely that Shokan had intentionally suppressed the information. There had been something almost coy in the way the imperial monk had parted with the smallest possible bits of information. Yes, perhaps he would return to the monastery in the woods tomorrow.

That left the Kiyowara case for today. He must go back and interview the servants. Someone must have seen something. Strange that Lady Aoi had insisted he suspected the wrong person when he had no suspects.

Or rather, they were all suspects: the heir, Katsumi, who was now Lord Kiyowara; his mother; Ono, if he was the mother's lover; and perhaps even that stiffly proper major-domo. In fact, the late Kiyowara could have been killed by anyone on the property that afternoon. It meant he would need to spend considerable time with the servants to find out who else might have had a motive or access.

He stopped his pacing when he reached this conclusion and clapped his hands for Seimei. The old man appeared promptly. When he saw his master's face, he smiled. 'You have found an answer, sir. Truly, there's blessedness even in adversity.'

'I'm afraid I'm sadly short of answers, Seimei. No, I only wanted to tell you that I'm off to revisit the Kiyowara mansion. I may be late. Please inform my wife.'

'Very good, sir. May misfortune turn into success.' Then he chuckled. 'The common people in the provinces believe that if a man has eyes and a nose, he may go to the capital. You have both and are already here.'

That made Akitada laugh, and he left in good spirits.

His hopes were dashed immediately when he reached the Kiyowara mansion and encountered a policeman at the gate. The policeman barred his way and demanded his name. When Akitada gave it, the man drew himself up and put his hand on his short sword.

'You are forbidden to visit, sir, by order of His Majesty.'

Akitada was stunned for a moment. Then he realized that the emperor had had nothing to do with this. Kobe had simply applied the standard formula to an order, and the policeman had recited it. Anger rose again and nearly choked him. He turned away.

What could he do without access to possible witnesses of the crime? And why force him away from the case? Was this again politics? It made him think that one of the Kiyowaras or the Minister of Central Affairs was guilty, and that the chancellor or one of his powerful sons was protecting a murderer.

If that was the case, it was sufficient warning for him to stay away. He would have to return the gold Lady Kiyowara had paid him. The thought that he was made part to a cover-up sickened him.

But perhaps someone was simply making sure he would be ruined. Akitada almost hoped that was all it was. As for the Kiyowara murder, there was still one thing he could try. He set out at a brisk pace for the home of Major-domo Fuhito.

The sun was setting over the western hills in a spectacular conflagration of sky and clouds, and the heat was marginally less breath-taking. Fuhito's house was one among several old villas in an equally old neighborhood. Akitada was familiar with this part of the city. Not only did his wife still own a piece of property here – a herb-, vegetable-, and flower-garden on the land where her late father's home once stood – but also some of the people in this neighborhood had played significant roles in his past cases.

As he walked beneath the trees shading the street with green branches that overhung the walls and fences, Akitada thought of Hiroko – not the Hiroko who was Lady Kiyowara, but the woman he had loved in vain. The familiar longing still twisted his heart. He had never known a more beautiful creature, and even now the memory still made him dizzy with desire. He had been tempted, had offered her marriage, but nothing had come of it. Worse, her memory was forever tied to another loss that was more painful than hers.

Akitada reined in his memories, saddened and feeling mildly guilty of disloyalty towards Tamako.

Fuhito could still be at work – Akitada had no idea what hours a major-domo kept – but his servants must be home. Akitada would wait. When he reached the house, he saw that here, too, many old trees grew behind the cypress fence, promising green coolness after the sweltering day. He used a bamboo clapper to strike a small bell at the gate.

As he waited, he looked around. It was a quiet, peaceful street that resembled Akitada's own and probably dated to the same time two centuries ago, though these lots were smaller, having been designed for lower-ranking officials and clerks. It was pleasant here, far from the clamor and clangor of the merchant quarters. Birds sang, and the scent of flowers drifted over the tall fence.

Akitada rang the bell again, more impatiently. Where were the servants?

This time, he heard a woman's voice call out, 'A moment. I'm coming.' Then the gate creaked open and a rattle sounded. He looked down at a short old woman who was leaning on a cane and peering back at him. 'Oh, dear,' she said, 'I don't know you. Are you lost?'

To judge from her clothing, she was an upper servant, perhaps Fuhito's housekeeper. Akitada smiled at her. 'I hope not. My name is Sugawara Akitada, and I came to speak to Fuhito.'

'He never comes home until dark,' she said. For her age – the hair she wore twisted into a bun at her neck was snow-white – she held herself still proudly erect, in spite of the frailty and hollowness of great age.

'Perhaps I might wait for him?' he suggested.

She hesitated, and he wondered if she was afraid to admit him because she was alone in the house. He prepared to reassure her of his good character when she smiled quite sweetly, made him a bow, and said, 'But of course, My Lord.' She stepped aside, and he walked into a garden.

Perhaps this place had once had a courtyard and outbuildings to stable a horse or two, and to keep a cart or small carriage, but these were long since gone. Instead a narrow path of large, flat stones wound through shrubs and among trees towards a partially hidden home. The scent of flowers and the song of birds seemed intense.

'Allow me to show you the way,' she said, since the path was narrow and custom did not allow a servant or a female to walk ahead of a man.

Akitada nodded and followed. 'How beautiful!' he said, looking around. 'Who made this garden?'

'My son did most of it, though the trees were here long before our time.'

'Ah, your son is a very talented gardener.'

She turned and smiled that charming smile again. 'Yes, Fuhito loves this garden. It gives him peace.'

Taken aback, Akitada asked, 'You are Fuhito's mother? I beg your pardon.' He searched his mind for a family name and failed.

She was clearly amused. 'You are wondering why I answered the gate? We live very simply here. Today my maid went to market to buy something for our evening rice. She doesn't trust me to do the shopping.' She chuckled. 'Or the cooking. Kosue is becoming very bossy in her old age.'

Akitada was charmed by the old lady, for 'lady' she surely was. Did she know why he was here? Apparently not. He wondered once again about Fuhito's background as he followed her down the winding path through cool and moist greenery and emerged into an open area around a small house. Apparently, there was a main house and a second, smaller pavilion. Both were old, but in very good repair, and Akitada suspected that they had been part of a larger compound.

All around him, lush shrubs and flowering plants spread, climbed, and cascaded from tall trees. Tamako would know their names, but he only recognized azaleas – still in bloom so late in the season – peonies, roses, and a late-flowering wisteria.

'I wish my wife could see this,' he said, looking all around.
'Then you must bring her next time.'

How simple and gracious that invitation was. She did not
know him, nor why he had come, yet she had done him the cour-
tesy of treating him as a welcome visitor. He was ashamed for
taking her for a servant, and worse, for suspecting her son of
murdering his master. Thanking her, he explained about the immin-
ent birth at his house.

She clapped her hands in delight. 'What happy news. You
must be overjoyed.'

Was he overjoyed? There was still a large element of fear
involved in the birth of his second child. But Tamako had looked
and felt much stronger lately, so he allowed himself some joy
and said, 'Yes, thank you. And you? Do you have other children? Or grandchildren?'

She shook her head. 'Alas, no. Fuhito is my only surviving
child, though no mother could have been more blessed in a son.
And he, poor man, still mourns his only child. Now, there are
only the two of us here.' She brightened. 'But don't listen to an
old woman's carping. If you have quite decided on waiting for
him, would you prefer to do so alone or in my company?'

He said quickly, 'Oh, in your company, of course. Thank you
for offering. And perhaps you would not mind showing me a
little of this wonderful garden?' He stopped himself, seeing her
cane and her great age. 'I beg your pardon. It is too much to
ask.'

But she looked so pleased and was so eager that he accepted.
She led the way, explaining graciously and with considerable
pride. 'My son has studied the art deeply,' she said at one point.
'He has a library of books, both in our language and in Chinese.
It has helped him deal with his grief.'

Akitada asked, a little diffidently because it was a personal
question, 'His grief? Forgive me, but he seemed calm and busi-
nesslike when we met. I confess I have had little chance to get
to know him well.'

She was silent for a long time. Finally, she said, 'My son was
widowed early, but this sadness concerns the loss of his daughter,
my granddaughter. Motoko was beautiful and young and full of
happiness. He loved his child entirely. Some would say too much.
She was his whole life. This garden makes a poor substitute.'

Akitada's thoughts flew back to the horrible death of his

beloved son Yori. He, too, had loved his child entirely. He still loved him. Taking a deep breath, he said softly, 'I know. They call it the darkness of the soul.'

She turned and searched his face. 'You also?'

He nodded. 'My five-year-old son. Last year, from smallpox.'

She reached out impulsively to touch his arm. 'Oh, I am so very sorry. And now you fear for this child?' Flushing, she withdrew her hand. 'Forgive me. That was quite improper.'

He managed a smile. 'Not at all. You are very kind. A kindness is never improper. And yes, I am afraid – for the child *and* its mother.'

She nodded. 'I shall remember them to Amida when I worship.' She sighed. 'Don't you think it is terrible when you have nothing left to fear?'

He thought about that for a moment because there was a good deal of pain in his fears, but he nodded. Old people became lonely if their children died before them. He was sorry for her even as his own heart lifted a little. Soon there would be another child in his home, another son to raise and to carry on his name, and this time the chances of his surviving into adulthood would surely be better. Yori had been a healthy child until the disease had struck him down. They would be more careful this time.

They finished their stroll through the garden.

Fuhito had created banks of flowering azaleas, a miniature mountain with a small waterfall that became a watery rill, winding about in more intricate curves even than the paths they walked. They passed over three different small bridges and walked beside a pond filled with water lilies. Tiny frogs swam there, and carp jumped for clouds of small gnats.

It was dusk when they reached the house again. The first fireflies sparked among the darkening boughs. Into that peaceful world broke the sudden rattle of bamboo from the gate.

'That will be my son now,' she said, and even in the fading twilight, Akitada saw her face light up. Perhaps she was not really so bereft that she had nothing to fear. She loved her son, and Akitada might take him from her.

Steps approached, and there was Fuhito, stopping in surprise – or terror, for he turned quite pale when he recognized Akitada.

His mother said quickly, 'See who has come. Lord Sugawara has honored our house with a visit and taken a great interest in your garden.'

Akitada smiled and nodded. 'Indeed, I have had great pleasure seeing this beautiful place. Surely this is what the Western Paradise must look like. You are to be congratulated.'

Fuhito bowed. 'Thank you, My Lord. The garden is a poor thing, a mere dabbling for the sake of passing time.'

Akitada explained his presence, and Fuhito nodded. 'Yes, Her Ladyship was very upset about the policeman at the gate. She would be even angrier if she knew that you have been forbidden access.' He turned to his mother. 'This concerns the death of His Lordship. We will talk in my room.'

Her smile faded, and she looked quickly from her son to Akitada. 'Of course,' she said softly. With a bow to Akitada, she walked quickly away.

Fuhito took Akitada into the main house. It was not only of modest size, but also sparsely furnished and nearly dark. In a corner room, he lit an oil lamp. Akitada saw that many unmatched old shelves and stands held books. Whatever former wealth the books represented was disproved by the bare wood floor and the flimsy, scratched desk and cheap writing set. There were not even cushions to sit on.

Akitada nodded towards the books and said, 'What a very fine library you have.' He hoped that Fuhito would unbend just a little. He was disappointed.

Fuhito's expression did not change. 'A few books are about gardening; the rest are what is left of my grandfather's and father's libraries. I found I could not sell them, or only for a negligible sum.'

Akitada asked, 'What happened?' then saw the other man's face and wished he had not asked. 'Forgive me. It's none of my business.'

Fuhito turned away. 'It doesn't matter. My father was disgraced. It was not a criminal matter, but he lost his rank and position. He committed suicide. I had to leave the university and find employment.'

'I am very sorry. The shadow of karma follows us every-where.' Akitada was himself all too well aware of the precarious nature of an official post, but at least his misfortune had not yet reached the level of destroying his family. Fuhito's story made him more determined than ever to fight for his future.

Fuhito hunched his shoulders and said, 'I wouldn't have minded so much as long as . . . if my daughter had lived.'

Akitada did not know what to say to that. He felt very sorry for the other man, but there was still the matter of murder. He sighed and asked, 'Could you answer a few more questions about your master?' Determined to stay until he had learned what he needed to know, he sat down on the bare floor.

Fuhito made a helpless gesture with his hands and sat down across from him. 'I apologize for the lack of comforts,' he said miserably.

'I'm quite comfortable. I take it from what you said earlier that Lady Kiyowara expects me to continue with the case in spite of the police?'

'Yes, I think so. She will be very angry with the superintendent.'

The way of heaven was just. Let Kobe deal with Lady Kiyowara's fury. The lady might well make him cease his opposition. She was quite formidable, and then there was her relationship to the regent's wife. Encouraged, Akitada began his quest anew. 'Have you found out anything else useful from the servants?'

'No. Nothing.'

'No disgruntled members of the household? No dismissed and angry servants?'

Fuhito looked surprised by the notion. 'Hardly. Servants do not lift their hands against their masters.'

'Oh, I don't know about that. Even the mildest and most obedient man can be pressed too hard and lose his self control.'

The major-domo shifted uncomfortably, but said nothing.

'Let's go back to the scene you found when you entered your master's room that afternoon. It's strange that there shouldn't have been a weapon that might have dealt the fatal wound. While it is barely possible that the murderer entered and left the room without being noticed, surely that becomes highly unlikely if he was carrying a weapon.'

'I'm afraid I cannot help you. It is, as you say, inconceivable.'

'If he or she entered from the garden—' Akitada paused to let the image of that sun-drenched landscape flash across his memory. The poet had been there, walking along the stream. And yes, it would have been easy enough to pick up one of the large stones that followed that waterway, slip into Kiyowara's room and kill him, then slip back out to replace it. Oh, if only he could go back there. There might still be traces of blood, or some hair, perhaps, on that fatal stone.

He came back to Fuhito, who was watching him nervously. 'The poet Ono – he's a particular friend to Lady Kiyowara. Are they lovers?'

The bluntness of that took Fuhito's breath away. He colored to his ears. 'I could not say, sir.' It was said flatly, before he had time to become angry. Then he glared at Akitada. 'Surely that is a very improper suggestion under the circumstances. Both you and I are in Her Ladyship's employ.'

'When it's a matter of murder, no question is improper. Are you yourself involved with her?'

Fuhito's jaw dropped. He was speechless.

'You must realize that it looks very much as if this murder is a personal affair. From the beginning, the most obvious suspects have been the son and his mother. I took on the case, assuming they are innocent. That means I must consider others who might have had motives and opportunity to kill the man.'

Fuhito brushed a hand over his face. 'I am a mere servant,' he said, 'and my position is such that I would not risk my livelihood by approaching my mistress with improper suggestions. She would not, in any case, tolerate it. As for her private life, I know very little about it. Her husband always showed her the greatest regard, but their relationship had become formal over the years. His Lordship loved his son and honored the mother. As for His young Lordship, he would not raise his hand against his own father. He is hot-headed but also gentle.'

'Hmm.' Akitada tried another approach. 'I'm told your late master engaged in affairs outside his marriages. In fact, he had a bad reputation with women. Lady Kiyowara might have felt threatened or decided to pay him back in the same coin. In the latter case, a lover would have a motive. In the former, a husband or other relative.'

Fuhito flushed again and shook his head. 'I cannot believe it of Her Ladyship.'

Akitada snapped, 'But you do not deny your master's habits regarding females? I expect you know all about it. Who better than you?'

Fuhito gasped. 'I?' His hands clenched convulsively. He asked in a shaky voice, 'Has my mother told you?' Then the words tumbled out. 'It's not true. There was no truth to it. I never believed—' He broke off and buried his face in his hands.

Akitada was stunned. What had he said? He had only assumed that a major-domo would be aware of his master's affairs. Whatever nerve he had touched, this must be important. It must be the secret of Fuhito's relationship with Kiyowara. Though he pitied the man and his mother, he could not let it pass.

'I think you'd better tell me about it yourself,' he said gently.

He had to wait until Fuhito calmed down and raised a distraught face. 'I lost my only daughter a number of years ago. Motoko was only sixteen. A mere child when she . . . she was raped. She could not live with that misery.' He gave a bitter laugh. 'They say suffering is like the forging of rough iron into a sharp sword. It has not been that way in our family.'

Akitada drew in a breath and glanced out through the open veranda doors at the elaborate landscape, then looked at the man's grief-torn face and wondered if losing a grown daughter to suicide was more or less devastating than having carelessly exposed a small son to smallpox. He said heavily, 'I am very sorry for your pain. Your mother mentioned your loss, but gave no details. I, too, lost a child. They say there is no greater grief. Can you tell me what happened?'

Fuhito's hands made a helpless gesture before he tucked them into his sleeves. His voice shook a little. 'Motoko was both beautiful and good. That summer she had just started to serve Her Ladyship and seemed very happy. They said later that the gods must have become jealous.'

This did not answer the question, or only partially. Akitada searched for a way to probe for what he suspected. In the end he was blunt. 'Given Lord Kiyowara's reputation with women, might he have been responsible?'

Fuhito flushed a deep crimson. He did not answer right away. Then he said, 'If I had thought that he had behaved improperly towards my child, I would certainly have spoken to him. The house was always full of guests in those days. Taking advantage of someone of her birth would have meant nothing to a high-ranking noble.'

Akitada considered this. It was possible. And it would explain why Fuhito had stayed in the Kiyowaras' service. Another dead end. He bowed his head. 'Thank you, and forgive me for bringing back painful memories.'

Fuhito nodded. They rose and walked outside. It was fully dark now, but someone, perhaps Fuhito's mother, had left a lighted lantern at the beginning of the path. Fuhito picked it up and lit the way to the gate. There they bowed to each other again, and Akitada walked out into the dark street. The gate rattled shut behind him, and the warm darkness received him like a stifling blanket of sadness.

And yet, was not the man who had nothing left to fear more likely to commit murder than anyone else?

THE TIGER AND THE RAT

They let Tora go first. He rushed across the short distance to the warehouse door, raised his foot, and kicked the door open. It splintered and flew back. He did not waste time trying to make out objects in the dim interior, but burst inside with an almighty yell.

The darkness was fetid with the stench of hops, sour wine, excrement, and blood. Shouts and curses erupted all around him. He lashed out at moving shadows, swinging the pole from side to side in powerful sweeps, making contact once or twice. The building filled with thuds, yells, and screams. People were running everywhere. Something hit him a glancing blow across one shoulder. He jumped aside, moving back from the melee because he was afraid of hitting his companions.

As his eyes grew accustomed to the half-light, he saw that the large space was partially filled with stacked bundles, casks, boxes, and handcarts. About eight youths, some armed with knives or sticks, milled in the center of the large room. A ninth was crawling out the door. All seemed less interested in fighting than in fleeing the building.

Cowards, Tora thought. Then he saw Jirokichi in the far corner, hanging from one of the rafters, lifeless and covered in blood.

Leaving the battle to the deaf mutes and the girl, he dropped his pole and ran to Jirokichi. There was a dark puddle of blood and piss in the dirt between his feet. He stank, and flies buzzed up when Tora got close. The Rat's toes barely touched the ground. Too late, Tora thought. Poor Rat. It had been all for nothing, and he did not know how to tell Hoshina. He pulled the knife from his boot and cut the rope around Jirokichi's wrists. There was blood everywhere on the body, and his hands slipped as he tried to ease Jirokichi to the ground. He fell with a thud.

As Tora bent over him, he felt a sharp kick to his backside and stumbled forward, falling across the body. He rolled off quickly and twisted around. The skinny youth loomed above him, his teeth bared in an ugly grin and his eyes bright with an almost mad joy.

'So,' he hissed, 'it's you again. I missed last time because it was dark. This time, you're out of luck, you bastard.' He raised a bloody knife and laughed.

Tora had dropped his own knife in the fall. The skinny youth had his foot on it.

In close encounters, knives can deliver nasty wounds even when you manage to avoid a fatal blow. Tora scooted away and scrambled up. The youth laughed again. He snatched up Tora's knife.

One for each hand.

Tora risked another glance around for his pole or anything else he might use to defend himself. There was nothing close enough, and nobody was paying attention to them. It was just him and the skinny bastard.

An uneven battle.

But Tora was still fired up with rage at finding Jirokichi dead and, worse, bearing marks of torture. He did not want this animal to live. Pulling off a boot, he flung it at the youth, who raised his right arm to knock it aside. Tora used the moment of distraction to jump, bending low and aiming his head at the other man's middle. He meant to knock him back and fling himself down on top to disarm and kill him.

It didn't work.

The other, being younger and lighter on his feet, danced away and then came at him, both blades slashing.

Tora recovered from the charge and backed away, hopping this way and that to avoid the knives. The youth followed, teeth bared, eyes shining in the dim light that came from the splintered doorway. Tora tried to reach his pole, but almost fell over Jirokichi's body again, and realized that he was being driven into the corner of the building.

The youth with the flashing knives knew it too and, sure of

his prey, got impatient and careless. He threw the knife in his right hand. This surprised Tora, who reacted too slowly. While the knife missed his chest, it went deep into his upper left arm. The pain was immediate and so sharp that he gasped. He felt the warm blood running down inside his sleeve. His arm and hand were limp and useless.

He thought briefly of pulling the knife from the wound and using it, but was afraid he might lose more blood and become completely helpless. There was no more time for maneuvers. He had to act quickly.

His opponent moved in for the kill, but had to shift the other knife from the left hand to the right, and Tora made a last desperate move. He closed his eyes, doubled up, and rushed forward like a maddened bull. This time, his head did connect with the body, there was a squawk and a satisfying hiss of air being expelled, then they were falling in a tangle of limbs, Tora on top.

If this trick had worked earlier, Tora would have had the use of his left arm to meet his enemy's right. But now his left arm had a knife in it and refused to obey. He had knocked the breath out of the youth, and his weight pinned him down, but the bastard still had a knife in his right hand.

Tora twisted to reach across and block the blow he knew was coming, but his left arm could not support his weight. He collapsed, expecting to feel the knife thrust deeply into his side or back. It would most likely be fatal. He was making an effort to roll away when suddenly a large, dirty foot slammed down and pinned the youth's hand and knife to the ground. There was a howl of pain.

Hands lifted Tora to his feet, where he stood swaying, feeling more blood pouring down his arm and hand. The ground felt unsteady. He realized vaguely that the foot belonged to Koichi, the girl's father, but Koichi's figure seemed to become hazy and melt before his eyes. Tora mumbled, 'Don't—' then felt suddenly very tired, so tired that he decided to sit down for a moment.

He woke to a strange fog. In it, he lay stretched out next to Jirokichi's corpse. He thought it odd that this should be so, but also diverting. He was curious to find out what would happen next. Then reason returned with a sharp pain in his arm. He sat up, groaning with the effort.

The girl came to kneel beside him, holding out a cup. He groaned again, but drank thirstily. It was wine, strong wine, and he almost lay back down again, but the wine settled into his stomach with a sharp and pleasant heat, and his head and sight cleared a little. He was still in the warehouse. The girl looked at him anxiously. He turned his head. The three deaf mutes sat just beyond Jirokichi's corpse, staring at him. Their clothes looked strange. One man lacked sleeves on his thick, muscular arms, and another wore only a short jacket over his loincloth.

Memory returned piecemeal: Jirokichi was dead. No, best not to look at him. The knife fight. He checked his left arm and saw that a thick bandage of checked fabric was wrapped around it. The knife was gone, and the bleeding seemed to have stopped. The fabric was familiar.

He cast a furtive glance at the girl's skirt. 'Thanks,' he said, with a nod to the bandage. A very shapely pair of knees and thighs were revealed by the drastic shortening of her dress. He grinned. 'I guess I owe you a new gown.'

She blushed a little and offered the cup again. Tora shook his head, then looked around. A few yards away, he saw another body. It looked like the bastard who had knifed him. He pointed. 'Who took care of him?'

'Dad.'

'Damnation! I needed to ask him about those fires. Where are the others?'

'They ran.' She frowned at him. 'Maybe Dad should've let Takeo kill you?'

'Sorry. You have a point.' Tora put the palms of his hands together and bowed his thanks to Koichi. 'Please tell your father that I owe him my life. I have a wife and a baby son. It will be good to see them again.'

Koichi's face remained passive, but he nodded.

Tora should have been thankful, but he felt mostly glum. Nothing good had come from their effort. They had been too late to save Jirokichi, and now he would have to go tell Hoshina, and then explain his knife wound to Hanae. He sighed and thought of getting to his feet. He was amazingly light-headed, and the arm throbbed unpleasantly. That was when he heard a strange sound from the corpse beside him. His hair bristled and he froze. Taking a deep breath, he decided to risk a quick look.

Jirokichi's eyes were slightly open and looked at him. Tora scooted away with a gasp. The sound came again, something between a groan and a grunt, and then the corpse moved its lips.

Jirokichi seemed less bloody than he remembered from his first glimpse of him hanging from one of the rafters. Someone had cleaned him up. He shot a glance at the deaf mutes and the girl and saw that the girl smiled. What was there to smile about?

Half afraid, he looked at Jirokichi again. The Rat had closed his eyes, and his head had rolled a little more towards him. And – yes, there was a sort of rasping breath coming from his bruised mouth. Disbelieving his eyes and ears, Tora turned to the others. 'He's alive?'

They nodded. Koichi gestured to his daughter.

'He's in pretty bad shape,' she said, 'but he's alive. They hurt his jaw and his belly. And they threw knives at his legs.'

Tora inspected the Rat more closely. Parts of the three men's clothing were wrapped around both of Jirokichi's blood-soaked thighs, and his jaw was swollen on one side. The eye socket on that side was also red and starting to swell, closing that eye. The ear closest to Tora was filled with drying blood, and more blood caked his gray-streaked hair.

Tora cursed softly. He looked at Koichi and said, 'The lousy bastards tortured him. Why'd you let them get away?'

Koichi spread his hands and shook his head.

The girl said, 'They've been bad, but they're our people. We came to help Jirokichi.'

'At least you got that bastard Takeo. He was the worst.'

She exchanged a glance with her father and gestured. He shook his head. Tora staggered to his feet and limped over, picking up his boot on the way. The skinny youth had been the leader of the gang. He had had his head split open by Koichi's pole or cudgel and was unconscious, but he was breathing.

They had not bothered to tie him up.

Puzzled, he returned to the group. 'You should've killed him for what he did to Jirokichi, but at least I can turn him over to the police. They'll have their own methods for making the scum talk.'

The girl looked at the others and translated. Koichi and his companions regarded Tora the way a man might look at a poisonous snake in his house. Tora realized that there had been a distinct cooling of their relationship for a while now.

He was in a difficult position. Having chosen the path of justice, he now owed his life to a member of a gang. He bit his lip, then said, 'Look, I realize you don't want the police involved in this, but there's the matter of the fires, and of Jirokichi. I promise to do my best to keep you out of it.'

Koichi shook his head and growled deep in his throat.

The girl said, 'No police. We did this for Jirokichi, not for you.'

'That bastard over there knows all about the fires. At least let me have a go at him.'

Koichi growled again. Tora saw that the other two looked ready to attack him. The girl said sharply, 'You'd better leave now.'

So much for his having saved Jirokichi and gotten a knife in his arm for his trouble.

Tora said, 'Jirokichi needs a doctor. He'll have to be carried home. I'll help, but I've only got one good arm.'

She said, 'That's our business. We were just waiting for you to come round and leave. There's nothing else for you to do here.'

'Look,' Tora blustered, 'I'm the one who found him. He'd be dead by now if I hadn't come. The bastards you're protecting would have killed him. If he's your friend, you owe me something, and I'd at least like some information.'

She shook her head. 'No. We don't work with the police, and we don't rat out our own.'

'I'm not the police.' But Tora saw their faces and knew that it was useless. How had they found out about him? His eyes went to Jirokichi. The Rat was watching him. 'You told them I was with the police,' he said accusingly. 'Damn you, Rat. I don't want your filthy gold, but I could've used some support.'

Koichi got to his feet with an angry grunt. The other two followed. Koichi pointed towards the door.

'You'd better go,' said the girl. 'And you'd better not come back.'

Words failed Tora. He took a step towards them and found he was still holding his boot. With a curse, he bent to put it back on. The vicious pain in his left arm made him sick to his stomach. He was in no shape to argue. Shaking his head, he stumbled out of the warehouse and into the sweet-smelling night air.

FAMILY MATTERS

Akitada had taken to sleeping in Tamako's room after spending that pleasant night with her. He did so for the companionship, not for sexual gratification. Perhaps he had also hoped to be there when the child came.

The first warning came sometime in the middle of the night. He woke because Tamako moaned beside him and then clutched his arm. Her fingers dug almost painfully into his skin.

'What? What is it?' he asked, coming awake slowly, then finding himself immediately in a panic. He had pent up his fears over the past days, pushing them aside, telling himself that Tamako looked and felt much better, and that all was quite well. Childbirth was a natural process. Women had children all the time and came through it very well. Tamako had survived the first birth in spite of some difficulties.

Yes, there had been difficulties, even beyond the immense snows that had isolated them. But then there had been Doctor Oyoshi, that kind and gentle man who had helped her through it and, more importantly, helped him as well. He had been a gibbering idiot by the time Yori was born.

And now it was about to happen again.

Tamako's grip on his arm gradually relaxed. 'The child,' she said, after the pain had passed away. 'It's coming this time. I've been feeling the pains for a while now. I'm sorry, Akitada, but could you wake Hanae and the others?'

The others were her maid Oyuki and Seimei.

Akitada scrambled out of the bedding. 'Yes, of course. Right away. Can I do anything? Are you thirsty? Do you want screens put up around you? What about lights?'

'No, Akitada. The women will see to it. You'd better make yourself a bed in your study. This will take a while.'

'Don't be ridiculous. I'll be right here.'

'Thank you, but there's no point to it. I'll be well looked after.' She bit her lips and closed her eyes, clutching at the bedding as another pain started. 'Now please go!' she gasped.

Akitada grabbed his robe and ran.

The maid was the first he shook awake. She slept in the eave chamber of Tamako's pavilion and knew immediately what was happening. Then he hurried barefoot across the compound to Tora's quarters and pounded on the door. Tora appeared, sleepy-eyed and clutching his bandaged arm.

'Sorry, Tora. Where's Hanae? The child is coming.'

Tora's eyes widened and he turned, but Hanae had heard and was already there, tying the sash on her gown and then twisting her hair back.

'Perhaps Tora had better go for the doctor,' she said. 'Sometimes it's quicker the second time around.'

Akitada saw the way Tora cradled his arm and shook his head. 'No. Seimei said he was to rest. That was a very nasty cut. I'll go myself. Just as soon as I wake Seimei and put on my boots.' Tora protested, but Akitada overruled him. 'I'll be glad to have something to do,' he said. 'You rest that arm and look after your son.'

Seimei was awake and gathering his herbal remedies. He greeted Akitada with a smile. 'A happy day, sir. And perhaps another son.'

'Perhaps,' said Akitada, too distracted to contemplate it. 'Hanae said it would be quicker than last time. That's good, isn't it?'

Seimei chuckled. 'I am sure Her Ladyship will think so. You are getting a doctor?'

Akitada nodded. 'I'm going myself. And I'd better get a monk, I suppose, if it's really urgent.'

'It is always best to take an umbrella before the rain starts. Don't forget that you will need some money, sir.'

Akitada hurried back to Tamako's room to make sure she was being looked after. He arrived just in time to hear her moaning again. He shuddered and was tempted to leave, but made himself creep closer. The women had set up screens around Tamako and covered them with white cloth. He peered over and saw that the bedding had been changed to white hemp, and that Tamako was draped in a tent-like white hemp gown. Her eyes were closed, and her face was flushed and covered with moisture. Oyuki knelt beside her, mopping sweat from her face, and Hanae was on the other side, holding her hand and murmuring encouragement. Tamako writhed and tossed her head from side to side. Her long hair was spread all over the bedding and the floor. Akitada fought rising nausea as he watched her agony, and he swallowed convulsively. He felt utterly helpless and unwanted.

When the pain passed, she relaxed. Breathing heavily, she
opened her eyes and looked up at Akitada blearily.

'Go away,' she said.

She sounded almost angry, and a shocked Akitada retreated
to the door. 'Is . . . is everything going well?' he asked.

Hanae called out, 'Yes, sir. But it will be best if you see to
the arrangements. It may not take long now.'

Akitada obeyed gladly. In his room he found money and his
boots. He put them on with shaking hands. Then he left, running
all the way to the doctor's small house half a mile away. He was
out of breath as he rang the bell. Nothing happened, and he
pounded on the door until the doctor's servant appeared.

'Quick,' Akitada said. 'Your master's needed.'

The servant seemed unsurprised. He asked the honored name
of the caller and the nature of the emergency, then left to inform
the doctor. Akitada paced anxiously until the physician appeared,
followed by his servant carrying his satchel. He dispatched them
to his home and breathed a sigh of relief.

At a more moderate pace, Akitada next proceeded to the small
temple where they had made arrangements for a monk to chant
sutras during the birth and later to say an appropriate prayer to
the Buddhas of the three worlds for the child. He had little faith
in this having any practical effect, but now that the time had
come, he decided to engage three monks instead of the one who
had been requested. He told himself that Tamako would be able
to hear the chants of three monks better and feel reassured. Then
he paid an additional three pieces of gold to have sutras recited
in the temple.

Having made such an efficient start, he decided to invite also
the neighborhood Shinto priest to say prayers and scatter rice
for good luck. The priest was a pleasant older man who was
unsurprised by the sudden urgency of the request. While Akitada
waited impatiently, he donned a striking black and red robe and
gilded head dress and took up a spear and a shield. Then he
called an assistant to carry a hamper with other paraphernalia.
They walked back together and arrived to the solemn chanting
and bell ringing of the three monks, who had positioned themselves on Tamako's veranda.

The Shinto priest inspected the premises, then performed
a ritual perambulation around Tamako's pavilion, reciting
spells, scattering rice grains, and holding up an amulet against

potentially lurking evil spirits at the four corners. Afterwards he took up his station in the courtyard, where he laid out a thick straw rope in a circle. In this circle, he danced and chanted while beating on the shield with his spear. His assistant accompanied him on a drum and occasionally twanged the string on a catalpa bow.

As Akitada observed these performances, dawn was breaking over the rooftops, and somewhere a cock crowed: a new day and a new life were beginning. He smiled to himself, content at having carried out his duties with such success, and went to see how his wife was progressing.

But when he crossed the threshold into Tamako's room, he was greeted by an atmosphere of heat, sweat, blood, and anxious activity. When Tamako screamed, Akitada grasped the door frame for support and stared at the rectangle of white-enshrouded screens, behind which heads bobbed up and down and tense voices muttered. Some crisis was at hand. It sounded as if things had gone very wrong. Perhaps Tamako was on the point of death.

Afraid to move closer, he called out, 'What is happening? How is my wife?'

The doctor bustled out from behind the screens, making shooing motions as if Akitada were a small child or pet dog who had wandered where he was not allowed. 'You must have patience, sir,' he cried. 'There's nothing you can do. Now go away, please.'

Akitada would have stood his ground for answers, but at this point loud shouting broke out in the garden. He turned and ran out. Some fifteen or twenty strange men were jumping about waving assorted weapons and screaming unintelligible words at the tops of their voices.

He gasped, 'What the devil—?'

Tora joined him, grinning. 'They're good, aren't they?' he shouted over the noise.

He looked so proud that Akitada was speechless. Tora roared to the men, 'Louder, brothers. Put your hearts in it. Don't let them get anywhere near.'

It dawned on Akitada that Tora had taken it upon himself to provide and drill a troop of helpers to scare away demons lying in wait to possess mother and child in their weakest moments.

The chanting of the monks on the other side of the building combined with the shouts of the demon-repelling warriors and the noise made by the Shinto priest and his helper in the courtyard. All of it nearly drowned out another scream from inside.

Nearly, but not quite.

The whole scene filled Akitada with sudden terror and revulsion. Tamako was dying – he was sure of it – dying in agony, and this horrible noise was her death chant. There had been chanting when Yori lay dying. The whole horror was repeating itself.

He turned away and staggered to his study, where he sat down, shivering with fear.

Seimei found him a little later. 'Come, sir,' he called from the doorway. 'The doctor said to call you.'

Akitada stared at Seimei's smiling face. 'Call me?' he asked dully.

'You're a father again,' crowed Seimei and shuffled away happily.

A father again!

And Tamako was alive? She must be. Seimei had been smiling. Akitada got to his feet and started for the door. Then he remembered. A father always welcomed his son with a sword. He took the Sugawara sword from its stand and, carrying it reverently in both hands before him, walked to Tamako's pavilion.

Outside, the shouting and chanting continued, but it made a happy sound now. Akitada was filled with joy and gratitude. The door to Tamako's room opened just as he got there – conveniently, since his hands were full and laying down the sword might have been a bad omen. He walked in, a broad smile on his face for the moment when he would see his son.

He was met by several gasps. The screens around Tamako's bedding had been moved aside so that he could see her lying there, looking pale and exhausted.

Someone snatched the sword from his hands. Akitada turned his head and saw that Seimei seemed to be hiding it behind his frail body. The old man looked apologetic and bowed immediately. 'Your pardon, sir. I should have mentioned . . . Please forgive an old man. It was the joy that overwhelmed me. It's a little girl, sir.'

A little girl?

Akitada was surprised and turned back to Tamako for

clarification. To his dismay, she had started crying. Now she rolled on her side with a wail.

'What . . .?' Akitada looked around at shocked faces, then strode to her side, knelt, and took her hand. 'Tamako, what is it? Are you in pain?' She snatched her hand away, but did not respond, and the sobbing increased. He looked for the doctor. 'Come here. Something's wrong. Help my wife.'

The doctor crept closer, looking a little uncomfortable, but he continued to smile. 'Nothing is wrong, sir. I'm afraid Her Ladyship thinks you're disappointed.'

Akitada was no wiser, but now Hanae came to place a small silk-wrapped bundle in his arms. 'Welcome your daughter, sir,' she told him.

He looked down at a tiny red face and moist dark hair. The baby's eyes were closed, the nose a mere button, and the rosy lips a flower bud. As he watched, the mouth opened slightly, and lips and tongue made wet sucking noises. Then a minuscule hand emerged from the folds of fabric. His heart contracted with a great surge of love. 'Oh,' he said, and 'oh' again, then he bent over the child and kissed her small head. 'A daughter.' He looked at Tamako with tears in his eyes.

His wife had stopped sobbing and looked back. A tiny smile tugged at the corner of her mouth. 'A daughter, Akitada. Do you mind so very much?'

He smiled, rocking the baby gently. 'Look, a daughter. Isn't she beautiful?' he said to the others. 'Who would have thought we'd have a daughter?'

Relieved laughter filled the room. They called out their well-wishes for the child's future health and happiness.

Through Akitada's head danced visions of a pretty little creature in colorful clothing skipping through his house, tugging on his hand, begging to be picked up, bringing her dear Papa small gifts of flowers and stones from the garden.

He muttered endearments and stroked the child's silky hair with a finger, admiring the perfect little hand. 'I have a daughter,' he said again, with such evident joy and satisfaction that Tamako laughed aloud.

'A little girl,' she said, her voice still thick from weeping. 'A little girl who will steal all your love from me.'

'Never,' he said fervently and reached for her hand.

FLOATING CLOUDS

Tora's wound worsened overnight. He had ignored it in the excitement of the birth, and the others had been too busy. He woke feverish and in pain. Hanae was spending the night in Tamako's pavilion to look after her and the newborn, and Yuki was with his mother.

Tora got up with a groan and went to their small kitchen to quench his thirst with some water. Then he unwrapped his arm and saw that the wound was oozing and surrounded by a swollen and angry redness. He soaked some rags in cold water and laid them on his arm. This soothed the pain a little, but did nothing to clear his fuzzy head. He needed Seimei to take a look and work some of his magic with herbs or salves or whatever, but he did not want to draw attention to himself at a time when the household was exhausted and when any extra care should be devoted to its mistress and the little baby girl.

Eventually, he rewrapped his arm as best he could and ventured outside to sweep the courtyard and clean up the garden. The sweeping proved impossible with only one arm, so he confined himself to whatever he could do in terms of tidying up. But even that was exhausting. He could not remember when he had felt so weak and tired. Eventually, he sat down on the steps to Akitada's study, leaned his head against a post, and closed his eyes.

Seimei found him there. 'What are you doing?' he scolded. 'Sleeping when so much is to be done? The courtyard looks terrible. Go and sweep it immediately. We will have company.'

Tora opened his eyes blearily. 'Can't,' he said.

'What? Did you drink yourself into a stupor?'

Tora sighed and got to his feet. He felt awful. 'What do you need me to do, old man?'

Seimei peered at him. 'What is the matter with that bandage?' He came closer, looked at Tora's face, then reached up to touch it. 'Amida,' he murmured. 'Here, sit down again. You have a fever.'

Tora obeyed gratefully. Seimei undid the bandage, pursed his lips, and shook his head. 'That looks bad. It may have to be cut again.'

Tora's heart sank. 'Not that. Can't you wrap some of your herbs around it, or dab on that stinking paste that draws out the poison?'

Seimei sighed. 'I can try, but we had better call the doctor. Now, back to bed with you.'

Tora would have preferred to doze fitfully through the morning but, true to his word, Seimei came to treat him with evil-smelling ointments, bitter infusions, and painful squeezing of the oozing wound. He was followed by an anxious Hanae, who hid her panic behind anger. She accused him of wanton carelessness in seeking out trouble, of allowing himself to get stabbed, of not caring for his injury, of not caring about her or his baby son.

Just when the worst storm had blown over, and he was trying to find a comfortable position to rest in, Seimei returned with the doctor. The bandages came off again; there was more painful poking and squeezing, much head-shaking and pursing of lips, and then the doctor left, promising to send a good barber along to cut into the festering wound.

They left, and Akitada took their place. Here at last, Tora found some sympathy.

'Does it hurt a lot?' his master asked, looking worried. 'Why didn't you tell us? You did far too much yesterday. I blame myself. I should have known that you needed to rest, but my head was full with preparations. I'm sorry, Tora.'

That brought tears to Tora's eyes, and he turned his head away. 'No, no, sir,' he muttered thickly. 'It's nothing. It doesn't even hurt.' That was a lie, of course. 'And I had a lot fun.' That was true enough. The memory dried his tears, and he turned back to Akitada with a grin. 'They were great, those fellows, weren't they? Oh, the racket we made! I swear we made the roof shake over Her Ladyship.'

'There wasn't an evil spirit anywhere near our place. I expect they'll keep their distance in the future, now that you've taught them some respect.'

'Right.' Tora chuckled weakly. 'And how's your lady today? And the little one? What will you name her?'

His master's face broke into one of his rare smiles. 'Both are well. You saw her. Isn't she the most exquisite little creature?

It's miraculous that we should have produced something so very beautiful. I don't believe there's ever been an imperial child to compare with her. We've decided to call her Yasuko. It's one of the names approved by the doctor of divination. What do you think?'

'It's a fine name, sir. And your daughter is as beautiful as her parents.'

Akitada laughed happily. 'As her mother, perhaps, but certainly not anything like the long-faced, scowling old dog who is her father.'

'Well, perhaps girls aren't supposed to take after their fathers.'

His master seemed to think this very funny also. 'Her mother tells me that she has an enormous appetite. Surely that means she's a strong child.'

He sounded a little uncertain about this. Tora knew that he would always fear losing another child. 'I could hear her voice all the way into the garden,' he said. 'I think she screamed louder even than Yuki did when he was born.'

'Really? Yes, she does have a very strong voice.' His master chuckled again.

Seeing so much happiness where there had been none for so long, Tora almost forgot the pain in his arm and the fierce headache that had developed over the past hour, and smiled back.

His master patted his good arm and said, 'You must rest now. Genba will be home soon, and meanwhile we'll manage quite well. I'm perfectly capable of raking the courtyard, and the women are busy sweeping the reception room and preparing festive delicacies for the guests. I'll stop in again a little later.'

Akitada had almost finished raking the courtyard. He liked the activity; it allowed him to think of his little daughter and of having once again a family. One of the first things he had done this day was to send a courier to the farm to inform his people there of the birth of the child and to call Genba home. In his joy, expense was nothing to him. The following days would bring many visitors.

There would be many happy times ahead: playtime with Yasuko, excursions into the countryside with Tamako once she was recovered, shared books, time spent on the veranda to admire Tamako's garden in its summer greenery as the baby played between them. He would play his flute for them . . .

Hanae broke into his daydreams. 'Sir? Sir, we have no foods to offer visitors, and the cushions in the reception room look very worn and dirty to me. Also, perhaps there should be more wine – and candles, in case some of your friends stay past dusk. Do you want me to go into the city?'

Akitada set aside his bamboo rake. 'No, you're needed here to help look after our patients and the two little babies. I'll see to it that provisions are delivered.'

Hanae did not argue. Poor girl, he thought, watching her run back into the house: we ask far too much of her and give her little credit.

He, too, went inside, changed into a decent robe, and helped himself to more gold from the money chest. Seimei was absent, most probably looking after Tora.

It was a glorious morning as he strode down the street outside his residence. A neighbor saw him and came running from his house to congratulate him. The good news had spread. Akitada was happy. He felt as though he were walking on clouds. The willows lining the canals on Suzako Avenue swayed gently in a light breeze. Children splashed in the water, and a pair of guards officers in their bright tunics trotted by on their fine horses.

When he reached Rokujo Avenue, he decided to simplify his chores by seeking out a few of the best food merchants, placing his orders, and having them delivered immediately. A silk merchant displayed handsome cushions in festive colors of rose and yellow. He purchased these on the spot. The merchant was very pleased to send his clerk with them to the Sugawara residence. All of this naturally involved a generous infusion of gold, but in Akitada's present mood that did not matter. What mattered was speeding up the process so that he could return quickly and look in on mother and child. In the market, he found young men offering their services to carry purchases or messages. Choosing the cleanest and most polite of these, he hired him for the rest of the day to answer the gate and perform other services. Loading the young man down with a number of other purchases, Akitada returned home, pleased that he had discharged his duties so quickly and efficiently.

He found Tamako in good spirits and his daughter asleep. Hanae, drawn and worried, reported that the doctor had looked in on Tora and sent his assistant for a man skilled in surgery. Between them, they had cut open Tora's swollen arm and removed

a good deal of blood and poison. Tora had not been coopera-
tive, but was sleeping now.

Tamako said, 'Make her go and tend to her husband, Akitada.
It isn't right that she should spend all her time here when I feel
perfectly well.'

Hanae protested that Tora was sleeping, and so was Yuki, who
was with him. She needed to see to the preparations for the afternoon's callers.

'All is in good hands,' Akitada assured her. 'The food will be
delivered already prepared. And so will the cushions and gifts
for well-wishers.'

Hanae looked doubtful, but left.

Akitada felt a pang of concern for Tora. But being relieved
of visiting him immediately, he spent a pleasant hour admiring
his sleeping daughter and chatting with his wife about his
purchases in the city.

'It must have cost a good deal,' she said at one point when
he had regaled her with a description of the delicacies he had
selected and the excellent wine he had tasted and ordered to be
delivered in ten large jars.

He waved her concern aside with a light heart and, seeing that
the baby was awake, he leaned over her to make faces and funny
sounds.

Yasuko looked back at him with wide eyes and no change of
expression whatsoever.

'She doesn't smile,' he complained. 'Possibly she's astonished
or sadly disappointed, but I cannot help my face. Do you think
I frighten her?'

Tamako laughed. 'She's much too young to smile.'

'Oh.'

He tickled the baby's neck and was thrilled when she seized
his finger with her tiny hand and attempted to suck on it. 'Look,'
he said, 'she's really very strong for such a little thing. Is she
hungry?'

'She'll cry when she is hungry.'

'Oh.' He looked at his wife and saw the amusement on her
face. 'I must have forgotten how it is with babies,' he said,
abashed.

Seimei interrupted this blissful moment with the report that
deliveries were arriving, and that the merchants expected to be
paid. Akitada parted reluctantly from his family.

In his study, he sat behind his desk, opened the account book, and rubbed some ink. Seimei showed the first claimant in.

She was a Mrs Kameyama, a middle-aged woman of portly stature in formal black silk. Her business catered for the parties given by court nobles and specialized in such choice delicacies as honey-glazed chestnuts, fried fish cakes, shrimp-filled steamed buns, pickled watermelon, and a variety of rice dishes. She recited a long list of items delivered by her men and ended with an exorbitant figure that made Seimei draw in his breath sharply. He hid the sound by clearing his throat with a little cough, but Akitada knew guiltily that he had been carried away with his order.

Seimei went to the money chest and counted out an amazing stack of gold pieces, bringing them to Akitada, who entered the expenditure in his book and paid the woman. She smiled and bowed her way out backwards as if he were an imperial prince.

As well she might, thought Akitada, when she carried away such a princely sum of money.

And so it went, as bill after bill was presented, and when the last merchant had left, Seimei reported the amount of gold and silver that remained. It was shockingly small. Not only had Akitada spent lavishly on this day, but the expenses of the previous one had also been costly.

Akitada and Seimei looked at each other. Akitada said, 'I had no idea that having a daughter would be so expensive.'

Seimei smiled. 'I am told it gets worse when they take husbands.'

'This gold I spent . . . I have not earned it yet. I have neither found Lord Kiyowara's murderer nor the abbot's disciple. I feel as if I had stolen the money.'

'Nonsense, sir. You will solve those cases quickly enough.'

Akitada was not convinced. He was forbidden to meddle in the Kiyowara affair, and the abbot's case had been in Tora's hands, but Tora was lying in his bed with an infected wound and a worrisome fever. He said, trying for a light tone, 'There is an appropriate proverb for this situation. I am surprised you haven't remembered it.'

Seimei raised his brows. 'Proverb, sir?'

'Yes. "Unjustly gained wealth disperses like floating clouds." I have been strangely out of touch with reality.'

Seimei shook his head. 'The gold cannot be said to be unjustly gained when you are working to earn it.'

Akitada sighed. Like the rest of his household, Seimei expected more from him than he felt able to produce.

What was worse, he could not make a start when there would be visitors who must be received and entertained, and Tora was far too ill to take up his duties.

The day passed slowly with social duties and frequent visits to Tamako and Tora. Tamako looked and felt well, but Tora was very feverish. When he saw Akitada, he asked what day it was, and when told, he tried to get out of bed to take up his duties. Akitada calmed him down with difficulty.

The stream of neighbors and friends bringing their best wishes continued throughout the afternoon and evening. Both humble and great, they came in their best clothes carrying gifts, some modest and others generous, and sat to chat a little about riots in the city and about Michinaga's resignation of all his posts to his sons. Most thought it very unfair that Michinaga should be blamed for the fires when the gods might be upset about any number of other matters. They looked forward to the many new appointments that would surely follow in due course. New people would rise to power suddenly. But they all avoided asking about Akitada's future.

Sometime towards evening, Seimei brought in a little package, wrapped carefully in rose-colored silk and tied with pale floss silk. He said with great emphasis and satisfaction, 'Compliments of the superintendent of police, sir, and his apologies for not being able to deliver it in person. He seemed in a great hurry.'

'Kobe brought this himself?' Akitada asked, amazed.

'With his best wishes for the honorable little daughter.'

'How very strange!'

Akitada unwrapped the parcel, half expecting some poisonous creature to emerge. But it contained only a child's fan, exquisitely made and painted with birds and butterflies playing among pink cherry blossoms.

Seimei peered at it short-sightedly. 'Dear me,' he said, 'that must have cost a good deal for such a bauble.'

'It's beautiful,' said Akitada and thought how very much it was like his image of his little daughter. With some regret, he added, 'Of course, we must return it.'

'Return it? Why?'

Akitada shot Seimei a look of reproach. 'Have you forgotten his insult? I'm surprised he dared send this.'

'Perhaps he thought the occasion warrants forgetting the past.'

'Never!' Akitada pushed the little fan away and rose to his feet. 'If he thinks he can wipe out all that he has said and done with a child's toy, he is very mistaken. Wrap it up again and send it back.'

'Sir, perhaps it would be better to reconsider. Superintendent Kobe has been helpful to you in the past, and at the present time he could still be useful. Why offend the man when he clearly still retains feelings of friendship?'

'Feelings of friendship?' Akitada looked at the old man in surprise and wondered if Seimei was becoming senile and forgetful. It was likely, considering his advanced age. Come to think of it, there had been other times when he had seemed out of touch with reality. The sudden thought of Seimei's approaching death filled him with sadness and calmed his anger. 'We'll leave it for the time being,' he said. 'Shall we go look in on Tora?'

Tora was clearly miserable. He raised glazed eyes and asked for water. He was not a water drinker. When Akitada touched his forehead, it was cold and clammy rather than dry and hot. When Seimei turned to pour some water from a pitcher into a cup, Akitada saw his face. It filled him with dread. He almost burst out with a question, but bit his lip. There was no point in scaring Tora.

He knelt beside his friend and supported his shoulders while Seimei held the cup to Tora's dry, cracked lips. Tora drank thirstily. When he was done, he croaked, 'Sorry, sir. Don't know what's come over me. I feel as weak as a baby.'

And in pain, to judge by his expression when he made the slightest move. But the water had refreshed him a little. After a moment, he tried a smile. 'A great day for you, sir,' he said. 'I bet you've been busy receiving guests.'

'Fairly busy. Even Kobe sent a token.'

'No! The big man came himself?'

'To the gate only.'

Tora tried another grin. 'He'll come around now, you'll see.'

Akitada shook his head. 'I don't think so. To change the subject, I'm free at the moment and thought I'd take up the search for the abbot's lost boy.'

Tora looked alarmed and struggled upright again. 'You can't. It's too dangerous. If it's that urgent, I'm sure I could get up in a little while.'

Akitada pushed him back gently. 'If I didn't know you better, I'd feel insulted,' he chided. 'Do you think I cannot handle it myself?'

Tora flushed. 'N–no, sir. It isn't that. The trail leads to those hoodlums, and I expect they're out to get me after what happened. If you show up asking questions, you'll have both gangs hunting you down.'

Akitada frowned. 'Gangs? I thought we were talking about some young troublemakers. Maybe it's time the police looked into activities around the Western Market. I assume that's where you made contact?'

Tora looked very uncomfortable. 'Hoshina has her wine shop there. She knows where Jirokichi is, and Jirokichi knows something about the fires. But the gangs hang out farther west from there.' He described the warehouse area and the Fragrant Peach. 'If you do go there, sir, you must take some police constables with you. The local warden is no use whatsoever. They all protect each other.'

Akitada attempted to get more information about his progress with the missing acolyte, but Tora had exhausted his strength. He rambled on about the fires, a serving wench and her boyfriend, and the young lord. He shivered a good deal and seemed to have trouble concentrating. At one point, he did grasp the urgency of all the questions and argued about getting up again. Eventually, his voice faded, and he closed his eyes with a sigh.

'Sir,' whispered Seimei, 'I think we'd better go now. I'll make him a strengthening broth for his supper later and mix in something to dull the pain and help him rest. After that we must hope that his strong young body will heal quickly.'

Akitada was very worried about Tora. He returned to his room and wandered out into the garden. It was dusk, and the warm air was heavy with the scents of summer. The sky was that lavender hue just before it would dull to gray. A few pale clouds scudded across it, their skirts still gilded by the last rays of the sun. One of the carp in the pool jumped and fell back with a soft splash. For a moment, the sound took his eyes to the thickening darkness below. When he raised them again, even that last faint light had gone.

The joy of the day had passed.

It seemed strange that nobody had become suspicious that the fires always started at night when most householders were asleep

with their hearth fires and lamps extinguished. Some had been
blamed on lightning. There had been thunderstorms around the
time of the fires. That, too, seemed strange. Why set a fire, if
the rain would put it out again? And why had the police not
investigated? Of course, if the arson was connected to extortion,
the victims might have covered up the truth for fear of further
retribution.

Akitada had reached that point in his rumination when Seimei
came out. The old man's face told him that there was bad news.
Akitada's thoughts flew to Tora, but Seimei said, 'A messenger
from the Board of Censors, sir.'

Akitada went inside and found a stiff-faced, stiff-backed young
man in the uniform of a lieutenant of the outer palace guard.
The lieutenant did not bother to salute. He demanded, 'Are you
Sugawara Akitada of the Ministry of Justice?'

Akitada's heart plummeted into his stomach. 'Yes, but I no
longer serve there.'

'You are to report tomorrow.' The lieutenant handed over a
rolled document, turned sharply on his heel, and marched out
of the room, followed by Seimei.

Akitada untied the ribbon and unrolled a formal letter. It
ordered him to appear before a committee of censors to answer
charges of 'acts against the public interest and for personal gain.'

His knees felt so weak he had to sit down. If he was found
guilty, he could well be banished from the capital. And even if
they did not go that far, he would never get another position.
His hopes of a new future for his family were gone, wiped out
as if they had never been – immaterial and fleeting as the clouds.

THE CENSORS

The *Danjōdai*, or Board of Censors, occupied buildings
directly across the street from the Ministry of Justice.
During the performance of his duties as ministerial clerk
and secretary, Akitada had had occasion to deal with these feared
investigators of all sorts of offenses committed by officials. Some
of those occasions had been most unpleasant, but none more so
than this one.

These days, the forty-odd censors had little to occupy them beyond inspections of the books of outgoing governors. Most of their judicial tasks had been taken over by the Ministry of Justice or the Capital Police. But the bureau persisted and guarded its ancient privileges jealously, reporting on officials from the sixth rank up and examining misdeeds of those below that rank. The censors enjoyed the status of the office, along with the income, without being overly burdened with work or responsibility.

But this made them doubly dangerous to Akitada, a former member of the Ministry of Justice. He would have to argue his case against their prejudice, and not only his livelihood, but also his honor was at stake.

He wore his second-best official robe and court hat and carried his notes in his sleeve. These he had reviewed during the sleepless hours of the night until he knew the points by heart, but such was his insecurity that he did not dare leave the details up to his memory. The mind plays tricks at the worst moments, and he could not afford to be struck dumb during the interrogation.

The sky was overcast. There had been talk that the long-awaited rainy season would finally start. The summer heat with its ineffectual thunderstorms had been enervating in the capital and disastrous for the rice farmers. Akitada eyed the clouds with misgiving. With his luck, he would arrive wet and bedraggled, his fine robe and trousers splashed with mud. He walked faster and managed to arrive dry, if out of breath and perspiring.

Lack of sleep and a general sense of impending defeat put him at a disadvantage, and things did not start well. A servant showed him into a small, airless room used as a waiting area, leaving the door to the hallway wide open. People passed back and forth, glancing curiously at Akitada, who began to feel like a condemned man on public display before his execution.

Eventually, the five official censors who would hear his case arrived also. They, too, looked in at him, some of them coldly, others frowning. Akitada bowed, recognizing a few faces: three were Fujiwaras and cousins of the emperor and the chancellor, the other two were unfamiliar. Not one of them looked as if he would deal fairly with a Sugawara.

He continued to wait. The perspiration on his skin dried into assorted itches, and the tie of his hat dug uncomfortably into the skin under his jaw. It seemed to take a long time for them to arrange themselves. Perhaps they were already discussing his punishment among themselves. Even exile became a distinct possibility. He thought of Sado Island and shivered in the warm, close air of the anteroom in spite of his heavy formal robe and full trousers.

At long last, the servant reappeared to call him into the hearing room. There had been a time in Akitada's life when he would have knelt immediately inside the door and touched his forehead to the floorboards. But he had risen in the world since then and was no longer a callow and timid youth. He swallowed his fears and walked in, head held high, telling himself that his past accomplishments had surely made him a better man than the five stiff, black-robed officials lined up on the dais.

Apart from the censors and himself, the room also contained a scribe, who sat to the side behind a low desk to take down the proceedings, and a secretary, who hovered behind the censor in the middle.

When he reached the cushion placed for him, Akitada bowed and said, 'I am Sugawara Akitada and hope to be allowed to explain the matter that caused the present inquiry.'

Waiting for a response, he looked from face to face. The chief investigator was one of the Fujiwaras and surprisingly young. He was flanked by the two other Fujiwaras, men in their forties or fifties with dull round faces and heavy bodies. The two men on the ends were the strangers to him: one elderly, with a neatly trimmed white beard, the other thin and long-jawed. They barely stirred or changed expression when his eyes met theirs. Were they waiting for more, for signs of abject humility, for pleading? He stiffened his resolve. They would not see him grovel or beg for leniency.

Finally, the young man in the center said petulantly, 'You may be seated.'

Akitada sat, removed his notes from his sleeve and placed them carefully before him. Then he looked up expectantly. He thought he saw some signs of unease; they looked at each other, fidgeted, frowned. Akitada said, 'I am at your service, gentlemen.'

More fidgeting. It occurred to Akitada that they found themselves saddled with a problem they did not know how to address. His self-confidence rose marginally.

The Fujiwara in the center was senior in rank even though he was the youngest. The colored strips on his court hat marked the upper fourth rank. He was in his twenties and still slender, unlike most of the chancellor's family. Akitada thought he looked the sort of young man who would have done well as an officer in the guard. Perhaps he wished himself there. Now, he clearly struggled to live up to his duties and resorted to bluster.

'You stand accused of very serious crimes,' he announced with a frown. 'I would have expected more humility under the circumstances.'

'I am guilty of no crime and have no reason to be ashamed of the way I have performed my duties,' Akitada returned, staring back.

This angered the young man. He leaned forward, pointing his baton at Akitada. 'What? Do you deny your transgressions while assigned to the Ministry of Justice? Do you deny that you have disobeyed your superiors? And that you have set yourself against the proper authorities by interfering in an official murder investigation? These are serious offenses, and there is strong suspicion that you may be guilty of the crime.'

Akitada regretted angering the man for the sake of self-respect. Puppies such as he could be dangerous even when they were ineffectual.

He bowed deeply and said, 'I deny the charges, My Lord. I am here today to serve his Majesty as I have done all of my life.'

His reply left the other at a loss how to proceed. He glowered, opened and closed his mouth, but found no words. Akitada scanned the faces to his right and left. Not one offered to speak. All looked irritated. A bad start.

The bearded older man bit his lip, then glanced towards his superior and said, 'Perhaps the scribe may read out the charges so that Lord Sugawara can respond to them. If necessary, the members of the Board can then question him as to details.'

There was a murmur of agreement.

The ranking Fujiwara flushed. 'Thank you, Akimoto. I was about to say so.'

It occurred to Akitada that the older man must be the career soldier Minamoto Akimoto. He had the look and was known for a fine military career in his youth. Akimoto did not look happy to be here, and that, too, might work against Akitada.

The scribe bustled up to help the chief censor find the correct document, and the reading of the charges commenced.

The account cited his angry outburst against his superior and the subsequent ill-fated visit to the Kiyowara mansion the day the counselor was murdered. Unnamed witnesses reported on Akitada's reaction to his demotion and his determination to find the man responsible.

Clearly, his former colleagues at the ministry had been eager to provide this information.

The document next outlined a long list of past offenses. For this, they had gone all the way back to the beginning of his career. Almost all of the examples fell in the category of disobedience or neglect of duty. They went on and on from his disobedience in attending criminal trials when he was still a mere apprentice clerk, to his other appearance before the Board of Censors upon his return from Kazusa when he had been charged with exceeding his powers in the investigation of missing tax payments.

Akitada clenched his hands inside the full sleeves and gritted his teeth in silence.

They had built a case against an arrogant official who had consistently overreached himself, disobeying instructions and behaving in the manner of someone so power-hungry that he would stop at nothing. The complaints of his previous superior, Minister Soga, featured prominently.

The reading eventually concluded. Akitada wished he could simply blank out the reminders of past struggles and disappointments. When the final word faded, he took a deep breath.

'If I may be permitted—' he started, but the ranking censor raised a warning hand.

'There is additional information,' he said, making a face. 'And it is of a most serious nature. It appears that you are about to be arrested for the murder of the late counselor.' He described how Akitada had found out that it had been Kiyowara Kane who had raised questions about Akitada's suitability to serve and had recommended demotion, how Akitada had then called on Kiyowara, clearly in anger, and how he had been seen rushing away only moments before the counselor was found dead in his office. 'Apparently, Sugawara then tried to cover up his crime by pretending to investigate the case.

It was a frightening catalogue of crimes and misdemeanors. When the chief censor stopped, the others looked at Akitada with fixed expressions that proclaimed his fate.

Akitada pulled his wits together and tried to stifle his anger.

'I am not guilty,' he said, glad that his voice was reasonably steady. 'My being there the day Kiyowara died was a mere coincidence. Any number of others were also there, and at least one of them had a much stronger motive to kill the counselor than I did. I merely wanted to ask him why I lost my position. I suspected that Lord Kiyowara must have based his judgment on the same old trumped up charges I have just been listening to. I could hardly have blamed him. He was a relative newcomer to the capital. But I thought there would be some gentlemen among you who knew better – or that you would at least have checked the facts. In fairness, I should be allowed to present the true record of my service to the emperor.'

The young Fujiwara sneered. 'Shouldn't you have done this in a more timely manner? The Board took care to notify you. I am very much afraid that this is just another example of your defiance of authority, and I for one refuse to waste any more time on this case.'

Akitada's heart sank. He would not be allowed to defend himself. His experience with similar cases in the past told him that there was rarely recourse once a verdict was given. Those who ruled the nation had no wish to alienate colleagues or to undermine the powers of another office. It was as ridiculous as it was frightening. Would they now also find him guilty of murder?

He bowed. 'My apologies,' he said. 'I did prepare these documents in my defense, but expected that I would present the facts in person.'

'Then you were wrong and should have informed yourself better,' snapped the young nobleman.

Akitada looked at them dumbly. There was nothing else for him to say. What were they waiting for?

The silence stretched.

It was again Akimoto who cleared his throat apologetically. He made a small bow towards his younger colleague and said, 'The senior censor is, of course, quite right, but perhaps in this instance we might make an exception. I'm somewhat familiar with Lord Sugawara's history and think we would all benefit from having a look at his version of the facts before we make our decision. A mistake made in haste would be embarrassing.'

The senior censor started to bluster, but there were murmurs of consent from some of the others. His face stiffened, and he said coldly, 'Since Lord Akimoto expresses concern, far be it from me to urge a speedy resolution. By all means, let us take our time. The chancellor will appreciate our thoroughness . . . if not our dilatory handling of the case.' He waved his baton, and the secretary approached to collect Akitada's notes. Akitada was told to return the following day.

He had no illusions that the intercession by Akimoto meant the case against him would be dismissed. If anything, it had rankled the senior secretary and would make him even more determined to find Akitada guilty – if only to make a point. What Akitada had gained was half a day's freedom, perhaps his last. The fee paid by Lady Kiyowara would have to be returned. He doubted that there was enough gold left in his money box. He must earn the Abbot's fee somehow.

The skies still hid behind clouds. It was warm, but there was the smell of rain in the air. He walked home to change his clothes. Seimei met him with an expression that was anxious and hopeful at the same time.

'Is it over, sir?'

'No. I'm to report again tomorrow. It doesn't look very good. For the moment, though, I need to get into old clothes. How's Tora?'

'The same.' Seimei's expression was bleak. 'I don't like this fever. We have tried everything. Where are you going?'

'To find out what it was that Tora stirred up and perhaps to earn my fee from the abbot. We'll have to return the Kiyowara gold.'

Seimei gasped and put a hand to his mouth.

'Don't worry.' Akitada felt guilty for having been so blunt. 'We'll weather this, as we have worse things. Just make sure that Tora gets what he needs.'

Seimei nodded. He tried a smile. 'At least Her Ladyship and the little one are thriving.'

Akitada patted Seimei's frail shoulder. 'There, you see? We mustn't despair. Now, can you help me find some rags suitable for associating with crooks?'

Seimei balked. 'You aren't thinking of looking for those young monsters who attacked Tora? They tortured some poor creature for days! You must not risk your life at this time. We shall cope.'

Akitada smiled. 'Don't worry. I shall be very careful.'

'Please, sir.' The old man's voice rose a little. 'Think of your wife and child if you won't think of yourself.'

They had a right to worry and that made it doubly hard, but Akitada had no choice. Guilt made him peremptory. 'Enough! This is no different from any other work I have ever done and certainly less dangerous than exile on Sado Island.'

That reminder made Seimei suck in his breath and turn away to look for old clothes for him. They were not precisely rags, but a dingy pair of trousers and a long jacket: comfortable, and indistinguishable from clothes worn by any poor man who had some business to attend to.

Since a sword would attract attention, Akitada pushed a knife in his sash under the jacket. If Akitada had not spoken harshly a moment ago, Seimei would no doubt have said that his master was jumping into a deep pool with a heavy stone in his arms.

THE RAIN

The distance to the Western Market seemed longer than Akitada remembered, but then he rarely had occasion to do much walking these days. At least the cloudy skies made the summer heat more bearable.

It was market day, an occasion that alternated once a week between the two markets on either side of the capital. After a lean and troubled year, Akitada had looked in amazement at the bustle of the eastern market. There, stands were selling sedge and bamboo blinds, paper fans, cotton or ramie cloth, religious objects and household vessels. Food sellers offered dumplings, cakes, noodles, soups, and stews. And entertainers were everywhere: a puppet master carried his stage on a tray tied around his neck; three musicians fluted and strummed and drummed; a young woman danced and sang; a storyteller entertained young and old; a fortune-teller sold his amulets; and acrobats performed their tricks among the shoppers. Here, the picture looked much bleaker. The goods were poor stuff, and most of the stands sold vegetables.

He found Hoshina's wine shop easily, but there his luck ended. Tora's description had suggested a flirtatious female, but he found a big, full-breasted woman, bustling back and forth among poorly-dressed customers.

She was in her thirties with a slightly pock-marked face and protruding front teeth. Her customers, though, seemed fond of her. They tried to pinch her bottom or lift her skirt as she passed and laughed uproariously when she slapped their hands away.

Eventually, Hoshina noticed him and stopped for his order.

'Wine.' He was hungry, but dared not try the food.

She appraised him for a moment, then said, 'You want the good stuff.'

He nodded. 'And I'd like to talk to you when you have a moment.'

She was surprised. 'That could be a while,' she said, eyeing him more closely.

'I'm in a hurry. It concerns Tora.'

Her face closed. She took a step away and scanned the crowded room. 'I'm busy. It's market day.' Her voice was tight and she left.

Akitada saw only ordinary working men snatching a quick bite or drink before returning to work. None of them were boys, but Tora's mention of the three deaf mutes probably meant that any of these older males could be members of a gang. Tora had pointed out that the deaf mutes and the girl had protected the boys from the police. Hoshina was probably afraid to talk to him.

He wondered what to do next when Hoshina was back with a flask and a cup. She held out her hand. 'Twenty coppers.'

It was dear, but Akitada gave her the money, saying in a low voice, 'Tora is very ill. That's why I came. It's urgent.'

Her eyes widened briefly, then flew around the room again. She leaned down to pour the wine and murmured, 'Later. After the market closes.'

That would not be until well after dark. Akitada asked in a low voice, 'How is Jirokichi? Can't you at least tell me where he is?'

She straightened, saying, 'How should I know? The bastard's left me. All men are bastards.' She flounced away, swinging her hips to a chorus of raucous shouts.

Had that been the truth? He looked after her and knew that he could trust no one in this matter. Something was afoot that was far more important than the disappearance of Shokan's protégée, and Jirokichi was at the center of it.

He tasted the wine. It had the strong flavor and murky consistency much loved by the common people. Leaving the rest, he walked out.

The clouds still hung low over the city. His mood had changed, and it seemed now that they cast a dull, depressing light on the city. He wished for rain because that would close the market early. He had not eaten all day, having been too tense about the hearing this morning. He looked at the foods offered by the few market vendors and settled for a bowl of noodles that he bought from a middle-aged woman who looked clean and was doing a good business.

He had chosen well. The noodles were plump, and the broth was nicely seasoned. Suddenly ravenous, he finished quickly and bought a second bowl. This earned him the woman's gratitude.

'Good, eh?' she asked with a gap-toothed grin.

'Very good,' said Akitada, slurping noisily.

'Hah.' She laughed. 'My old man, he says he only keeps me for my noodles. Better than fresh sea bream, he says. You're not from around here, are you, sir?'

So much for trying to pass as a poor man. 'I don't come here very often,' Akitada said vaguely, then changed the subject by nodding at the lowering sky. 'You must be worried that the rain will close the market early.'

She glanced up and shook her head. 'Not likely. It'll hold off till dark.' Her bright eyes looked Akitada over more closely. 'So what are you doing in this part of town, if you'll forgive a nosy woman's question?'

She was a chatterbox, but there was a twinkle in her eyes and her friendliness was generous. Akitada chuckled and decided to ask a question or two himself. 'You have sharp eyes. I was hoping that I wouldn't be taken for an official. I'm looking for a young monk. His name is Kansei. He seems to have run away and his abbot is nearly frantic with worry.'

She cocked her head. 'Now why would he run away? Plenty to eat in a monastery. Besides, where's his faith in the Buddha?'

'Not all boys go willingly into a monastery. Sometimes the father or mother hope to gain blessings. Or perhaps they cannot afford to feed a child.'

She nodded, looking thoughtful. 'Is he a child then? They do run sometimes.' She turned away to stir her pot of noodles and serve a customer. 'Poor boy,' she said when she turned back.

'Why do you call him poor? As you said, the acolytes lead better lives than the children of the streets.'

She frowned. 'Maybe. How old is this boy then?'

'Well, he's not precisely a child. I believe he's about seventeen. The abbot thinks he got bored and joined a street gang.'

Her eyes widened. 'Oh, that's bad. They're young devils, if you ask me. And you should see how much money they have to throw around. Gold, even. Now, where would boys that age get gold? And they have no respect for working people. We all keep an eye out for them. They come here and take whatever they want and don't pay. And if you make a fuss, they dump your food and dishes in the dirt and kick them around. Devils! I've seen them knock down a poor old man and laugh. One day they beat up a constable right over there.' She pointed towards some leaning stands, their covers of woven reed mats supported by thin bamboo poles. 'They pulled up those poles and were jumping around pretending to be stick-fighters. The man whose stand it was called the market constable, but they beat up the constable and he ran away.'

Akitada shook his head. 'I see what you mean. Were they arrested?'

She uttered a bitter laugh. 'Arrested? The police won't touch them. The constable who got beaten up, he quit and left town. The one we have now disappears whenever they show up.'

'But vendors still do a good trade. The gang can't be too bad.'

'As I said, we keep an eye open. Take my word, they're as bad as can be.'

Yes, perhaps they were. The stick-fighting incident might have been a prank that got out of hand, and the rest was mere hooliganism, but the fact that they had gold to spend suggested that they earned it by committing far more serious crimes. Akitada said, 'I take it you haven't heard about any young monks joining them?'

'Oh, no. How could such a one forget the Buddha's teachings and do such things?' She eyed Akitada's empty bowl. 'You know, that reminds me: one of my best customers is a woman whose son is a monk. She comes regular and always eats three bowls of my noodles.'

He quickly handed his bowl over for a refill.

'You looked like you needed some food,' she said with a satisfied nod as he raised the bowl to his mouth. 'Like I said, this woman, she loves my noodles. Only the rich can afford to put on fat like that. She says she's come down in the world, but that her son will be a great man some day and she'll live in a mansion with many servants again. She put her boy in a monastery to have him taught because she can't afford a university.'

It was a stretch, but Akitada asked anyway, 'What's her name?'

'She's just a customer, but I'll ask her next time. You'd know her anywhere. She's so fat she's got to lean on a child to walk.'

That image made Akitada feel uncomfortably full. What had he been thinking of to let this clever noodle woman con him into buying three bowls? He quickly handed back the empty bowl, paid, and walked away.

Noting glumly that the clouds just seemed to hang there, he decided to spend the time until the market closed by checking out some of Tora's other recent haunts.

He found the warehouses easily, and like Tora he smelled the characteristic sour odor of fermented rice. The gang's warehouse looked deserted, its gate leaning drunkenly and only confused tracks marking the dry dirt in front. Looking up and down the narrow lane first to make sure he was alone, Akitada slipped into the yard.

His steps sounded overly loud as he walked up to the splintered door. He reminded himself that the worthless rascals were responsible for Tora's festering wound and reached down to pull the knife from his boot before opening it. There was a sudden clatter in the darkness, and he jumped back. When nothing else happened, he walked in cautiously, letting his eyes adjust to the murk. Something darker than the gloom materialized near his feet with a yowl and streaked off to the outside. Before he could catch his breath, a second shadow flew past and also disappeared outside.

Cats.

Ashamed, he took a deep breath to calm the frantic beating of his heart and looked around. The light was minimal, but the warehouse did not seem to contain any other creatures. He put the knife back in his boot and circled the open space. An unpleasant smell joined the yeasty one of malt. The odors of rotting flesh and excrement.

He walked gingerly, looking at the scuffed and bloodstained

dirt floor, until he reached the larger stains beneath the iron hook that must have held the captive Jirokichi. A few flies still remained and buzzed up lazily. No one seemed to have attempted hiding the evidence by cleaning up the place.

It sickened him that what had happened here would go unpunished. Neither he nor Tora could go to Kobe to report.

Akitada made a half-hearted inspection of the few remnants of the sake trade. Evidence of formerly stored rice was everywhere. When he picked up one empty, broken bag and shook it, a few dark purple grains fell out: malt rice, used to start fermentation. They joined other dark droppings on the dry, sandy floor. Mice or rats had been at work, and that explained the cats he had disturbed. A number of rice wine casks and large vats were empty, and so were various boxes. The handcarts that had once served in delivering goods to brewers were mostly in need of repair. The warehouse had not been used for its intended purpose for a while, yet it might be interesting to find out who owned it.

Its more recent occupants had left their own marks. The remnants of past meals still coated some earthenware bowls, and sake cups lay scattered on the ground. Someone had left a colorful jacket behind, and a pair of dice rested in one of the sake cups. Near the door was another small pile of items: a closed charcoal brazier with a handle, the type maids used to carry live charcoal from one building to another; two stoppered earthenware pitchers; and a cloth bag.

Akitada picked up one of the pitchers. It was full. So was the other. He thought at first they must contain rice wine, but when he pulled out the wad that stopped the narrow mouth, the liquid inside was dark and viscous and smelled like cheap oil. Lamp oil was a useful item if the gang had spent much time here after dark, but two large pitchers of oil were certainly a lot to keep one small lamp lit. He checked the cloth bag. It contained stuffing of the type used in quilted covers and winter clothing, plus a small container of flints. The charcoal brazier was empty except for some ashes.

There was no longer any doubt. He was standing in the headquarters of the gang that had been setting the fires. A small group of street kids had terrified the capital into believing that the gods were punishing the country. Could they have hoped to topple the chancellor's government? It was not likely. But when Tora and Jirokichi had come too close, they had caught Jirokichi and tried to kill Tora. They would have succeeded if another gang had not interfered.

That was interesting, but not reassuring. The young 'monk' Akitada hoped to restore to Abbot Shokan was most likely involved up to his handsome ears. If caught, he would be arrested and sent into exile and probable death.

And Shokan would be grievously embarrassed by this discovery and furious with Akitada.

He paused to listen. He was not safe here.

Something in the air of the warehouse changed subtly. It seemed dimmer, and there was a moldy smell. Akitada sniffed and looked around without being able to account for it. Then he heard a faint rushing sound, not unlike the distant roar of the sea. A soft plinking noise came from right above his head. He looked up into the darkness of rough beams. The plinking repeated, then multiplied, became a steady drumming . . . and he realized he heard the rain on the roof.

Finally, it had come, rushing and gurgling, to soak the land.

Akitada ran outside to watch it falling in silvery sheets, pock-marking the dry earth, covering the roofs and walls of buildings with glossy darkness. The trees turned a deeper green and danced gently in the shower.

His spirits lifted. The rain seemed to him to wash away the evil he had found inside. Surely that meant the gods had not forsaken them. There would be a good rice harvest after all. And the fires would cease.

He let the warm drops run down his face and lifted his hands to the cloudburst. The world became misty. The warm earth and the many roofs of the city that had been baking in the sun gave up their heat in steam. Finally, the summer rains had come.

Laughing softly to himself, he walked away from the warehouse. Even for him, hope was still possible.

He arrived at the Fragrant Peach drenched, but full of new energy and determination.

He knew from Tora's report that this dirty dive was a hangout for criminals. These days, criminals organized much like tradesmen and merchants did. They formed brotherhoods that protected their members. Akitada thought that Tora had tangled with two different gangs: the one to which the three deaf mutes belonged, and the other, made up of young men in their early twenties or younger. The precise connection between the two gangs was not clear. The deaf mutes had attacked the arsonists to rescue Jirokichi, but they had then allowed the youths to escape. He would have to be careful.

He was not the only one who had ducked in from the shower that continued outside. The atmosphere was dim, smoky, and smelled of wet dog. Several damp locals sat chatting around a fire that put out more smoke than light, and the young waitress was serving them wine and bowls of pickles.

Since she played a significant role in Tora's story, Akitada watched her a moment and decided she was a hardened criminal in spite of her youth and prettiness. They started their lives of crime young in these unsavory parts of the city. Even though she had seemingly helped Tora free Jirokichi, Akitada placed no trust in her.

The other customers were poor laborers, though a few looked like cut-throats. None were younger than twenty years.

He walked forward looking for a place to sit and saw that there was another part of the room: a raised section covered with worn mats. A single oil lamp cast its light on a youth. Akitada's jaw dropped. There, in lonely splendor and apparently at his ease, sat the young Kiyowara heir.

THE PIT

Akitada did not know what to make of it. One of the 'good people' here, in such a place? It was impossible.

But his heart rose. Whatever had brought the Kiyowara heir to this low dive, finding him was a gift from the gods. He had caught the son alone, without his family's protection and in circumstances that might make him talk.

Of course, if the censors heard about it, his fate was sealed, but his prospects were poor already and he might just get to the bottom of this mystery in time to avert being arrested for murder because he was expendable while a relative of the chancellor was not.

He strode across the room with angry determination and stepped on the raised section.

Young Kiyowara looked up at him blankly.

'What are you doing here?' demanded Akitada, sitting down across from him.

The young man said nothing, but stared at Akitada as if he were an apparition.

'Does your mother know you go slumming in this part of town?'

'My mother?' the other asked, still dumbfounded.

'Hey.' The young waitress appeared at Akitada's elbow. 'This is a private room. Go sit someplace else.'

The raised portion could hardly be described as a room, being open to the rest of the wine shop on two sides. 'We have private business,' he snapped. 'Bring me some wine.'

She looked at His young Lordship, who seemed more befuddled than ever. 'What private business?' she asked the boy, who shook his head helplessly.

Akitada growled, 'Don't tell me you've forgotten. I was supposed to investigate your father's murder.'

The girl gasped, and the young man turned perfectly white. 'M–my f–father's murder?' he stammered. 'Who s–sent you here?'

The girl now grasped Akitada's arm and pulled sharply. 'You'd better leave or I'll call my father,' she threatened.

Akitada shook her off. 'Go and get me that wine.'

She hesitated. The youth said nothing. He looked frightened. Reluctantly, and with several backward glances, she left.

Something did not feel right about this. Akitada looked the terrified youngster over. His robe, while of good silk with an intricate blue and white pattern, was not only worn, but also torn and stained in places. Perhaps it was meant as a disguise of sorts. Under the circumstances, that was almost funny. In any case, the clothing did nothing to hide the handsome face with its slanting eyebrows and pointed chin.

So what was Katsumi doing here, hanging out with thieves and robbers?

Then a memory surfaced. Had not Tora insisted the young lord had a double in the western city? On the one occasion that Akitada had met the young lord, the youngster was in the background and had taken no part in the conversation. Still, if this was another youngster, the two were startlingly similar.

But why had he cast this youth into a panic when he had

mentioned the Kiyowara murder? If he was indeed someone else, he could not know of the crime.

Akitada asked more gently, 'Are you Katsumi?'

The boy looked around as if for help. Then he shook his head.

'Who are you and what exactly is your relationship to the Kiyowaras?'

The youth panicked. He shot to his feet. 'I don't know what you're talking about,' he cried and bounded off the platform.

'Oh no, you don't,' Akitada cried and went after him. But the youth was dodging customers in a full run for the door.

The wine shop became very quiet.

Akitada tried to follow, but someone put out a leg and he stumbled, caught himself, was tripped again, and fell full-length to the floor. He heard laughter.

Furious, he scrambled up and looked at sly faces. 'How dare you? That youth may be a killer. The next person who interferes with me will have to deal with the constables.'

It was the wrong thing to say. Three burly men suddenly blocked his way. The rest watched, snickering. A dirty bearded man sitting near Akitada took a deep mouthful from his wine flask and spat it at him.

Akitada tried to shoulder past the bullies. They did not budge. Neither did they speak. They eyed him like hungry dogs.

In a moment, the situation had become dangerous. He would have to fight his way out. Bending down, he pulled the knife from his boot. 'Get out of my way,' he snarled. Their eyes widened at the sight of the knife, and suddenly the path to the door was clear.

As he flung himself outside into the sheeting rain, Akitada blamed himself for his foolish mistake. These were not people who respected authority. More to the point, he had no authority any longer, and he could not call on the police for assistance. He was very lucky to have escaped real trouble.

The street was empty – and why not? Too much time had passed, and the youth had long legs and lots of stamina. Akitada put the knife back in his boot and ran to the street corner to check the side street. He found it empty and ran back the other way, past the Fragrant Peach. At the alleyway next to the wine shop he stopped to peer into the gloom. On this rainy day, late afternoon resembled dusk. It was nearly dark between the overhanging roofs of adjoining buildings. Water poured from the

eaves and splashed into puddles and ditches below. Was that a
movement at the far end? He heard the faint sound of a gate or
door closing over the rushing of waters.

The youngster must be hiding behind the buildings. Akitada
plunged into the narrow passageway. Halfway down, he was
about to slow down and reconsider when a heavy, wet cloth
dropped over his head. Akitada struggled against the evil-smelling
thing, but strong arms pulled it tight and then bound his flailing
arms to his body. He kicked out, but was jerked up roughly and
thrown over someone's back. Gasping for breath, he tried to
shout for help, managing only muffled grunts. The need for air
grew urgent, and he tried to throw himself off the man's back.
A short struggle later, he struck the ground painfully. He managed
to catch a breath, then something struck his head, and blinding
pain was the last thing he felt.

Akitada regained consciousness in the dark and knew instantly
what had happened. The smell of the suffocating cloth was still
in his nostrils, his head hurt terribly, and his arms and legs were
tied. At least he could breathe again. Total blackness surrounded
him. His fuzzy head at first made him think he had been struck
blind, but then he realized he was a prisoner in some dark, moist
place with earthen walls.

With the realization came panic. He was transported back on
Sado Island, chained in the underground chamber of the mine.
He retched, then vomited. His head throbbed worse than before,
and he felt dizzy. He vomited again and regained enough control
to move away from his vomit.

This brought him up against another dirt wall. His wrists were
tied behind his back. Even if his captors had left him the knife,
he could not have used it. He pulled on his bonds, but only
managed to tighten them. The rope was wet and intractable.
Maneuvering about by pushing with his legs, he verified that he
was in a pit less than a man's length in either direction. He could
sit and even kneel, but there was not enough headroom to stand
up. His prison's ceiling seemed to be made of rough wooden
planks. Something heavy kept them in place, for he could not
lift them by pushing upward with his shoulders.

The effort made his headache worse, and he collapsed in a
corner. For a while now, he had been vaguely aware of some
movement near him. Now it happened again, the merest slither

and scrape. A primal fear made his heart race. Leaning against the dirt wall, he fought down a second panic attack and listened.

Nothing.

Yet still there was the acute sense that he was not alone in a pit that was barely large enough for a man. Tora, who believed in ghostly spirits that played tricks on humans, would have thought that he was buried with some sort of demon, but Akitada did not believe in demons.

He tried to put his fear from his mind and thought about the situation.

The darkness meant little. Night could have fallen while he was unconscious. He seemed to have enough air, and it was reasonably fresh. Perhaps with the morning light he would see chinks in the boards above, but this pit might not be in the open. The floor underneath him seemed to be of stone, covered with a thin layer of dirt. It smelled vaguely of rotting vegetables. Most likely, this was one of those storage pits used to keep fruit and vegetables during the winter months. That and the moistness of the dirt walls made him think it was in someone's backyard. But his captors would hardly have put him where he might attract notice by shouting for help. He decided to wait before trying that. If they had posted a guard, he might get killed.

His captors had surely come from the Fragrant Peach. There had been more than one: big men, just like the three silent customers who had blocked his way in the wine shop. He had probably fallen into the hands of one of the gangs that ruled the western city. What did they plan to do with him? The possibilities that crossed his mind made his blood run cold.

There was neither food nor water in his prison. Perhaps they meant to leave him here to die. He fought off the horror of such a slow death by piecing together the events before the attack.

He thought about the youth who looked like the Kiyowara heir. Surely he was part of the gang, along with the young waitress and most – or all – of the customers of the Fragrant Peach. What plot had his visit threatened? How had he managed to get into such trouble by looking for the abbot's missing protégé? Nobody would go to these lengths to keep a boy from being returned to a monastery.

But they might do so to help a murderer escape.

The youngster's reaction when Akitada had mentioned the Kiyowara murder at the very least implicated him. Had

Kiyowara's murder been political? And could it be that the gangs were working for some powerful nobleman in the government? Who among the illustrious men competing for positions would use criminals to further his ambitions?

At this point Akitada's thoughts became hopelessly tangled and he dozed off.

When he woke again, his situation had worsened. He now sat in about a foot of water and something furry perched on his right shoulder. He gave a violent jerk, and the creature plopped into the stinking water. It splashed around frantically, then caught hold of his pant leg and climbed on to his knee. Disgusted, he shook it off again, but then regretted his cruelty.

It was only some small helpless creature trying to save itself from drowning. They were both caught down here. He decided his companion was probably a rat that had been foraging in the old vegetable cellar when he was tossed down and the exit covered with boards and heavy weights. He could keep his head above water, but the rat was not so lucky. This time, when the rat regained its perch on his knee, he let him be.

He had no idea how long it had taken for the water to rise this far, but it added a new fear. He need not worry about dying from thirst; he was more likely to drown in this hole.

Self-pity seized him. He would never see his baby girl again, would not see her grow, would never return to Tamako and the others. They would not know what had become of him. Perhaps they would eventually assume that he had committed suicide because he was disgraced.

How would they manage?

A new misery broke into his maudlin thoughts. He had to relieve himself. That forced him to his knees, and from there into a standing crouch, which brought his back against the boards above. Though it was repellent to add to the filth in which he and the rat existed, he had no choice. No matter how thirsty he got, nothing could make him drink this water. The rat splashed about trying to climb his legs.

While he was up, he tried again to push upward against the boards. Again he failed. Panic rose, and he doubled his efforts, struggling desperately, slipping in the mud and falling several times, hoping that he had not squashed the rat. He gained nothing by this except that the flow of water increased from a trickle to a steady small stream filled with dirt and mud. It became likely that one or more of the walls of his prison would cave inward under the water pressure and bury him. Drowning was one thing; being suffocated in mud quite another.

He gave up trying to shift the weight above and sat down to work on his bonds. The rat eagerly climbed into his lap and leaped to his shoulder. He was becoming attached to his companion. The creature's will to survive against all odds inspired him. Through the thin, wet fabric of his shirt he could feel the rat's every breath, perhaps even the rapid beating of his heart.

The rat might, of course, be a female, but he liked to think of it as a male. How desperately he fought for his life! Perhaps, not having human intelligence, he felt an even greater panic. And yet, what did a rat have to lose? A constant struggle for food – his only joy outside the brief pleasure of mating – and always the threat of predators and killers, dogs, cats, and humans alike.

'I can't see you,' he told the rat, 'but you're filled with the spirit of survival. Tora would have thought you a demon in the dark and feared you. Yes, you are a little demon, the way you fight and cling to life.' He chuckled. 'Now that we are intimately acquainted, you'll need a name. I'll call you Demon, shall I?'

The rat turned on his shoulder, perhaps to hear better, and tickled his ear with his whiskers. Akitada laughed.

He wondered if he was going mad.

He took a lesson from the rat and focused on escaping death. It was not clear how he could free himself, but if he was to die, he wanted to die fighting for his life.

Like the rat.

With his hands tied behind his back, he could do little except to work his bonds loose by pulling and stretching, or to cut the ropes by rubbing them against something sharp. He had already tried and failed to loosen them, and it seemed unlikely that the rat could be trained to gnaw the ropes apart. The thought made him laugh again. There was not enough time in any case. He shook his head, causing the rat to squeak in protest.

Perhaps the knock on his head had addled his brains, or the fear of a very unpleasant death had made him silly.

Tora had once managed to escape death by cutting his bonds with a pottery shard. Akitada started to search the floor of his prison.

His fingers just reached the muddy floor under the water he

sat in. Straining, he felt about in the mud, moving around until he had covered every section of the floor. It seemed to take a long time, exhausted him, and turned up nothing but a few pebbles and small stones too smooth to do any good. Amazingly, the rat had clung on patiently, as if he knew the human was trying to save them.

And all the time, the water was rising.

Having failed to find a useful tool on the floor, he knew he must turn to the walls next. He dreaded the effort of raising and lowering himself slowly along the muddy walls.

Leaning back to gather strength, he thought he heard a faint sound, as if someone had shouted in the distance. Akitada struggled up, slipped, and sat down hard in the cold water, the rat scrambling to hold on to his shoulder. He raised his voice, bellowing for help until his throat grew sore and he had to stop.

Nobody came. Nobody heard him.

Yet the small and distant sound gave him new hope. If he could free his hands, he could scratch and scrabble at the seam under the wooden cover. Since fresh air reached him, there must be chinks. He would work more dirt loose.

But first came the slow and painful exploration of the dirt walls, covering each time only an area wide enough for his bound hands to search. Standing, he could not quite reach to the top with his hands. The slow work sitting, then kneeling, and finally standing in a bent-over position, strained his muscles and exhausted him. He slipped many times back into the water. After every third effort, he allowed himself a brief rest. Throughout, the rat adjusted its precarious hold again and again, complaining in high chirps.

'Be quiet, Demon,' he said once. 'I'm trying to save your miserable life along with mine.' After that, he imagined, the rat's complaints diminished.

At some point during his efforts, his mind seemed to clear miraculously, and he saw how the murder must have happened and what its real motive had been. He was so startled that he stopped working for a few long moments, overwhelmed by the human suffering that had led to the crime.

But there was no time. The water was rising faster. It already reached the middle of his chest when he was sitting. Soon he would no longer be able to rest.

He found what he was looking for in the third wall. A sharp

piece of flinty stone protruded slightly from the dirt. He thanked the gods that it was embedded at a point where he could work on his knees.

'Now, Demon, we have a chance. Sit tight.'

The rat chittered softly and wrapped its tail around Akitada's neck.

Using his fingernails, Akitada exposed a little more of the sharp edge, then raised his arms enough to press the rope against it and started rubbing. The rat bobbed up and down and adjusted his tail a few times, but he seemed to take this activity for an amusing diversion.

To his relief, Akitada felt the first strand of roping part quickly and worked even harder. Another strand parted, and the bonds around his wrists loosened slightly. By now his shoulders were sore, but he did not care. He leaned into his work, scraping the rope against the flint as fast and hard as he could.

His increased effort caused the flint to come loose and fall into the muddy water. Akitada felt like weeping. He sagged back into a sitting position and felt about without much hope of finding the flinty bit of stone. He did not, but this effort caused the rope to loosen further, and now he strained to break the remaining strands. They gave, and he brought his arms to the front, cradling his sore hands and wrists against his stomach while the throbbing pain in his shoulders and arm muscles slowly eased.

The cold and fetid water nearly reached his armpits now. He had no time to lose. Staggering back up, he explored with both hands the seams along the wooden cover. The rat squawked once or twice in protest, but managed to hold on. He found where most of the water came in, a steady flow. Something was slowly draining into his pit. Akitada wondered if it was still raining. The long-desired rain was doing its best to kill him.

On the opposite side, he managed to insert his whole hand between the wooden cover and the ground above. Here he scratched at the dirt, scraping it inside where it splashed into the water. At some point, the rat lost its precarious perch and plunged into the water, which reached Akitada's upper thighs by now. Akitada stopped scraping and instead felt around for the animal. He found the rat when he sank his teeth into his leg in a desperate effort to save himself. Detaching the creature, he dropped him inside his shirt, a wet, irritable presence that moved about to find a comfortable place as Akitada returned to his work.

His neck and back began to hurt from standing in this awkward position, but soon he could reach outside the pit to his elbow and find the edge of the wooden cover. A large loose splinter caught in his skin, and he broke it off to use for a digging tool.

More fresh air came in, and he could hear some sounds, the rain splashing, a bird's cry, a dog barking in the distance. He worked away feverishly.

And then he heard muffled voices.

He shouted, 'Here. Please help. Over here!'

At first there was only silence like last time, but then a male voice shouted, 'Who's that? Where are you?'

The voice was vaguely familiar, but Akitada did not think about that. 'Here! I'm in a pit. I think there's dirt on top of a wooden cover. Can you follow my voice? Hurry, please. The water's rising.'

It was indeed. His pushing against the cover must have let in more water, for he was now immersed to above his waist. With his body bent over, there was little room left between his face and the top of the rising water. And he could not feel the rat any longer.

'Sir? Is that you? Please call out again!'

Genba! Yes, of course. Genba had come back.

'I'm here. I can hear you clearly, Genba. A few more steps.'

Suddenly the cover above him slid back, then tilted inward, bringing wet soil with it and pushing Akitada down into the water. He fought wildly, but the weight on his back was too heavy.

Then hands reached for him and pulled him out, and Genba cursed and thanked the gods all in the same breath.

Akitada choked, coughed, spat out muddy water, received a couple of painful thumps on his back and a good shaking, and finally drew a decent breath. Genba cut the rope around his ankles while wishing every torment of hell on the perpetrators.

Akitada stood swaying in the dark, or rather in the dusk, for it was getting light, and the steady rain washed the mud off his face.

The rat!

'Genba,' he croaked. 'Go look in the pit . . . There's a rat . . . Fish him out if he's alive.'

'What?'

'Go!'

Genba walked over to the pit, lifted the cover, and reached in. 'What do you know?' he said, straightening up. He sounded amazed and held the rat up by its tail. 'It really is a rat. Ouch.'

The rat had twisted up to bite him. He dropped it and sucked his finger. Akitada gasped anxiously, but the rat found its feet and scurried away.

They were in some derelict yard behind a warehouse. Rainwater gushed from the warehouse roof into a ditch. From a breach in the ditch, a small and steady stream had made its way to the pit.

Nearby huddled silent, staring men with lanterns – four constables, their red jackets nearly black in this rain. He wanted to ask how they came to be there, but his strength finally left him utterly and he collapsed.

KOBE

Genba asked anxiously, 'Sir? Sir, are you all right?'

Sitting up with Genba's assistance, Akitada took a ragged breath. His throat still hurt from the near drowning and the gritty filth he had swallowed along with the water. His body also hurt, particularly his bad knee, but he shook his head, as much in wonder that he was still alive as to deny any injuries. 'Tired,' he croaked, then raised an arm to point at the constables. 'What . . . brought them?'

'When you didn't come home by dark last night, Tora got very upset and tried to get up to go look for you . . .'

'Tora – how is he?'

'Better. The fever is coming down, but Seimei wouldn't let him get up.' Genba grinned. 'No need. I was there by then. And by the way, congratulations on your new daughter. She's a beautiful child. A princess.'

Relief and a tentative joy washed over Akitada. He was alive, and so was his family. Nothing else mattered. He tried a smile. 'Yes, yes. Thank you. And thank you for saving my life.'

Genba gave a rumbling chuckle. 'I did little enough, sir. It was all Superintendent Kobe's doing. And he and I just followed Tora's directions.'

'Kobe? You went to Kobe?'

'Yes, sir. Tora did say you wouldn't like it, but I could see I would need help.'

Akitada digested that. The amazing thing was that Kobe had agreed to help. But perhaps he had been more interested in catching the gang. Sitting in the drizzle on the wet ground, Akitada considered the situation while idly picking mud from under his finger nails. Genba shuffled and cleared his throat.

Akitada looked up. 'Oh. You did right. I owe my life to all of you.' For the first time, he looked at his surroundings. It was still only half light, but he recognized the outline of the abandoned warehouse.

He rose unsteadily and took a few steps towards the gaggle of policemen. They were wet and had tired faces, but they grinned. Though perhaps it was his muddy appearance they found amusing.

Akitada called out, 'Thank you. That was excellent work.'

A dry voice said, 'Was it? It seems to me they had a very easy time of it.'

Akitada turned.

Kobe looked as wet and tired as his men. His eyes widened. 'You look terrible,' he said. 'Where were you?'

Akitada nodded his head towards the muddy crater. 'In there.'

Kobe stepped closer and looked. 'The dear gods in heaven,' he exploded.

'They took exception to my asking questions of a young man in the Fragrant Peach.' Akitada tried another smile. 'Thanks for coming to the rescue.'

Kobe nodded. He looked uncomfortable and blustered a little. 'You do wander into danger with the utmost unconcern. But that doesn't excuse this. We've arrested everyone in the Fragrant Peach and sent them to jail. Time enough to get to the bottom of this in the morning. There was no young man, though, just an under-age girl.'

Akitada nodded. 'She's the daughter of the owner. He and two of his friends are deaf mutes. I doubt you'll get anything out of them. She is normal and protects the young male. His name is Tojiro. He ran. They caught me when I followed him.'

Kobe frowned. 'Was it that damned Kiyowara case again? You never would listen. See where it got you this time. I hear the censors have their claws into you because of it. And you with a new child to support.'

Akitada hung his head. 'It was another case,' he said wearily. 'I was trying to earn money I had already spent. A question of honor rather than stubbornness.'

Kobe was not to be distracted from his lecture by mere ideals. 'Whatever it was, the risk was too great to follow your usual obsession with solving a puzzle. Your duty is to your family first. If you needed money, all you had to do was ask me.'

The accusation was unfair, but Akitada felt tears come into his eyes at the offer of money. He was glad the light was still faint and his face was wet from rain. He was too tired for this. Hiding his emotion, he said, 'Perhaps you'd better dismiss your men. You don't need witnesses to read me a lecture on duty.'

Kobe muttered an apology and turned to the policemen. 'What are you standing around for, you dolts? Get on with it. Dismissed.' The men bowed and shuffled off.

Turning back to Akitada, Kobe said gruffly, 'Come, we need to get you to a bathhouse.'

To Akitada's dismay, Kobe decided to have a good soak himself. Akitada wished for nothing so much as sleep.

At this early hour, the bathing area was still empty except for a couple of attendants. They stripped. Akitada was only half awake. They sluiced themselves off, then attendants scrubbed them vigorously. This revived Akitada somewhat as his blood coursed through his body and his skin tingled. When they finally submerged their bodies in the large tub of steaming water, Akitada leaned back with a sigh and closed his eyes. His lacerated fingers burned at first in the hot water, but the pain in his knee subsided, and his sore muscles relaxed. A greater contrast between his condition in the pit and his present bliss seemed unimaginable.

'Don't go to sleep – at least not yet,' Kobe said loudly.

Akitada blinked at him through the steam. 'What?'

'You're still angry with me?'

Akitada was embarrassed. 'No.'

'I apologize. I had to try to stop you. You were headed into deep trouble. Of course, nothing I said made a difference, but I had to try.'

Overcome by the apology, Akitada said nothing for a moment, then muttered, 'Don't be silly. I also said some unforgivable things.'

Kobe persisted in trying to explain his motives. 'I was afraid that you wouldn't consider the dangers. You never do, you know.'

'I know you thought me foolhardy. Perhaps you even thought me a fool.'

'Never a fool.' Kobe sighed. 'I expect I'll be called in today. My dismissal is overdue.'

Akitada sat up. 'What? Why?'

Kobe chuckled mirthlessly. 'It seems I, too, am disobedient.'

Akitada's disobedience went back to the very beginning of his career in government, and yet he had managed to hang on – until now. 'How did you offend?' he asked.

'I think they'll call it 'interfering in official policy'. I insisted that your only offense was trying to solve a man's murder.'

'You made someone angry by helping me?'

Kobe gave him a crooked grin. 'It was the right thing to do, so don't feel responsible.'

Akitada stared at Kobe. Their uneasy banter had turned serious.

Kobe's lips twitched again. 'Don't look so worried. If anything, you've done me a favor. This is my chance to retire to my family's estate in the country. I'll be leading the simple life. Hunting, fishing, and sitting on the veranda on a summer night to compose poems to the moon.'

'You could always have done that.'

'Ah, but others had expectations. My aged father wished to brag about his son in the capital. My wives liked their carriage rides to visit other ladies. My sons hoped to make brilliant careers. My servants . . . Well, you know what servants are. They take personal pride in their masters' worldly success.'

Akitada felt slightly sick. 'Think how many enemies I've made in your household alone.'

'Well, we must all bear the burden of our karma.' Kobe said lightly, then changed the topic. 'Let's get you home.'

By the time he reached home, tiredness had seized Akitada to such an extent that he staggered. Genba had to restrain Trouble's enthusiastic greeting. Akitada clutched the banister for a moment to steady himself. This was not good. He had to face the censors in a few hours.

Genba offered an arm, and Tora came, looking drawn and pale. Akitada was ashamed of his weakness. He pulled himself together, refused assistance, chided Tora for being out of bed, and patted Trouble's head.

'I'm fine, sir,' Tora said, then added fiercely, 'Genba told us what happened. I'll get the bastards that did this, if it's the last thing I do.'

Akitada wanted to protest, but Seimei joined them, looking anxious. And at the door of the house stood Tamako in her rose-colored gown, the one he liked so well, and he forgot everything else.

Though he was dreadfully tired, he found that he could walk quite well and went to her with a smile. It was not proper, but there were no strangers present, and he took his wife into his arms. For a moment, they clung to each other.

'Are you well enough to be up?' he murmured into her scented hair.

And she asked, 'Are you hurt?'

They answered together, and laughed.

'I'm just tired,' he said, releasing her. 'And you?'

'Quite well, as you see.'

'And our daughter?'

'Come and see for yourself.'

They went to Tamako's room, where he held his daughter until she fell asleep. He told Tamako about the pit, trying to make it sound like an adventure. The rat featured prominently in his account of their efforts at escape. It was in vain. Tamako shuddered in horror. Fortunately, the maid brought in the morning gruel, and they ate together and talked about Trouble's latest offenses. For a short while he almost forgot the pit, as well as the dreaded hearing. But Seimei came soon enough to remind him to change into his court robes.

When he got up, Akitada found that he could barely stand. Every muscle and bone in his body, so recently soothed by the hot bath, now protested again. He gritted his teeth so Tamako would not notice, but as soon as he was out of her room, he shuffled like an old man. He had never felt less ready to fight for his reputation.

He was still struggling with his full court trousers, and trying to keep the food down, when the sound of a horse and voices outside announced a visitor. He hurried into his robe as Genba admitted the same guard officer who had brought the summons from the censors.

This time, the young man bowed. He presented a letter from Minamoto Akimoto, who told him that the hearing was postponed.

He apologized for the delay, which was caused by the censors needing more time to review his documents.

The gods were not without pity.

Akitada took off his court robe and spread his bedding. He was asleep instantly.

When he woke, he blinked at the cloudy sky above the treetops and wondered what time it was.

Somewhere in the distance he heard male voices in conversation. Suddenly worried that he had slept away the whole day, he got to his feet, rolled up his bedding, and went to look for Tora, who had received short shrift earlier. After that, he would pay Kobe a visit.

He saved himself a trip. Kobe and Tora sat on the front veranda, chatting amiably.

'I'm afraid I fell asleep,' Akitada said sheepishly. Kobe looked as tired as before.

They smiled at him. Kobe said, 'Seimei refused to wake you, and Tora came to keep me company. They look after you well.'

Akitada sat down beside them. 'Yes. Too well. I meant to come to see both of you.' He rubbed a hand over his face and found stubble. 'What time is it?'

Kobe peered at the sky. 'Probably the first quarter of the hour of the horse.'

'So late,' muttered Akitada, remembering at the same time his duties as a host. 'It's time for the midday meal. I hope you'll share my simple meal.'

Kobe nodded. 'Thank you. Tora and I were quite finished discussing his adventure when you came. You have nothing to add, do you, Tora?'

Tora shook his head. 'Only to say again that I don't think Jirokichi's involved. I think he stumbled on the arson by accident.'

'Perhaps,' Kobe said. 'We must find the fellow. I'll have his girlfriend brought in.'

'She promised to talk to me,' Akitada said. 'I never got back.'

Tora said, 'You must've laid it on thick, sir. She wouldn't give me so much as a comment on the weather when I talked to her.'

'I told her you were at death's door after saving this Jirokichi's miserable life.'

Tora snorted. 'Well, I'd better go feed my son.' He bowed to Kobe and walked away. Akitada was relieved that he looked much better.

He and Kobe went to Akitada's study, where Seimei waited with a tray holding wine and cups. 'Will you want refreshments, sir?' he asked Akitada.

'The superintendent reminds me that it's time for the midday rice. Have cook send us something.'

After Seimei left, they looked at each other in silence for a moment.

'You had a close call,' Kobe finally said.

'Yes. I'm not sure Demon and I would have survived, if Genba and your men had not come when they did. The water was nearly to my head.'

Kobe raised an eyebrow. 'Demon?'

Akitada chuckled. 'There was a rat in the pit. He perched on my shoulder when the water rose.'

'Dear heaven.'

'He gave me courage. Did you find the youngster I was chasing?'

Kobe shook his head. 'I've put more men on it. They're systematically combing that part of the city. Tora says he's one of the arsonists.'

'Perhaps, but he was not with the others when they tortured that poor little thief.'

Kobe grimaced. 'Jirokichi. They call him the Rat. You have a fondness for rats, it seems. He has a reputation, that one. It's surprising that he was tortured by a gang. Thieves generally protect each other.'

'Tora says Jirokichi works alone, and those juveniles were bent on revenge for an earlier incident. What is strange is that one gang apparently turned on the other to set him free. I think it means those boys work outside the organization. You found the evidence of arson in the warehouse?'

Kobe nodded. 'So far, the older men and the girl haven't talked, but I've postponed serious questioning until I can be there. We're still rounding up all the street boys in the area.'

'It struck me as significant that the gang freed Jirokichi and then let the young devils run. Perhaps one of the gang has a relative among the arsonists.'

'Perhaps. But the protection racket run by the organization

has been threatened by the fires. Merchants stop paying if their shops burn anyway.'

They sat in silence, pondering this, until Seimei and Tamako's maid brought in trays of food. There was rice, a vegetable dish, fried bean curd, and pickled melon.

Akitada was hungry and ate with relish, but Kobe only picked at his food. He said suddenly, 'Do you think the fires have a political purpose, that they are directed at Michinaga and his sons?'

'Yes. But it's hardly something I can meddle in.'

Kobe sighed. 'I have to meddle in it, and I'm no more fit to face the consequences than you.'

'I know. But you must inform Chancellor Yorimichi, at any rate. Can you talk about your investigation of the Kiyowara murder?'

'Yes.' Kobe speared some melon with a chopstick and chewed. 'As I said, the suspicion falls on the son. He was overheard quarreling with his father. When we asked him about that, he was evasive and looked frightened. So far his mother has protected him, and word has come down from the chancellor's office to handle the family gently.' Kobe grunted his disgust.

'What about the weapon?'

'No sign of it, but we could not very well search the mother's pavilion. Whatever it was, it crushed the skull in several places. Most of the damage was to the front of the head. You would think Kiyowara would have defended himself against the attack, but perhaps the first blow was unexpected and struck with great strength. A man, even a young man, could deliver such blows in anger. And he kept striking after his father was down.'

Akitada tried to imagine Katsumi in a violent rage and failed.

Kobe asked, 'What will *you* do about the case?'

'I cannot return to the residence, but mean to talk to the major-domo again. He lives outside. I'll let you know if there is any new information.'

Kobe pushed his bowl aside. It was still half full. 'Well, I'd better go and arrest the son.'

Akitada said quickly, 'Don't! There might be another explanation. Let me ask a few more questions.'

'Very well, but it cannot wait much longer. I'll be following up the business of the arsonists until I hear from you.'

Akitada reached across his desk and opened a small box,

taking from it Tora's amulet. 'Tora found this in the street after
he collided with one of the young rascals. I believe it may belong
to the youth Tojiro.' He waited until Kobe had opened the pouch
and looked at the amulet inside. 'I want to know more about
that boy who looks like Katsumi. This is a religious object. I'll
start with Abbot Shokan, I think. He has lost an acolyte and has
been suppressing information.'

Kobe reinserted the amulet and handed it back to Akitada. He
frowned. 'Do you think this Tojiro is related to the Kiyowaras
or that he is the abbot's missing lover? You can't have it both
ways.'

Yes, that was the problem. Back in the pit, with Demon
perching on his shoulder, it had seemed entirely feasible. Akitada
said evasively, 'I wish I knew. Perhaps it's a family keepsake.
And Tojiro keeps appearing in both cases.'

Kobe gestured towards the amulet. 'You have only that amulet
and a vague resemblance to young Kiyowara. It seems far-
fetched.'

'Yes. I had not meant to tell you this much.'

Kobe chuckled and got up. 'Well, let me know what happens.
It's time I went to see what our prisoners have to say for
themselves.'

THE SANDALWOOD TREE

I t rained off and on throughout the day, but Akitada enjoyed
the excursion. He was finally back on his own horse. The
animal was his single weakness for luxury, and he had stead-
fastly turned down astonishing offers for it from wealthy and
powerful men.

Besides, the rain had cleansed the air over the capital, which
had been heavy with the stench of smoke and wet rubble for
weeks. In the country, the farmers tended their fields, opening
sluices to control the abundance of water that had gathered in
ditches and holding ponds. The crops looked green and healthy.

Later, in the forest, dripping branches released their moisture
in a sibilant cadence, and small birds groomed themselves among
the wet branches.

Abbot Shokan received Akitada eagerly. 'You've found him,' he cried. 'I knew it. If anyone could, it would be you. Come, come. Sit and tell me. Did you bring him back with you? But no, they would have told me. When will he return?'

Akitada sat, waiting out the effusion. Perhaps his lighter mood had shown in his face. He rearranged his expression. 'I am very sorry to disappoint Your Reverence, but if I have found your acolyte, I have misplaced him again.'

Shokan's face fell. 'What can you mean?'

'I believe I found him briefly, but he escaped. At the moment, the police are looking for him. He seems to be involved in setting all those fires that have plagued the city for so long.'

Shokan's lower lip trembled. 'That cannot be,' he muttered. 'He would never . . . It would be a betrayal of all his principles . . .' His voice trailed off, and he shot Akitada a frightened glance.

'I think Your Reverence knows that the crown prince has enemies at court and in the nation.'

Shokan tried to look blank. 'What? I cannot imagine what you mean. You must do what you can to rescue the boy if he is arrested.'

'I am afraid I cannot do that, Reverence. But Superintendent Kobe is a fair man. He will not hold him, if the youngster is innocent.'

Shokan sat for several long moments, staring at Akitada. 'Then he's lost,' he said heavily after a while and bowed his head. 'He showed such promise. They say the sandalwood tree is fragrant in its first leaves. That is the way he came to me, a young sandalwood tree. Oh, the corruption of this world must be terrible if it swallows up even the innocent children.'

Akitada was uncomfortable in the presence of such grief coming from an old, fat man who had led a life of ease. He thought it hypocritical, though clearly the emotion was real. Perhaps this was what happened to those living 'above the clouds'. They no longer had any connection with the poor, the laborers, the market women, the prostitutes, and all the innumerable peddlers, traders, and entertainers that scratched out a living from each other and from those just slightly better off than they.

It was even doubtful that this imperial prince-turned-cleric knew anything of Akitada's world.

His voice harsher, he said, 'Surely a man of Your Reverence's status in the political and spiritual spheres can intercede and change even a condemned man's fate. In fact, you never needed me for that.' He reached in his sleeve and brought out the amulet. Placing it before the abbot, he asked, 'Have you ever seen this?'

The abbot snatched up the little pouch and removed the amulet with shaking fingers. 'Yes,' he said. 'Yes. It's Kansei's. I gave it to him.'

'My retainer tangled with one of the arsonists as they were running from the fire. He dropped it.'

The abbot clutched the amulet to his chest. 'The man could have stolen it.'

Akitada lost his patience. 'The boy is now known as Tojiro. I think it is time, Reverence, that you told me the truth about his background.'

Abbot Shokan seemed to shrink into himself. 'I have not lied to you,' he said softly. 'I wanted only the best for a child given into my care. And you are wrong about what I can do for him. My hands are tied by my vows. I cannot interfere in legal matters.'

Akitada did not believe this for a moment, but he softened his tone. 'Without knowing his story, I cannot go to Superintendent Kobe to speak on his behalf.'

Shokan gave him a hopeless look. 'Then he has already been arrested.' For a moment it looked as if he would cry like a child.

Akitada did not set him straight.

Shokan said dully, 'A woman who claimed to be his mother brought him here. That is the truth. He was five and already beautiful. She – her name was Ako – wanted him to receive an education and offered to pay a small sum every year for his upkeep. She did not keep her word, but in time I saw his lively intelligence and began to take a personal interest in him. He seemed to like his life here, and when he was twelve, we decided that he should become an acolyte. His mother agreed readily.' Shokan made a face. 'A greedy woman. She wanted money. That such a child should have been born to her!' Shokan sighed heavily and wiped his eyes. 'I paid what she asked. He grew more beautiful every year, but he took little interest in the austerities of our lives, and he ran off all too often. He said he went to see his mother. If so, she had a bad influence on him. I decided to postpone his tonsure.'

And that, of course, explained why the young acolyte looked no different from any other boy. Akitada was not sure if he liked the abbot's story. It might be true that Shokan, being cut off from the world, had taken a fatherly interest in a poor child and furthered his education, and that the boy had been tempted by the livelier world outside the monastery. It was equally possible that the boy had been forced into a sexual relationship he had no taste for and had run away. But he could not ask these questions and therefore focused on something else. 'Are you certain that the woman was really his mother?'

Shokan said quickly, 'No. I wondered many times, but the boy claimed she was.'

'And you really have no idea where I might find her?'

'None. I never saw her again after I paid her, and the monk I sent to look for her said she had disappeared. I confess I did not look very hard for her.'

'Are you aware of any connection between the boy or his mother with the Kiyowara family?'

'Kiyowara? No.'

Akitada, doubting Shokan's memory, said, 'Kiyowara was the Junior Controller of the Right. He was murdered a few days ago.'

Shokan blinked. 'Really? I take little interest in worldly matters. Kiyowara? He must be one of the new men. There is too much violence. We live in the latter days of our faith. What makes you think Kansei had any connection with the man?'

'He bears a rather striking resemblance to the young Kiyowara heir. Could he be the murdered man's son?'

Shokan looked astonished and then a little excited. 'I have no reason to think so, but I always felt that he was an unusual child. It surely would make this an extraordinary story.'

Stranger things had happened, Akitada thought, but he decided that he must ask another man about this. He took back the amulet, promised to keep Shokan informed about the boy's fate, and left.

As he walked back to get his horse, it occurred to him that he might as well talk to the monk who had come to his house. He had surprised him with his disapproval of the acolyte and the abbot's concern. He looked around and saw a group of small boys sitting under a pine tree. They were peering at a small bamboo cage.

Akitada joined them and admired the large, fierce-looking cricket inside. With the ease of upper-class children, they instantly included him in their discussion.

'Maro caught him. We're going to catch another and make them fight,' said one.

'He'll be a vicious fighter,' said another.

Their ages ranged between five and nine years. Maro was an older boy, but it was the youngest who was most impressed with the insect's viciousness. The child was very much as Yori had been before his death. The pain of that memory was still sharp, but Akitada reminded himself of the little girl at home. Would she catch crickets some day? Perhaps not. Girls were more likely to collect fireflies. After an exchange of a few observations on crickets and other small creatures, he asked, 'Would one of you know where I might find Saishin?'

They looked at each other and made faces. Maro got up reluctantly. 'I'll take you, sir,' he offered.

'Thank you. That's very good of you,' Akitada told him. They started across the monastery compound. 'Do you by any chance remember the boy Kansei?'

Maro nodded. 'He was one of the big boys. He was very disobedient,' he said, 'but His Reverence liked him, so he got away with it.' He sounded matter-of-fact and a little envious.

'Ah. What sorts of things did he do?'

'Well, he ran away a lot. And then the monks would have to go search for him and that made them cross.' Maro grinned. 'And he didn't do his sutra readings. And he'd go into the woods with a bow and arrow and shoot birds and things. The monks said he'd come to no good.'

'And Saishin? He didn't like Kansei much either, did he?'

'Oh, Saishin hated him. We think it's because His Reverence liked Kansei the most, even though Saishin is the best monk we have.'

'The best? Really?'

The boy nodded. 'Oh, yes. He performs more austerities than anyone, and he's forever praying. See? There he is now.' Maro stopped and pointed at the dark figure of a monk seated outside one of the temple halls. Saishin was in meditation pose, his hands on his knees, his eyes closed.

Maro said in a whisper, 'I'll leave you then, sir,' bowed, and ran off at top speed.

Akitada decided that the boys had liked Kansei. There had been that small note of admiration in Maro's tone when he had mentioned Kansei's disobedience. They did not like Saishin.

Akitada approached the seated monk. The sound of his steps crunching the gravel did nothing to interrupt his meditation. Akitada was forced to clear his throat.

The hooded eyes opened slowly and looked at him. Saishin's expression did not change.

'You may recall coming to my house not long ago,' Akitada said.

After a disconcertingly long moment, Saishin nodded. 'I remember.'

'It occurred to me that you might have some information that would help us find the lost boy.'

'It is not likely.'

'Was it you who saw Kansei with some other youths in the market?'

'Yes.'

Akitada snapped, 'Look, His Reverence wants the boy found. The least you can do is make an effort. Do you want me to go back and tell him you refused to answer my questions?'

Saishin did not react to this threat. He said in the same flat tone, 'That would be a lie.'

'You don't want him found and returned to the monastery. Am I right?'

This time the pause was even longer. Saishin blinked and said, 'It would be better for the monastery if he did not return.'

'Why?'

'He doesn't belong.'

'That's nonsense. He's been living here since he was five years old.'

'He doesn't belong.'

'You mean he wouldn't make a good monk?'

'That, too.'

Akitada bit his lip. 'Can you at least describe the boys you saw with him?'

Saishin frowned. 'Scum. Criminals. Sometimes there were only two, sometimes five or six. They were his age, but bad. They had knives and the scars from knife fights. Devil's spawn, all of them.'

'No doubt,' Akitada said dryly. 'Do I take it that you kept a regular watch on the market area in order to keep the abbot informed about Kansei's company?'

Saishin flushed. 'I may have combined other errands with keeping an eye on one of our acolytes.'

And that meant that Saishin had done his best to blacken the boy's reputation with the abbot. It might be immaterial, but Akitada kept it in mind.

'What about the boy's mother. Do you know where she lives?'

'No. His Reverence asked me to find her, but she had moved away.'

Akitada gave up and got his horse.

At home, Trouble greeted him with the usual exuberance, but Genba and Seimei had their heads together studying a piece of paper.

Akitada dismounted and waited for Genba to take his horse to the stable. 'Where's Tora?' he asked, looking around.

'Tora got tired of sitting around so he offered to go to run an errand for cook,' Genba said. 'He'll be back soon.'

Seimei still stood with the piece of paper in his hand. 'What is it?' Akitada asked. 'Did someone bring a message?'

Seimei came and said, 'After a fashion, sir.' He held out the scrap of paper. It was dirty and crumpled, and Akitada hesitated to take it. 'It was wrapped about a large stone and thrown over the back wall,' Seimei explained.

Akitada took it and smoothed it out. The writing was in a good hand. It said, 'Beware of fire.'

THE GRATITUDE OF RATS

Tora carried the shopping basket over his good arm, but his true errand did not involve shopping. The rain had let up, but the streets were muddy. Apart from some puddle-jumping urchins, people seemed to slink about like half-drowned rats.

The market was closed today, and he found Jirokichi's girl-friend in a nearly empty wine shop, listlessly sweeping the dirt floor. She stopped when she saw Tora and looked him over. 'I thought you were at death's door,' she said. 'Your fine friends lie a lot.'

'My fine friends never lie, though they may worry more than need be.' Tora did not sit down and had no smile for Hoshina. 'I want to see Jirokichi now,' he said.

She did not refuse him, but glanced at the lone customer in the corner. 'I can't leave,' she said.

'Then tell me where he is.'

'He's much worse off than you are,' she said.

Tora just gave her a stare. 'I don't care. I want to see him.' He raised his voice. 'Now!'

She turned away and went over to the customer. 'Sorry, Jinzaemon,' she said. 'I've got to lock up. Come back tomorrow, please.'

The man was elderly and timid. He got up obediently and shuffled out. Hoshina locked and barred the door. Then she filled an earthenware pot with the stew that remained and took the empty cauldron outside.

Tora waited impatiently. When she returned with the clean cauldron, she set the rest of the shop to rights, then placed the earthenware pot in Tora's basket and told him to follow her.

To his surprise, Hoshina took him to the other side of the capital where affluent and law-abiding people lived. There in the Seventh Ward, they entered a substantial house of the type normally occupied by minor officials or clerks working for the government. Tora doubted that her wine shop earned enough to support this lifestyle and gained a new respect for Jirokichi's abilities as a thief.

Hoshina called out, 'I'm home. I've brought Tora.'

Jirokichi's voice came from the back of the house. 'You're early. Did you say you brought Tora?'

Hoshina turned from the flagstoned hallway into a kitchen, where she deposited the stew pot and Tora's basket. 'Come,' she said.

Jirokichi reclined near the open veranda door of the main room. He was leaning on an armrest and had a quilt across his lap. His face was turned towards them, but hard to see against the watery light coming from outside.

Tora's eyes went past him to an extraordinary garden, now glistening with moisture from the recent rain. Lush green cabbages grew next to a patch of healthy onions; cucumbers and beans climbed up a bamboo trellis; and enormous mounds of leaves cradled golden melons. Among all that bounty pecked some chickens, and two fat ducks poked their heads out of a bamboo cage.

Jirokichi laughed at Tora's amazement, 'Welcome to my

humble abode, my hero. Hoshina and I are just a pair of humble farmers. How are you?'

Tora, seeing him lounging at his ease, scowled. 'Alive, no thanks to you, Rat.' But now he saw the effects of the vicious beating on Jirokichi's face. His nose and mouth were heavily scabbed and swollen, one eye was still closed and black, and his body bore colorful bruises wherever his skin was bare. He moved only with difficulty and grimaced at the slightest change in position. Tora sat down and softened his tone. 'And how goes it with you?'

Jirokichi gave him a lopsided grin. 'It goes. It'll be a while before I'll be able to earn an honest gold piece again, but in time perhaps some slight activity will be possible.'

Hoshina snapped, 'No more activity for you. You're retired.'

Jirokichi winked at Tora. 'She loves me. Can you believe it? And she thinks love gives her the right to mistreat me. Hoshina, my dove, some of the special wine for my friend.'

Tora looked after her. Jirokichi was right. Hanae bossed him around much the same way Hoshina did Jirokichi. It was strange that women treated the men they loved like bad little boys.

But he was here for a purpose, and the visit was long overdue. Reaching inside his shirt, he brought out a small package. He laid it down in front of Jirokichi. 'Your gold. Count it.'

Jirokichi pushed it back. 'You shame me,' he said. 'I owe you my life. Twice.'

Tora snapped, 'I told you I don't want your gold. I want to know about the fires.'

Jirokichi looked away. 'I know,' he said. 'And I'll tell you. I pay my debts, and this one . . . Well, it could cost me my life, but I owe you that. Very probably the knowledge will cost you yours, so be sure you know what you ask for.'

'How the devil can I know, if you won't tell me?'

Hoshina returned with wine and cups. 'I brought home some of the bean stew. Do you want to eat?'

Tora shook his head, but Jirokichi smacked his lips. 'Your good bean stew? Excellent! Tora will eat when he tastes it. The beans are from our garden.'

Hoshina left.

'Well?' said Tora, getting angry again.

'Those boys, the ones that caught me?'

'Yes, what about them?'

'They've been working for a rich merchant in the Fifth Ward.'

Suddenly, a vivid memory surfaced: a fat man huddled with some street kids. He stared at Jirokichi. 'Watanabe?'

Jirokichi looked offended. 'You've known that all along? Then why bother me?'

'I didn't know I knew it. I saw him talking to some young rascals.' Tora scowled and clenched his fists. 'And that fat toad pretended to feel sorry for those poor bastards dying. Oh, he'll be sorry for what he's done.'

Jirokichi looked nervous. 'Better leave it be.'

'You're a great coward, Jirokichi. How did you find out?'

Jirokichi fidgeted. 'You won't tell the police, will you?'

'I have to.'

Hoshina came in and set down three bowls of stew. She joined them. 'You cannot do that, Tora,' she said. 'They'll arrest Jirokichi.'

Light dawned a second time. Tora grinned. 'You mean you were breaking into Watanabe's house when you found out?'

They both nodded. Jirokichi raised his bowl and slurped noisily. 'Hoshina,' he mumbled, chewing, 'you're an artist. Eat, Tora. It's delicious.'

Tora sniffed his bowl cautiously, then tasted the soupy broth. It was good, but Jirokichi was clearly besotted with anything Hoshina did. He ate a little and said, 'I hate to mention it, but Superintendent Kobe plans to question Hoshina. So it's pretty well too late. Besides, I don't know how to tell him about Watanabe without bringing up your name, but maybe I can make a deal.'

They looked at each other. Jirokichi sighed. 'Well, I'd made up my mind to tell you anyway. One night I was getting ready to help myself to some of Watanabe's gold . . . For the poor, you know. Make sure the superintendent understands that it was for the poor.'

Tora cast up his eyes. 'Of course.'

'I was sitting on a beam right above his money chest when there was this loud pounding at the back door. Watanabe gets up and goes to answer it, cursing under his breath, and I creep into a corner of the roof to hide. He brings in three of the bastards – Takeo, Togo, and Chako. They want money from him for some work they've done.'

Tora interrupted, 'Was that the night they caught you?'

Jirokichi raised his bowl and let the vegetables in the bottom drain into his mouth. 'Yes. They saw me coming from the house. I thought I was dead, but the devils took their time.'

'But you already knew someone was setting the fires.'

Jirokichi heaved an aggrieved sigh. 'Are you going to let me tell the story? Yes, I knew Takeo and those young devils were setting fires. Most of us in the business suspected. But it wasn't just a lark. They were being paid. They bragged about it. Said they worked for those above the clouds and laughed like it was a joke. You know, the fires of the gods? Only, it wasn't the gods they meant. And there I was, caught in the house of their employer. I tell you I was so scared I almost wet my pants. Anyway, Watanabe goes to open his money chest, giving me a good view of piles of gold and silver that would feed the whole western city for a year. He hands the scum a few gold pieces and tells them to be more careful next time. They leave, he goes back to bed, and I take off without touching his gold.' Jirokichi made a face. 'Only, in the rush to get away, I didn't look where I was going, and the bastards caught me in the street outside.'

Tora digested that. 'Any idea why Watanabe wants to burn down businesses?'

Jirokichi shook his head and eyed Tora's half-filled bowl. 'That money chest was full. Watanabe's a money lender. I bet he's working for one of the great lords.' He suddenly looked angry. 'That's the way it is in the world. The nobles borrow ready cash for their expensive lifestyles from men like Watanabe in exchange for protecting them from the law. There's no difference between that and a protection racket.' He gestured to Tora's bowl. 'Are you going to finish that?'

Tora was far enough removed from his own humble beginnings to be taken aback by Jirokichi's comparison. 'The great lords don't burn down the city when they don't get their money,' he said sourly and pushed his bowl towards Jirokichi.

Jirokichi flared up. 'Hey, that wasn't the gang's doing. That was Watanabe and his hired boys.' He seized Tora's bowl and ate.

'Maybe, but if your friend Koichi and his buddies are such good guys, why did they let those young devils escape?'

Jirokichi put down his bowl. He looked glum. 'Turns out Takeo's Koichi's son. Koichi's a good man, but he's a father. He hit Takeo hard for what he did to me, but he couldn't let him be taken by the police.'

'So Takeo's still loose?'

Jirokichi nodded glumly.

Tora sneered. 'Well, they caught his sister. She keeps company with a kid called Tojiro. What about him?'

Jirokichi burped. 'Don't know him. Don't keep up with the family except to nod to Koichi when I see him.'

Hoshina said, 'Don't get them into trouble.'

'Too late for that,' said Tora, getting up. 'When they tried to kill my master, the police arrested Koichi and the girl. They'll make them talk, and that means they'll get the young bastards, too.'

Jirokichi gulped, shook his head, and shrank into himself. 'I'm sorry we met,' he said heavily, then turned away to look out at his garden.

Tora looked down at him. 'And I should've let them kill you,' he snarled and stalked out.

Hoshina ran after him. 'He doesn't mean it, Tora. He'll come round, you'll see. But they're his friends. His people.'

Tora stopped and looked at her. 'And I'm not. Fair enough. And we should never help someone who isn't one of us, right?'

She hung her head. 'Nobody helps people like us.'

'I did,' Tora grunted and left, slamming the door behind him.

THE CONFESSION

Akitada frowned at the note. 'What does it mean?'

'We think it must be a warning, sir,' said Seimei.

'Or a threat,' said Genba. 'Somebody's going to set fire to this place.'

Akitada's heart sank. He should have expected it. Kobe had arrested some of the gang. Now the rest had declared war. He glanced around at his home – ancient, time-blackened and shaded by enormous trees, a continuous drain on his finances, and a place he loved dearly. He could not lose it.

Seimei was still confused. 'Who would send such a thing to us?'

Akitada explained. 'The way it was delivered, it may announce retaliation because Tora and I have interfered with criminal activities in the western city.' He turned to Genba. 'It doesn't say when. We'd better fill buckets with sand and water, warn the neighbors, and stand watch tonight.' He thought of Tamako and the baby, of Tora's little son. Tomorrow they would take the women and children to his sister Akiko in the country.

He glanced up at the cloudy sky. Perversely, the clouds were too high for rain, and they scudded along too quickly on a fresh breeze. It was perceptively cooler than it had been, and thunderstorms were unlikely. With this weather, it would be dark sooner than normal.

Akitada folded the paper and put it in his sleeve. 'I have an errand and will drop this off with Superintendent Kobe on the way. If those hooligans operate in the usual manner, we needn't expect trouble until the hour of the rat or later.' He cast a worried glance towards the house. Tamako was getting stronger every day, but a sudden scare might dry up her milk. He did not want to risk that. 'Better not alarm the women yet. Tell my wife I'll be back in time for the evening rice.'

Seimei looked dubious but bowed, and Akitada turned on his heel to walk out of his gate again.

He went quickly along Horikawa Avenue, hurrying because he felt uneasy, and arrived at Kobe's office out of breath. To his disappointment, Kobe was not in, and the officers and men seemed very busy. Akitada left the note and an explanation with an assistant. Then he turned south to Nijo Avenue to make his way to the residential area where Fuhito lived. He did not relish this errand, but wanted to get it over with.

As last time, the major-domo's mother admitted him. He noticed the change in her almost immediately. She held herself as taut as a bow string.

Her expressions of the usual courtesies and her congratulations on the birth of his daughter were almost painful in their stiffness.

As last time, Fuhito was not home yet. They took the path through the lush foliage of the outer garden, now shimmering with moisture from the recent rain and shaking a soft shower of drops on them. Feeling awkward, he commented on the benefits of the recent soaking.

'The garden becomes oppressive in the rainy season,' she said.

Her voice shook a little, and so did her hands. Taking him directly into her son's study, she left him to wait alone. Outside, moisture still dripped from the roofs, making odd musical patterns of small sounds.

He thought about the change in her and decided that she was terrified of him.

Something had happened to put her in a panic.

Impatient with the delay, Akitada got to his feet and started pacing. He should be at home, looking after his family. A sound from the garden made him pause to listen. Somewhere a gate closed, and Akitada hoped that Fuhito had returned, but he heard nothing else.

A moment later, Fuhito's mother brought a tray of refreshments, and Akitada realized he had been wrong. Nobody had come, but someone had left.

He sat back down, and she knelt to serve him.

'I thought I heard a gate,' he said, 'and hoped your son had returned.'

Her hand jerked, and she spilled a little wine as she filled his cup. Apologizing, she dabbed at the moisture with her sleeve. 'It must have been my maid. My son is not back yet.' She sounded strangely breathless. Pushing the cup and a small bowl of nuts a little closer to him, she murmured, 'Please forgive this poor food.'

Akitada looked at her sharply. She looked positively ill. 'There is nothing to forgive,' he said. 'I am the one causing trouble. Perhaps this is not a good time.'

'It is no trouble,' she murmured. To his shock, tears began to course down her cheeks. She did not brush them away. Neither did she explain or withdraw. She sat there, silently weeping.

He rose nervously. 'Please allow me to call someone.' He went to the door and clapped his hands.

In the distance, a voice shouted, 'Coming,' and soft shuffling footsteps announced a small woman even older than Fuhito's mother. She fussed over her mistress and led her from the room, leaving Akitada alone, wondering who had left by the gate. He was sure Fuhito's mother had told him on his last visit that they had only the one servant.

Perhaps it had been Fuhito himself, taking flight because he expected to be arrested, but Akitada did not think so.

He was proved correct a moment later when the front gate

opened with the familiar clatter of bamboo, and Fuhito's firm footsteps approached the house.

'I'm home, Mother,' he called out, and then there was the sound of muffled voices, his mother's high and agitated, Fuhito's soothing, until the house fell quiet again. After a moment, steps approached, and the major-domo walked in.

'My Lord?' he said, bowing. 'What gives me this honor? I did not expect you again.'

Akitada did not return the greeting. 'There are some unanswered questions,' he said vaguely.

Fuhito hesitated. 'I'm afraid that Her Ladyship does not wish the matter pursued,' he said. He was still standing, as if he expected Akitada to cut his visit short and depart again. 'She said the police will handle matters from now on.'

Akitada raised his brows. 'Really? In that case, I shall satisfy my own curiosity.'

Fuhito fidgeted. 'I don't think it would be wise for me to speak, sir. It might be seen as disobedience by my mistress.'

Akitada was becoming irritated. 'Sit down, Fuhito,' he snapped in his best court-hearing manner. 'It seems you have a grandson, your master's son by your daughter. I believe Tojiro is slightly older than his half-brother Katsumi.'

Fuhito's legs gave way and he sank to the floor. He was very pale and opened and closed his mouth several times, searching for words.

Akitada looked at him and dreaded what he had to do. He decided to get it over with quickly. 'I think you quarreled with Kiyowara about the boy. If he has an obligation to this son and refused to acknowledge it that would constitute a powerful motive for murder and explain the furious attack that killed him. Did you kill your master?'

He can deny it, thought Akitada. I hope he does. In spite of his knowledge, he felt great pity for the man.

The sound of steady dripping fell into the silence like funereal music and reminded him of the old lady's tears. Four generations of a family destroyed by the selfishness of an ambitious nobleman. The Fujiwaras and their connections had spread their poison throughout the land, at first disenfranchising the old order and then, once they had what they wanted, finishing the process by tormenting its descendants. There was little difference between the Sugawaras and Fuhito's family. His own fall from fortune had already begun. Why should he play into the hands of the authorities by revealing Fuhito's guilt?

Fuhito surprised and disappointed him. After a long silence, he asked, 'How did you find out?'

Akitada did not answer. There was still time for the man to deny the deed.

Fuhito looked at him with moist eyes. 'Yes, Tojiro is my daughter's son. You were right. Lord Kiyowara . . .' He paused, searching for words. 'Kiyowara seduced her when she was only fifteen and in his mother's care.' He raised a shaking hand and brushed it over his face. 'No,' he said fiercely, 'it was not a seduction. The truth is that he raped her brutally, raped a child! Not once, but again and again, until his mother found out and put a stop to it. They sent her home. But she was with child by then and tried to drown herself in the pond. Then she tried to hang herself with her sash. In my despair, I went to him and confronted him with what he had done. At the time he could not afford a scandal. He was afraid I would talk and agreed to install her in his household as a secondary wife. She gave birth to his first son there, but the birth and her misery were too much, and she died a day later. The child is Tojiro.'

Silence fell again. Fuhito sat hunched into himself, his thin hands clutching his knees, his eyes staring holes into the flooring.

Akitada waited a decent time, then asked, 'What happened next?'

Fuhito started and went on: 'My daughter's maid Ako was with her at Kiyowara's house. After my daughter's death, she looked after my grandson until they were sent away. Tojiro was not yet a year old when Lady Kiyowara gave birth to Katsumi.' Fuhito sighed. 'My master called me in to tell me that the first lady wanted Tojiro to be raised by us. My mother and Ako looked after him for the first years. His Lordship settled some income on us and promised to do more for the child when he was older.' Fuhito spread his hands helplessly and looked at Akitada. 'The boy's future was at stake. It made up for what happened to his mother. We hoped his father would not forget his promise.'

'And did Kiyowara remember?'

Fuhito did not answer that. Instead he said, 'When Her Ladyship's sister married His Excellency, the present regent, things changed again. Lord Yorimichi wasn't regent or chancellor then, but everyone knew he would be because he is Lord

Michinaga's oldest son. Tojiro was five when his father told me to enroll him at Seikan-ji, a monastery outside the capital. Ako was to take him and claim she was his mother. I did not like it, but his father insisted he would receive a good education there. I knew he was more afraid than ever his relationship with my daughter would become known.'

Fuhito had remained in the service of the man who had dealt with his daughter and grandson in such a dishonorable manner because he had hoped that some day there would be a better future for the child. That did not altogether excuse him from having abandoned the child himself. Akitada firmed his resolve.

'I take it Tojiro objected to becoming a monk.'

Fuhito's head sank again and the hands clutched his knees. 'Yes, but that was not until much later. Tojiro ran away from the monastery the first time when he was thirteen. He went to Ako, who was living in the western city on some money I paid her. One day the foolish woman told him something of his background. He came to me to argue his case. I explained and begged him to be patient a little longer. His father had just accepted his new position. I told him that he would soon be able to do something for his son. Alas, this last time Tojiro fled, he was in despair. I saw that he could not remain in the monastery and went to His Lordship to plead his case. My master became angry with me and the boy. He said that he wanted nothing to do with Tojiro. That we had been paid. I could see that all my hopes had been in vain. He would never acknowledge Tojiro.'

Fuhito paused a moment, then spoke quickly, as if he were afraid he would lose his courage if he paused. 'I remembered my poor child's fate and all of Kiyowara's empty promises and lost my temper. I accused him of breaking his word. He laughed in my face, mocking my family and my dead daughter. I could not think straight and lashed out at him. I just smashed my fists into his head and face again and again, and when he fell down, I kicked him until he stopped moving. When I gained some awareness again, I saw that I had killed him.'

A heavy silence fell.

Akitada had not thought that it would be so easy to get a confession. Fuhito, for all his humble position, was still a gentleman and would not shame his family by cowardly lies. The daughter's fate was a powerful motive for murder, one that had perhaps simmered for decades. Now that he thought about it, neither Fuhito nor his mother had said in so many words that the young girl had committed suicide. They had merely let him think so.

Akitada asked, 'Where is Tojiro now?'

The major-domo raised his head and looked at him. 'The boy had nothing to do with it. I beg that you will keep him out of it. Let it be me who pays the price. I promise to cooperate fully.'

'I'm afraid Tojiro is suspected of being part of a gang involved in setting the fires. He will almost certainly have to answer questions.'

Fuhito became agitated. 'Tojiro got mixed up with some boys when he stayed with Ako, but that was only because he envied them their freedom. He was a child. He still is a child.'

Akitada got up, suddenly tired and defeated. 'I am sure he'll explain it all to the police. I think you've been giving him shelter here. If he returns, please convince him that it is better if he gives himself up.'

Fuhito rose also. 'What will you do?' he asked anxiously.

Akitada's stomach contracted. He had to turn the man over to the police. Regardless of Tojiro's fate, Fuhito would be jailed, tried, and sentenced to exile. His family property would be confiscated, and his family would be sent into the streets to beg. All that could be done was to delay the arrest a little longer. He said reluctantly, 'I'm afraid you will be arrested and eventually tried for Kiyowara's murder. If you can, it would be best to make some arrangements for your mother and grandson quickly.'

Fuhito looked around the room as if trying to memorize it. He made a sound that was half groan and half acquiescence. Raising his hands to his face, he swayed for a moment, then straightened his back, lowered his hands, and bowed. 'Thank you, for your considerate behavior, My Lord.' And with that, he turned and led the way to the gate.

Akitada walked homeward quickly. The wind had picked up, and there was again the smell of burning in the air. He hoped he would not be too late.

FIRE WATCH

To his relief, all was well in his quarter. Tora opened the gate, his face breaking into a wide smile. 'Wait till you hear what I found out,' he cried.

Akitada, still breathless and thinking of the threat to his family and his tragic errand to Fuhito's house, ignored this. 'Is all well here? Did Kobe send an answer?'

Tora's face fell. 'All's well, and no, no word from the superintendent. Did you expect to hear from him?'

Akitada growled, 'I expected better than that. A police cordon around my house would be nice.'

Tora cheered up. 'Don't worry. We'll handle the little bastards if they come. I hope they do. I'll show that sack of shit Takeo what's what.'

Akitada said sourly, 'You're hardly in any shape to fight.'

'I'm fine. Now listen. I know who's been running that arson gang. Jirokichi finally came through.' Tora clapped his hands in glee. 'We've got them. You can turn them over to the police and collect your reward. Jirokichi's a miserable specimen, but this time he lucked out.'

'Get to the point.' Akitada's eyes were on Genba who was filling buckets and large pots at the well. The number of containers was pitifully small.

'There's a rice merchant called Watanabe in the Fifth Ward. He's been paying those kids to set the fires. Jirokichi thinks he's working for someone in the government.'

'A rice merchant setting fires? It sounds far-fetched.'

'Jirokichi was in his house and watched him pay off the three creeps who run the gang. Takeo was one of them. They caught Jirokichi leaving. That's why they tortured him, to find out what he knew.'

Akitada was even more doubtful about this news. 'Did they actually talk about setting fires?'

'Umm, no. Not in so many words. But you can see—'

'You're accepting the word of a thief. If he told the truth, he would have been dead by now. It's just a bunch of hoodlums terrorizing merchants and tormenting the weak.'

Tora snapped, 'Well, they tried to kill him. Maybe they couldn't find his hideout. I couldn't.' He took a deep breath. 'All right, don't believe me. I'll tell Kobe myself. I think he'll listen.' He turned on his heel and stalked away.

Muttering under his breath about Tora's manners, Akitada went to check on his family. Tamako was nursing the baby, and Hanae sat near her. She was feeding Yuki small bits of melon with a pair of chopsticks. They looked calm and happy.

'There you are,' said Tamako with a smile. 'Please forgive my not rising to make you a proper bow.'

She was teasing. They had both become very casual about such conventions between husband and wife. In fact, they behaved almost like equals these days. He liked that.

He went to sit next to her, peering at his daughter's rosy face. That small and tender dark head against Tamako's white breast was to his mind one of the most perfect things of his world. He reached out a finger to caress his daughter's silken hair and let it stray to Tamako's warm skin. 'I will hold you to proper protocol later, wife,' he murmured. 'You mustn't think that you can forget your duty to your husband because you're a mother again.' Tamako blushed and bent her face more closely to the baby's.

'Should I leave?' Hanae asked, eyeing Akitada with raised brows.

They said 'no' together. Tamako still looked embarrassed, even though she smiled, and he wished he could take his words back.

He desired his wife more than ever, but it was too soon. Besides, he would not be able to come to her bed tonight anyway.

He left the women and went to discuss the arrangements with his retainers. In the morning, Genba would go to hire sedan chairs. Seimei and Tora would accompany the women and children to his sister Akiko.

Tora protested immediately.

Akitada said, 'Your arm is not healed enough for you to use your sword.'

Tora glared. 'I'm not useless,' he snapped.

Akitada tried to soothe his anger. 'Someone has to guard the women on the journey.'

'Very well, but I'll return as soon as they are settled.'

Seimei cleared his throat. 'I'd like to stay also, sir.'

Akitada threw up his hands. 'Then who will look after my family?'

Seimei bowed his head and agreed to travel with the women.

Next, they considered how best to guard the house during the night. Only one of the buildings was close enough to the wall so that firebrands could be thrown on to the roof. That was the small house Tora and Hanae occupied. Since the front courtyard and the gate could be watched from there, Seimei would be installed on its porch with a small gong by his side to give an alarm. Akitada and Genba would patrol the rest of the property continuously during the night hours. Tora, who could not be expected to use his sword arm yet, would sit on the ridge of the stable roof to watch the street in front of the residence and the rest of the compound.

Akitada was frustrated that there was no word from Kobe. They could only hope that the night would remain quiet. After that, the women and children would be in a safe place. He inspected the stores of water and sand, and found them inadequate, but there was nothing he could do about that. Perhaps the good soaking from the rain would slow a fire down.

They managed to keep their worries from the women. Akitada shared his evening meal with Tamako and mentioned casually that he wanted to do some work on their accounts and would sleep in his study.

By the end of the hour of the boar, the household had retired. It was fully dark outside, and the lights inside the house had been extinguished. Akitada and Genba took turns walking the grounds. Because of the overcast skies, the darkness was intense.

Akitada finished the first watch and was relieved by Genba. Sitting down beside Seimei, he said softly, 'I'm very sorry for putting you and the others through this. You must be tired. Why don't you go to bed? The three of us can manage.'

'The old need little sleep, sir.'

Seimei sounded alert, and Akitada was grateful for the company. He leaned back against the porch railing, looking up at the dark sky and the even blacker outlines of trees and roofs. 'Do you think that murder can ever be a moral option for a man? That it would be not only cowardly but also wrong to go on living without killing?'

After a moment, Seimei's voice came from the darkness.

'Master K'ung Fu-tzu says, "To see what is right and not do it is cowardly." Do you plan to kill someone, sir?'

'No. But I have met such a man: a man who has killed. It troubles me, and I wonder what to do.'

'Ah. When a frightened bird hides in his sleeve, even the hunter does not kill it. You feel pity for this murderer. That is like you, sir.'

'But what shall I do, old friend? If I act the way I have been taught by my ancestors, and by the rules of the ancients and by the law I must serve, I will bring tragedy to the innocent along with the guilty. What does your Master K'ung Fu-tzu have to say about that?'

Seimei chuckled softly. 'They say the master was quite free of words like "shall", "must" . . . or "I".'

'Lucky man!'

They fell silent. Akitada thought about Fuhito. Something nagged at him: something that did not fit, was still not explained. From the far distance came the sound of the palace bell marking the next hour. If they came tonight, it would be soon. Restlessly, he got up to check Tamako's pavilion. She had left its doors open to the coolness of the night breeze. He wanted to close them, but was afraid to wake her. Instead, he went to sit on her veranda steps and listened to the night sounds and his daughter's soft mewling in her sleep.

He thought he heard Genba's step at one point. A little later, there were the sibilant sounds of a whispered exchange. Who was he talking to?

The whispering troubled him enough to get up and check. He found nothing and returned to Seimei. After a while, Genba emerged from the darkness like a large shadow.

'Nothing so far, sir,' he muttered, sitting down.

'Did you talk to someone just now?' Akitada asked.

'No. You said "no talking".' Genba sounded astonished.

'I thought I heard whispering.'

Genba got to his feet again. 'Where? I'll go have a look.'

'No, you rest. I've already checked. I must have imagined it.'

Akitada started his second round. He trod the familiar paths of his garden and listened for unusual sounds, but heard nothing. The same silence prevailed in the front courtyard and behind the stable. Only the restless moving of the horses could be heard. Akitada climbed the ladder and raised his face above the roof edge. Tora crouched near the ridge, his head lifted slightly. When he recognized Akitada, he shifted closer.

'All's quiet, sir,' he hissed.

'Good.' Akitada climbed back down and resumed his circuit. He hoped Tora did not think he was checking up on him. A moment later, he passed behind Tora's house and thought he smelled burning again. But the odor was very faint; probably a remnant of last night's cooking fire.

Near Tamako's pavilion he heard a rustling in the shrubbery and seized his sword, but it turned out to be the neighbor's cat. He chased it to the wall and saw it momentarily outlined against the faintly lighter sky before it dropped down. Suddenly, the night seemed full of unfamiliar noises. He peered up to the top of the wall again. There was a slight reddish tinge in the sky towards the west. He decided to climb up to Tora's rooftop again to get a better view of the city.

But as he retraced his steps, Tora's warning shout came, and a moment later Seimei's gong sounded. He broke into a run and heard another cry – this time from behind him, from Tamako's pavilion.

A woman's scream.

Seized with terror, he turned back, flew up the steps to the veranda, and burst into Tamako's room, cursing the fact that he had not made sure her doors were locked. It was pitch dark. The baby whimpered and someone sobbed. Tamako? A paler shape moved in the room.

A young male voice, filled with hate, said, 'Don't come any closer or they die.'

Akitada froze. He still could not see, but the baby's whimper turned into a wail, and Tamako's anguished crying filled the darkness. He was seized with a helpless rage. He heard sounds of struggle and the man's curse and moved towards them, afraid that his action was all wrong, that it was exactly what their attacker had expected and would repay with death, but there was no alternative. Death had always been part of the plan.

He held the sword close to his body for fear of hurting his wife or child. Groping forward with his free hand, he touched Tamako's silky hair (a deeper darkness against her pale under-gown) and grasped her shoulder to pull her away and to the side. She cried out, 'He has Yasuko.'

The dark shape of their attacker moved farther away. 'Yeah, I've got the kid – so stay away, dog official.'

Yasuko's crying became a heart-wrenching bawling at the top of her small lungs.

'Light a lamp,' Akitada called out to Tamako. Then, forcing himself to speak calmly, he said, 'Don't hurt her. She's only just been born. Who are you?'

'None of your business.'

Behind Akitada, light sprang up. He saw a skinny youth in a bright red jacket, his back against the wall, a knife in one hand, and the bawling child pressed against his chest with the other.

'No closer,' he hissed and put the knife's point against the baby's neck.

Tamako pleaded, 'Please, please, please . . .'

Akitada clenched the sword to his side. 'You're Takeo,' he said, still trying to keep his voice steady. 'What do you want?'

When he heard his name, surprise flickered in the other's eyes. 'I want the bastard that got my family arrested.'

'Your family tried to kill me.'

'I thought it was you. You know what they do to them in jail? I know. They beat you until your blood soaks through your clothes and you lose consciousness. Then they let the flies and ants feed on you.'

Yasuko squirmed and bellowed. Akitada kept his eyes on her. *Dear heaven, don't let her be injured.* 'Better than drowning a man in a pit,' he said.

Takeo flared up, 'They didn't know that. They would've let you go after a bit – only, by then the police were all over the place.' He glanced over at Tamako, who was kneeling on the floor, her hands raised towards the baby. 'You took my family, and now I'll take yours . . . and you get to watch.' With a cruel smile, he looked down at the squirming child in his arms.

Akitada saw the knuckles of the hand that held the knife whiten. 'Wait,' he cried. 'Your quarrel is with me. Let them go.'

Takeo nodded at Akitada's sword. 'You think I'm stupid? A knife against a sword? You nobles are all alike. You think we're nothing. You think we have no brains or courage or fighting skill.'

'Then show me your courage. I'll throw away my sword and take you and your knife on bare-handed, and I'll still win,' Akitada boasted.

The youth hesitated. Akitada saw the temptation in his eyes

and held his breath. Except for the baby's hiccuping whimpers, the room had gone still.

Takeo measured him. 'Throw it out into the garden.'

'First you let them go.'

'No.'

Tamako got to her feet and took the few steps to Takeo, her hands outstretched for her child.

Akitada walked to the door of the pavilion. 'Well?' he asked. 'Are you an honorable man?'

Takeo sneered, 'Are you?'

There was nothing to be gained by arguing any longer. Akitada flung the sword away as far as he could. At the same moment, Tamako snatched the baby and rushed to him. He stepped aside to let her pass, and she ran into the garden.

They were alone now, he and the youth with the wicked-looking blade. Akitada moved to block the doorway and saw Takeo's face. Yes, he had just been tricked. Letting Tamako escape meant that she would give the alarm. He would have to be quick.

The cries of 'fire' and the sound of the gong still sounded in the distance. He heard the frightened sounds of horses. Tora and Genba had their hands full fighting the fire.

Takeo came with a shout, the hand with the knife raised, his eyes on Akitada's throat.

Akitada could not move aside. His family was in the garden. He had no choice but to meet his attacker and knock the knife aside.

But the youth was agile and ready for the maneuver. He danced sideways, lowering the knife. When he came again, he slashed upward towards Akitada's belly. Akitada reacted almost too late. As it was, the knife cut neatly through his sash. It dropped to the floor, and his robe swung open in front, hampering his movements. But it also gave him an idea. He pivoted, swinging the robe wide and forcing Takeo back. Akitada now had enough space to slip the robe off and use it like a whip to lash out at his foe.

Takeo laughed at this move and skipped nimbly aside. When he rushed him again, Akitada caught the slashing blade in the folds of his robe. A swift kick and a jerk of the robe, and Takeo sprawled disarmed on the floorboards.

As Akitada snatched up the knife, a woman's voice shouted outside. His heart skipped. He turned to look, saw a reddish glow of flames from the stable roof, and had his feet pulled from under him.

The back of Akitada's head hit the floor and the world turned black. He felt Takeo's weight on his chest and his hands on his throat. He could not breathe. Struggling for air, he bucked and rolled, found the knife still in his hand and shoved it hard into his attacker.

The hands around his throat went slack. Akitada pushed Takeo off. They got to their feet together, Akitada coughing and Takeo bent over with both hands pressed against his belly, his face pale in the flickering fire light. Dazed, Akitada looked at the bloody blade in his hand and then back at the youth. Takeo had not moved, but now his knees slowly buckled. The expression on his face changed to surprise. On his knees, he vomited a stream of blood. He tried to stagger up again, but fell and rolled, his body going into spasms. He vomited again – a great fountain of blood all over Tamako's polished floor – and then lay still.

Akitada paused only to make sure he was dead, then ran outside, shouting, 'Tamako?'

'Here.' She came from underneath the veranda, holding the child. Her eyes were anxious. 'Are you hurt?'

'No.' She had stayed close, he thought, when every instinct should have driven her away. The baby was quiet now, and a new fear seized him. 'The child?'

'She was only frightened.'

He suddenly felt like laughing out. 'So was I,' he said and took them both tenderly in his arms.

For a moment, Tamako allowed it, then she said, 'Akitada, the fire. Hanae and Yuki.'

He released her and took her hand. 'I'm sure they're fine. Come. I cannot leave you here.' He looked around and found his sword, and they walked together towards the fire.

Tora's house and the stables were fully aflame. In the fire-light and smoke, shadows moved eerily about the buildings.

'The horses,' Tamako moaned.

'Genba will have got them out,' Akitada said and hoped he was right.

At that moment, a figure rushed at him. They collided, gasping, and moved apart. In the red light of the flames, Akitada saw the youth Tojiro with a cudgel in his hand. He pushed Tamako behind him and raised his sword.

ANOTHER CONFESSION

'Don't, sir,' Tojiro gasped, stepping back. 'I tried to help.'

Akitada said, 'With a cudgel in your hand?'

Tojiro looked at his hand and flung the cudgel into the shrubbery. 'I was afraid the others would try to make trouble.'

'Trouble?' It was a ridiculous word to use in view of the murderous attack by Takeo and within sight of the hissing flames that the gang had set. Akitada took a step forward and held out his left hand. 'Take off your belt.'

Tojiro looked puzzled for a moment, then saw Akitada's belt-less robe and undid his own, holding it out to Akitada. 'Please make use of it, sir.'

Akitada took it. 'Turn around and put your hands behind your back.'

'Why? What are you going to do? I swear I didn't mean any harm. I came to help and— Didn't you get my note?'

Akitada raised the point of his sword towards the youth's neck. 'Turn!'

Tojiro obeyed. Akitada passed his sword to Tamako and used the belt to tie Tojiro's hands. 'You'll be handed over to the police,' he said. 'I'm thoroughly fed up with your antics.'

When Tojiro turned around, there were tears in his eyes. He said softly, 'Yes, sir. I expected it. But I didn't come to set a fire. I came to tell you that it was I who killed my father.'

For a moment Akitada doubted he had heard right. Another confession? And why would this youth confess to murder, but not to setting fires?

There was no time to consider the implications now. He took back his sword from Tamako, then grasped Tojiro's arm roughly and pulled him along towards the courtyard. He had no idea what he would find there and was prepared to shed more blood if any of their attackers remained.

But peace had returned, even if order was still elusive. Red-coated policemen and neighbors' servants who had come to help put the fire out milled about. Akitada's two horses were tied up to the well.

Seimei saw them first and came to meet them. 'Are you all right, sir? And My Lady and the little one?' he asked anxiously with a glance at the bound Tojiro. 'Did he attack you?'

'We're unhurt. I caught this one on the way here. The other one is dead. He attacked my wife and child.'

Seimei and Tojiro gasped. Seimei said, 'It is a miracle everyone escaped. What monsters the young have turned into.' He glared at Tojiro with such disgust that the young man paled.

Tamako asked, 'Is everyone else safe? Hanae and Yuki?'

'Yes. Well, Trouble got singed pretty badly when he bit one of the gang and was beaten back with a burning torch. Hanae is in the main house with Yuki, tending to the dog's wounds. I'm afraid the stable and Tora's place are a total loss.'

'Poor Trouble,' said Akitada. 'What a very brave dog he is. Where is Tora?'

'At his place, looking to see if he can salvage anything.'

Genba joined them, his face a picture in red and black. He was covered with soot and sweat. 'What happened to you, sir? We were worried. The police finally showed up. After it was all over and we'd driven the bastards away and nearly put out the fire.'

Akitada glanced at the smoking ruins of the stables. 'Never mind, Genba. We're alive. Take this fellow to the kitchen, tie him up, and lock him in.' Turning to Tamako, he said, 'You and Seimei better stay in the main house.' He called a couple of the constables and asked them to guard his family.

Then he went to inspect the damage. The stables were gone, along with saddles and feed for the horses. He found Tora on the pile of smoking rubble that had been his quarters. He was kicking charred and smoking timbers aside.

'I'm very sorry, Tora,' Akitada called up to him. 'We will rebuild it. Better than it was. I'm glad you're safe.'

Tora swung around. He was black with soot. 'What about My Lady and the little one?'

'They're well, the gods be thanked.' It had been a disastrous night, but at that moment Akitada felt again a relief so great that he seemed to float. 'Come and leave that for later. We are safe, and that is all that matters. We need a cup of wine and something to eat.'

Tora climbed down reluctantly. 'I had about ten pieces of gold saved up,' he said gloomily. 'First I get robbed, and now this.'

'Never mind. I caught Tojiro a moment ago. And I had to kill Takeo.'

Tora brightened. 'Well done! Looks like you got all the excitement. Takeo was a piece of garbage, and Tojiro's not much better.'

They were crossing the courtyard on their way to the main house when Kobe arrived.

The superintendent paused to shake his head at the devastation, then came quickly to Akitada. 'I didn't get your message until a few hours ago,' he said.

Akitada saw that Kobe looked exhausted and still wore the same clothes. 'You haven't been to bed since I saw you last?'

'No. More unrest in the city, and then an attack on the western jail. Koichi's friends decided to spring him by setting fire to the jail.'

'That must be what I smelled earlier, before the fire here. Did anyone get hurt?'

'Three prisoners died. They were shackled.' Kobe's face was bleak. 'It was terrible, the screaming. I wish I'd retired to my farm last year. What about your family?'

'We're safe now, but I had to kill a youth, and another is tied up in my kitchen.'

Kobe's lips quirked in the briefest of smiles. 'You've been busy yourself. Let's have a look.'

They stopped first at Tamako's pavilion. When Kobe saw the dead youth and Akitada showed him the knife he had held to the baby's neck, Kobe sucked in his breath sharply. Then he examined the body.

'But he died from a knife thrust into his side,' he said. 'Didn't you have your sword?'

'I did, but I told him that I would fight him barehanded.' Akitada realized that this sounded like bragging and flushed. 'It was the only way he would relinquish my daughter. I was lucky that he was young and naive,' he added.

Kobe stared at him. 'It sounds horrible. Let's see the live one.'

Genba unlocked the door to the small kitchen building. As they walked in, they saw Tojiro trussed up against one of the beams that supported the roof. He looked defeated.

Akitada had promised Fuhito time to arrange his affairs, but Tojiro had changed all that, including the way Akitada felt about his grandfather's confession. He was convinced now that Fuhito had tried to protect his grandson. Much would depend on Tojiro's explanations.

Kobe stood over the boy with a frown. 'You're the one they call Tojiro?'

Tojiro looked up at him. 'Yes.'

'How old are you?'

'Sixteen.'

Akitada was taken aback. Given the boy's lifestyle, he had thought the youth to be at least seventeen, if not older. But he was tall and very handsome under all that dirt. No wonder Koichi's daughter had fallen for him.

Kobe asked, 'Parents?'

Tojiro hesitated and glanced at Akitada. Then he lifted his chin. 'My father was Kiyowara Kane. I killed him. My mother is also dead. She was one of his wives.'

Kobe's jaw sagged. 'What? Don't tell outrageous lies. You won't like the taste of the bamboo whip, my boy.'

Akitada said quickly, 'He's telling the truth. He is Kiyowara's oldest son by a secondary wife.'

Kobe was shocked. 'You mean the Kiyowara heir is this one's younger brother? Where did he come from all of a sudden?'

Akitada hedged. 'I think the story is a little complicated. The point at the moment is that he has just confessed to the murder. I haven't had time to get details yet, but his grandfather is the Kiyowaras' major-domo, Fuhito. He also confessed to the crime.'

Kobe gave Akitada a long look, but said nothing. He turned back to Tojiro. 'Is that true? Did you kill Lord Kiyowara?'

The boy's chin came up again. 'Yes.'

'Why?'

'He wouldn't acknowledge me. He was hateful and said things about my mother. I hit him and he fell. He hit his head on the desk, I think. I saw blood and saw that he was dead and I was glad.' Tojiro spoke quickly, with a passionate sincerity. His eyes shone with pride.

Kobe turned back to Akitada. 'Can this be? Why did none of the servants report seeing him?'

'He looks very much like his brother. I think they saw him, but took him for Katsumi.'

A brief smile passed over Tojiro's face. 'I got on Katsumi's horse and galloped out of the gate. Nobody paid attention.'

Akitada was not at all sure what to make of this boy. 'Did you by any chance run away from Seikan-ji?'

Tojiro flushed. 'How did you know?'

'The abbot is looking for you.'

'Well, he'll have to manage without him,' Kobe snapped. Drawing Akitada back outside, he said angrily, 'I must say, you should have informed me of all this before.'

Akitada felt guilty. 'I intended to, but I've only just realized what happened. Someone delivered a threat here – at least I took it for a threat. Tojiro claims he was warning me – and I postponed reporting to you in order to look after my family. Fuhito confessed late yesterday.'

Kobe mellowed a little. 'I see. I was fairly busy myself then. Which one of them did it, do you think?'

'I would bet the grandfather lied to protect the grandson. He loves the boy and feels guilty for what happened to him.'

'Very well, we'll sort it out later. The boy will be taken to the eastern jail, and I'll have my men remove the body from your lady's pavilion. Then I have to leave. I wish I could offer help with the clean-up, but we're stretched very thin.'

'I understand.' Akitada glanced back over his shoulder towards the kitchen building. 'You know, I feel there is something not quite right about Tojiro's confession. I'd like to pay another visit to the Kiyowaras if you will permit it.'

Kobe thought a moment, then nodded. 'By all means make sure. And collect your fee for clearing them of suspicion while you're at it.'

A WOMAN'S HONOR

A kitada stayed only long enough to see his family settled and hire laborers to remove the charred timbers and rebuild the stables and Tora's small house. The simplicity of their construction and the tips he promised set them to working with speed and enthusiasm.

He changed out of his dirty clothes, bathed, and set off for the Kiyowara mansion in his second-best robe.

Servants, still in mourning, received him. Fuhito was absent.

A sense of unease and subdued excitement filled the air. Akitada asked to speak to Lady Kiyowara and her son.

He waited in the same waiting room as the last time. Outside, the day was pleasant. The rain had taken away the dry heat that had oppressed the city for so long. The Kiyowara gardens were green and fresh in the sun, and the water in the little rill ran high and clear over the large round stones.

Akitada was not happy with the outcome of the case. Not only did he not like to see Fuhito and his family suffer further at the hands of arrogant aristocrats like the Kiyowaras, but he was also dissatisfied with both confessions. Fuhito had been too adamant that Tojiro was completely innocent, and Tojiro had confessed much too readily to the killing. In addition, the boy's description of how he had murdered his father had not rung true. It was as if both were trying to protect the other. Fuhito was quite likely to sacrifice himself for his grandson. Akitada did not know Tojiro very well, but from what he had seen, the youngster had shown both courage and principles. The truth was, he hoped to find that someone else had killed Kiyowara.

His wait was shorter than he had expected. A servant came and took him to the reception room. Lady Kiyowara was with her son, but this time her cousin, Lady Aoi, attended her. This audience was markedly more casual than the last one and differed also in the fact that the young lord now had the seat of honor. His mother sat to his side, and Lady Aoi – still in her beads and amulets and with her hair disheveled – sat farther back.

Akitada bowed to young Katsumi, who seemed to be trying valiantly to appear manly and self-assured, but would not meet Akitada's eyes. When Akitada had also bowed to his mother, he said, 'There have been certain developments. Someone has confessed to Lord Kiyowara's murder. I have come to make my final report.'

The young lord glanced nervously at his mother. She said, 'That is most satisfactory,' and clapped her hands for a servant. A sense of relief was almost palpable in the room. A middle-aged man appeared, and she instructed him to bring a money box from her room. Then she told Akitada, 'I speak for my son and myself when I say that we are grateful to you. I have sent for the rest of your fee. Please proceed with your report.'

Akitada had become uncomfortably aware of Lady Aoi's piercing stare. Unlike the Kiyowaras, she reminded him of a coiled snake. She seemed to be shouting at him, *Don't!* He tried to ignore this and began.

'From the beginning, it was clear that the murderer or his accomplice belonged to his household.' Lady Kiyowara frowned, and Akitada said quickly, 'I'm sorry, My Lady. It was simply impossible for any outsiders to have entered the property in the middle of the day unnoticed by the servants. There was one exception to this, but for the time being, let us eliminate any and all political enemies of the late lord. It is true that Prince Atsunori, the Minister of Central Affairs, stopped by, but he cannot be considered either an enemy or someone who would dirty his fingers with murder.'

Lady Kiyowara started to object, but the servant returned with a small box, identical to the first one Akitada had received. She dismissed him, then said, 'Go on.'

'Allow me first to tell you a story from the past.' Akitada spoke of Fuhito and his young daughter, of the birth of the young woman's son, and of Lord Kiyowara's promise to acknowledge the boy. He watched their faces as he spoke. He had expected outrage and denial, but there was none. He found it especially interesting that young Katsumi did not seem in the least surprised.

Lady Kiyowara looked down at her hands and said bitterly, 'It is no secret that my husband had many women. He may also have many children. What is that to us now?'

The young lord shot her a glance and moved uncomfortably.

Akitada said, 'It is important because it is Fuhito who confessed to your husband's murder. He claims that the broken promise to acknowledge his grandson is why he killed your husband.'

Lady Aoi sucked in her breath at the news of Fuhito's confession, but her cousin only sighed. 'Poor man. I do not blame him. I am sure he was dreadfully provoked.'

'I am not done, My Lady, for only a few hours ago, his grandson Tojiro, your son's half-brother, also confessed to the murder.'

Lady Aoi moved abruptly. Her beads and bangles made a harsh, dry sound. Lady Kiyowara turned and said, 'There is no need for you to stay, cousin.'

Lady Aoi did not answer. She only shook her head, her eyes burning into Akitada's with a fierce intensity.

Lady Kiyowara turned back. 'Well, no doubt the police will

straighten it all out,' she said, pushing the money box towards Akitada. 'In any case, that finishes our arrangement. Please accept this in appreciation of your work.'

At this point, the young lord exploded. 'No. We're *not* finished, sir. I will not allow you to blame my brother. It was not his fault. My mother has paid you to shift the guilt on him. Well, I'll pay you twice that amount to clear his name.'

'Katsumi,' cried his mother, 'watch your words. It is not wise to be associated with your father's killers.'

Akitada admired the boy for his speech, so he only said mildly, 'I neither shift guilt on an innocent man nor clear a guilty one.'

The youth glared. 'Then you may as well arrest me too, for I helped him.'

His mother snapped, 'Nonsense, my son was nowhere near my husband the afternoon he died. Katsumi had gone out to exercise his horse.'

Katsumi ignored her. 'I've known my brother for months. He spoke to me one day and told me who he was. I knew it was true because we look alike. After that, we used to meet often when I went out riding. I taught him how to ride my horse. The day of my father's death, I let him in through the back gate. It was I who encouraged him to speak to my father, and I also let him take my horse to escape.'

Lady Aoi started swaying back and forth and muttering, 'Oh, no . . . Oh, no . . . Oh, no.' They all looked at her. She paid no attention and fell to reciting prayers.

Lady Kiyowara was very pale and at a loss for words. Her fan had fallen into her lap. She shook her head in disbelief.

Katsumi faced Akitada with the same defiant sincerity Tojiro had shown when he had confessed. 'Well? What will you do?' he demanded.

Akitada sighed. 'You will have to speak to the police, of course, My Lord. It does you honor that you are standing by your brother. I think he, too, is a young man of principle and courage. It is a pity that the father of two such young men should have been their very opposite.'

Lady Aoi suddenly rose, towering over them like a vengeful deity. 'Not only men have principle and courage, Lord Sugawara,' she said, her deep voice vibrating with passion. 'We women have had to bear the violence of men and their ruthless rape of our bodies. We have borne their ill-begotten children and raised them while their fathers took other women. And yet we have been patient and hoped that our sons would not turn out to be the monsters their fathers were. We, too, have honor.'

Akitada sat transfixed. Here, finally, was the truth. He hardly dared breathe. He had suspected something of the sort all along, though not necessarily of this odd and wild creature. And yet, he thought, who more likely? She was a woman of rank, an astonishing and exotic beauty in spite of her eccentric appearance and her tall stature and deep voice – or perhaps because of them.

Lady Kiyowara looked terrified. She pleaded, 'Oh, Aoi! Don't.'

Aoi ignored her. Her eyes did not leave Akitada's. 'Kiyowara's sons may be males, but I will not let them take the blame for this,' she said. 'You, Lord Sugawara, were wrong from the start. I came to your house and told you so, but you would not listen. That boy and his grandfather are innocent, because I killed Kiyowara.'

There was a pause. Strangely, no one contradicted Lady Aoi. The young lord had turned to watch her, but Lady Kiyowara sat silent, hanging her head.

Lady Aoi went on: 'I paid my cousin a visit, and on the second night her husband came to my room and defiled me, a shrine virgin. A man would not hesitate to avenge such a dishonor, but I am a woman and he was my cousin's husband. Still, I went to speak to the monster when I saw the boy leaving his room in a panic. I took up one of the large stones from the garden stream to defend myself and entered Kiyowara's study. He was getting to his feet, holding his head. When I charged him with the rape, he laughed and taunted me, saying that I had liked it and come for more. That's when I raised the stone and struck him. The fool did not think a woman would have the courage or the strength to attack him, so he did little to defend himself, and I kept striking to make sure he was dead. So there you have the truth. I am proud that I did what hundreds of women before me should have done to spare others after them.'

Akitada believed her. He said, 'Lord Kiyowara committed a very serious offense against you and the gods you serve. I admit it did not occur to me that he would rape a woman of your sacred calling under his own roof.'

Lady Kiyowara said bitterly, 'My husband enjoyed rape. Normal relations were not to his taste. He wanted women who resisted him. I grew afraid of bringing good-looking young women into my service, but I, too, had thought he would respect a shrine virgin.'

Lady Aoi, suddenly quite calm, sat back down. 'I don't care what happens to me. It was my karma to kill an evil man.'

'Nothing will happen to you,' her cousin cried. 'The regent won't permit you to be punished when he hears the story. He will regret having given my husband his wealth and power.'

'I hope so,' said Akitada.

If ever a man had needed killing, it was Kiyowara.

THE RUNAWAY

From the Kiyowara residence, Akitada walked to police head-quarters, where he hoped he might still find Kobe. There was no particular rush, since with Lady Aoi there was no fear of flight or other aggression, but he wanted to see if he could get Tojiro released.

Kobe was in, eyes bloodshot and puffy and hands shaking with fatigue.

'You need sleep,' said Akitada, who wasn't exactly feeling rested himself.

Kobe ran a hand over his face as if he meant to wipe away the signs of exhaustion. 'I intend to go home shortly. That is, unless you bring more work.'

Akitada smiled. 'I hope not. Or rather, it won't be pressing. I bring you a third confession.'

Kobe threw up his hands. 'Why is everybody so eager to take credit for Kiyowara's death?'

'His conduct made many enemies. If the oppressed are system-atically tormented by the strong, they take pride in their revenge.'

Kobe sighed. 'I was joking. Who is it this time?'

'Lady Aoi, Lady Kiyowara's cousin.'

'The shrine virgin? But why would she make such a claim? Never mind. She's said to be slightly mad. Surely you did not believe her?'

'She is far from mad, and I do believe her. Kiyowara raped her the night before she killed him. A woman like Lady Aoi does not allow her honor to be defiled without avenging herself. She spoke up when she heard of Tojiro's confession. She saw him leaving Kiyowara's study and found Kiyowara inside, just getting up from where he had fallen. It seems he only cut the back of his head when Tojiro pushed or hit him. She confronted him with the rape, and Kiyowara taunted her. She says she used a stone from the garden to hit him and that she continued to hit him until he was dead. How does that fit with your coroner's opinion?'

Kobe nodded slowly. 'It fits. It fits exactly. He had a minor wound to the back of the head, which was little more than a cut. It bled. Then there were larger, rounded wounds to the front: to his forehead, face, and temple. Some of those bled also. The wounds to the front of his head, according to the doctor, killed him.' He fell into abstracted thought. 'This is difficult,' he muttered. 'We cannot arrest her. As a shrine virgin, she is under the emperor's authority.'

'Well, perhaps you could claim that Kiyowara fell and injured himself. That is at least partially true.'

Kobe frowned. 'I shall have to report the truth and leave the decision up to His Majesty.'

'Well, then. Can we let Tojiro go?'

Kobe raised his brows. 'What about the fire setting?'

'I've begun to have some doubts about that also. What does he say?'

'He confirmed that the boys worked for Watanabe, but that was all.' Kobe got to his feet with a groan. 'Come, let's go see him now.'

Akitada hesitated. 'It can wait.'

'I won't sleep until this whole business is unraveled.'

They walked across to the jail. At the gate, they found Fuhito peering inside as if his gaze could bring forth his grandson. He was leaning against a pillar and looked terrible. His face was tear-streaked.

Akitada stopped. 'Major-domo? What are you doing here?'

Fuhito started. 'Oh. It's you, sir. They've arrested Tojiro and won't let me see him. I told them that it was I who killed Lord Kiyowara. Please, sir, would you see what you can do?'

Kobe said irritably, 'It would be helpful if both of you stayed with the truth. Your lie won't help your grandson.'

Fuhito looked at him, taking in the uniform and the rank

insignia. He bowed. 'Begging your pardon, sir, but my grandson is innocent. The fault is mine alone.'

'Nonsense. Both of you lied to protect the other. Neither you nor your grandson killed Kiyowara.'

Fuhito turned absolutely white. His knees buckled, and he sat down abruptly in the dirt. Akitada bent to help him up and found that the old man trembled violently.

'Is it true?' he asked, clutching at Akitada's hands. 'It is not a trick?'

'It's not a trick.'

Fuhito staggered up. 'But who? And how?'

Kobe looked at Akitada and shook his head slightly.

Akitada said, 'When Tojiro struck his father, he fell and hit his head. He was unconscious, and the boy panicked. I think, later, your grandson decided that you must have gone to finish the job. Both of you thought the other was the murderer.'

'I believed him.' Fuhito ran a trembling hand over his face, wiping away the tears. 'And I found the body.'

'Someone else went in to speak to Lord Kiyowara after Tojiro left.'

Fuhito frowned. 'But—' He stopped when he saw Kobe's face.

Akitada said, 'I think you'd better tell him.'

Kobe glowered at Fuhito. 'If you tell anyone, I'll have you and your grandson thrown in jail for lying.'

Fuhito raised both hands. 'I don't want to know, sir.'

Akitada said, 'You will have to know or you'll think a terrible injustice was done. Lady Aoi confessed to killing Lord Kiyowara because he raped her.'

Fuhito's hands still shook a little and he tucked them under his arms. 'Oh,' he said. 'Oh, I see.' He shook his head. 'Terrible. What will happen to Tojiro?'

Kobe said, 'There is still the matter of your grandson setting fires. We were about to ask him about that. You can come along.'

A guard unlocked Tojiro's cell. They found him sitting with his elbows on his knees on some old straw mats. Nearby stood a slop bucket. The boy was chained to the wall.

When he saw them, and his grandfather with them, he got to his feet. 'I'm sorry for what I've done, Grandfather,' he said quickly. 'Please do not concern yourself.'

Fuhito sobbed as he went to take the boy in his arms. 'Hush, Tojiro,' he said. 'You did not kill your father. And neither did I.'

Tojiro looked astonished and checked with Akitada and Kobe. Akitada nodded, but Kobe said, 'You have been cleared of the murder charge, but there are many other things still to be explained.' He glanced at the stinking slop bucket. 'In my office. Guard, take his chains off.'

They gathered in Kobe's office, along with a clerk to take notes. Fuhito could not stop weeping, but he did so silently, wiping his face surreptitiously with his sleeve.

Kobe began the questioning. 'What is your true name?'

'Kiyowara Tojiro.'

Akitada produced the amulet in its silk bag and tossed it to Tojiro. 'This is yours. Given to you by Abbot Shokan. What happened to your religious name?'

Tojiro flushed. He did not touch the amulet. 'I took back my own name. I'm not cut out to be a monk.'

Kobe snapped, 'That's pretty obvious, considering you went straight from the monastery to a life of crime.'

Tojiro shook his head. 'I never committed a crime.'

'What about the people you associated with? Koichi and his family are involved in the protection racket. And those youths you ran around with did worse than that. They have tortured and killed people.'

Tojiro shot his grandfather an uneasy glance. 'Seiji and Ako gave me a place to stay after I ran away. And Koichi and Haru were good to me. I didn't know at first that Takeo was . . . Well, that he could be violent and that he was a thief. Koichi only collects payment for services. That's no crime.'

Kobe snorted. 'What happens when a client doesn't pay?'

Tojiro said uncertainly, 'Nothing. He doesn't get protection.'

'And then he finds out just how badly he needs it, right?'

Tojiro looked away. 'It wasn't Koichi who set the fires. That was Takeo. Koichi punished him when he found out, and Takeo left home. Koichi was very angry.' He paused. 'After Takeo left, Koichi asked me to find out what he was up to.'

Kobe expressed his disbelief with another snort of derision.

Akitada asked, 'Was it on one of those occasions that you ran into Tora and robbed him?'

Fuhito sucked in his breath sharply. 'Tojiro?' he asked. 'Did you do that?'

Tojiro cried, 'No, Grandfather. It wasn't like that. I'd been following Takeo and his friends. I saw them set that fire, and they saw me. I didn't want them to catch me. That's when I ran into someone and we both fell down. I was picking up his coins to give them back, but he grabbed me before I could do so. Then the others came and I ran.'

Fuhito growled, 'What happened to the coins?'

Tojiro looked down at his clenched hands. 'They caught me on the next street and took the money away from me. I let them think that I'd been stealing so they'd believe I'd become one of them.' He looked up at Akitada. 'I'll return the money. All of it. Tell your man I'll find work and pay it all back.'

Fuhito pleaded, 'He's not a bad boy. He's just fallen into bad company, and that is my fault. Could you accept his promise and mine that the money will be returned?'

Akitada nodded. 'But that doesn't clear him in the matter of the arson.'

Tojiro cried, 'I told you. I was only watching them. Koichi was worried about Takeo.'

Kobe pursed his lips. 'As your grandfather said, you kept bad company. Why should we believe you? Running away from a monastery is one thing, but most boys would go home to their parents and not join a gang of criminals.'

Fuhito covered his face. 'I abandoned him,' he sobbed. 'I told him I would not take him back, that he had to return to Seikan-ji and be a man. That his future depended on it.'

Kobe greeted that with a doubtful, 'Hmmm.'

Akitada asked, 'Why could you not stay at Seikan-ji as your grandfather had asked you to? You were treated well and got a good education, didn't you?'

Tojiro glanced at his weeping grandfather, then at Akitada. 'You wouldn't understand,' he said dully. 'I had to get away. I cannot be a monk. Nobody liked me. Every day they told me I must prepare myself to give up the world, that the world is nothing-ness and corruption and misery. But I knew better.'

Akitada suppressed a smile. When he was Tojiro's age he, too, had run away. He had run from an authoritarian father and a cold and hostile mother to find affection elsewhere. He said, 'Abbot Shokan expressed a great fondness for you,' letting Tojiro interpret his words.

Tojiro moved his shoulders uncomfortably. 'He was all right,' he conceded. 'Only, that made everyone else hate me the more.'

Akitada and Kobe made eye contact. Akitada willed the

superintendent to be generous, and after a moment, Kobe said, 'Will you help us bring the guilty to justice?'

Fear flashed in Tojiro's eyes. 'I'll give you the names of Takeo and his friends, but I'm not getting Koichi and Haru in trouble.'

'Takeo is dead, and we already have Koichi and his daughter. We need the other boys.'

Tojiro jumped up. 'You've arrested Koichi and Haru? They haven't done anything. I told you. Koichi only collects fees for a man who's served in the eastern armies. His name is Sergeant Umako. Sergeant Umako keeps small merchants safe from criminals, and they pay him a small fee every month. Besides, he and Haru own the Fragrant Peach in the western city. It's Takeo who's been trouble, not his family.'

Akitada and Kobe exchanged looks again. Kobe smiled. 'Koichi and his two deaf mute friends work an illegal racket. If those merchants don't pay their fees, someone burns down their houses.'

'No. You're wrong.' Tojiro clenched his hands and looked from one to the other. 'I know better. They're not criminals. I told you I've been staying with Seiji and Ako. Ako's married to Seiji.'

Fuhito sighed deeply. 'Because I told my grandson that I would not take him back the next time he ran away, he went to my daughter's former maid, Ako. I did not know she was married.'

Tojiro said, 'They were kind to me. You just don't know how hard it is for people like them. They're good people.'

'Hmmm,' muttered Kobe, looking from the distraught boy to his distraught grandfather. 'Whatever they are, I think we'll turn you over to your grandfather for the time being. Just don't run away again or I'll see to it that you go to trial.'

Fuhito threw himself on his knees before Kobe. 'You may take my life if Tojiro escapes or does any mischief whatsoever. Tojiro, show your gratitude!'

Tojiro, looking a little confused, knelt and bowed.

Akitada cleared his throat. 'Good, that settles that. Can I rely on your visiting the abbot together to explain the situation and apologize?'

Tojiro nodded, and Fuhito said, 'Yes, of course. It is all my fault anyway. I am very sorry that His Reverence has been troubled.'

Akitada thought of Fuhito's old mother, and of the empty house in its beautiful garden. Three lives had been salvaged. Of course, their future was by no means clear. But there was hope that the friendship between the two sons of the late Kiyowara might bridge the gulf their father had created, and perhaps the new lord would make use of Fuhito's learning and help his brother rise in the world.

EPILOGUE

Towards the end of the summer, the political disarray that had begun when Michinaga relinquished his powers to his sons finally sorted itself out, but none of that affected Akitada. In the general amnesty in honor of Michinaga's service to the nation, Koichi and the others were freed.

Lord Kiyowara's death was officially due to a fall. Of all the news that circulated, only one rumor was of interest: Lady Kiyowara's cousin Aoi had asked for imperial permission to resign her shrine duties and return to her family, and this had been granted.

One day, not long after Koichi and his daughter had been freed, Kobe sent Akitada a note that the police had found the rice merchant Watanabe hanging from one of the rafters and his wife dead from strangulation. Watanabe had left a letter explaining that he was taking this way out for himself and his wife because he could not face the shame of his actions. He claimed that some of the fires had been set on his orders because certain merchants owed him money or had in some other way offended him, but that the youths soon discovered the fires caused enough distraction to allow them to steal money and valuables from empty houses.

On the surface, this sounded believable, but Akitada would always believe that a high-ranking nobleman had ordered the fires to influence the succession. It would have been easy enough to force Watanabe's suicide before he could talk to the police.

Justice is frequently elusive.

Akitada concentrated on his own problems. Crews were clearing away the construction debris around his new stables. Reconstruction had been speedy, thanks to Lady Kiyowara's final payment. The small house belonging to Tora and his family was already finished, and Hanae was busy moving in new household goods and furnishings.

Tamako's pavilion had been cleaned, and thick new mats covered the floor where Takeo had died. Fortunately, Akitada's wife was not given to imaginary terrors and had moved back in with baby Yasuko and her maid.

Into this satisfactory state of affairs rode the censor Minamoto Akimoto with a small retinue of uniformed imperial guards. The workers dropped their tools and gaped. An excited Trouble chased, barking, around the horses, causing half of them to shy. It was a while before the dog was caught and Akitada could properly welcome the old warrior.

He did so with fear in his heart. He had been lulled into a sense of security even though the censors were not done with him.

Still, Akimoto was smiling, so perhaps the news was not all bad.

Akitada took him to his study, where Seimei was working on the accounts. Seimei excused himself, and Akimoto looked around at all the books generations of Sugawaras had accumulated. He said, 'You must be a remarkably learned man. It grieves me all the more that you should have been treated so shabbily.'

Perhaps this was just a kindness before giving bad news. Akitada said, 'Bookishness does not compare with military service, Lord Akimoto. The nation is deeply indebted to men like you. I merely shuffle papers.'

Akimoto cocked his head. 'You do yourself a disservice. I have read the documents describing your service very carefully, and it seems to me that you are no stranger to the sword yourself.'

It was generous, especially from a man who had spent his life on battlefields, but Akitada shook his head. 'That was never by choice, sir. And I was younger then.'

The much older Akimoto chuckled.

Seimei returned with wine and served them. Akitada was glad that some of the good wine was left. The rebuilding had once again brought them to the brink of penury.

Akimoto sipped appreciatively. 'You must forgive me,' he said. 'I should have said right away that I've come on official business for the Censors' Bureau, and that you have been cleared of the charges against you.'

Akitada, slightly dazed with relief, refilled the wine cups. 'Thank you, sir. That is very good of you, but surely personal visits are not part of your duties.'

'I volunteered. Somebody has to apologize, and I find that the older you get, the easier this becomes.' He chuckled again. 'The others were embarrassed, and our esteemed chairman withdrew in a huff.'

Akitada, remembering the pompous young Fujiwara, laughed. 'I had prepared myself for dire news. Apart from the birth of a little daughter, I seem to have tumbled from one disaster to the next lately.'

Akimoto raised his cup. 'My felicitations. To your little daughter and your lady wife.'

They drank, smiling at each other. 'It seems I'm a very lucky man after all,' Akitada said.

'I bring other good news also. You have been reinstated at the ministry. I made a point of seeing your minister to report the findings of the censors. He was distraught over what happened to you and begs you to return. Official word should reach you soon.'

Akitada was glad, but then he remembered Kobe, whose position was in danger because he had tried to help him. 'By any chance, is there news about Superintendent Kobe?' he asked.

Akimoto said, 'Kobe is to be reconfirmed in his position by the new administration.'

Perhaps it was too much good news, thought Akitada as he climbed the steps to the Ministry of Justice a week later. He would find it impossible to work under Munefusa, but a man with a family to support must make sacrifices.

It was late in the morning, and the hallways of the ministry were empty. Akitada went first to Munefusa's old office, assuming it would be his, but here he found a stranger busily writing notes on a document. The man looked up with a frown. Akitada apologized and went to see the minister.

The minister's secretary was another stranger. What had happened to Munefusa? When Akitada gave his name, the secretary bowed quite deeply and went to announce him.

Fujiwara Kaneie came out himself to receive Akitada. He was smiling, but clearly embarrassed. Akitada felt much the same. He owed the man an apology for his extremely rude behavior.

Kaneie took him into his office and poured some wine that was standing ready.

'My dear Akitada,' he said, 'it is good to have you back.' He managed to sound both sincere and apologetic.

Akitada steeled himself for his own apology. 'I behaved atrociously to you, sir, and beg your pardon for my rash words. I assure you, I regretted them as soon as I left this room.'

Kaneie gave a nervous laugh. 'Not at all. You were very angry. I should not have blamed you for that. I, too, regret what I said.' He paused a moment, then added, 'You know, I would have explained if I had been allowed to do so. Even now, my dear Akitada, I am restrained from speaking. It was all very unpleasant, and I was extremely relieved when new instructions arrived, rescinding the earlier orders. Please allow me to apologize on behalf of my superiors.'

'Thank you, sir. I'm very glad to have your trust again.' He hesitated. 'But I'm not quite sure what the arrangements are. There was a stranger in my office.'

Kaneie looked puzzled. 'A stranger? Munefusa should have left your old office ready for you.' He shook his head. 'That man, Akitada. You can have no notion what a horrible muddle he made of things. We had some very difficult cases, and I think all the findings will have to be rewritten. I would have fixed matters, but you know I have no head for the finer points of the law. You have been missed.'

'Where is Munefusa?'

'Munefusa and a number of clerks have been dismissed. It seems he was second cousin to Kiyowara Kane and gold changed hands to ... umm ... contrive false charges against you. Munefusa will face the censors.' He added, 'There are all sorts of rumors. I hear the Minister of the Right will resign – officially as part of the reorganization of Michinaga's retirement, but he is a known enemy of the crown prince.' Fujiwara Kaneie smiled and got up briskly. 'But all is finally back to normal here. Come and let me introduce you to your staff.'

The news stunned Akitada. So his demotion had not been some dark plot directed at him by his unknown enemies. It had merely been due to a greedy upstart using his personal connections to advance himself. He was not sure if that made it better.

His 'staff' consisted of three men: two junior clerks and one senior. The juniors were recent graduates and looked pleasant enough. The senior was well known to him. He was Shinkai, the same elderly man who had run after him to express his regrets the day Akitada had been dismissed. This pleased Akitada until he saw the enormous, nearly toppling stacks of documents on his desk.

'Umm, yes,' said the minister, 'I'm afraid things have stacked up a bit under Munefusa.'

As if he had heard his name called, the door opened and Munefusa himself appeared. He paled when he saw them and attempted to retreat.

'Come in, Munefusa,' snapped the minister. 'I expect you wish to apologize to Akitada for your unconscionable lies about him.'

Munefusa inched in and bowed. He flushed and avoided looking at Akitada. 'I did not know Lord Sugawara would be here,' he said. 'I came for my notes.' He swallowed and added in a murmur, 'I shall need them to refresh my memory.'

'Ah, yes,' said the minister. 'When will you appear before the censors?'

Munefusa mumbled something inaudible and scurried to a shelf to pick up a thin book. He dashed back to the door so quickly that he tripped over his feet and nearly fell out of the room.

They all burst into laughter.

Akitada returned home full of the good news and found that his house had been decorated with many-colored flags and sheets that fluttered gaily in the summer breeze. They turned out to be clothes and blankets of all sorts. Apparently, Tamako had decided to air out the clamminess left by the recent rains.

He found her working among the clothes chests with her maid and told her his news.

'Really?' she said, distracted. 'I suppose that means you'll be away from home again every day.' Realizing that her response was less than warm, she gave her husband a radiant smile. 'I've become accustomed to having you around.'

Akitada spied the baby Yasuko abandoned in a half-emptied trunk and went to pick her up.

'Oh,' said Tamako, 'would you mind very much entertaining your daughter for a little?'

'Not at all.' He cradled the baby in his arms, smiling down

at her. 'It will be an honor.' But then the seriousness of this responsibility struck him. 'What shall I do if she starts crying?'

'Oh, Akitada,' his wife teased, 'how can you be so nervous when she is your second child? In any case, I just fed her. She'll be asleep soon.'

He carried his daughter carefully to his room, decided it was too dark and dull for a child and snatched up his bedding roll with one hand before walking out on to the veranda. There, in the shade of the sun-warmed wall of the house, he made a little nest of the quilt and placed her inside. Then he sat down next to his daughter to admire her. She gazed back calmly, pursing rosebud lips.

What was she thinking of her father with his long face and beetling brows? She did not look frightened, but detached, as if waiting to see if he would prove acceptable.

He pointed to the garden, the sky, a small bird on a branch, telling her about them. He promised her that some day they would feed the goldfish in his pond together.

She appeared to listen, but remained distant – or so it seemed to him. Not knowing how to bridge the gulf, he sighed.

Then he remembered his flute. The memory brought sadness because he had played it for Yori's departed spirit right here on this veranda. But his little son had loved the sound of the flute from the time he was an infant.

Akitada went to get it. Sitting back down beside Yasuko, he played a few soft notes and saw her eyes widen. He tried a happy little melody, and the pursed mouth relaxed, a dimple appeared in her cheek, and her eyes crinkled at the corners. She made a soft gurgling sound. Could this be a smile? An almost laugh?

He lowered the flute, but the baby frowned. The corners of her mouth turned downward.

Quickly, he raised the flute again and played and, yes, the smile returned. A genuine smile! She was smiling at him. No question about it.

Filled with pride and happiness, he played song after song until long after his daughter had fallen asleep.

HISTORICAL NOTE

In the eleventh century, Japan was ruled by an emperor and court nobles in the capital, Heian-kyo (modern Kyoto). The Japanese government was originally patterned after Chinese models, but by this time it was no longer a meritocracy as in T'ang China, but rather in the hands of a single powerful family, the Fujiwaras. At the time of this novel, the man in power was Fujiwara Michinaga. After a century of marriage politics that placed Fujiwara daughters into the imperial bed, the family had become so closely connected to imperial power that emperors were encouraged to abdicate once they produced heirs so that a Fujiwara grandfather or uncle could rule as regent for an under-age emperor. When Michinaga retired as regent in 1017, he had ruled the government for upward of twenty years, the last four as regent and chancellor. He was the grandfather of two emperors, father-in-law of three emperors and one crown prince, and father of two regents and many of the ministers. For contemporary accounts of the life of Fujiwara Michinaga and Fujiwara politics, see *Okagami, The Great Mirror*, (trans. Helen McCullough) and *A Tale of Flowering Fortunes* (trans. William McCullough & Helen McCullough).

The business of government was carried out by officials working out of a number of ministries and bureaus that surrounded the emperor's palace. Other court nobles served as governors of the provinces. These men were often self-serving politicians who aimed at building their private wealth via lucrative appointments, and they contributed greatly to the weakening of the central government over the next two hundred years. Much of the senior officials' time was spent on court ritual, while lower-ranking members of the aristocracy carried out the day-to-day business of administration.

Japanese customs mixed native traditions with those of China. The official government language (used almost exclusively by men) was Chinese, but Japanese flourished in the hands of poets and court ladies who kept journals and wrote novels. Lady Murasaki's novel *Genji* was written during the first decade of the eleventh century.

Heian-kyo was originally laid out in a grid in the Chinese
manner: that is, following directional laws that placed the
imperial palace and government buildings in the center of
the northernmost section and divided the rest of the city into
a right and left half, each with its own administration. By the
eleventh century, the western (or right) capital had fallen on
evil times and the city had begun to spread across the Kamo
River to the east. The city itself had few religious institutions,
but many monasteries and temples dotted the mountains to
the north and east.

Buildings were constructed almost exclusively of wood, with
bark or tile roofs. For that reason, fires devastated the city peri-
odically and had become so frequent by the eleventh century
that emperors left the imperial palace, and many nobles moved
out of the city and across the Kamo River. Even given the problems with wood construction and the use of open flames for
heating, cooking, and light, there were too many fires to be
accounted for by accidents. In fact, many fires were set by thieves,
who used the chaos caused by dousing flames in order to break
into nearby empty houses.

Law and order was supposedly kept by the imperial and metro-
politan police: a semi-military force that engaged in arrests,
investigations, and prosecution by judges who were part of the
system. The police also maintained the city's two jails. In addition, each city ward had a warden who kept order in his own
area. In spite of this, crime flourished in the city and even in
the imperial palace enclosure. Poverty contributed, but part of
the problem was that emperors frequently declared amnesties
and liberated all the jail inmates because they wished to please
the gods or avert some disaster. In addition, Buddhism forbade
the taking of a life, regardless of the seriousness of the crime
committed.

The native Shinto religion coexisted peacefully with
Buddhism, which was a later import from China. That Akitada
should have visited a Buddhist monastery headed by an abbot
with imperial blood was by no means an uncommon case. Many
emperors and princes took clerical vows. Some of the Buddhist
temples shared space with important Shinto shrines, and emperors
made pilgrimages to worship at both. Akitada encounters a Shinto
shrine virgin and a Shinto priest. Shinto *kami*, or gods, are closely
related to the imperial descent and to rice culture. Imperial

princesses always served as virgins at the important Ise and Kamo shrines. But there were many shrines and many kinds of female attendants. Some were shamans and could be powerful and dangerous because they transmitted the words of the *kami*. They were adept at casting spells, foretelling the future, speaking for the dead, and exorcizing evil spirits. Akitada's reservations against hiring a female shaman illustrate the fact that many of these women wandered the country, engaging in licentious behavior and earning a living by fortune-telling and public dancing.

Marriages in upper classes were polygamous: that is, a husband could have many wives. They held different ranks, depending on their backgrounds, and some were merely concubines. In addition, men frequently carried on outside affairs. Marriages could also be dissolved on the husband's word. But women were able to own property. That fact and the influence of their fathers protected them to some extent. Those without personal wealth or family protection did not fare so well. Lady Kiyowara is Kiyowara's first lady because she belongs to a powerful family on her own account, and her son is the heir even though he is not the firstborn like Tojiro, the son of a lower-ranking wife.

The rituals performed to assure the safe birth of Tamako's child involved Buddhist and Shinto rites and clerics, as well as the popular customs associated with keeping evil spirits at bay. For a more complete description of such parturition rites, see *The Diary of Murasaki Shikibu*, where Lady Murasaki describes in detail the activities accompanying and following the birth of an imperial child. Many of these had to do with the fact that childbirth was considered one of several forms of pollution (death was another) and the belief that a woman in labor was a favorite prey of all sorts of evil spirits.